The daughter of a town marshal, **Linda Lael Miller** is a *New York Times* bestselling author of more than one hundred historical and contemporary novels. Linda's books have hit #1 on the *New York Times* bestseller list seven times. Raised in Northport, Washington, she now lives in Spokane, Washington. Visit her at www.lindalaelmiller.com.

Brenda Jackson is a *New York Times* bestselling author of more than one hundred romance titles. Brenda lives in Jacksonville, Florida, and divides her time between family, writing and traveling. Email Brenda at authorbrendajackson@gmail.com or visit her website at brendajackson.net.

#1 *New York Times* Bestselling Author

LINDA LAEL MILLER

STATE SECRETS

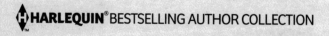

HARLEQUIN®BESTSELLING AUTHOR COLLECTION

ISBN-13: 978-1-335-94124-4

State Secrets

Copyright © 2018 by Harlequin Books S.A.

The publisher acknowledges the copyright holders of the individual works as follows:

State Secrets
Copyright © 1985 by Linda Lael Miller

Tall, Dark...Westmoreland!
Copyright © 2009 by Brenda Streater Jackson

Recycling programs for this product may not exist in your area.

Printed in U.S.A.

CONTENTS

STATE SECRETS

Linda Lael Miller

For Mary Clare Kersten.

Thank you for your encouragement,
your diplomacy and your blue pencil.

Chapter 1

The tall man ran one hand through his dark hair and shifted uncomfortably in his seat. Despite the heavy woolen overcoat he wore, he was still cold. Swift indigo eyes scanned the first page of the dossier. "So what, Walt?" David Goddard bit out, frowning. "She's the president-elect's third cousin. Since when do third cousins qualify for Secret Service protection?"

Walt Zigman made a contemptuous, impatient sound. Apparently, this assignment wasn't exactly dear to his crusty old heart. "It isn't protection, Goddard," he snarled. "Remember that. This is a surveillance project."

David sat back in his chair, drawing his right ankle up to rest on his left knee. "Surveillance," he muttered, suppressing an unprofessional urge to fling the file on Holly Llewellyn back into the mess that littered Walt's desk. "That isn't our—"

"I know, Goddard," Walt interrupted, falling into his own chair and reaching into one ink-stained shirt pocket for a match to light the cigar stub that was always in his mouth. "I know. I tried to give this thing to the Bureau. I even tried the CIA. But they both threw it right back in my lap. Anything connected with the president or his family is our bailiwick—according to them."

David breathed a swearword. He was tired and he could still feel the bite of the crisp November wind outside. He wanted to get out of Washington and have Thanksgiving dinner in Arlington with his sister, Chris, and her family. He wanted to spoil her kids and lounge in front of her fireplace. "Okay, Walt. So Ms. Llewellyn is our problem. Why am I the lucky one?"

Walt chortled. "Born under the right star, I guess. Come on, Goddard, how bad can it be? You spend a few weeks—maybe a few months—in Spokane. You get the lady to like you. And you make damned sure she's really what she claims to be, and not a courier for that brother of hers."

David had the beginnings of a headache. He opened the dossier again, skimming the rundown on Holly Llewellyn. Twenty-seven years old. Blond. Blue-eyed. Five feet, seven inches tall. A one hundred twenty-three pound pain. "What makes you think she's running secrets? It says here she writes cookbooks."

"Middle Eastern cookbooks," David's supervisor imparted with dramatic import.

David's mouth twisted into a wry grin. "That alone should convict her," he mocked.

"Dammit, Goddard, keep your sparkling wit to yourself. Can't you see that we've got the makings of a scandal here that would make Watergate seem insignificant?"

"A scandal?"

"Yes! How would it look if the new president's cousin turned out to be a traitor? Isn't it bad enough that her brother sold out? She could be cut from the same cloth!"

David sighed. "That's unlikely, Walt. It says here that she's written a book about Scandinavian meatballs. Good God, maybe she's spying for the Swedes!"

"Stow it."

"Or the Danes. You've got to watch those Danes, crafty little devils, one and all."

"Goddard!"

"She wrote *Fun With Tacos,* too, I see," David pressed on dryly. "Do you think she's working for the Mexicans? Holy guacamole, Batman—do you suppose they're planning to rush up here and take back Texas?"

Walt was leaning into the desk, his meaty hands braced against the edge, his cigar stub bobbing up and down in outrage. "I'm glad you think this situation is funny, Goddard, but it just so happens that the next president of the United States doesn't agree with you! This little lady happens to have a bona fide, card-carrying traitor for a brother!"

David flipped through the rest of the dossier, not so hastily this time. His headache was worse. "Craig Llewellyn," he muttered.

"You remember him, don't you, Goddard?" Walt gibed, going to stand at the barred window of his dingy little office.

Remember? David remembered, all right—how could he help it? Craig Llewellyn's defection had never made the national news, by some miracle, but every federal agent in the country knew the sordid story. "Being Llewellyn's sister doesn't make the lady a security risk, Walt," he pointed out quietly.

"Maybe not. If she wasn't related to our next president, I wouldn't be worried. If she hadn't just spent two months in Iran, I wouldn't be worried. As it is, I'm *damned* worried."

"You'd think the opposition would have caught on to this before the election…" David speculated, thinking of the outgoing president and the no-holds-barred campaign he had conducted.

"They didn't," Walt broke in. "I'll expect your first report early next week."

"Right." David stood up and stretched. Every muscle in his long frame ached with residual cold. "Is this operation covert, by the way, or do I just knock on Ms. Llewellyn's door and flash my identification?"

Clearly, Walt Zigman had a headache, too. "That was a stupid question, Goddard. You've been on White House Detail too damned long. Spent too much time walking the first lady's dog. Of *course* it's covert!"

David shrugged, feeling weary. Maybe Walt was right; maybe he was getting soft. Instead of thinking about this case on every level, a part of him was anticipating a day at Chris's place. The kids would be watching the Macy's parade on TV. The smell of roasting turkey would be everywhere….

He reached for the dossier. "Can I take this?"

Walt waved impatiently. "Yeah, yeah, that's your copy."

David tucked the file under one arm. He supposed it was the forthcoming holiday that was distracting him, stirring up bittersweet memories and half-formed hopes, making him feel far older than his thirty-four years. He tried to imagine Marleen, his ex-wife, roasting turkey or settling a band of freckle-faced rug rats in front of the tube to watch a Thanksgiving parade and couldn't. "You having dinner here, Walt?" he asked, his hand on the doorknob. "Tomorrow, I mean?"

Zigman grinned around his cigar stub. "Nope. Going to New York to see my daughter. Happy Thanksgiving, Goddard."

David laughed, though he had a bereft feeling inside. He thought of Marleen studying chimpanzees in Borneo and wondered if she remembered that she'd once wanted to raise an entirely different kind of monkey. "I'll call you on Monday."

"Right."

David stepped out into the wide, familiar hallway, with its lighted paintings and expensively shabby carpeting. In front of the Oval Office, two agents guarded the heavy double doors. He nodded and they nodded back, their faces solemn.

Downstairs, David left the White House by a side door, then strode through the snow-dusted parking lot to his car. At one of the high wrought-iron gates, he showed his ID, even though he was going out, not in, even though he knew the young Marines on duty, knew their wives and their kids and their collar sizes.

Again he felt lonely. Even quietly desperate. As the White House gate clanked shut behind him, he turned up the car radio in a belated effort to cover the sound.

Holly Llewellyn placed the elegantly scripted invitation in the center of the kitchen mantelpiece. Hands tucked into the pockets of her cozy blue jogging jacket, she stood back to admire it.

"Imagine," said her friend and secretary, Elaine Bateman, from her chair at the cluttered trestle table. "Being invited to the White House! An inaugural ball! Good heavens, Holly, what are you going to wear?"

Holly's bright, aquamarine eyes danced with mischief and she withdrew her hands from her pockets to push her chin-length blond hair atop her head. "Nothing," she crooned, striking a cheesecake pose.

"That ought to cause a sensation!"

Holly made a face and went back to the printer set up on the end of the trestle table. She began printing out the pages of "Ka-bobs for a Crowd," the initial chapter of her new book. "I meant that I'm not going," she pointed out. "After all, Toby is in school and I've got my classes to teach and this book to finish. These recipes all have to be tested and retested, you know. And there's my newspaper column—"

"Excuses!" Elaine cried, ignoring the finished manuscript, *Soups are Super,* that she was supposed to be indexing. "Good Lord, Holly, how many times does a person's cousin get elected president? I can't believe you'd miss a chance like this! Besides, you've got until January."

The rhythmic whining of the printer was giving Holly a headache; she closed her eyes and ran her hands down the sides of her trim-fitting jeans. "I'm not going," she repeated sharply.

Elaine sighed in a way that made Holly regret her tone of voice. "Okay, Holl. No problem. Listen, tomorrow's Thanksgiving—do you mind if I take this home and work on it there? I've got a turkey to stuff and ceramic pilgrims to set out in strategic places."

Holly laughed, able to look at her friend now. "Go," she said. "And leave the manuscript here. It will keep until Monday."

Elaine beamed triumphantly, gathering the stack of blue-penciled pages into a neat pile. "You were always a soft touch for ceramic pilgrims." She grinned. "Are you sure you don't want me to work Friday?"

"Positive."

Elaine looked worried now, her wide green eyes watchful. "You and Toby have somewhere to go for Thanksgiving, don't you? I mean, you're not going to sit here and brood or anything, are you?"

Holly felt a tender sort of exasperation. "We're spending the day with Skyler's parents, worrywart. Hie thyself home, before that husband of yours tries to stuff the gobbler on his own. Remember last year? He cut himself on the giblets."

Elaine laughed. "Roy means well," she said, taking her coat from the antique wall rack beside the back door. Shrugging into it, she tossed her glossy brown hair back over her shoulders. "How was he to know that a partially frozen turkey neck can be lethal?"

"How indeed?" Holly chuckled, wondering why she felt so sad. Skyler's parents were nice people; she and Toby would both have a good time at their house.

"Happy, happy," Elaine sang, opening the door to leave and letting in a rush of frigid November air. "See you Monday."

"Monday," Holly confirmed, smiling hard. But when her friend was gone, she sat down on the long bench beside the trestle table and sighed.

Just then Toby scrambled in from the other direction, still wearing his jacket, earmuffs and mittens. His "Moon Boots" made puddles on the redbrick floor, and he was waving a multi-colored construction-paper turkey in one hand. "Look what we made, Mom! Look what we made!"

From somewhere in the depths of her, Holly summoned up another smile. "Wow!" she crowed. She didn't bother to correct the little boy, to remind him that she was his aunt and not his mother. She never did that anymore.

The seven-year-old was trying to peel off his winter garb without crumpling his purple, green, pink and black turkey. The cold glowed in his plump cheeks and his china-blue eyes sparkled.

After ruffling his irresistible corn-silk hair with one hand, Holly aided him by taking the bedraggled, paste-crusted turkey while he wrestled out of his jacket.

"I've never seen a turkey quite like this," she remarked.

Toby laughed and Holly felt a pang at the sound; he was so like her brother, Craig. Poor, hunted Craig. "I wanted him to be different, Mom!" For a moment, the child looked sheepish. "Besides, all the brown and gold and orange paper was gone."

Holly walked to the huge side-by-side refrigerator and attached the turkey to its surface with magnets. To make room, she had to take down the previous month's construction-paper pumpkin. "No matter," she said. "I like this bird. He has character. Are you hungry?"

"Starved," the little boy exclaimed, and there was a scuffling sound as he made a place for himself at the paper-and-book-littered table.

Holly plundered the refrigerator for lunch meat, sliced cheese, lettuce and mustard. She thought ruefully that another trip to the supermarket was in order.

Carrying the armload of sandwich supplies over to the counter, Holly set everything down to open the old-fashioned wooden bread box.

"We're still going to Skyler's place tomorrow, right?" Toby asked without looking at her.

Holly was closing the bread sack, tucking it back into its nook. She sighed. "Not exactly. We're going to his parents' house, remember? They live in the country."

"Oh."

"You don't like Skyler very much, do you, Toby?" she ventured, buttering a slice of bread, adding cheese and lunch meat and a lettuce leaf.

"Are you going to marry him?" the child countered, watching Holly with pensive eyes.

It was a fair question, but since Holly didn't know the answer herself, she could hardly offer one to Toby. "I don't know. I like Skyler."

"A lot?"

Holly thought. "Yeah. I like him a lot."

"Do you love him?"

Holly's knife clattered in the mustard jar. "Well—"

"You're supposed to love somebody if you're going to marry them. The way Elaine loves Roy. She's always kissing him and when he says something, she looks at him like every word is real important."

Holly paused, feeling oddly shaken, and gave her nephew a lopsided grin. "You've been watching Dr. Phil again," she teased.

Toby looked puzzled. "Huh?"

"Never mind. How was school today?"

The little boy sighed. "I didn't get any orange paper."

"I remember," Holly replied, putting the finished sandwich on a plate and carrying it to the table. "How come that happened, anyway? Were you late for art class or something?"

Toby was gathering up the sandwich in eager hands. "I had to talk to the principal."

"Toby Llewellyn! Did you get into trouble?"

"No," Toby said through a mouthful. "He wanted me to talk about the new president next week at assembly."

A jolt of mingled alarm and fury raced through Holly; she had to take a deep breath before she could speak calmly. "What? How did he know—"

Toby shrugged. "Maybe there was something in the paper. Mr. Richardson was pretty disappointed when I told him I didn't know the president."

Holly was pacing the floor, her hands tucked into the hip pockets of her jeans. The celebrity of being a cookbook author was one thing—only a select group of people cared one way or the other, of course—but this shirttail relationship to the future president could get to be a real problem. Suppose reporters started taking an interest? Suppose what Craig had done got talked about? Toby could be hurt or even put in real danger!

"Did you see any newspaper people, Toby? Did anybody ask you questions?"

Toby shook his head. "Can I watch TV?"

Holly nodded somewhat impatiently. "You'll tell me if anyone you don't know tries to talk to you, won't you, Toby?"

"Sure. Is there any lemonade?"

Agitated, Holly forced herself to stop pacing. There

was no reason to panic, no reason. After all, she and Craig were only distantly related to the new president.

"Mom?"

"Cocoa. I'll make you a cup of cocoa. It's too cold for lemonade."

"Okay," Toby agreed amiably, on his way out of the kitchen. A moment later, as she searched the cupboard for a saucepan in which to prepare the cocoa, Holly heard the television set in the next room blaring. Her hands trembled as she collected the milk, salt, sugar and chocolate.

Oh, my God, she thought. *Craig, what have you done to us? What have you done to all of us?*

She reflected on her brother's problems as she made the cocoa and carried it into the family room to Toby. The telephone shrilled and Holly jumped, startled out of her skin. She raced back into the kitchen and grabbed up the receiver. "H-hello?"

"Hello, kitten," said the familiar masculine voice on the other end.

Holly sank into the chair at her small desk, her knees wobbly. Skyler. It was only Skyler. She was so glad that she didn't even ask him not to call her by that silly, condescending nickname. "Hi," she said.

Skyler cleared his throat. Skyler always cleared his throat when he was about to suggest something he expected Holly to oppose. "Listen, Holl, I was wondering—why don't you and I and the kid just drive up to my folks' place tonight, instead of waiting until tomorrow? I could close the shop early."

Holly bit her lower lip, considering. She hated the way Skyler always referred to Toby as "the kid," as though he didn't have a name. But confronting him about it had about as much effect as asking him not to call her "kitten." Which was none at all.

"Holly?" Skyler prompted when the silence grew too long. "Are you still there?"

"I was just—I was just thinking."

"Is it that hard to decide?" he snapped, impatient now.

Holly drew a deep breath and let it out slowly before answering. "No, Skyler, of course not. But, well—"

Skyler made an exasperated sound. "I suppose you're afraid I'll want you to sleep with me. In my parents' house, Holly? Give me some credit, will you?"

He was being unusually defensive, Holly thought, but then sex was an issue between them. While Holly was certainly no innocent, she wasn't ready for that kind of intimacy, not with Skyler Hollis at any rate. "Sky."

"Well? That is what you were thinking, isn't it?"

Holly sighed as she rubbed her aching temples with a thumb and forefinger. "Yes. And I refuse to discuss it over the telephone."

Skyler's struggle for equanimity was almost audible. "Right," he said presently. "Do I pick you up tonight or not, Holly?"

"What time would we leave?"

"I can be ready in about an hour and a half. We could eat dinner on the way if you'd like."

Holly found herself smiling in spite of the odd tension Skyler always managed to inspire in her. "That sounds like a good idea. I really don't feel like cooking."

Skyler chuckled. "Little wonder."

"On the other hand, I've got a freezer full of experimental ka-bobs. Test run from yesterday."

"I'm in no mood to be a guinea pig," Skyler retorted quickly, and there was a disturbing note of conviction in his voice. "I'll see you at—" he paused and Holly could imagine him looking at his thin gold watch "—six-thirty."

"Six-thirty," Holly confirmed, and after a few perfunctory words of parting, they both hung up.

Somebody should have said, "I love you," Holly thought as she left the kitchen.

Skyler stood before the mantelpiece, frowning at the invitation to the inaugural ball. He was a tall man with sleek, fair hair, an altar-boy face and elegant, long-fingered hands. The owner of a very successful stereo-and-television dealership, Skyler was prosperous, and his tailored gray slacks and tasteful cashmere sweater were meant to convey that to even the most casual onlooker.

Holly stood watching him, waiting, her hands in the pockets of her black corduroy skirt. With it she wore high leather boots, a burgundy blouse and her black velvet blazer. Her hair, cut in a layered, easy-care style, glistened, and her makeup was perfect.

"You didn't tell me you knew—" Skyler began, pensively, turning to frown at her.

"I know lots of famous people, Skyler."

"Yes," Skyler mused, one perfect golden eyebrow arched in speculation, "but shaking somebody's hand on *The Today Show* and getting invited to an inaugural ball are two different things."

Holly folded her arms and allowed herself a wry smile, though inside she felt shaky. She always did with Skyler; his very presence seemed to evaporate her self-confidence. "Howard is a distant cousin, Skyler. I didn't mention it because I didn't think it mattered."

"Howard! You call the next president of the United States 'Howard'?"

Holly shrugged. "It's his name, Skyler."

"Still—"

Suddenly Holly was impatient. "I'm not going to the ball anyway," she said, reaching for her purse, which sat on the corner of her desk. "Shall we go? The traffic will be horrendous and it's still snowing."

Skyler nodded distractedly, but even as they left the kitchen, he kept casting his eyes back to the invitation. "Right," he said.

Once Toby and his suitcase, which also contained Holly's things, had been tucked into the tiny back seat of Skyler's sleek, sporty car, and the boy had been carefully buckled in by a seat belt, Holly glanced quickly at her old-fashioned brick house and felt a sweeping, dismal sort of loneliness.

Mentally, she shook herself. Good heavens, she was acting as though she would never see her cozy home again.

The traffic, as Holly had predicted, was terrible. The number of cars leaving the city was equaled only by the number of cars coming in, and the snow swirled and spiraled in front of the windshield, making it almost impossible to see.

"We're in hyperspace!" Toby cried in delight. Out of the corner of her eye, Holly saw Skyler grimace and tighten his grasp on the steering wheel.

She let her head rest against the back of the seat and closed her eyes. Skyler Hollis was what her mother might have called a "catch," with his good looks and his flourishing business, but his antipathy toward Toby, carefully hidden though it was, disturbed Holly. She wondered if he felt that way about all children or just her nephew in particular.

An hour and a half later, when they had eaten at a roadside restaurant and were again on their way, Toby asleep in the back seat, she broached the subject. "Do you want children, Skyler?"

He glanced at her and then turned his attention back to the hazardous road. "Of my own? Most men do, Holly."

Holly sat up a little straighter. "Of my own," he'd said. "In other words, you wouldn't accept Toby?"

Skyler's clean-shaven jaw worked for a moment, and his narrow shoulders grew tense. "Your brother will probably come back for him one day, Holly. You told me that yourself."

Holly sighed and looked out the window at the fierce flurries of snow. She had told Skyler that, it was true. But now she had grave doubts that her brother would ever actually reclaim his son or be in a position to take care of him. After all, Toby's mother was dead, and though few people knew it, Craig was a wanted man, suspected of espionage. It was possible, in fact, that he wasn't even in the country.

"Craig won't come back," she said quietly, after a long silence.

"How could he not come back?" Skyler demanded angrily. "You've got his kid!"

His kid. When Skyler said that, used those simple, everyday words, it always sounded inhumane. "And I want to keep him, Skyler. Craig is in no position to be a real father and besides, I love Toby. I love him very, very much."

There seemed to be nothing to say after that. Skyler shoved a classical CD into the slot on the dashboard and the car was filled with thunderous Beethoven.

Chris's kitchen was a bright, warm, cluttered place. The walls were graced with shining copper utensils and a fire crackled in the huge wood-burning stove in one corner of the room. Two long shelves held the largest collection of cookbooks David had ever seen.

Frowning, he took down a copy of *Fun With Tacos* and studied the colored photograph of the author on the back cover. Tousled, honey-colored hair, enormous blue-green eyes. Holly Llewellyn.

"Taking up the culinary arts?" Chris asked mischievously, standing beside him.

Startled, David thrust the thin volume back into its place on the shelf and shook his head.

Chris, a lovely woman with dark hair and eyes, laughed warmly and hugged her brother. "We live in a new age, you know. Men are actually cooking, among other things."

A new age. David's mind caught on those words—he was uneasy, even jumpy. He had the strangest feeling that he was on the edge of something momentous, something that would change his life forever. He took Holly Llewellyn's cookbook down from the shelf again, turned it over and studied the captivating face on the back.

Llewellyn, he thought, if you turn out to be a fink, I'm not going to be able to take it.

Chapter 2

Holly looked with a jaundiced eye at the mechanical department-store Santa Claus nodding beside the escalator. Thanksgiving is over, she thought ruefully, so bring on Christmas.

In the toy section to her left, a horde of shoppers were engaged in a good-natured battle of some sort.

Reaching the next floor and the cookware section of the large store, Holly found Elaine already there, her hair pinned to the top of her head, a clipboard in hand.

"What's going on downstairs?" Holly asked irritably. The weekend with Skyler and his parents had been a disaster.

Elaine chuckled but did not look up from the list she was going over. "They got in a shipment of Webkinz."

Shrugging out of her winter coat, Holly assessed the room. The store had done a good job of setting up;

there were tables, aprons and even chefs' hats for all the students. In the cooking area, where Holly would demonstrate the fine art of baking fruitcake, an assortment of copper utensils had been set out on the counter.

She peered at Elaine's clipboard. Normally, twelve students were accepted for her popular cooking classes, but this time the list showed thirteen names. "David Goddard? Who the devil is that?"

Elaine gave her friend and employer an understanding, patient look. "There's always room for one more, right?" She grinned. "The guy was so eager...."

Holly was annoyed and tired. All she wanted to do was spend the night at home, in front of the TV or better yet, in a hot bath with a book. Anywhere but in this posh downtown department store, teaching thirteen people how to bake fruitcake. "Elaine," she began stiffly, "this is a popular class. There is a waiting list several months long, in case you've forgotten. So where do you get off letting some bozo walk in and sign up just because he's eager?"

Elaine colored prettily. "Actually, he's better than eager. He's a hunk."

"Great! You let him in because he was good-looking!"

Elaine shrugged. "What can I tell you? I looked up into those navy blue eyes and I could not deny the man ten lessons and a chef's hat."

Holly muttered an expletive and flung down her purse and coat. "I'll be glad to deny him for you," she snapped, washing her hands at the gleaming steel sink that was part of the store's fully equipped kitchen. "Where is he?"

"Downstairs, I think, in the toy department," Elaine replied, unruffled, as she checked the supplies of flour, sugar and assorted other ingredients against another list on her clipboard. "He said something about buying a couple Webkinz for his nieces."

Holly found an apron and put it on over her jeans and cotton shirt. Despite repeated pleas from the store's publicity director, she refused to wear a chef's hat. "I don't know why I agree to do these cooking classes, anyway," she muttered.

"You have a contract with the store," came the blithe reply from her secretary. "And they pay you big bucks."

"Thanks for reminding me."

Elaine looked up from her clipboard and made a face. "Anytime, boss."

Holly couldn't help it; she had to grin. "I don't know how you put up with me. I've been a grouch all day and I'm sorry."

Elaine sighed. "A weekend with Skyler Hollis would do that to anybody. Everything checks out, Holly. Could I go now? Roy and I are going to have dinner out and then do some early shopping."

"Go. Leave me here to tell the hunk that he can't learn to bake fruitcake." Holly paused and assumed a pose of mock despondency. "The help you get these days."

Elaine laughed. "When you see him, you'll let him stay. Believe me, God was in a good mood the day He threw this dude together. Everything is definitely in the right place."

"Elaine Bateman, you are a happily married woman!"

The pretty brunette was pulling on her coat. "Yeah. But I'm not blind," she twinkled, before taking up her purse and starting off toward the escalators.

Holly was alone for about five minutes, and then

a heavy, earnest-looking man arrived. She asked his name—it was Alvin Parkins—and checked it off on Elaine's list. One by one, the other students came, some of them bringing copies of Holly's books to be autographed.

And then he showed up. Number Thirteen. The intruder. At the very first sight of him, Holly's stomach did a nervous flip.

He was tall and his hair was very dark, neatly cut, and his eyes were a piercing navy blue, just as Elaine had said. He wore blue jeans, a soft white sweater and a brown leather jacket and under each of his powerful arms, he carried a plush toy.

Holly lifted her chin, squared her shoulders and approached him. "Mr. Goddard?"

He tilted his head slightly, in acknowledgment or greeting or both. His cologne was musky and Holly found herself trying to identify it by name.

Holly glanced at the toys, trying to delay the moment when she must tell this man that there simply wasn't room for him in the fruitcake class. "Mr. Goddard— I—" Holly cleared her throat. "The fact is, Mr. Goddard, that there just isn't…there just isn't room in this class for another person. I'm sorry."

He set the toys down on one of the tables and calmly removed his jacket. He didn't look as though he planned to go anywhere. "I'm sorry, too. That it's a problem, I mean. But your secretary took my money and told me I had a place in good old Fruitcake 101 and I'm staying."

Holly felt the color rising in her face. "You're going to be difficult, aren't you?"

David Goddard smiled and folded his arms, stirring

that appealing musky scent and touching something deep inside Holly. "If necessary," came the simple reply.

To hide her annoyance, Holly looked down at her watch. It was time to start the class and all the other students were there, ready to begin. It wouldn't do to make a scene in front of them and besides, Elaine had told the man he could participate. "All right, then," she muttered, "you can stay."

"Thank you," he replied, and the deep warmth in his voice soothed Holly somehow, taking away the anger that had arisen at his stubbornness.

David Goddard proved to be an attentive student, listening closely to every word Holly said, watching every move she made. She could almost feel the steel-trap agility of his mind.

When the class was over and Holly was cleaning up, he stayed behind to help. Without a word he rolled up his sleeves and began running hot water into the sink.

Holly gathered mixing bowls and spatulas and bread pans and brought them to the counter. It was odd, the feeling she had—as though they were old friends instead of strangers, washing dishes together in a homey kitchen instead of a busy department store.

"This is quite a setup," he remarked, up to his elbows in hot, soapy water.

Holly found herself smiling. "I know. I was impressed the first time I saw it, too." *And the first time I saw you, Number Thirteen.*

"Did they put all this in just for you?"

She shook her head and took a dish towel from a top drawer. "I think it was a demonstration kitchen at first—you know, so people could see how the appliances would look in a home setting. When I started to become well-known, Cookware and Books put their heads together and came up with the idea that I should teach classes here."

David smiled. He had a nice smile, she noted, a smile touched with humor. Full of straight white teeth. But what was that sad detachment in the depths of his ink-blue eyes?

"Doesn't that take up a lot of your time? Teaching, I mean?" he asked.

Holly dried a lacquered copper mixing bowl to a red-gold shine. She liked the way it looked, so bright and cheery. "I guess it does. I travel a little, write my books. And I keep up a weekly newspaper column, too." She paused, then shrugged. "I like teaching, though. I get to meet new people that way."

"You don't meet people when you travel?"

She smiled again, wearily. "Not really. I take classes in other countries, and sometimes I'm the only student. It's precise, exhausting work and I usually don't even get to see the sights, let alone strike up lasting friendships. What do you do for a living, Mr. Goddard?"

"Call me David or I'll never tell," he retorted, and even though his glance was pleasant, Holly had a feeling that he was stalling, for some reason.

"All right. What do you do for a living, David?" she insisted, watching him.

The navy blue eyes were suddenly averted; he was concentrating on scrubbing a baking pan. "I'm in law school at Gonzaga," he finally answered.

The answer seemed incomplete somehow. David Goddard was in his midthirties, unless Holly missed her guess. Surely old enough to be through with college, even law school. On the other hand, lots of people changed careers these days. "What kind of lawyer are you planning to be? Corporate? Criminal?"

He took up another baking pan. "Actually, I'm taking review courses. I graduated several years ago, but I haven't been practising. I thought I'd better brush up a little before I tackled the Bar Exam again."

"The Bar Exam? I thought you only had to take that once."

"It varies from state to state. I didn't study in Washington."

He was hedging; Holly was sure of it. But why? "Where did you study?"

David still would not look at her. "Virginia. Do they pay you extra for washing dishes?"

The sudden shift in the conversation unsettled Holly, as did something she sensed in this man. In a flash it occurred to her that he might be a very clever reporter looking for a story. Her cooking career usually didn't generate a lot of interest, but being third cousin to the next president of the United States just might. And what if he knew about Craig?

Holly paled and withdrew a little. "I can finish this myself," she said stiffly. "Why don't you go?"

Now the inky gaze was fixed on her, impaling her, touching that hidden something that did not want to be touched. "Is there a sudden chill in here or am I imagining it?" he countered.

Holly kept her distance. Gone was the feeling of companionship she had enjoyed earlier. There was danger in this man; there was watchfulness. Why hadn't she noticed that before? She fielded his question with one of her own. "Why would a lawyer want to learn to bake fruitcake?" she asked.

David went right on washing, his hands swift and strong at the task. "For the same reasons the other people in this class do, Holly. There was a bookkeeper, if I remember correctly, and a construction worker—"

"Maybe a journalist or two," she put in sharply, glaring at him now.

"A journalist?" He looked honestly puzzled for a moment, and then a light dawned in the blue depths of his eyes. "You think I'm a reporter," he said.

"Are you?"

"No," came the firm and immediate reply. And Holly believed David Goddard, though she couldn't have explained why.

"You really want to bake fruitcake?" Did she sound eager? Lord, she hoped not.

David laughed and touched the tip of her nose with a sudsy index finger. "I really want to bake fruitcake."

They finished cleaning up and David lingered while Holly put on her coat and reached for her purse.

"Was there something else?" she asked, trying to keep her voice level. For some reason Number Thirteen had a strange effect on her.

"Yes," he answered. "I plan to walk you to your car. It's late and I don't want you to get mugged."

Holly felt warm. Protected. Though she cherished her independence, it was nice to have someone looking out for her that way. "Thank you," she said.

Her car was in a parking tower in the next block, isolated and in shadow. It probably wasn't safe, walking there alone, but she hadn't thought of that in her hurry to get to the store and conduct her class. She was glad David was with her.

He waited beside her sporty blue Toyota until she

had found her keys, unlocked the door and slid behind the wheel. Toby's model airplane, a miniature Cessna flown by remote control, was on the seat, and she moved it in order to set down her purse and the small notebook she always carried.

"Is that yours?" David asked with interest, his eyes on the expensive toy.

"Actually—" Holly grinned "—it belongs to my nephew, though I do admit to flying it now and then up at Manito Park."

Again there was an unsettling alertness in David, as though he was cataloging the information for future reference. But why would he do such a thing?

"I have a plane like that," he said, and Holly ascribed her instant impression that he was lying to weariness and an overactive imagination.

David Goddard was a kind, attractive man, not a reporter or an FBI agent. She was going to have to stop letting her fancy take over at every turn or she would become paranoid. She said goodbye, started the car and backed out of her parking space.

There was a light snow falling and Holly drove up the steep South Hill at a cautious pace, her mind staying behind with David Goddard.

He *could* be a reporter, she thought distractedly as she navigated the slick, slushy streets. He could even be an FBI agent hoping to find Craig.

Holly laughed at herself and shook her head. "You'd better take up writing fiction, Llewellyn," she said aloud. "You've got the imagination for it."

But even as she pulled the car to a stop in her own driveway, even as she turned off the engine and gathered up her purse, her notebook and Toby's airplane from the seat, she couldn't shake the conviction that David Goddard was something more than a second-time law student who liked to cook.

Inside the house, Holly found her housekeeper and favorite baby-sitter working happily in front of the living room fireplace. Madge Elkins was a middle-aged woman, still trim and attractive, and her consuming passion was entering contests.

Now, she was busily writing her name and address on one plain white 3-by-5-inch piece of paper after another.

"What are you going to win this time, Madge?" Holly asked pleasantly, putting down the things she carried and getting out of her snow-dampened coat.

"A computer system," Madge replied, tucking a paper into an envelope and sealing it with a flourish. "Printer, software, monitor, the whole shebang."

Another person might have laughed, but Holly had known Madge for several years and in that time had seen her win more than one impressive prize in contests. A car, for instance, and a mink coat. "Is Toby sleeping?"

"Like the proverbial log," Madge answered, gathering a stack of envelopes, all addressed and stamped, into a stack. "You had a couple of phone calls—one from Skyler and one from a man who wouldn't leave his name."

Again Holly felt uneasy. "What did he say? The man who wouldn't give you his name, I mean?"

Madge shrugged, fussing with her contest paraphernalia. "Just that he'd call back. Skyler wants you to call him."

Holly was suddenly testy. If Skyler wanted to talk to her, he could darned well call back. She saw Madge to the door and then headed off toward the kitchen, planning to take one of her experiments out of the freezer and zap it in the microwave. She'd been running late before cooking class and hadn't had a chance to eat dinner.

Just as the bell on the microwave chimed, so did the telephone. Muttering, Holly dived for the receiver, afraid that the ringing of the upstairs extension would awaken Toby.

"Hello?" she demanded impatiently.

The voice on the other end of the line was haunted, shaky. "Sis?"

Holly's knees gave out and she sank into the chair at the desk. "Craig! Where are you? What—"

Her brother laughed nervously and the sound was broken and humorless, painful to hear. "Never mind where I am. You know I can't tell you that. Your phone might be bugged or something."

"Craig, don't be paranoid. Where are you?"

"Let's just say that this call isn't long-distance from Kabul. How's Toby?"

Holly deliberately calmed herself, measuring her tones. She was desperate not to panic Craig and cause him to hang up. "Toby is fine, Craig. How about you?"

"I'm all right. A little tired. More than a little broke."

Holly closed her eyes. So that was the reason for his call. Money. Why was she always surprised by that? "And you need a few bucks."

"You can spare it, can't you?" Craig sounded petulant, far younger than his thirty-six years. "You're a rich lady, sis. Didn't I see you on *Ellen* a few months ago?"

"Craig, come home. Please?"

He made a bitter, contemptuous sound. "And do what? Turn myself in, Holly? Give me a break—I'll be in prison for the rest of my life!"

"Maybe not. Craig, you're not well. You need help. And I promise that I'll stand by you."

"If you want to stand by me, little sister, just send a cashier's check to the usual place. And do it tomorrow if you don't want me to lose weight."

"Craig, listen to me—"

"Just send the money," he barked, and then the line went dead. Holly sat for five minutes, letting her ka-bob get cold in the microwave, holding the telephone receiver in her hand and just staring into space.

Finally she hung up, forced herself out of the chair and took the ka-bob from the microwave. Although she ate, she tasted nothing at all. The ka-bobs she had taken such pride in making might as well have been filled with sawdust.

David Goddard locked the two Webkinz into the trunk of his rented car, shaking his head as he remembered the way he'd had to scramble for them. He sighed, then grinned. The kids would like them, so it had been worth a few scars.

On his way back to the parking garage's lonely elevator, he passed the place where Holly's Toyota had been. Instantly, his mind and all his senses brimmed with the scent and image of her.

He reached the elevator and punched the button with an annoyed motion of his right hand. Walt Zigman was full of sheep-dip if he thought that woman was capable of espionage. Holly Llewellyn was harried and she was haunted, but she was nobody's flunky.

The elevator ground to a stop; the doors swished open. David stepped inside and punched another button. He smiled to himself, thinking of the first fruitcake he'd ever put together in his life. It was a good thing no one had bothered to taste it; his cover would have been blown then and there. He'd been too lost in Holly Llewellyn's aquamarine eyes to concentrate on baking.

Baking. He rolled his eyes. For this I went to law school, he thought. For this I walked the first lady's dog.

He reached the first floor of the parking garage, where there was a wine shop and an old-fashioned ice-cream parlor. Ice cream, in this weather? David shivered and lifted his collar before stepping back outside, onto the street.

At the corner, he paused. Gung ho Christmas shoppers surged past him when the light changed, carrying him along. He went back into the department store where Holly had taught her class and again braved the toy department. This time he bought an airplane, a model that would fly by means of a small hand-control unit. Manito Park, she'd said.

Half an hour later David entered his apartment, acquired only two days before, with mingled relief and reluctance. It was a small place, furnished in tacky plaids. The carpet was thin and the last tenant had owned a dog, judging by the oval stains by the door and in front of the fold-out sofa bed. At least he had a telephone. David went to it and, with perverse pleasure, punched out Walt Zigman's home number.

It was after one in the morning on the East Coast and Walt's voice was a groggy rumble. "Who the—"

"Goddard," David said crisply, grinning. "I said I'd report Monday. This is my report."

Zigman swore fiercely. "Goddard, did anybody ever tell you that you're a son of a—"

"I met her."

"Holly Llewellyn?" Walt's interest was immediate. Clearly, he was now wide-awake. "How did you manage that so fast?"

"Simple. I bought yesterday's paper and read the food section. There was a write-up about her new class."

"Her new class in what?"

David closed his eyes. There was no way out of this one. "Fruitcake," he answered reluctantly.

Zigman laughed. "Fitting," came his rapid-fire reply, just as David had expected.

"You're getting corny in your old age, Walt."

"Did you find out anything?"

David unzipped his jacket and flung it down on the couch. It covered the toys and the model airplane in its colorful box—he'd be up half the night assembling that sucker. "Sure," he snapped. "She fed me grapes and poured out the whole sordid story of her life in the underworld."

"Don't be a smart—"

"I met her. That's all. But I can tell you this much, Walt—she's no traitor. I'm wasting my time here."

"You're getting paid for it. Keep your eye on the ball, Goddard. When it's time for you to come back to D.C. and follow the new first lady around, I'll let you know."

This time it was David who swore. "Tell me, Walt," he began dryly, "does she have a dog?"

"Three of them," said Walt with obnoxious satisfaction. "By the time the new first family takes up residence, you'll be back on good old Pennsylvania Avenue, passing out poochie treats."

"You're funny as hell, you know that? In fact, why don't you take your goddamned job and—"

"Goddard, Goddard," Walt reprimanded in his favorite fatherly tone. "Calm down, I was just kidding you, that's all. You're a damned good agent."

Agent. If he hadn't felt like screaming swearwords, David would have laughed. "I didn't work my way through law school so that I could walk dogs, Walt."

"You really are unhappy, aren't you?"

"In a word, yes."

"We've been through this before."

"Yeah. Good night, Walt."

"Goddard!"

David hung up.

After a few minutes he hoisted himself up off the fold-out couch, dug the stuffed animals out from under his coat and set them on the scarred counter that separated his living room–bedroom from the cubicle the landlady called a kitchen.

Thinking of his nieces and how they were going to enjoy the Webkinz, he began to feel better.

Presently, David took a TV dinner out of the tiny freezer above his refrigerator and shoved it into the doll-sized oven. While it was cooking, he stripped off his clothes, went into the bathroom and wedged himself into a shower designed for a midget. After drying off with one of the three scratchy towels the landlady had seen fit to lend him, he went back to the living room and dug his robe out of a suitcase. Someday, he promised himself, he was going to write a book about the glamorous life of a Secret Service agent.

After consuming the TV dinner, he set about putting the model airplane together. It was after midnight when he finally gave up, washed the glue from his fingers, folded out the sofa bed and collapsed, falling into an instant sleep.

Chapter 3

It was very bad luck that, after a quick visit to her bank that bleak Tuesday morning, Holly encountered David in the neighborhood branch of the post office. Or was it luck?

Holly looked at the carefully wrapped parcel in his arms and decided he was only mailing the Webkinz he'd bought the night before to his nieces. No doubt he lived nearby and it made sense that he would be here.

"Don't you have classes today?" she asked as they waited in line, stiff pleasantries already exchanged.

David smiled wanly. "One o'clock," he answered. He hadn't looked at the address on the envelope Holly carried, as far as she could tell, but she held it against her coat all the same.

Soon enough, it was Holly's turn at the window; she laid the envelope addressed to Craig's go-between girlfriend on the counter and asked that it be registered. While she filled out the form and paid the small fee, David had ample opportunity to study the address, but there was no helping that. She couldn't very well turn around and say, "Please don't look at this envelope. I'm sending money to my brother, who is a fugitive, you see, and there is a chance that you might be a reporter or even an FBI agent." So she said nothing.

"See you tonight?" David asked in a deep quiet voice as she turned away from the window to leave.

Holly hadn't even thought about the classes; she'd been too intent on getting that cashier's check sent off to Craig. "Tonight," she confirmed, but her mind was on the letter she had just mailed. It would reach its destination, Los Angeles, within a day or so. Had she done the wrong thing by making it easier for Craig to keep on running? She knew she had.

She would have left then, but David caught her arm in one hand and stayed her. "Are you all right?" he asked, ignoring the impatient post-office clerk, who was waiting to weigh and stamp the package he still held.

Holly nodded quickly and then fled. In her car, she let her forehead rest against the steering wheel for a moment before starting the engine and driving away. As she pulled into a supermarket parking lot a few minutes later, she was still trembling. She loved Craig; he was her brother. But she almost wished the FBI would catch him. That way there wouldn't be any more lying, any more hiding, any more guilt.

She got out of the car, locking it behind her, and went into the supermarket. Think about the couscous you've got to test today, she told herself. Think about the spices you'll need. Don't think about Craig and especially don't think about David Goddard. It was a co-incidence that he was in the post office just when you were. It was a coincidence!

That seemed unlikely, but by the time she had chosen a cart and gotten out her shopping list, Holly had convinced herself that she was being fanciful again. Paranoid, like Craig.

He was wearing a navy blue football jersey with white numbers, jeans and polished leather boots. Holly, exhausted from a day of making couscous over and over again, gave herself a mental shake. What did she care what David Goddard wore, for heaven's sake?

Her beautiful aquamarine eyes looked hollow and smudges of fatigue and worry darkened the flawless skin beneath. David ached for her. Things were going to get worse, maybe a lot worse, for Holly Llewellyn before they got better.

If they ever got better.

Again he lingered, quietly helping her with the mess left behind by thirteen people struggling with a complicated German recipe. I'll have to go through this eight more times, Holly thought dismally. All the rest of this week. All of next week.

"Coffee?" David asked, drying his hands on one of the pristine towels provided by the store.

Holly found the idea oddly appealing, considering that, on at least one level, she was afraid of David Goddard. "I don't know, I…"

"Please?"

She felt the pull of his blatant masculinity and tried to field it with words. "You didn't take your fruitcake home last night," she said. "The janitor must have thrown it away."

David folded his arms and arched one eyebrow. He saw through what she was doing; she just knew it. "I threw it away myself," he replied, watching her. "I was afraid you might taste it and flunk me on the spot. Now, are we going for coffee or not?"

Holly couldn't help the nervous, weary chuckle that escaped her. "I'll make you a cup at my place." Now what made her say that? She never brought men to her house; only Skyler came there and he usually invited himself.

"Great," agreed the alarming David Goddard before she could take back the offer. "I'll follow you in my car."

Holly put on her coat, thinking that the kitchen table at home was still littered with reference books and parts of the manuscript Elaine had been indexing all day. The remains of that day's couscous experiments probably covered the counters, since Madge wasn't supposed to clean until the next morning; tonight she was only baby-sitting.

Reaching the parking garage, Holly was jarred to find that David's car was next to her own. Not for the first time, she had the unsettling feeling that he always knew where she was and what she was doing. But that was silly. He was a gentleman, that was all. A rare enough animal these days.

"You wanted to make sure I didn't get mugged," she guessed distractedly as he unlocked the door of a small, ordinary brown sedan.

David executed a teasing salute, but Holly was looking at his other hand. The car keys he held were affixed to a chain bearing the insignia of a nationally known rental agency. He rented his car? That seemed odd, just as the vehicle itself was odd, unsuited to him in a myriad of vague ways.

Puzzled, Holly got into her own car, started the ignition and, doubts notwithstanding, led the way to her sizable "cottage" on Spokane's quietly elegant South Hill.

"You rent your car," she said the moment they were in her living room. Not "welcome to my house," not "take off your coat," but "you rent your car." Holly felt stupid.

"Yes," David confessed readily. "Mine is in the shop."

Of course, Holly thought, but she was still bothered on a subliminal, barely discernible level. She drew a deep breath and forced herself to smile. "About that coffee I offered. This way to the kitchen."

David followed her across the shadowy living room, lit only by the dying fire in the hearth, and even though he was walking behind her, she was aware that he was taking in a tremendous amount of information just by looking around.

"Be prepared for a mess," she chimed, to cover her uneasiness. "My assistant and I spent the day making couscous."

They entered the kitchen and Holly stopped so swiftly that David nearly collided with her from behind; she felt the hard wall of his body touch her and glance quickly away.

Madge was at the sink, just finishing an impromptu cleaning detail, but her presence wasn't what caught Holly so off guard. Skyler was sitting at the table, sipping coffee. Why hadn't she noticed his car outside?

He looked up and there was a challenge in his brown eyes as they assessed David Goddard. "I don't believe we've met," he said coldly, rising from the bench at Holly's table to glare at David.

Skyler was acting like a jealous husband and it infuriated Holly, but before she could say anything at all David crossed the room and extended his hand to Skyler.

"David Goddard," he said in crisp introduction.

Madge took in the scene with bright, interested eyes, but did not say anything. Neither did Holly, who was too taken aback by the intangible storm that was suddenly raging in her quiet, cozy kitchen.

"Skyler Hollis," came the grudging reponse.

David took in Skyler's sleek blond hair, elegant green sweater and custom-made slacks in one swift, indigo sweep. "Did you ever appear in *GQ* magazine?" he asked.

Madge made a chortling sound and turned back to the sink. Holly rolled her eyes heavenward and then stomped over to the counter, where the coffeemaker waited.

"I own a stereo store," Skyler announced, either missing the reference to his wholesome good looks or choosing to ignore it. "What do you do, Goddard?"

David, Holly saw in a quick glance over one shoulder, gave a slow smile. "I'm learning to make fruitcake."

"Fruitcake," Skyler huffed, scowling. "I meant, what do you do for a living?"

"I'm a door-to-door salesman," was the icy and totally false reply. "I sell air fresheners. You know, those little bowls with the flowers in them—"

"Here's your coffee," Holly broke in archly, setting David's cup down on the just-cleared trestle table with a resounding thump. "Skyler, do you need a refill?"

Skyler shot her a look and carried his cup to the sink, where he thrust it into the hands of a sedately amused Madge Elkins. "No!" he barked.

"Am I breaking up a meaningful relationship?" David asked, lifting his cup in an unsuccessful attempt to hide a grin.

Skyler's look darkened; he leaned back against the counter and stubbornly folded his arms.

Holly was embarrassed and exasperated. "Skyler Hollis, will you just sit down, please? David is—"

"I know what David is," Skyler snapped before he stomped out of the kitchen. Seconds later, the front door slammed.

"I'm sorry," David said.

"I could swear I saw smoke coming out of that man's ears," Madge put in, receiving a swift look from Holly for her trouble.

The housekeeper smiled and shrugged, then took her leave without waiting for an introduction to David Goddard.

They were alone. Holly sighed heavily and fixed her gaze on her own cup of coffee.

"Are you in love with Skyler—what's his name? Hollis?"

The directness of the question brought Holly's gaze shooting up from the dark brew in her cup to David's face. "In love with him?" she echoed stupidly.

"You do realize, I hope, that if you marry that guy your name will be Holly Hollis?"

Holly burst out laughing. "You know, I never thought of that. I guess I'd just have to go on calling myself Llewellyn."

David's impossibly blue eyes were filled with gentle

humor. "I really am sorry if I caused any trouble, Holly. If you want me to apologize to Hollis, I will."

"No," Holly said quickly. Perhaps too quickly. "Skyler had no right to act that way," she added moments later, in more carefully measured tones. "He has no claim on me and if I want to bring a friend home for coffee…"

"Is that what I am, Holly? Your friend?"

Holly clasped her hands together in her lap. She was twenty-seven years old, an adult, but she suddenly felt like a fifteen-year-old on her first date. "I hope so," she said softly.

Graciously, David changed the subject. The muscles in his forearms worked as he reached for the sugar bowl and added a spoonful to his coffee. "You aren't even thirty yet, unless I miss my guess," he said. "How did you happen to accomplish so much by such a tender age?"

Holly was comfortable with the subject of her career, at least. She pushed aside the strange suspicions she had about this man who sat across the table from her and allowed herself to forget, for a little while, her worries about Craig and her impossible relationship with Skyler Hollis. "I was lucky. My grandmother wrote cookbooks, you know, and she taught me a lot. And I worked hard."

"You must have spent a lot of time with your grandmother," David remarked, watching her.

"My brother and I lived with her, along with our mother. Our father was killed in an accident when I was seven," Holly blurted out in a rush. There, she thought. If he asks about Craig, I'll know something is wrong.

She held her breath.

"Your mother and grandmother are both gone now?" David asked gently.

Holly was unaccountably relieved, though her throat tightened when she answered. "Grandmother passed away, yes. Mother married a missionary doctor and we don't see her very often."

David's rugged face seemed to grow taut for a moment. "You've never been married?"

Holly shook her head. "I almost was, once." Strange. She could think of Ben now, without hurting. "What about you?"

David laughed, but there was no amusement in the sound or in the ink-blue flash of his eyes. Holly knew before he spoke that he'd once been hurt, and very badly. "I got married during my second year of law school," he said. "Marleen was a graduate student in Animal Sciences."

There was anger as well as pain in his voice. Holly deduced that Marleen had not died, as Ben had. "And?" she prompted.

"And she's now in Borneo studying chimps. She finds them endlessly fascinating and far less demanding, I would imagine, than a husband."

The bitterness in his tone stung Holly profoundly. David still loved Marleen despite his anger; she was sure of it. And for some reason, that hurt. "I'm sorry," she said, getting up hastily to go to the coffeemaker and bring the decanter back to the table, where she refilled her own cup and then David's.

"Don't be," David replied succinctly. "Marleen is happy."

But what about you? Holly wanted to ask, though, of

course, she didn't dare. She put sugar into her coffee—something she never did—and kept her eyes averted.

"You said you were almost married once. What happened, Holly?"

Holly's throat constricted again. "My fiancé was killed," she managed to say. "He was working on a construction project in Alaska and...and he fell."

"You loved him a lot, didn't you?"

Holly nodded. "I wanted to die, too, at the time. And I was so angry."

There was a short, companionable silence. The coffeemaker made gurgling sounds and the fire crackled on the kitchen hearth. David's hand came, strong and warm, across the tabletop, to shelter Holly's hand.

It was then that Toby shuffled into the kitchen, looking sleepy and rumpled in his cherished Spider-Man pajamas. "Is it time to go to school, Mom?" he asked, befuddled.

Holly's eyes darted involuntarily to David's face, then shifted to her nephew. "No, sweetheart, it's still night. Go back to bed."

Toby gave David a curious look. "Who's that?" he demanded.

"This is Mr. Goddard, Toby. He's a friend of mine, a student in my cooking class."

Toby assessed David again. "You cook?" he wanted to know.

David laughed and the odd tension Holly had felt was broken. "Not very well, slugger," he retorted kindly, "but I'm learning."

"I'm not going to learn," Toby said firmly, drawing just a bit nearer to David, sensing, as Holly did, that this was a man who liked children.

"Oh, yeah? Why not?" David asked. And he sounded truly interested, not patronizing. "Don't you think men should cook?"

Toby shrugged, not exactly sure what he thought. "Mom cooks enough stuff. Do you think men should cook?"

David thought. "Yeah," he answered presently.

"Why?"

"Because they get hungry."

Toby grinned. "Wanna see my airplane?"

David looked to Holly for her permission; she liked him for doing that. She nodded.

"Sounds interesting," the man said to the boy, and then they were off to Toby's room to inspect the radio-controlled Cessna. The sound of their retreating voices gave Holly an odd feeling of well-being. Which was immediately spoiled by the ringing of the telephone.

She answered with a brisk and biting, "Yes?"

"Who is that Goddard guy?" Skyler demanded without preamble.

Holly drew a deep breath, then let it out again. Control, she must maintain her control. "David is a friend of mine, Skyler." Sugary acid slipped past her resolve, dripping from every word. "I am allowed to have friends, aren't I?"

"Not men!"

"Good night, Skyler," Holly sang, and then she set the receiver firmly back in its cradle.

Seconds later, the telephone rang again.

"Hello?" Holly said sweetly.

"Don't you ever hang up on me again, Holly Llewellyn!" Skyler shouted.

Of course, Holly had no choice but to do exactly that.

She then adjusted her answering machine to pick up on the first ring. If Skyler chose to call again, he would be cordially invited to leave his name, number and message. If he felt called upon to deliver a lecture, he would get only an electronic whirring sound in reply.

Holly was at the sink when David returned to the kitchen; though she didn't hear him, not consciously at least, she was aware of him in every sense. She stiffened as he came toward her, his boots making a melodic sound on the hard brick floor.

"Holly?"

She turned to face him. She couldn't keep her fingers from clenching the counter behind her.

David stopped, looking stricken. "You're afraid of me."

"Y-yes."

"Why?"

How could she explain, when she didn't understand it herself? She was afraid of David Goddard, and yet his nearness was causing every nerve-ending in her body to jump and crackle like naked electrical wire. Not even Ben—tender, laughing, lost Ben—had ever affected her in quite that way.

"Holly?" he prompted.

Holly felt very silly and not a little old-maidish. She blushed and gave a nervous, shaky laugh. "It's not as though I think you're... I mean... I know you're not—"

He was closer now. Holly could feel the heat and the strength of him. He was not yet touching her, but God help her, she wanted him to. She wanted him to hold her and kiss her and— He did. He kissed her. He cupped his gentle, strong hands, one on each side of her flushed face, bent his head and kissed her. His lips were soft and cautious, making no demands.

A strange warmth filled Holly, stabbing her in some places, soothing her in others. She trembled when his tongue persuaded her lips to part for him and she moaned at his thorough, masterful yet entirely tender conquering.

And his body was warm and hard against Holly's, pressing, igniting licking flames of unfamiliar, unexpected passion. It hadn't been like this with Ben, she reflected frantically. Not even when they actually made love.

David drew back suddenly, with an obvious effort. "I'd better leave," he said in a hoarse voice, his eyes not quite linking with Holly's.

She was wounded and still breathless. "David—"

At last he looked at her, and she saw anguish in the depths of his eyes, along with a cold, self-directed anger. "I'm sorry," he rasped, reaching for his jacket.

Holly wanted to cry. She wanted to laugh. She didn't know what she wanted to do, except make love to David Goddard and have him make love to her. And that wasn't possible, of course, because they'd only known each other for a day and because Toby was sleeping upstairs. "Don't be sorry. You didn't do anything wrong."

"Didn't I?" he asked, speaking more to himself, it seemed, than to Holly.

Holly couldn't believe the crazy things that were going on inside her, the aching, melting sensations. The howling hunger. And her breasts. Her breasts quivered with a need to be fondled, their tips still at eager attention. What was happening to her?

"Will you come and have dinner with Toby and me tomorrow night, David?" she heard herself ask.

A log fell in the fireplace, sparks snapping. The silence was terrible and so was Holly's suspense. Which would be worse: his refusal or his acceptance?

"Yes," he said finally, and with some reluctance. "I know better, but I'll do it."

"Seven?" Holly asked with a calmness that amazed her. "We could go on to class afterward."

David wasn't looking at her; it seemed that he couldn't. The telephone jangled but the answering machine picked up instantly. The silence was heavy, pulsing.

"Seven," he said hoarsely, and then he was leaving, striding away from Holly with determined motions.

After she'd heard the front door close and the engine of his car start up with a fierce, revving sound, she could move again. She locked the house and turned out the few lights that still burned, then made her way upstairs.

Her bed looked as it always had—the same Pennsylvania Dutch quilt covered the practical flannel sheets beneath. The same brass headboard glistened in the light from the lamp on her dresser. The same two pillows waited, neither having ever borne the weight of a man's head. Not Skyler's certainly. Not even Ben's.

The bed was unchanged, but Holly's feelings about sharing it were vastly different. Tonight it looked lonely and cold rather than spacious.

Shaking her head, she went into the small bathroom adjoining her room, washed her face, brushed her teeth, stripped off the black slacks and red sweater she had worn that night, and finally the wispy panties and bra underneath.

Holly stood naked before the full-length mirror on the back of her bedroom door. She saw a well-proportioned if unremarkable body, curved in some places, hollowed in others.

She permitted herself to remember that long-ago summer, between high school and college, when she and Ben had given in to the dizzying, constant demands of their youthful bodies. She had not soared, as books and movies had led her to believe she would, but she had not been traumatized, either. Ben's lovemaking had been gentle and pleasant, if not truly fulfilling.

But now, as the result of one brief kiss, Holly knew that, with David Goddard, her body would respond with abandon. It would sing. It would quiver.

The prospect was completely alarming.

With flouncing motions, Holly stormed over to her dresser, wrenched open a drawer and pulled out a long T-shirt-style gown. She quickly put the garment on, as though that would dispel the crazy hungers, the yearnings, that had lain dormant until one particular man had kissed her.

Determinedly, she got into bed and settled into the warmth of the soft flannel sheets. Unable to sleep, she tossed this way and that, plumping her pillows, lying down and sitting back up again.

After almost twenty minutes of this, Holly faced a very disturbing fact. Sure as the sun would rise in the morning, sure as the December snows would fall, David Goddard was going to make love to her. It was inevitable; it was inescapable. The self-control she needed in order to feel strong and safe would desert her.

Tears burned in Holly's eyes and flowed down her cheeks. She would be changed forever and then she would be left because David was not what he seemed to be, not what he claimed to be.

All her instincts warned that this was true and yet she could feel herself sliding toward him, careening down some steep psychological hill. And there was nothing to grasp, nothing to break her fall.

She rolled over and sniffled, tucking both hands under her face the way she had as a little girl. Skyler. She would think of Skyler and everything would be all right.

What did Skyler look like? She couldn't remember. After dating the man for months, she couldn't remember!

"Oh, damn!" Holly cried into the quilt edge that was bunched in her hands. Again she tried to summon Skyler's face to her mind but it wouldn't come; instead, she saw David's dark hair, David's strong jawline, David's ferociously blue eyes.

"Who are you, David Goddard?" Holly wailed inwardly, her mind full of shimmering tangles of fear and joy, happiness and dread. Who are you?

Except for the wild, thunderous beating of her own heart, there was no answer.

Chapter 4

David bent and tapped the side of the glass fishbowl with an impatient index finger. The two goldfish floated, one above the other, just staring at him, their shimmering fan-shaped tails barely moving.

"You guys are really boring, you know that?" he complained in an undertone. "I bought you to give this place some color and flash and what do you do? You just sit there, watching the world go by. Swim, dammit!"

The fish regarded him implacably, still hovering midway between the surface of the water and the bottom, with its blue rocks and shifting plastic fern and dime-store diver.

"No class," David grumbled, turning away and wrenching the damp sweatband from his forehead in one irritated movement.

Still breathing hard from his customary morning

run, he stumbled into the bathroom and took a quick shower. Later, as he dried himself and dressed—in the living room, for God's sake—he wondered how the hell he was ever going to impress Holly Llewellyn with a place like this.

Draping a towel over his shoulders because his hair was still dripping wet, he took in the goldfish, the un-made sofa bed, the spots on the carpet. No class. Like those seventy-nine-cent goldfish, the place had no class.

The telephone rang and David, who had been in-dulging in a fanciful nostalgia for his real apartment in faraway Georgetown, was startled. He put images of good art, the hot tub in his bathroom and the ivory fire-place out of his mind as he lunged for the instrument.

"Goddard," he answered, and the long-distance buzz coming over the wire told him that he'd been right. This was his call from Washington.

"Zigman here," Walt replied. "The Bureau staked out the address in L.A., Goddard, but they must have muffed it somehow, because Llewellyn didn't bite."

David had a headache. He had hoped the FBI would be able to collar Llewellyn immediately; like a child about to have a sliver pulled, he'd wanted the whole thing to be over with. "He was an agent himself once. He probably knows the signs."

"Yeah."

"Does this mean I can drop the case and come back to Washington?" Part of David hoped it did, while an-other part wanted to watch Holly Llewellyn forever.

"Hell, no. The little lady sent him a letter, didn't she? You saw it with your own eyes, Goddard. That means she's in fairly regular contact with our boy, doesn't it?"

David resented the "little lady" reference. Holly was

so much more and the phrase seemed to demean her. "Holly is a woman, Walt. With a brain."

Zigman's laugh traveled three thousand miles to annoy David as instantly as if he'd been in the same room. "Goddard, you are going soft. Don't get to liking this broad too much. She's in line for an indictment herself, you know."

"For what?" David snapped.

"Christ," Zigman swore impatiently. "For aiding and abetting a fugitive. Are you going to wake the hell up, Goddard, or do I have to send somebody else out there to handle this thing?"

David bit back all the fury that surged like bile into his throat. He'd never been pulled from a detail in all the time he'd worked for the service, and he wasn't about to start now. Besides, he couldn't be sure how another agent would manage the situation. And it was delicate. Holly's emotional state was delicate. "I can handle it," he said.

"Wouldn't have sent you if I didn't think you could," Walt replied in smug tones. His cigar stub was probably bobbing up and down in his mouth, and David wished he could be there to squash it into the man's teeth. "Keep a sharp eye out, Goddard. Llewellyn could turn up there. If he does, I want him busted. On the spot."

The thought made David half-sick, and he closed his eyes. His wet hair was dripping cold trails down his neck and he began drying it with one end of the towel. He could imagine the look on Holly's face if he casually wrestled Llewellyn to the floor in her living room. "Yeah."

"Can you handle him by yourself or do you want a detail? The Bureau has an office in Spokane—"

"You keep the Bureau the hell out of this, Walt! I mean it!" The outburst was too sudden, too emotional. David drew a deep breath and stopped toweling his hair to sigh. "Llewellyn is a former agent," he reiterated a moment later, when he could speak more moderately. "If he sees a bunch of three-piece suits and crew cuts watching his sister's house, how do you think he'll react?"

"He'll split, just like he did in L.A."

"Right." David sighed again, running one hand through his hair. "Let me handle this, will you, Walt? If I need the Bureau, I can always call them in."

"All right," Walt agreed in his gruff, wry way. "But you remember why you're there. It isn't to make fruitcake, Goddard. Or time."

David's headache was infinitely worse. "Yeah," he agreed after a long, long time. "I'll remember."

"Good," came the brisk reply. "When do you see the broad again?"

Enough was enough. He'd let that word pass once; he couldn't do it again. "Don't call her that again, Walt. If you do, your nose will be where your right ear is now. I'll see to it."

Zigman swore and rang off.

David held the receiver in his hand for a long time, doing some swearing of his own. Craig Llewellyn was going to show up in Spokane, he could feel it in his bones. It was only a matter of time. Holly was going to be destroyed by the inevitable arrest, by David's deception.

Why the hell had he accepted the dinner invitation, dammit? Suppose there was a replay of that episode when he'd kissed her, in the kitchen? What then? David had spent most of the night reliving that ill-guided indulgence and imagining all the sweet pleasures that could have come after it.

He shook his head, trying to dislodge the thought, but his body recollected perfectly. Heatedly. He'd had his share of women, of course, but none had ever made him feel quite the way Holly did. She could reach past the hard finish painted over him by his Secret Service training. She could so easily reach past it.

Maybe Walt Zigman was right; maybe he was losing his ability to be objective. Maybe he was getting soft.

David allowed himself one rueful, humorless chuckle. *Soft* was definitely not the word. Not where Holly Llewellyn was concerned.

The day was a full and busy one, but it took forever to pass, all the same. Instead of thinking about her newspaper column, as she should have been, every turn of Holly's mind seemed to lead to David Goddard.

Elaine was gathering together the leaves of the manuscript she had been working on, preparing to leave. "What time is the hunk coming over?" she asked.

Color leaped into Holly's cheeks and pounded there. "What hunk?" she asked tightly, a little annoyed that Elaine could read her preoccupation so easily.

"Don't give me that. I'm talking about your date with David Goddard and you know it. What are you serving? What are you wearing? Do you want me to take Toby home with me for the evening?"

"Once your questions start coming, there's no stopping them, is there?" Holly countered, still flushed. She took the disk containing her pitiful effort at a cooking column from the computer and shut off the machine with an angry flourish.

Elaine was not intimidated, but she did back off just a little. "I could take Toby home," she offered again. "Roy and I enjoy him so much, and—"

"Toby is staying right here!"

"Why? Do you need him as a buffer, Holly?"

Holly had been halfway out of her chair; now she sagged back into it. "I wouldn't use Toby that way, Elaine," she said, but the doubt in her voice bothered her.

"It's all right, you know, to want time alone with an attractive man. It's not going to scar Toby's pysche or anything."

In spite of herself, Holly chuckled. Elaine did have a way of lightening a situation. "Last night," she confessed after a few moments of reflection, "David kissed me."

"So?"

"So it was weird, Elaine. The earth moved. Bells chimed. All the corny stuff you see in movies and read about in books—it all happened."

Elaine beamed. "That's great!"

"It is not," Holly insisted, her face set and serious again. "It's terrible. That man is dangerous, Elaine."

"Dangerous? Why?"

Now Holly felt foolish and she couldn't quite bring herself to meet her friend's eyes. "He's not like Skyler. He's—"

"Thank God for small favors."

Holly was putting her computer disk into its paper folder, turning off the printer, clearing her desk. Anything to keep from looking directly at Elaine. "You don't like Skyler, do you? I can understand why Toby doesn't, but you should."

"He's all right," Elaine conceded with a heavy and somewhat dramatic sigh. "It's just that he's so, well, you know, safe. Boring."

"He's reliable, that's what he is," defended Holly. "I might marry him."

"If you do, you're crazy. You don't love Skyler, Holly."

"How do you know?" Holly demanded. But she wished with all her heart that she could love Skyler, truly want him. Even need him. It made her mad that she couldn't.

"If you loved him, ninny-brain, you wouldn't be all hot and bothered because David Goddard is coming to dinner. You haven't thought straight all day."

Holly slumped. "I'm not 'hot and bothered'!" she lied in a plaintive wail.

Elaine only laughed. "Let me take Toby home with me. Please? I promise to give him the most nutritionally balanced TV dinner in the freezer, and I'll bring him home after your class lets out."

Holly hadn't even thought about the class. Dear Lord, that was one more thing to add to the worries she already had, like what she was going to serve David Goddard for dinner and what she was going to wear. She wanted to look attractive, but not predatory....

It was as though, by their long and friendly association, Elaine had learned to look right inside Holly's brain and read her every thought. "Wear something sexy. Leopard skin, maybe."

Holly laughed. "Leopard skin? This is a quiet, casual dinner, not a movie about barbarians! And I have no desire to look 'sexy.'"

"Pity," Elaine said, looking entirely serious. "A woman ought to wear something sort of Frederick's-of-Hollywoodish once in a while."

Holly only shook her head, amazed. She wanted to ask if Elaine herself ever wore such garments but didn't quite dare.

"Hey, Tobe!" Elaine yelled, shaking off the look of deep thought, beaming again. "Come on! You're coming home with me tonight!"

The TV, blaring in the family room, went silent. The next sound, in fact, was a little boy's whoop of delight. Toby bounded into the room, already struggling into his jacket, his face shining. "Do you think Uncle Roy will play Donkey Kong with me?"

Elaine gave the child a conspiratorial smile. "Yes. But you must promise to let him beat you at least once."

Toby squared his small shoulders manfully and looked charitably reluctant. "Oh, all right. But just once."

There was a whoosh of goodbyes, Toby planting a quick, wet kiss on Holly's cheek, and then a swirl of cold air when the back door was opened. And they were gone.

Holly sighed, and as an aching sense of loneliness grasped her, she took herself firmly in hand. "Frederick's of Hollywood!" she muttered irritably as she went to the freezer to take out falafel and couscous experiments from last week's chapter of her new cookbook.

She slammed the foil-wrapped packages down on the countertop, near the sink. If David Goddard didn't like eating experiments, the heck with him. What did he think this place was, a restaurant? Why, if he said one single word, she would...she would...

Holly sighed. Who was she kidding? She put the foil packages back into the freezer and took out the special beef stroganoff she'd been saving in case Skyler's parents decided to come to Spokane on one of their infrequent visits.

After straightening the kitchen and throwing together a green salad, she raced upstairs to take a shower and exchange her jeans and madras shirt for something more—more what? Sexy?

Still dripping from her shower, wrapped only in a bright pink bath sheet, Holly shoved the white cashmere suit back into the closet. It was too clingy, that was all. Entirely too clingy.

She brought out a flowing blue dress, interwoven with tiny silver threads, that she'd picked up in Iran only the month before. Even then she'd had no idea where she would wear such a thing, but she hadn't been able to resist the gown's quiet elegance.

She returned that garment to the closet, too. After all, it had that deep neckline and it was too formal. Whatever she chose would have to do for the cooking class she had to teach after dinner, she reminded herself.

Finally, Holly settled for tailored black slacks and a soft mulberry sweater. Not exactly suited to making Belgian fruitcake, she thought, but at least she would look halfway decent when David arrived and she could always push up the sleeves later, when it was time to conduct her class.

Hurriedly, she brushed her hair, applied her makeup and brushed her hair again. She allowed herself one cool misting of the expensive perfume she'd once bought on a dash through the Paris airport.

When the rites of womanhood had all been performed, she stood back from the mirror to look at herself. Her lipstick was crooked, and she wiped it off and reapplied it, this time using a lip liner. "Color inside the lines, now," she mocked herself.

David arrived promptly at seven o'clock, just as they'd agreed. Not a moment before and not a moment after. Something about this small precision bothered Holly, but she pushed the feeling aside.

There was a fire crackling in the living room fireplace and the table in the rarely used dining room had been set with pretty china and her grandmother's silver. David looked impossibly handsome in his gray slacks, creamy white sweater and navy blue jacket. No indeed, this was no time for silly doubts.

"Come in," she said, stepping back.

David smiled, but the look in his eyes was weary. Perhaps he'd had a hard day at law school. He extended a bottle of wine and then took off his coat. "Where's Toby?" he asked, and the expression in his indigo-blue eyes was suddenly expectant.

Holly was a bit embarrassed. Now she was going to have to say that Toby was spending the evening at Elaine and Roy's, and it would look as though she'd been setting the scene for a steamy seduction. Why, oh, why had she lighted the fire and set the table so carefully? "He had a previous engagement," she said.

"Good," David replied smoothly.

"Good?" Holly echoed, confused.

David laughed. "A man's got to have a social life," he answered, and Holly remained off-balance because she didn't know whether he meant that Toby needed a social life or he did.

They ate in the dining room, with the candles lit—

Holly had been too shy to light them, so David had done it—with the wine and the good china and the glint of the aged silver flatware. Holly hadn't entertained a man in this particular way in as long as she could remember, and she was uncomfortable and distracted, not knowing what to do or how to act. The fact that she silently flogged herself for being silly didn't help; she still felt like a fifteen-year-old about to go to her first prom.

"Do we have time to sit by the fire for a while," David asked easily, setting his wineglass aside, "or are we off to tackle the mysteries of Belgian rum sauce?"

Holly laughed, even though the thought of sitting in front of a romantic winter fire with a man—with *this* man—patently made her nervous. "We have a few minutes."

He stood up, but instead of coming around to pull back Holly's chair, as Skyler would have done, he started gathering up dirty dishes. Holly was disappointed for a moment, but then she decided that one act was as considerate as the other and began to help.

Holly waited, every nerve screaming, for him to kiss her. He didn't do it while they were clearing the table, of course, and in the kitchen he kept the dishwasher door between them as they put the china and silverware inside. Was he shy or something?

Holly's cheeks stung with color. Elaine was right, she castigated herself angrily, you're hot and bothered!

Once the dishwasher was churning away, David caught Holly's hand casually in his and led her back to the living room as though it were his house. As though they had all the time in the world.

"Maybe we shouldn't—" she sputtered, lifting his

hand so that she could peer at the watch on her own wrist. "It's getting late—"

David sat down on one of the soft Indian pillows facing the fireplace and pulled Holly after him. She tumbled against him, and her heart lurched into her throat at even that small contact, driving the breath out of her lungs and causing a curious ringing sound in her ears.

She settled herself primly on the other pillow, careful not to look at him. She knew that she would see the familiar, quiet amusement shining in his navy blue eyes.

"Holly."

She swallowed, knotting her hands together in her lap. "What?"

"Look at me."

She looked at him because doing otherwise would have been foolish and petulant. Even infantile. "So, I'm looking already," she said.

He laughed and that was at variance with the look in his eyes which, instead of humor, betrayed a reluctance of some kind. A hurtful reluctance.

Holly was stung. David wanted to resist her as badly as she wanted to resist him! Wasn't she attractive? Did he find her— David bent his head and kissed her, and an almost inaudible groan rumbled up through his chest and brushed against her lips. He was only nibbling at her mouth, tasting it as though it were a delicacy to be savored. He muttered something, and to a dazed Holly, it sounded as though he'd said, "Why?"

She couldn't think of that now. She couldn't think of anything except the havoc that reluctant kiss was causing inside her. She shivered and placed her hands on his strong shoulders, where they moved of their own accord to caress his neck.

He kissed her in earnest then, his tongue exploring the sweet depths of her mouth, enlisting her own to respond in quick, fevered parries. His hand moving gently up and down the length of her thigh caused the flesh hidden beneath to quiver.

Holly wanted to die and she wanted to live forever. She wanted to stop and she drew him nearer, allowing him to shift her body and his own so that they were both prone before the crackling fire.

His hand left her thigh to move up over her hip, underneath her soft mulberry sweater, over the flesh at her waist, over her rib cage. He freed her from his sorcerer's kiss to nibble gently, provocatively, at her earlobe and her neck.

"I want you, Holly," he said in that forthright way of his, his voice a gruff caress against the base of her neck.

Holly shivered, even though there was a heat pulsing inside her that made her long to fling off her clothes. "David, I...we..."

"I know." He chuckled, and his hand had found the catch at the front of her bra. There was a feeling of sweet, wanton freedom as her breasts were released, and then his fingers were soothing her, searching out a nipple that already awaited them at strictest attention. "Tell me to stop."

If Holly hadn't been so bedazzled, she would have slapped him. "I can't..." she admitted, her words falling away to a groan as he found that arching nipple and rolled it gently between his fingers.

He drew her sweater slowly upward, his hand cupping the captured breast, shaping it for conquering. When he bent his head to lave the throbbing peak softly with his tongue, Holly gasped with pleasure and arched her back in reflexive surrender.

"We...can't do this..." he managed to say as his mouth blazed a path from the conquered breast to the one that awaited sweet defeat. "We can't..."

"I know," Holly agreed. But when his tongue touched the untended nipple, she knotted her hands in David's rich, mink-soft hair and held him close.

Holly Llewellyn was to wonder many times, sometimes with regret and sometimes with relief, what would have happened if the telephone hadn't rung when it did. Its cold, jarring jangle made David thrust himself away from her as if in fury.

Stung and shaken and still needing, Holly hastily fixed her bra and stumbled off at a half jog to answer.

"Hello!" she gasped, winded and embarrassed. She could see David from where she stood and he was just staring into the fire, his broad back rigid.

"Sis?"

Holly wanted to cry. Not now, she thought frantically. Oh, God, not now! She lowered her voice. "Hello, Craig."

"'Hello, Craig'? Is that all you've got to say?"

Holly stiffened, very conscious of the man sitting before the fireplace. Her breasts were still heavy and warm with passion, their peaks moist. She tried to breathe properly. "What should I say, Craig?" she asked petulantly, forgetting this time to keep her tone at whisper level.

"I tried to pick up the money," Craig rushed on angrily, frantically. "Guess what? There were crew cuts all around Cindy's place!"

Holly trembled, then drew a deep breath. "Crew

cuts?" she repeated, confused. David's back stiffened almost imperceptibly, or was that a trick of the firelight? He didn't appear to be making the slightest effort to hear what was being said, but appearances could be deceiving.

"FBI agents. Holly, they were everywhere! Did you turn me in?"

"Of course I didn't!" At this outburst, David turned his head, assessing Holly with a look she could read all too well: it was full of stark, angry pity.

"Just listen," Craig rasped. God in heaven, how desperate, how hunted, he sounded. "I'm going to need money, Holly, and if I have to come there and get it, I will!"

"You can't do that! Toby would be—"

"Toby. Always Toby. Don't you ever think about anybody besides that kid, Holly? What about me? I'm your brother, remember?" Craig stopped to draw a harsh breath and then began to cough. It was a frightening sound.

"You're sick!" Holly exclaimed, watching David. He had turned his eyes from her again and was now gazing into the fire, one knee drawn up under his chin. "Craig, please—turn yourself in. They won't hurt you, I swear it!"

"I'll call again tomorrow!" Craig roared impatiently, and then he slammed the receiver down so hard that Holly flinched. She was on the verge of tears when she placed her own receiver in its cradle.

The silence in the living room was complete, except for the snapping merriment of the fire. David looked at Holly but did not rise from his seat near the hearth. Holly closed her eyes momentarily, in a vain effort to shut out the reality of Craig and his problems, then drew a deep breath to steady herself.

"Y-you're a lawyer," she began, speaking as casually as she could. "If someone is wanted by the law, and another person…a person close to them…knows where they are and sometimes gives them money…"

David rose slowly to his feet with the grace of a predatory animal, but he kept his distance. And it was more than a physical distance. "Then that person is guilty of aiding and abetting a fugitive," he said evenly. "They could, under some circumstances, be imprisoned."

Holly trembled and bit her lower lip. When she closed her eyes against the possibility, her already precarious balance was affected and she swayed. David was instantly clasping her shoulders, holding her upright. And while there was a gentleness in his touch, there was little sympathy.

"I can help you, Holly," he said hoarsely. "If you'll just allow yourself to trust me, I swear I can help you."

Holly longed to pour out the whole ugly story, to tell him how scared and confused Craig was, to explain that he hadn't meant to do all those awful things. But she didn't dare. The fact that she had almost given herself to David moments before, making a joyous offering of something she held dear, changed nothing.

David Goddard was still a stranger.

Chapter 5

The rest of that week was dismal for Holly. She couldn't concentrate on her work and she was short not only with Elaine but with Toby. When Skyler called, offering an innocent-sounding invitation to lunch, she all but bit his head off.

In the evenings, of course, she taught her cooking class, and David was always there, always attentive—and never friendly. He might have been a total stranger, answering what casual questions Holly could contrive to ask with flat, clipped banalities. Not once did he stay to help with the cleanup, as he had those first two nights, and he certainly made no effort to contact her outside of class.

Holly was devastated and she was scared, too. Craig had nearly been caught in Los Angeles. How could the FBI have known where he would be if not for David's seeing the address on that letter she'd mailed? And that night, that shattering night when they had almost made love, David had said, *"I can help you, Holly. If you'll just allow yourself to trust me. I swear I can help you."*

He knew; she was sure he knew. And as far as Holly was concerned, that was reason enough not to see him again. Ever.

Except that she needed him, wanted him. Perhaps, though she couldn't often bring herself to examine the possibility rationally, she was even beginning to love David Goddard.

On Friday night, Skyler called to ask her out for dinner and a movie. Holly refused, pleading a headache, and went to bed early, setting the answering machine because Skyler had a tendency to be persistent. The telephone rang twice during the night, and a sleepless Holly timed the calls at eleven thirty-five and twelve-ten.

The next morning was one of those springlike days that sometimes creep into winter. Though there were still ragged patches of snow on the ground, the sun was bright and the sky was a painfully keen shade of blue.

The weather did much to bring Holly out of her doldrums, and to make up for some of the stresses of the past week, she suggested to a rather wan and distraught Toby that they take his airplane to Manito Park and fly it.

"I'm going to the Ice Capades this afternoon," Toby reminded his aunt, running his spoon glumly through the dish of oatmeal before him. "My whole class is going."

"I remember," Holly said softly. It hurt, this restraint between herself and Toby. It was a sad, pulsing ache. "You'll be back in plenty of time, I promise."

Toby brightened. "Okay," he chirped. "Let's hurry up with breakfast and go!"

His ebullience made Holly laugh, easing the bereft feeling inside her. "Let's do that. Be sure to wear your mittens because it's cold."

Toby nodded. As he passed Holly's desk, his oatmeal gleefully abandoned on the trestle table, he stopped. "Mom, there's messages on the machine. The light is flashing."

Holly glanced uneasily toward the telephone. Between Craig and Skyler, it was getting so that she didn't like to answer the thing at all. It wasn't likely that David had left those messages, she told herself, and she was in no mood to hear a lecture from Skyler or a lot of pathos from Craig. "I'll listen later. Right now, I'm in the mood to fly your Cessna."

"Me, too!" Toby agreed, and he was off again, in search of the warmer clothes he would need for a morning in the park.

Perhaps too conscientious for her own good, Holly went to the answering machine and frowned down at the little red light blinking so industriously, her finger poised over the "play" button. What if the calls had been from Craig and he was in terrible trouble? What if—

She stopped herself, sighed and drew back her hand. It could wait. Whatever it was, it could just wait. Any kind of hassle at this moment would be too much.

The park was sunny, and in places patches of green-brown grass dappled the grubby snow. There were lots of children around, their laughter ringing in the ice-cold air, and a goodly number of parents, too.

"I wish I'd brought my sled," Toby said wistfully,

watching as some of the children pushed and pulled each other on Flyers and plastic saucers.

Something twisted inside Holly as she watched her nephew; despite all his friends at school, he was a lonely child, often feeling separate from the others. Alone. While Holly's own childhood had been far from ideal, she had had Craig. Toby had no one near his own age.

The little boy squinted up at her, a grin forming on his face, and the toy Cessna seemed huge in his small hands. "You thinkin' about my dad?" he asked directly.

Holly was stunned. Lately it seemed as though she went around with all her thoughts written on her forehead, so clearly did people read them. "How did you know that?"

Small shoulders, hidden beneath the weight of a down-filled snowsuit, moved in a shrug. "You get a sad look on your face when you think about Dad."

"We were very close once," Holly admitted distractedly, having to look away for a moment because of the tears that stung her eyes.

"Dad's a bad man, isn't he?" Toby probed seriously, his mittened hands working awkwardly with the airplane.

Holly shook her head so suddenly and so hard that her neck ached—as did her heart. "No, Toby. Your dad isn't really a bad man, though he has done some bad things. He's sick, Toby, and pretty confused."

"He doesn't want me."

Holly knelt in the snow, which crackled beneath the worn knees of her oldest jeans, and clasped Toby by the shoulders. "It isn't that way at all, Toby. Your dad loves you. But when people have the kind of troubles he does, they just don't seem to have room in their lives for other things and other people."

Toby's face was scrunched up in the battle against unmanly emotion. "I liked Mr. Goddard a lot. How come he didn't come back? Does he have problems, too, like Dad?"

Holly closed her eyes for a moment and drew a deep breath. "No, Toby. I don't think he has the kind of problems that your dad has. As for why he didn't come back—"

"He was a fool," put in a deep, masculine voice.

Holly and Toby looked up simultaneously, squinting against the dazzling winter sun, to see David standing over them. He wore a dark blue ski jacket and jeans, a contrite expression on his face and held his own model airplane in his hands.

"Hi!" Toby whooped, overjoyed.

While Holly was glad enough to see David herself, glad enough to shout, in fact, she was a little injured by Toby's enthusiasm toward the man. It was as though a hopeless day had just been saved at the last, cliff-hanging second. And there were all her misgivings, too...

"Truce," he said gruffly, extending one hand to Holly, the plane tucked under his opposite elbow now. "Please?"

Holly swallowed. It was sheer, foolhardy madness to get further involved with this man and she knew it, but she couldn't quite bring herself to refuse what she knew he was offering. "Truce," she croaked out, after what seemed like a long time.

Eyes of an impossibly dark blue swept over her so swiftly that she could almost believe it hadn't happened, and then they shifted to Toby. "Hi, slugger. Ready to fly?"

Toby was literally beaming. Again Holly found his obvious fondness for David Goddard unsettling. What would happen when David went away? What if he did something that would hurt Craig and thus Toby, too?

"I'm ready!" came the exuberant answer.

David proved to be a lousy pilot, always dropping his hand-controls or sending his somewhat odd-looking model airplane plunging into bushes, but Holly was too amused to chalk this up as another reason to be suspicious of him. After all, he'd only said he owned a model plane, not that he was proficient at flying one.

In any case, David's ineptitude only seemed to endear him further to Toby, who patiently demonstrated again and again how to handle the craft properly. Holly stood back and watched, full of mingled dread and tender inclinations. She was glad, even relieved, when Toby offered her a turn with his airplane, for that gave her something to think about besides David Goddard and all the wonderful, terrible things that could come of allowing him into her life.

As the small airplane glided and dipped and roared overhead in a perfect circle, following the commands Holly gave it with her handset, Toby and David both applauded. Privately, she was surprised that she hadn't sent the thing crashing into a tree; her fingers wouldn't stop shaking.

Finally the morning ended; it was time to take Toby home, give him lunch and let him have a few quiet minutes before driving him to the Coliseum, where he would join his classmates for the afternoon performance of the Ice Capades.

Leading Toby toward her car, she glanced uncertainly at David. What would happen now? Did he want to talk? Would he just leave, or would there be a renewal of the dangerous attraction that seemed to be sweeping them together?

Holly felt stiff, almost formal. Walk away and don't look back! screamed her mind. This man is dangerous! But her heart said something entirely different. "We enjoyed seeing you again," she ventured aloud.

David's lips curved into a half grin, one that said he understood her feelings because they so closely paralleled his own, but his blue eyes were sad. "Toby will be busy this afternoon?" he asked evenly.

"I'm going to the Ice Capades!" the little boy crowed before Holly could assemble a polite answer.

David's indigo gaze touched the child with real affection, then sliced back to Holly's face. "I need to talk with you, Holly," he said quietly. "To be with you. Will you have lunch with me?"

"Sure she will!" Toby announced with loud confidence, scrambling into the back seat of Holly's car, setting his airplane and handset on the seat and buckling himself into the seat belt.

David laughed, but that quiet ache was still visible in his eyes. "Please," he said.

Holly swallowed hard and nodded. "Shall I meet you somewhere?"

"I'll pick you up at your place in an hour or so, if that's all right."

Holly nodded again and got into her car, busying herself with the fastening of her seat belt and the turning of the ignition key. Anything so that she didn't have to look back and see David getting into that rented car of his, that car that didn't suit him. She couldn't bear the strain of wondering about him anymore, of weighing his motives all the time. No, just for this one day she was going to enjoy what she felt, without letting doubt spoil it.

While Toby consumed soup and a sandwich, his appetite made sharp by a morning of fresh air and exercise, Holly exchanged her Saturday jeans for a pair of fitted gray slacks, her T-shirt and poncho for a classic navy blue blouse with a tie at the throat and a charcoal velvet blazer. She brushed her hair carefully and put on makeup, too, telling herself all the while that she wasn't trying to be attractive for David, not at all. It was just that as something of a local celebrity, she had an image to maintain.

Why she hadn't been concerned with that image earlier in the day, when she'd gone to a public park in her oldest clothes, wearing no makeup, was a question she didn't bother to examine.

When she returned from dropping Toby off at the Coliseum, David was waiting in front of her house. And he was driving a different car.

Holly parked her own Toyota in the driveway, locked it and went toward him, taking in the sleek lines of the red Camaro sitting at the curb. David got out, looking devastatingly handsome in jeans and a cream-colored bulky-knit sweater, and came around to open the car door for her.

"What happened to the rented one?" she asked. "The brown sedan?"

David shook his head, but he went back around the car and got in on his own side before answering. "I told you my car was being fixed, Holly. This is it."

Again, Holly was unsettled. This car looked and smelled so new, how could anything have been wrong with it?

"Don't weigh everything I say, Holly," David said, watching her. "I'm a man, not a mystery to solve."

Holly said nothing. She couldn't deny that he was a man, but the part about his not being a mystery was certainly open to debate.

Lunch, eaten in a plant-filled restaurant overlooking Riverfront Park, the site of a world's fair and Spokane's coveted antique carousel, was a stilted affair.

Holly was as annoyed as she was self-conscious. Hadn't David said he wanted to talk to her? No, in fact, he'd said he *needed* to talk to her. So why didn't he?

His glass of white wine seemed to fascinate him; he turned it in one strong, sun-browned hand, watching the ebb and flow. The silence lengthened.

"I thought you said we were going to talk!" Holly blurted out impatiently. What was it about this man that undid her so? She felt sure that it was more than her rising attraction to him, more even than her doubts about his motives for spending time with her.

He chuckled and the sound was hollow and humorless. "You're in a lot of trouble, aren't you, Holly? Or, I should say, someone very close to you is. Why won't you let me help you?"

Holly bit her lower lip. She wasn't about to make any admissions about Craig and her involvement in his many troubles, but she wanted to. She wanted to let everything pour out. "I don't need any help and I'm not in trouble," she said stubbornly when David's indigo eyes impaled her with an unspoken challenge. "What gave you that idea?"

He made an exasperated sound. "I'm not an idiot, Holly. I was there when this person called, whoever they are."

If Holly felt alarm, she also felt a paradoxical sort of comfort. Could it be that, for all her imaginings, David really didn't know that her caller was Craig? "I think we should leave," she said stiffly.

"Fine," David replied, setting his wineglass down with a jarring thump and rising from his chair to draw back Holly's.

The flesh on the back of her neck tingled as it was brushed briefly by the hard wall of his midsection. Even that small contact stirred the melting warmth deep in Holly's middle and made her heart beat at a faster pace.

She was still shivering when they reached his car.

"Take me home, please," she said, struggling not to fling herself into his arms like some helpless bit of fluff and sob out all the things that were tormenting her.

"Don't worry," he replied in a terse whisper.

But, at the house, he lingered. Against her better judgment, Holly invited him inside for coffee. Just passing through the living room, where they had so nearly made love the night Craig called and ruined everything, made Holly's face burn.

She was grateful to reach the cookbook-cluttered, sensible kitchen. What could happen here?

Too late, Holly remembered the first soul-jarring kiss. That was what could happen here.

She busied herself with the coffeemaker, filling the decanter with cold water, putting a new filter and fresh grounds into the basket. She was so very much on guard that her shoulders ached.

"Holly."

She stiffened as she felt David approach, but could not bring herself to turn around and face him. His hands closed over her shoulders and began gently working the taut muscles there.

"Scary, isn't it?" he asked in a low voice, his breath brushing Holly's ear and part of her cheek.

"Wh-what?" Holly hedged. She knew she should break out of David's hold, but she didn't have the spirit to do that. Besides, the massage he was giving her felt so good.

"The way we need each other."

Holly lifted her chin, barely able to keep from letting her head roll as the muscles in her shoulders were forced to relax. "I don't want to need anybody," she managed to say.

"Neither do I," came the prompt, gruff reply. "But there it is."

He was close, the length of his body comfortingly hard and strong against Holly. Suddenly his hands stopped working her shoulders to cup her breasts with a bold gentleness that caused her to draw in a swift, audible breath.

"D-David—"

His thumbs were stroking her nipples through the thin fabric of her blouse and the gossamer bra beneath. "Let me make love to you, Holly," he said hoarsely, his lips now touching the outer rim of her ear and making every part of her leap with a stinging desire. "If we don't, I'm going to go crazy."

Holly trembled, her head falling backward to press into David's broad shoulder, her eyes closed. "At least you're still sane," she admitted, breathless. "I'm already over the edge. I must be, to do this…"

The delicious torment of her breasts stopped; he turned her swiftly to face him. And new torments, even sweeter than those that had gone before, took over as he kissed her. Holly's knees quivered, threatening to give out, and David supported her by pressing closer, fairly pinning her to the counter's edge.

When he drew back, he searched her face with that same broken, needing look in his eyes. "Holly?"

Flushed, Holly nodded, and that was answer enough for David. He lifted her up into his arms and, at her direction, mumbled into his neck, carried her upstairs and into the bedroom. There, he dropped her summarily onto the rumpled covers, and she had cause to be embarrassed again because she had forgotten to make the bed.

To hide that, she tried to make a joke. "You boldly go where no man has gone before, I'll say that for you."

The indigo gaze impaled her. "Are you saying that you've never…"

Hastily, coloring again, Holly shook her head. "No. My…my fiancé—"

He sat down on the bed beside her, his fingers woven together, hands dangling between his knees. "It's all right, Holly. Just tell me one thing: is this really what you want? If it isn't, I'll leave right now and we'll pretend that none of it ever happened."

Holly did not want David to go. She wanted him to hold her, kiss her, love her. But she couldn't say any of those things because her throat was constricted.

David must have read her need in her eyes and in the flush on her cheekbones, for he kicked off his polished boots and stretched out on the bed beside Holly, wrapping one arm around her, holding her close. She loved the clean scent of his hair and skin, the tender threat of his powerful body.

Eventually he kissed her again, tentatively at first, as though he expected her to push him away. When she didn't, the kiss deepened and with his free hand he began to caress her, cupping his other hand at the back of her head. After a very long time, she felt crooned in sleepy surrender, arching her back just slightly in acquiescence.

When the blouse had been opened completely and laid aside, David unfastened her bra. Her breasts moved with voluptuous freedom, the peaks tightening in response to the fate that awaited them and the coolness of the air.

David continued to caress her, brushing the wanton nipples with his fingertips, charting the rows of her ribs, circling her naval. And all the while, he kissed her, seeking every depth and secret, consuming even as he cherished.

After a time, he kissed the line of her jaw, sampled her earlobe, traced a path of fire down the white length of her neck. When he found her breast and took the nipple full in his mouth to suckle, Holly arched her back again, electrified, and gasped out a senseless cry of welcome.

Meanwhile, his hand undid the tricky buckle on her belt, the button of her slacks and the zipper. Holly felt the fabric of both the slacks and her panties sliding downward and gloried in the sensation.

David left the sensuous warmth of her breasts to brush his lips down the length of her rib cage, first on one side and then on the other. He drew her slacks and panties down and away and kissed the hollows of her hips, making lazy, white-hot circles with the tip of his tongue.

Holly moaned with her need of him, so dazed she could barely see. When he shifted away from her and off the bed, she was stricken, until she realized that David was only removing his own clothing, that he would come back to her.

"Are you sure, Holly?" he asked softly as he stretched out beside her again, part of his lean, powerful body covering and making promises to hers.

"Yes," she managed to say.

He kissed her again, deeply and desperately, and their tongues engaged in a savage, fevered battle. His knee prodded her legs gently apart and then he was poised above her, bracing himself with his hands.

"God in heaven, Holly," he muttered hoarsely, "how I've wanted you…from the first…"

Holly's hands were moving up and down the sleek, rippled expanse of his back. She wanted to say something poetic, something memorable, but her arousal was such that she could do no more than gasp his name.

David groaned and entered the sweet sanctum of her body, carefully and with a tenderness that deepened the love Holly already felt for him. He moved slowly at first, rhythmically, sheathing and unsheathing, reacquainting her with the long-forgotten feel of a man's possession.

Holly's few experiences with her fiancé long ago had done nothing, nothing whatsoever, to prepare her for this. This was a glorious, blinding joy, one that centered all of her heart and all of her soul on the singular joining of this man's body with her own. She moved in time with him, making a soft, unselfconscious sound in her throat, a crooning, needing sound.

David's lips were everywhere, brushing her eyelids, tracing the line of her jaw, tasting her mouth. His tongue circled her lips in a way that was somehow territorial and fiercely arousing, and the pace he had set for her body increased by degrees until they both seemed to be hurling themselves at each other, frantic for a oneness that would consume them both.

When that moment came, David growled, his eyes closed, and shuddered upon Holly while she cried out and thrust her hips upward to enclose him as completely as she could.

They both sank into a sleeplike state for a time, their breathing ragged, eyes closed. David's fingers, tangled in Holly's hair, moved soothingly against her scalp. Then, suddenly and with devastating determination, he thrust himself free of her, cursing under his breath as he wrenched on his clothes.

Holly, shameless only moments before, now felt tawdry. She clasped the edge of the quilt covering her bed and pulled it over herself.

"David, what is it?" she finally dared to ask, watching wide-eyed as he completed the angry rite by jerking his boots back onto his feet.

He might have stormed out without saying anything at all if Holly hadn't spoken when she did, but then he froze, his back turned to her, rigid and impassive. "It was a mistake," he muttered at length.

"It was your idea!" Holly cried, wounded.

David lowered his head but did not turn around to face her. "Yes. It was my idea," he conceded raggedly.

"You feel guilty, don't you, David?"

Now he turned and met her eyes. "I'm sorry, Holly. I wanted you so badly I lost my head."

"You lost your head?" Holly was suddenly energized, electrified. But this time it was fury, not passion, that surged through her. Heedless of her nakedness, she flung back the quilt and bounded off the bed. "I beg your pardon?" she screamed.

David silenced her by laying three fingers gently, ever so gently, over her mouth. His eyes were dark with some pain that Holly couldn't understand and couldn't share. But whatever it was, she would gladly have traded her own confused, hurt feelings for it.

"Believe me when I tell you, Holly, that I've never wanted or needed a woman the way I needed you just now. Never. But it was a mistake. We can't let it happen again."

It would have hurt less, Holly was certain, if he'd slapped her. "What do you mean, it was a mistake? It was…it was…"

David kissed her forehead, wiped away the tears gathering at the corners of her eyes with practiced thumbs, then turned to walk away. He closed the door quietly behind him, but Holly waited until she was sure he was out of the house before flinging herself face-down on the bed to cry.

Chapter 6

The telephone rang. Sitting up on the bed, brushing her tangled hair back from her face, Holly reached out for the receiver, overriding the answering machine downstairs. Please, God, she prayed, let it be David.

"I left you two messages last night!" Craig blurted out the moment she said hello. "Don't you return your calls anymore, or is it something I said?"

Craig. Holly settled back on the pillows, which still bore the scent of David, and sighed. "I'm sorry, Craig. I was busy and—"

"You were *busy?* Good God, Holly! Remember me? I'm your brother, the man who is in trouble?"

Holly's throat was thick with despair, and her head ached. "We all have problems, Craig," she reminded him quietly, thinking of David Goddard.

"Sure, Holl. I know you're probably all torn up about

whether to pay your Keogh Plan before the end of the year and what color to paint your toenails."

The sarcasm, following the scene with David as it did, was too much. "Listen, Craig. I care about you and you know it. I do everything I can to help you. But you're the one who got yourself into this mess—kindly remember that!"

He subsided. "I know. Holly, I'm so scared."

Tears smarted in Holly's eyes, sudden and hot. It was a surprise because she had been certain that there were none left to cry. Images of another Craig, bright and fit and funny, rose in her mind. Dear God, what had happened to change him this way? During the troubled years after their father's death, when their mother had been so confused and distracted, he had been Holly's strength, her lifeline.

"I know, Craig, I know. I beg of you, give yourself up."

"I can't, Holly. I just can't. You don't know how these guys treat a fink—"

"Craig, they're not going to hurt you. I'll have a lawyer present. You're still a citizen and you still have rights."

"Not anymore, I don't," he muttered. "I've had dealings with al-Qaeda, Holly, and they know it."

"Why, Craig? Why did you turn to...to those people? Why did you do it?"

He made a strange sound and Holly was shattered to realize that he was crying. "I have a habit, Holly," he finally said.

Dread electrified Holly, and she bolted upright. "What kind of habit?" she whispered, her eyes wide and burning. "Dammit, Craig, *what kind of habit?*"

"Cocaine," he said.

"Oh, God," Holly groaned.

"Listen, I need money. Cindy managed to bring me what you sent, but that's gone now."

"No."

"What did you say?" Craig sniffled, and his voice sounded angry again.

"I said no, Craig. I'm not giving you money to buy poison! I absolutely will not!"

"Holly, I need—"

"You need help and I haven't been giving it to you! Oh, God, how could I have been so stupid—"

"Get the money, Holly. Send it to this address—" He rattled off a post-office-box number in a small Oregon town. "I mean it, Holly. If you don't, I'll be home for Christmas. And not to turn myself in."

"What are you saying?"

"I'm saying, sister dear," he answered with tart patience, "that if you don't help me I'll take Toby on the road with me. That's what I'm saying."

"No! I won't let you! I won't let you expose him to that, drag him around the country—"

"You won't be able to stop me, Holly. I know where he goes to school, and I know where you live. And remember I'm a former federal agent—I'll find the kid no matter where you try to hide him."

"Craig!"

"Send the money," he said. He repeated the address once more and then hung up.

Slowly, her hand trembling so hard that she had to make several attempts before she could manage the task, Holly replaced the receiver in its cradle.

She sat there on the bed, cross-legged, her head in her hands, until she heard Toby downstairs. "Mom!"

he yelled exuberantly, probably still excited from his afternoon at the Ice Capades, "I'm home!"

Holly quickly leaped off the bed, found herself a robe and went down the stairs.

Toby was waiting at the bottom, his beloved face alight. "Geez, Mom," he said, barely able to stand still, "the ice show was great! They had the Flintstones and—" He stopped, taking in Holly's bathrobe and mussed hair with concern. "Are you sick, Mom?"

"No, darling, I'm not sick," Holly answered swiftly, forcing a smile to her face. "How did you get home, by the way? I thought I was supposed to pick you up."

"David brought me!" Toby sang, spreading his mittened hands for emphasis.

Holly swayed backward, just slightly, stunned. How could she have missed seeing David, when he was standing only a few feet away? Why hadn't she sensed that he was near?

"I hope you don't mind," David said quietly, but there was much, much more that his eyes were saying. They looked haunted, hollow.

Holly's temper flared, fanned by her fear, and she shifted her eyes to Toby's trusting, upturned face. "Don't you ever, ever get into anyone's car but mine, young man!" she hissed.

Toby retreated a step, looking as though she'd struck him. "But, Mom, David—"

David laid a quieting hand on the child's shoulder. "No, Tobe. She's right. We made a mistake, you and I."

Toby was not appeased. He darted one furious look at his trembling aunt and dashed off into another part of the house, probably to take solace in the late-afternoon cartoons he loved to watch on television.

"What are you doing here?" Holly half whispered, watching David, loving him even though her every instinct commanded her to tear out his hair.

"I couldn't stay away. Bringing Toby back from the ice show seemed the perfect excuse, so I did it. I'm sorry, Holly. I didn't mean to undermine your authority."

Holly held her chin high, but inwardly she was all too conscious of her appearance. "You are very, very good at finding excuses to keep tabs on me, aren't you, David?"

There was a thunderous silence, and David averted his eyes for a moment before meeting Holly's glare directly. "I love you, Holly."

Nothing he could have said would have surprised Holly more; she came a step nearer and her hand tightened on the banister until her knuckles ached. "What did you say?"

"Don't make me say it again, Holly. I already feel like enough of a fool as it is."

"Thanks a lot!"

"Just get dressed, will you? We need to talk, you and I. Not fight, not make love. Talk."

Holly stared at him for a few minutes and then, too confused to deal with anything, turned and dashed up the stairs. Safe in the shower stall, with hot water pouring down over her head and her newly awakened body, she rested her face against the tiled wall and tried to catch her breath.

David made himself at home in the kitchen, conscious of the glum little boy sitting slumped at the trestle table. "Your mom didn't mean to yell at you, Tobe," he said, finding the coffee and the filters before pouring cold water into the top of the coffeemaker.

"She's sure grouchy lately! And it's almost Christmas, too!"

David smiled somewhat sadly, and then turned to look directly at Toby, leaning back against the counter, the coffeemaker chortling behind him. "Sure enough, it is almost Christmas. Time to get a tree."

Toby brightened a little, but he was still miffed. "Yeah, I guess." His eyes strayed to Holly's desk, to the answering machine there, its light blinking frantically. "She never listens to her calls, neither."

For the first time since high school, David Goddard blushed. David Goddard, who had guarded presidents. "She's been sort of busy."

The child bounded off the bench, a study in impatience, and stomped over to the machine. Before David could intercede, he had pushed two buttons on the machine. There were two brief messages from Holly's brother, followed by a long conversation that told David more than he really wanted to know.

Craig had a cocaine habit. He needed money. And he was in a town in Oregon, watching a certain post-office box. When he began to talk about taking Toby from Holly, David strode across the room and turned off the machine abruptly.

Toby's eyes were brimming with tears, and his color, high from the cold weather outside and his time at the ice show, drained away. "I want my mom!" he blurted out, fleeing the room.

David swore and cast one despairing look at the ceiling before leaving the house. Five minutes later, from a phone booth outside a supermarket, he called the FBI.

* * *

Skyler, arriving unannounced, frowned at Holly. "My God," he muttered, "you look terrible!"

On this dismal Sunday morning, a soft snow was falling; a fire was crackling on the kitchen hearth. "Thanks, Sky," Holly said, stepping back to admit him to her kitchen. "A compliment always gives a day that little extra something."

"Don't be difficult," Skyler chided, taking off his stylish muffler and shaking it, a look of disapproval on his face. "I bring great tidings and all that."

Holly could have used some great tidings to offset the problems she was having with Craig and the confusion she felt over David's disappearance the day before. He'd seemed so eager to talk, but when she had finished her shower, dressed and gone downstairs, he had already left the house. After a quick search, she'd found Toby in his room, sobbing into his pillow, and the little boy had refused to tell her what was wrong.

Finally, he had fallen asleep. When he woke up later, Holly had offered him dinner, but he had refused. He was still silent this morning, and his mood added to Holly's growing collection of worries.

"So, what glad tidings do you bring?" she asked, going to the coffeemaker and helping herself to her third cup since getting out of bed an hour earlier. After pouring a cup for Skyler, she sat down at the trestle table and nodded for him to do the same.

He took in her drawn face and the smudges under her eyes with puzzled concern. "Holly, what's wrong? You look—"

Holly held up one hand to stop him. "I know. Terrible."

"You're still in your bathrobe!" he marveled, shocked. Skyler didn't believe in looking less than one's best at any time of the day or night.

"Toby had bad dreams last night," she said, as though that were an explanation. She didn't add that she had been tormented by nightmares, too—when she had been able to sleep at all.

Skyler shrugged, looking helpless and a little annoyed. "What you need, what you both need, is a day in the country. Holly, let's drive out to my folks' farm and cut down a Christmas tree."

Holly knew that she shouldn't go, that she would be encouraging Skyler's affections if she went. Even though her involvement with David Goddard was an unholy mess, she didn't want to do that.

On the other hand, a drive in the wintry countryside would certainly be a pleasant distraction.

"Skyler, I—"

He sighed, and his fondness for Holly was naked in his eyes. "I know, Holly. You've been seeing someone else. Surely it isn't so serious that you can't spend a day with me?"

Holly's heart twisted slightly. The truth was, her entanglement with David was so serious that she *had* to spend a day with Skyler. If she stayed around the house, waiting for David or for another of Craig's devastating phone calls, she would surely go insane. And Toby needed the outing just as desperately as she did.

Gently, she reached across the table and closed her hand over Skyler's. She was surprised to find that he was trembling just a little. And she was saddened by what that probably meant. "I have been seeing David regularly, Sky. And I do care about him a great deal."

"I'd guessed that by the way you kept turning me down whenever I asked you out, Holly."

"I'm sorry," Holly replied softly, and she truly was. She had never wanted to hurt Skyler or anyone else, but she clearly had done just that.

"Say you'll come with me today, Holly. We'll find a couple of Christmas trees and Mom has a great dinner planned."

Skyler looked so hopeful that Holly wanted to cry. "Okay," she said. "Just give me a few minutes to get dressed and throw some breakfast together."

Skyler wasn't looking at her but into the depths of his coffee cup. "Don't bother with breakfast, Holly. We'll stop and eat on the way out of town."

Holly left the table, but she paused in the doorway of the kitchen, looking back at Skyler. Her throat ached and her answer came out sounding hoarse and raspy. "You're a good friend, Skyler Hollis. Do you know that?"

Skyler said nothing at all. After watching him for a silent, painful moment and wishing that things could be different, she hurried upstairs to get dressed.

"I'd like it better if David was taking us," Toby grumbled when Holly stopped by his room to ask him to get ready to go and find a Christmas tree.

So would I, Holly thought sadly, but she said, in a voice that quivered just the slightest bit, "Please don't be difficult, Toby. We need a dose of fresh air, you and I, and we're going to have it. Get ready, please. Skyler is treating us to breakfast."

Glumly, Toby went about obeying. Just as glumly, Holly went on to the bathroom to take her shower.

* * *

The day with Skyler was, for Holly, a bittersweet experience. They were two people who knew that their relationship was going nowhere, and were trying to be cheerful despite it. All the same, it was a pleasant day, at least for Holly, giving her the time she needed to paste herself back together and think.

During breakfast she pondered Craig's cocaine problem and his threat to take Toby away. While she was frightened by the things her brother had said, she began to suspect that the part about stealing his son was just hysteria. Deluded though he was, Craig couldn't possibly believe that he would be capable, under the circumstances, of taking care of a child.

As for the cocaine, well, while it was certainly a horrible shock, it did explain a lot about Craig's treason. And that's what it was; Holly forced herself to accept the fact. It was treason.

After that, she was unable to finish her hearty breakfast, no matter how much a subdued Skyler might urge her. But what she had already eaten helped Holly considerably. She felt stronger, better able to cope.

Toby, too, was coming out of his curious mood, however reluctantly. He enjoyed eating in restaurants even when it involved spending time with Skyler.

When they left the restaurant, snow falling all around them and with an easy day ahead, Holly was able to put most of her problems out of her mind and chat with Skyler. Toby sat in the back seat, armed with a pocket trivia game, shouting out an occasional question.

Skyler, in Holly's view, was uncommonly patient. "The Lone Ranger's uncle!" he called out once, in exuberant answer.

"Wrong," said Toby smugly, in the often-insensitive way of children. "It was Pinky Lee!"

Skyler rolled his eyes and tossed Holly a beleaguered look. She laughed because if she hadn't, she would have cried.

After an hour and a half of trivia, they reached the dairy farm owned by Skyler's parents. The Hollises were friendly people, and they greeted both Holly and Toby with comforting warmth. Hanging behind them, though, on the porch that stretched all the way around that carefully painted, solid old Victorian house, stood a young woman Holly had never seen before.

"Hello, Mary Ann," Skyler greeted the guest somewhat self-consciously. "How are you?"

A fetching blush rose in Mary Ann's pretty cheeks. "I'm all right. You?"

Skyler risked one broken glance at Holly and cleared his throat. "I'll get by," he answered gruffly.

Holly looked at Mary Ann again and hoped devoutly that Skyler would fall in love with her, here and now. It was obvious that the dark-haired, blue-eyed woman adored him—perhaps she and Skyler had grown up together and perhaps Mary Ann had always cared for him....

She brought herself up short. Fantasies. She was just weaving fantasies in hopes of making it easier to end her own relationship with Skyler.

"Mary Ann and I found some real good trees," Skyler's father announced cheerfully, and a glance at his leathery, good-natured face told Holly that he knew more about his son's relationship with the city lady than he was letting on.

Again Holly felt guilty. It was going to be so hard,

telling Skyler she didn't want to see him anymore, even though he must certainly have guessed it from their conversation that morning.

After a round of coffee in the huge, high-ceilinged farmhouse kitchen—Toby, of course, had hot chocolate—everyone except Mrs. Hollis set out for the woods.

It was a bracingly cold day, and here in the country the snow was cleaner and, alas, deeper, making the jaunt to the woods rather hard going for Holly. Flinging back an occasional polite look, Mary Ann kept to the lead with Skyler and Toby.

Wearing high rubber boots and a heavy, plaid woolen coat that smelled pleasantly of tobacco smoke and hay, Mr. Hollis stayed beside the lagging Holly. Something in his manner inspired confidence, and Holly, feeling an innate need to talk with someone older and wiser, ventured, "Mary Ann and Skyler must have known each other for a long time."

Mr. Hollis smiled. "Since kindergarten," he replied, keeping his voice low, as Holly had, so that no one else would overhear. "I'm afraid it's pretty obvious that Mary Ann has her cap set for him. 'Bout broke her heart when he went away to the city to start that store of his. Mine and Mother's cracked a bit, too, as it happens."

Holly was saddened. Skyler was the Hollises' only son, though he did have one sister. Probably, his parents had hoped that he would want to take over the family farm someday. "I'm sorry," she said.

"Ain't your fault," came the quick reply, and a smile lighted the older man's eyes as Mary Ann picked up a handful of snow and flung it at Skyler, who shouted in good-natured protest and then returned the volley.

Toby, never one to stand on the sidelines, gathered up ammunition of his own and joined the battle.

"Mother was real pleased with that cookbook you sent up, the one with your autograph in it. She shows it to all her friends."

Holly didn't know what to say to that, beyond "thank you"; she wedged her hands into the pockets of her old coat and sighed, slogging grimly along in the wake of the escalating snow war up ahead. Skyler's, Mary Ann's and Toby's laughter mingled, a bright song in the chilly, snow-flecked air.

"That's a fine boy you have there," Mr. Hollis persisted. Perhaps he sensed her need to talk and her paradoxical difficulty in doing so.

"Thank you. Toby is actually my brother's son, but I forget that most of the time, he seems like my own."

"Reckon if you take care of him and love him, then he is your own. It's the day-to-day of it that matters, you know."

"Yes," Holly agreed, thinking of Craig, remembering when he had been a fine father to Toby. But that had been several years ago, before Craig's wife, Allison, had died. Before his habit had driven him to sell out his own country.

"You don't say much, do you?"

Holly laughed. They were almost out of the pasture and into the stand of pine trees and Douglas firs that was their destination. "I'm usually more sociable," she said. "I'm sorry."

"No need to be sorry." He paused and caught her elbow in his strong, work-worn hand. His eyes were kind as they touched Holly's face. "A person's got to follow their heart, Miss Llewellyn. And sometimes it don't lead where they'd like it to, but they gotta go after it anyway."

So he did know that the relationship between her and Skyler was over. If it had ever really existed at all.

"I'm hoping that Skyler will find someone else soon," she said, her voice trembling a little. Cool snowflakes collected on her eyelashes and chilled her cheeks, and Holly glanced ahead at the laughing Mary Ann. "Maybe…"

Mr. Hollis looked pleased, and he gave a guffaw of laughter. "Maybe so," he agreed.

As if to lend the theory credence, Skyler lunged at a gleefully shrieking Mary Ann and threw her down into the snow, rubbing a handful in her face. She came up sputtering and laughing, making exuberant threats. Toby, having watched all this with mingled delight and uncertainty, hurled a questioning look back at Holly.

It's all right, she told him with her smile, and his face was again alight with the joys of the day.

There was a bewildering array of trees to choose from, but Holly, her jeans snow-sodden to her knees, was not inclined to be persnickety. Skyler shook out a fragrant fir that stood about seven feet tall and appeared to be symmetrical, and she nodded in answer to the question in his eyes.

Mr. Hollis handed over the small hatchet he carried, saying he was "too derned old" for such carryings-on, and Skyler chopped down the tree.

With Toby frolicking at his heels like a puppy—for this was proof that Christmas, that most elusive of childhood days, was truly coming—Skyler began dragging the tree back toward the house.

"Don't you want a tree for yourself?" Holly asked

him, ignoring the territorial looks from Mary Ann.
These, she supposed, were her just due for falling into
step beside Skyler.

"I'll get one another time," he said softly.

Holly knew then that he had contrived the whole
idea of tracking down a Christmas tree for her benefit;
after all, it was still three full weeks until the holiday.
He had seen how upset she was, sensed that she was
frazzled and overwrought, and tried to help.

A feeling like love but sadly different twisted in her
throat. "Thank you, Sky," she said gently.

Skyler only shrugged, but when he shifted his attention to Mary Ann and started teasing her his voice was
a determinedly cheerful boom.

Mary Ann gloried in the attention, though she pretended to be outraged, and Toby jumped and leaped
in the scratchy snow trail left in the wake of the fallen
tree, his cheeks pink, his china-blue eyes shining. How
mercifully innocent he was just now, Holly thought,
how unaware he still was of the complications that lay
ahead in the process of growing up.

They ate a sumptuous dinner of fried chicken,
mashed potatoes and country gravy, biscuits, and green
beans that Mrs. Hollis had put up herself. She and Mary
Ann talked so easily about farm things; the prices they
could get for cream and eggs, the patterns they would
use for sewing their Christmas dresses, whether to plant
peas on St. Valentine's Day or later on, in March.

Holly listened with interest and a sort of weary nostalgia, and when the meal was over, she volunteered to
do the dishes. Mrs. Hollis, having worked in the kitchen
all day, was obviously tired.

Skyler and Mr. Hollis and Toby went outside to tie

the Christmas tree to the roof of Skyler's car, and Mrs. Hollis retired to the living room to "put her feet up for a spell." Mary Ann, her eyes looking everywhere but at Holly, stayed to help with the dishes.

Holly felt a need to put Skyler's friend at ease. After all, Mary Ann belonged here, fitting in better than Holly herself ever could.

"You and Sky have been friends for a long time," she said quietly, taking up a flour-sack dish towel when Mary Ann had elbowed her away from the sink.

Now Mary Ann's dark, beautiful eyes swung to Holly's face, confused, but wary and full of challenge. "I love Skyler," she said in a low, earnest voice.

Holly smiled. "I know," she answered. "Toby and I won't be back here anymore after today."

There was a silence while Mary Ann absorbed that statement and dealt with it in her own way. Finally, she turned a bright smile on Holly. "It was good to meet you all the same," she said.

Holly laughed, and after that, the two women worked in swift accord, putting the kitchen right again in no time at all.

Chapter 7

Toby's eyes were round and sleepy as he looked up at Holly, and he yawned. "Let's decorate the Christmas tree," he suggested, valiant in the face of his fatigue.

Holly laughed and rumpled his hair. "Tomorrow, sweetheart. After school."

With an acquiescent shrug, he turned and scampered up the stairs, stopping midway to look at Skyler and say, "Thanks for taking us to the country. It was real neat."

Skyler shoved his hands into the pockets of his jacket, looking ill at ease and shy. He didn't truly belong in this house any longer, and that saddened Holly even though she knew it was for the best. "You're welcome, kid," he said.

Holly suppressed a tired smile. Some things didn't change. "Will you stay for coffee, Skyler?" she asked.

He shook his immaculately groomed head. "I don't think that would be a good idea." Toby was gone by then, busy getting ready for bed. "It's over, isn't it, Holly?" he added in a sad voice.

"Yes," she said quietly. "I'm sorry."

There was a painful silence, and then Skyler sighed and shrugged his shoulders. When he met Holly's eyes again, he was smiling with an obvious effort. "I'd better bring in the tree before I go. Where do you want it, Holly?"

Holly gestured vaguely toward the living room, and Skyler cleared his throat as though he might say something more. Then he ran one hand through his neatly styled hair, something Holly had never seen him do, and turned away without speaking at all.

The tree stood in the corner of the dimly lit living room, leaning, lushly green and fragrant, into the corner. There were no decorations on its boughs just yet, and to Holly, all alone now that Toby was asleep and Skyler had gone home, it was a forlorn sight.

She sighed, knowing that for all the exercise and fresh air of the day just ending, sleep would elude her. She turned off the living room lights and went into the kitchen, where she poured a cup of coffee and sat down at the trestle table.

"Coffee," she mocked herself, lifting the cup. "Just what your average insomniac needs before bed."

It was then that the flashing light on the answering machine caught Holly's eye. Resigned—one couldn't shut out the world forever—she stood up and crossed the room to her desk, pressing the button marked Play.

The first voice on the recording was Elaine's, saying that she had the flu and might not make it to work the next day. The second belonged to Holly's housekeeper, promising to come in to clean on Tuesday.

Holly frowned. This was strange. What had happened to those two brief messages from Craig? He'd said he'd called twice.

A third voice came on, jolting her out of her reflections. David's voice.

"Holly, call me, will you please? My number is 555-6782. It's important, so don't worry about the time."

Holly stood frozen in that lonely kitchen, such a busy place in the daytime but so echoingly empty now. Why should she call David after the way he'd treated her? Hadn't he made love to her and then said they'd made a mistake and left her alone with her confusion and her conscience? And then he'd come back, saying that he loved her, saying that they needed to talk—and disappeared before they could!

Something besides the two vanished calls from Craig niggled at the back of her mind but she couldn't quite grasp what it was.

David answered on the first ring, not with a hello but with his name. And that bothered Holly, too.

To cover her uneasiness, she blurted out, "David, if this is a game, I don't want to play! You said we needed to talk before, and then you just left!"

His sigh came, a raspy sound, over the wire that linked them together so tenuously. "Something came up, Holly, and I had to leave. I'm sorry."

Holly sank into her desk chair, turning the telephone cord in the fingers of one hand. "Toby was very upset, David. Do you know why?"

David hesitated and finally said, "No."

He was lying. Holly knew he was lying. But why? Whatever doubts she might have about David Goddard, she was absolutely certain that he would never do or say anything to put Toby in such a state. "You said you wanted to talk," she prompted coldly.

"I do. But not over a wire. Holly, could I come over? Please?"

Holly sighed and glanced ruefully at the Seth Thomas clock on the kitchen mantelpiece. "It's late, David—after eleven."

"Do you think you'll sleep tonight if we don't talk?" he asked.

Holly felt her face flushing. "That's all we're going to do—provided I agree to your visit, that is. Toby's home and—"

"I didn't ask you to go to bed with me, Holly," came the patient reply. "I really do want to talk with you. In person."

Holly's face grew hotter still, and she closed her eyes as memories of David's lovemaking washed over her in a heated, crushing wave. Perhaps that was what gave her the courage to refuse—if it was courage. "We can talk tomorrow, David. I've had a long day, and I'm tired."

"Holly—"

"Tomorrow," she said firmly.

"Tomorrow." He sighed, and then the line went dead. Holly hung up the telephone, frowned at the answering machine for just a moment and then went upstairs to bed.

Surprisingly, she slept soundly that night, without the dreams that had been troubling her so much.

Getting Toby off to school in the morning was a madness of lost textbooks and half-eaten oatmeal, as usual. Elaine called to say that she was still sick and definitely wouldn't be over.

Once she was alone, Holly eyed the work waiting on her desk with trepidation. Her newspaper column was due in two days and needed to be extensively rewritten, but she couldn't work up the self-discipline necessary to do the job.

It was almost a relief when David knocked at the glass panes in the kitchen door and then let himself in at Holly's somber nod. By that time, she had lugged the huge boxes of Christmas tree decorations down from the attic and was going through the newspaper-wrapped contents in search of the red-and-green stand.

"I'm sorry about last Saturday, Holly," he said quietly.

Holly's face heated again, and then chilled. There was a guilty, reluctant look about David, as though he had something important to say, something that he dreaded saying.

"That's okay," Holly lied, turning her attention back to the ornaments and the pieces of the large crèche left her by her grandmother. "Have some coffee."

"Where were you yesterday?" David asked, finding the cups and rattling the coffeemaker's glass decanter against the mug when he tried to fill it.

It gave Holly a perverse sort of pleasure to answer, "Skyler took Toby and me up to his parents' farm to look for a Christmas tree."

David was silent for so long that Holly finally had to turn around and look at him. Still wearing his brown leather jacket, he was watching her with unreadable indigo eyes, leaning back against the counter as he sipped the too-hot coffee.

"Are you in love with him, Holly?"

Holly sighed, unwrapping one of the three wise men and turning the large porcelain figure in her hands. "No. In fact, I told Skyler last night that we shouldn't see each other anymore."

There was another silence, broken at long last by David's noncommittal, "I see."

And suddenly Holly was furious. She whirled, the wise man still in her hands, and cried, "Dammit, David, you said you wanted to talk! It was your idea, remember?"

A half smile curved his lips. "Isn't that what we're doing? Talking?"

"No, damn you, it isn't! We're…we're shadowboxing!"

David sighed, set his steaming mug of coffee aside and shrugged out of his jacket, laying it over the back of a kitchen chair without particular concern. Holly had a feeling that he was used to expensive things, which the jacket obviously was.

"You're right," he said. "We are sparring. Holly, I meant it when I told you that I love you."

Holly's hands were trembling; she set down the endangered wise man. "So you did," she finally croaked out, keeping her head averted because there were sudden, inexplicable tears in her eyes and she couldn't bear for him to see them. "But something is terribly wrong between us, David. I know it. I sense it. You're keeping something from me."

He came to her then and clasped her shoulders in his hands. His throat worked fruitlessly for a moment, as though it were difficult for him to speak. "Whatever happens, Holly, remember that I love you. When we made love the other day—"

Holly pulled away from him, both drawn to him and frightened. "When we made love, you said it was a mistake," she reminded him, wounded by the memory.

The Christmas-tree stand was uncovered, and she pulled it out of the box. David took it from her hands and put it aside.

"Look at me, Holly."

Holly didn't want to obey, but she did. She had to.

"I thought I loved Marleen," he said slowly, his hands on Holly's shoulders again, firm and strong. "When she left, I hurt for a long, long time. And then it got so that I didn't feel anything, didn't want to feel anything. I had a lot of affairs, Holly—I'm not denying that—but until I met you I didn't think it was possible for me to really care about another woman."

One tear sneaked down Holly's face and she brought one hand up between David's arms to wipe it away. "Still something is wrong… I…"

He bent and kissed her briefly, tenderly. "Just trust me, Holly. I know that's a lot to ask, but I'm asking you."

"Something awful is going to happen!" Holly cried, frantic.

"Maybe. Sometimes things happen that are very painful at the time, but they're still for the best. And I'll be on the other side, waiting for you."

He was being so damned cryptic! Holly wanted to pound his chest with her fists, to claw out his eyes. Unfortunately, another part of her wanted to take David by the hand and lead him upstairs to that bed where they had made such sweet love, where she had been transformed, if only temporarily, into a woman with no problems, no doubts, no pain.

David caught her chin in his hand and lifted her face so that she had to look directly into his eyes. "I love you," he repeated slowly. "Whatever happens, I don't want you to forget that, Holly. Promise me that much."

She swallowed hard. "Tell me what you know, David. Who you are. What do you want—"

"I want you."

"You are being deliberately obtuse!"

He smiled, but it was a sad smile, and something vital lay broken in his eyes. He released Holly and took up the Christmas-tree stand, turning it slowly in his hands. "I'll set the tree up for you, if you want."

Holly bit her lower lip and then nodded. It was obvious that she wasn't going to get any more information out of David, but God help her, she didn't want him to go. Not yet.

"Thank you," she managed to say.

Setting the tree in its stand proved to be just what David and Holly needed to lighten the impossible weight of the situation. By the time Holly was finally willing to admit that the tree was as straight as it could possibly be, they were both laughing.

While David was washing the pitch from his hands, Holly impulsively lighted a fire in the living room hearth and put on instrumental Christmas music. As if to accommodate her oddly festive mood, a soft snow began to drift past the windows.

I'm crazy, Holly thought. I'm definitely certifiable. Half an hour ago, I was crying and now, just because David and I put up the Christmas tree, I'm lighting fires and playing music and setting the stage for something that shouldn't happen.

David returned, a cautious smile on his face. Without saying a word, he caught Holly's hand in his, sat down on the couch and pulled her gently into his lap. He smelled deliciously of fresh air and pine, and his blue eyes, often so disturbing, were as warm as the snapping fire on the hearth.

"I love you, David," Holly blurted out without stopping to think. How could she think when he was holding her that way, his hands making tender circles on her shoulder blades?

He laughed. "At last you admit it."

Holly was honestly surprised that she hadn't said the words before. God knew, the truth of them had been as much a part of her as her breath and her heartbeat, almost from the first. "David—"

He turned her on his lap and kissed her. "Shh. It's Christmas."

Holly was gasping by the time the kiss ended. She knew that her hair was probably mussed and her cheeks flushed. "It is *not* Christmas—"

David's face was buried in her neck, his lips making tantalizing forays along its pulsing length. "Woman," he groaned, and the word was at once a reprimand and the most flagrant praise. "You argue about everything."

The buttons on Holly's blouse were opening, one by one, and his mouth was following the ever-deepening vee of bared flesh intrepidly. Heat so intense that it bordered on pain surged through Holly as he explored the rounded side of one breast and nuzzled that side of her bra down far enough to bare what he sought.

"Ooooh," she groaned as he took brazen nips at the aching nipple and then suckled it. And all her doubts fled before the flames of her passion and his.

As David undressed her, never really ceasing his tender assault on her throbbing senses, all memory fled. By the time he had subjected her to the scandalously delicious release meant to prepare her for final conquering, Holly couldn't have recited her own name.

He did not enter her gently this time, but with a thrust that was fiercely pleasurable for Holly. Her hands moved wildly over the muscle-ridged expanse of his bare back, pleading, urging.

There was something sweetly wicked about making love on the living room couch, and Holly's passion was heightened by it, as, she sensed, was David's.

When the moment of scalding release came, it enfolded them both. David was kissing Holly as they moved together, and his moans of tender defeat echoed inside her mouth, mingling with her own fevered cries.

They lay entwined for some time afterward, their breathing ragged, their hearts pounding as though to break past flesh and bone and be bonded together.

This time, to Holly's enormous relief, there was no talk about their lovemaking being a mistake. And this time David did not leave her.

No, they showered together, laughing and flinging soapsuds at each other at first, later slipping into passion again. They made love a second time, their bodies still slick with water, on Holly's bed. After that, they dressed and made a tongue-in-cheek agreement to behave themselves.

When Toby got home from school, he found them in the living room, sorting the lights that would set the freshly cut Christmas tree aglow. His greeting to David was a whoop of delight and a hurling of his small, solid body into the man's arms. David laughed and pretended to be falling under the weight, and Holly, watching them both, was more certain of her love for this enigmatic man than ever before.

They worked, the three of them, until dinnertime, transforming the fragrant tree into a thing of glory. By the time the last glass ball was hung and the last strand of tinsel had been draped from just the right bough, it was dark outside.

"You can fix dinner now, Mom!" Toby announced magnanimously, his eyes on the shimmering wonder of the Christmas tree. "Us men are starved."

David laughed and shook his head. "Us men," he corrected Toby with mock sternness, "are going for take-out chicken. Your mom has done enough for one day."

Holly's eyes linked with David's and she blushed. That "enough" didn't bear recounting. "You don't have to go out. We've got lots of food in the freezer."

"Yuk," Toby complained. "I'm tired of ka-bobs. I want to go with David to get chicken."

Both of her men stood watching her, waiting for her approval. "Okay," she relented, smiling even though she tried to look insulted. "But you stay with David, Toby Llewellyn. Don't go wandering off and don't ask for two desserts. Or for pop."

Toby flung David a beleaguered look. "I'm not allowed to eat much sugar," he complained.

David chuckled and rumpled Toby's corn-silk hair. "You're so abused. Tell me your sad story in the car, will you?"

And after David had kissed Holly soundly but briefly, they were off.

Holly sat alone in the living room with the lamps turned off, admiring the lights of the Christmas tree. "When it comes to glow, Tree," she said aloud, "you've got nothing on me."

David liked being with Toby, and he had certainly enjoyed the day. Still, Craig Llewellyn was much in his thoughts as he navigated the snow-slicked roads in the Camaro he had rented after returning the brown sedan.

The little boy, fastened firmly into the seat belt on the passenger side, chattered on and on about the Christmas tree, the day they'd flown model airplanes in the park and the trip to Skyler Hollis's family's farm. David listened patiently, though in actuality he was going over the facts Walt Zigman had given him during their last telephone conversation.

Craig Llewellyn had managed to elude the FBI in that little Oregon town, just as he had in L.A. He was smart, Llewellyn was, and slippery. But he wasn't smart enough.

David knew that he would appear in Spokane very soon. And he was worried about Llewellyn's threat, overheard the day Toby had impulsively turned on Holly's answering machine and replayed her conversation with her brother. She obviously didn't know that David had heard the recording; maybe she didn't even realize that the machine had been on when she'd picked up the telephone.

He glanced at Craig's son and wondered how cocaine could have been bigger than such a treasure of a child. God, if this boy were his own...

David stopped himself. Once this thing with Craig actually broke, there would probably be little left of what he and Holly shared. She would hate him and so would the boy. It was a grim irony that he'd chosen her of all people, to fall in love with.

David seemed subdued when he and Toby returned with the take-out chicken. His eyes dodged Holly's and his contributions to the conversation were few and far between.

"What's wrong?" she asked, when a grumbling Toby had been settled at the trestle table to do his homework, and they were alone again beside the Christmas tree.

"I guess I'm tired," he said.

Holly was on the verge of tears. Was he going to spoil the day, after all they'd shared? Was he going to start talking "mistake" again?

"I guess you're shutting me out," Holly argued evenly. "And I don't understand it, David. Not after today. You can't make love to me and then treat me as though I'm some bad habit you wish you could break."

The word *habit* hung between them, or so it seemed to Holly. But David couldn't know about Craig's confessions to her concerning cocaine; there was no way he could know that.

"I can't do this problem!" Toby wailed from the kitchen. "Somebody help me!"

"I'll do it," David volunteered, his eyes still averted. And a moment later, he was turning his back on Holly and striding off toward the kitchen. He remained there until Toby's homework was done and it was bedtime.

While Holly appreciated the help David gave Toby— math was her secret nemesis—she felt a bit put out, too. How had things changed so completely, just in the time it took David to go and buy the take-out chicken?

When she came downstairs, having tucked Toby into bed and heard his prayers, David was sitting in front of the living room fire, staring ponderously into the flames as though some drama were being played out there.

Holly needed a moment to think, to collect herself; where this man was concerned, she had a way of plunging over emotional precipices, of saying and doing all the wrong things. Turning into the kitchen, she suddenly halted, stunned.

Craig was standing there, leaning casually against the counter, a cup of hot coffee in his hand. He looked so ragged and thin, with a fevered light in his eyes that made Holly despair.

"Craig," she whispered.

He toasted her sardonically with a lift of his coffee cup. "You didn't send the money," he said.

Holly could barely breathe, so great was her shock at seeing this wasted parody of the man who had been her brother. His filthy army fatigue jacket seemed two sizes too large and his eyes were sunken and haunted. "Craig, I couldn't," she said, keeping her voice low for fear that David would hear. "I didn't have a chance. You only called on Saturday…"

Craig's eyes swept the room, as though he might be assessing the value of things he saw there. "That guy helping Toby with his homework. Who is he?"

"Keep your voice down! He's still here!"

Craig's thin shoulders lifted in an impertinent shrug. "What's his name and where did you meet him?"

Holly sighed, half-sick with surprise and confusion, afraid that David would hear Craig and, conversely, afraid that he wouldn't. "His name is David Goddard and I met him in a class I'm teaching."

"I thought so. I remember him from the good old days."

"You—you what?"

"I remember him. He's a Secret Service agent, Holly. Or didn't he tell you that? I'll bet he asks a lot of questions about your misguided big brother, doesn't he?"

The room swayed around Holly, rising and falling, tilting at stomach-clenching angles.

"You mean you didn't even suspect?" Craig taunted in leisurely tones. "He must be pretty good."

Holly had suspected; she *had*. So why was it such a brutal surprise? She groped for the trestle table's sturdy edge, collapsing onto the bench. "Oh, my God. My God."

"The Secret Service doesn't usually handle this sort of thing," Craig speculated idly. "Must be connected to our dear cousin Howard, the never and future king."

It happened then; David came through the doorway. Holly heard him, felt him there, but could not look at him. Or at Craig.

"Llewellyn," he said, and Holly supposed it was an offhand greeting, though David had given the name no tone at all.

"Goddard," Craig replied calmly.

Holly looked up then, afraid. Suppose Craig had a gun? Suppose—

"Would you leave us alone, please?" Craig asked her companionably. "We're old friends."

Holly hadn't the strength to rise from that bench at the trestle table, and even if she had, she still would have stayed.

She darted a look from one expressionless man to the other, praying that there would be no violence, praying that Toby wouldn't stumble in.

David didn't so much as glance in her direction, and when he spoke again, he addressed Craig. "This can be easy, Llewellyn, or it can be difficult. The choice is yours."

Craig laughed and then horrified his stunned sister

by pulling a pistol from beneath his tattered army coat and laying it on the table. "I'll take it easy," he said. "Besides, the bushes outside are probably crawling with crew cuts by now. I'm not so far gone that I don't know you guys have been watching this place."

David took up the pistol deftly and unloaded the chamber, slipping the bullets into his pocket. His gaze slid to Holly just for a moment, and there was nothing in it to indicate that they had ever laughed together, ever been lovers.

When he went to the door to admit the inevitable agents, Holly sagged against the table's edge and covered her face with both hands.

Chapter 8

By morning, the news of Craig Llewellyn's "dramatic" capture was all over the newspapers. It was on television; it was on the radio. And it was in Elaine's face when she returned to work, largely recovered from her flu and wide-eyed with concern.

Holly sat blindly at the trestle table, a newspaper spread out before her.

Elaine took off her coat and sat down on the bench across from Holly. Being a true friend, she didn't ask why she had never heard anything about Craig before. "Are you going to let Toby go to school today?"

Holly sighed. "I don't know. Oh, Elaine, I don't know anything."

"It must have been awful."

Images of FBI agents surging into her kitchen throbbed in Holly's mind. Images of David, so cold, so quiet, so determined. "At least Toby slept through it all," she managed to say.

Elaine's hand came across the table to squeeze Holly's. "David Goddard—"

"Don't mention that man's name in this house, Elaine! Not ever again!" Holly flared, her eyes filling with tears of betrayal and fury.

"You were in love with him," Elaine said flatly. "I thought so."

"He wasn't in love with me!" Holly wailed. "Oh, Elaine, it was all an act from the first! I should have known—I *did* know but I wouldn't listen to my own instincts."

"That's very hard to do sometimes," Elaine comforted quietly. "Did David tell you that he cared for you?"

"Yes! But he lied—he only wanted to find Craig!"

"Maybe he didn't lie, Holly. Maybe he meant what he said."

"He lied. He wanted my brother." Holly was calmer now, though her heart was still thick with despair and raw sobs lurked beneath her carefully modulated words. "He lied."

"Well," Elaine said, "one thing is for certain—we're not going to get any work done today. And I don't think Toby should go to school until things quiet down a bit, do you?"

Holly shook her head. Eventually, the little boy was going to have to face the things his father had done, but she wanted him to hear the truth directly from her, and not on the school grounds. "C-could you take him home with you, just for the day? I'm afraid there will be reporters…"

"You know I'll do anything I can to help. What about

your class tonight, Holly? Are you going to go ahead with that, or shall I call everyone and tell them the course has been canceled?"

Again Holly shook her head. "I'll go crazy if I don't keep on working."

"What if David comes to class?" Elaine asked softly.

"I don't think even he would have that kind of gall. But if he does show up, I have a few things I want to say to him, you can bet on that!"

"It might be better to listen to what he has to say, Holly. I can't believe he—"

"Believe it. I was just something above and beyond the call of duty to him, Elaine. A means to an end."

Elaine looked as though she might want to say more, but she held her tongue. The telephone began to ring and she leaped up to answer it, her voice crisp and in charge.

"Do you want to talk to the press, Holly?" she asked after a few words with the caller, her hand over the mouthpiece.

"No!" Holly cried.

"I'm sorry," Elaine said into the receiver, "Ms. Llewellyn has no comment." With that, she hung up and turned on the answering machine to record a similar message for any future callers, setting it to pick up automatically.

And it was then, of all times, that Holly remembered what it was that had eluded her before, concerning the answering machine. After leaving those two vanished messages, Craig had called her again and the machine had been on. It would have recorded both sides of the conversation between her and her brother.

David Goddard had listened to that conversation, and he had erased it from the machine! He would have heard Craig mention the town in Oregon, the cocaine habit. And when the FBI had failed to find her brother there, he had no doubt deduced that Craig was desperate enough to come to Holly.

Which explained, of course, why he had spent the day there. Putting up the Christmas tree. Making love to Holly, going out for fast food so she wouldn't have to cook. And, finally, helping Toby with his homework. All very neat and professional.

In that moment of realization, if David had been standing before her, Holly was certain she could have killed him without hesitation.

Elaine had gone upstairs to fetch Toby, and the back door burst open and snapped closed again so forcibly that Holly was startled out of her grisly reflections.

Madge Elkins, the housekeeper, was turning the lock and getting out of her coat at the same time. "Good Lord, there must be a hundred reporters and TV people out there, Holly. They chased me up the driveway!"

Like an automaton, Holly got up from the bench and went to the window over the sink. Sure enough, the backyard was full of paparazzi. So, probably, was the sidewalk out front.

If they step on my tulips, Holly thought ferociously, stomping through the house. And there they were, dozens of them, with cameras of every sort in their hands and avid looks on their faces.

Holly flung open a window in the living room and yelled, "Get out of my flower beds!" Before so much as one question could be asked, she slammed the window shut again, so that their sudden burst of words only bounced off the glass, a dull, babbling sound.

In the kitchen, Elaine and Toby were getting ready to

make a break for it. Holly knelt in front of her nephew and held his small shoulders in her hands, hurting for the confusion and fear in his face.

"Tobe, everything is going to be okay," she said in a voice that didn't sound the least bit like her own. "It really is."

"Why are all those people out there? What did we do?"

"We didn't do anything. Toby, your dad was arrested last night and they want to ask us about him. You don't have to say anything at all to them—just stay close to Elaine."

Toby's eyes were wide and frightened. "Dad was arrested? Why?"

There was no choice but to be honest. Now, at this late date, Holly wished she had told Toby about Craig to prepare him for this inevitable disaster. "Your dad has a lot of problems, Tobe. Remember that day in the park, when I told you that he does bad things sometimes?"

"They put bad people in jail!" Toby protested, his lower lip jutting out.

"The police are not our enemies, Toby. It might not seem so right now, but being arrested was the best thing that could have happened to your dad. Now he'll get the help he needs."

Toby was clearly still confused, but he was calmer. Madge, on the other hand, was fidgety, standing at the kitchen window and peering out.

"I don't know if you should try to get past them, Elaine," she fretted. "It might be better to stay here."

This particular dilemma had been gnawing at Holly, too. She kissed Toby's forehead and stood up again, wondering what to do. It was then that David appeared at the back door, his breath a white fog in the winter air, his face set and determined. Holly would certainly not have admitted him, but Elaine did just that, before she could protest.

He barely glanced in Holly's direction, speaking instead to Elaine as he distractedly ruffled Toby's hair and then drew the child against him. Not knowing of David's part in this debacle, the little boy held on to the man as if for dear life. "What's the plan?"

Holly simmered, too furious to speak, but Elaine answered David's question as though he had every right to be there, every right to ask such a thing.

"I want to take Toby over to my place, but we're not sure about shuffling him through that crowd."

David, still not sparing so much as a look for Holly, nodded crisply and reached down with one arm, lifting Toby to ride on his hip. He smiled, actually smiled, into the child's trusting face. "Tell you what, slugger. I'll take you to Elaine's car. You just pretend those people aren't even there, okay?"

"Do they want to hurt me?" Toby asked in a tone that twisted Holly's heart.

"No way," David said confidently. "They want to ask you questions, just like your teachers do at school. But we don't have time to talk, do we?"

"No." Toby grinned, wrapping his arms around David's neck. "We don't want to talk."

David's eyes shifted to Holly's then, meeting her gaze squarely. And the expression in those fathomless indigo depths said that he was not apologizing for Craig's capture.

Holly would not have expected him to do that. Craig was a sick man and his arrest, as she had told Toby in other words, was, though painful, the end of a long nightmare. No, it was the way David had used her that hurt. The way he had insinuated himself into her life, caused her to care for him and lied again and again, both by word and by action, about his own feelings.

Now, though he hadn't said a word, he was asking her permission before plunging into the crowd of TV and newspaper people. Seeing the trust in Toby's face, knowing it would be better if he spent the day away from the house, she was forced to give that permission. She nodded, letting her eyes tell David Goddard that despite this concession, the distance between them could never be bridged.

With Elaine at his heels and Toby perched on his hip, David opened the kitchen door and went out. Madge fretted and fussed at the window; she was braver than Holly, who could not bear to look.

"They made it!" the housekeeper crowed after a few seconds of terrible suspense.

"D-David isn't on his way back in here, is he?" Holly ventured to ask, wringing her hands.

"No," Madge replied, apparently innocent of the intrigue that had just taken place between her employer and the man in question. "His car must be out front, because he went the other way. Maybe he's going to follow Elaine and Toby to make sure they aren't bothered en route."

The possibility that some of the reporters might trail after Elaine had not occurred to Holly until then, and she was jarred by it. "You don't suppose they will, do you? You don't suppose these…these people will bother Elaine and Toby?"

"They'll stay here," Madge said confidently, her face

still pressed to the window. One of her hands waved in an annoyed gesture. "Get out of there!" she shouted to someone outside. "You'll crush the lilac bush! You! Yes, you! Leave that birdbath alone!"

Despite everything, Holly had to laugh at the ludicrous comedy of it all. She poured herself a cup of coffee and went to her desk in the corner of the room, as though this were any ordinary day. The way the answering machine kept picking up on phone calls proved, of course, that it wasn't, as did the horde Madge had ordered away from the birdbath and the lilac bushes. Until Elaine called to say that they had arrived at Roy's mother's house out in the Spokane Valley, she left the machine's volume up so that she could hear each caller.

Grasping the receiver quickly, she spoke with Elaine and, for a few moments, with a gleefully excited Toby. It seemed that the whole matter had become an adventure to him, which was a relief to his aunt. After glorying in the fact that he didn't have to go to school that day, he hung up, and Holly pushed the volume button on the machine to its lowest setting before starting to work on her column.

Toward midmorning the media people got tired of standing around in the cold weather and began to straggle away, a few at a time, until the yard and driveway were empty again.

One would almost have thought that nothing abnormal had happened at all, Holly reflected as she worked on her cooking column and Madge dusted and vacuumed in another part of the house.

The answering machine was a reminder, of course; the moment one message had been left, another caller would try to get through.

But when Holly finished her column, which was surprisingly good, she thought, under the circumstances, she began to think about David again, and how he had betrayed her. How he had seduced her.

She didn't quite dare to go outside, but if she didn't work off some of her anger, and soon, she knew she was going to be tearing her hair. Staunchly, Holly went upstairs and exchanged her jeans and sweater for her workout clothes. She pinned up her hair, drew a deep breath and made her way to the family room just off the kitchen, where the mini-trampoline was kept.

Rolling it out of a closet, she set it on its sturdy legs. She switched on the TV to a cable channel devoted exclusively to old movies and bounced furiously on the trampoline while watching Claudette Colbert win Fred MacMurray's heart.

Holly ran, she did jumping jacks and then she just bounced again. Up and down, higher and higher she went, but she couldn't escape the fact that she loved David Goddard, no matter how hard she tried to distract herself.

The housekeeper, like Elaine, seemed kindly disposed toward David. Or, at least, she let him into the house when he knocked tentatively at the kitchen door.

"Where is she?" he asked.

The woman went back to the table, where she had been eating lunch and following the details of Craig Llewellyn's arrest on the screen of a TV roughly the size of a postcard. "In there," she gestured toward the inner doorway, "trying to bounce herself through the family room ceiling."

David frowned and wedged his hands nervously into

his pockets before going to the doorway to investigate. Holly's soft blond hair was pinned up haphazardly, her breathing audible even over the television set she was watching.

Her back was turned to David and she didn't hear his approach, for she kept right on bouncing. Bouncing. A shimmering film of perspiration shone from beneath the loose tendrils of honey-colored hair at the nape of her neck. "Don't you trust him, Claudette," she sputtered out. "All men are rat finks."

David felt a lot of things at that moment: sympathy, regret and, most of all, a desire to wrench Holly Llewellyn off that damned jogger-thing and make love to her on the family room floor.

He rounded Holly and stood before her, inwardly bracing himself for what he knew was coming.

Her beautiful aquamarine eyes, somewhat swollen and red, widened at the sight of him. He felt like Benedict Arnold crashing a party at George and Martha's place. At least she'd stopped that damned bouncing.

"Get the hell out of my house!" she hissed, her perfect cheekbones flaring to the color of her pink pants, her hands clenched into fists at her sides.

"No. I'm not going anywhere until you get down off that thing and talk to me."

"I'll call the police!"

"I don't think so. Besides, I probably have more sway with them than you do." He turned, admired Claudette Colbert's unique face for one steadying moment and then switched off the TV. "Get down, Holly," he ordered, facing her again.

She bit her lower lip, flashed him a look of beleaguered hatred and began to bounce again. Slowly. Defiantly.

It was giving David motion sickness. With a muttered curse, he grasped her and wrenched her down. She stumbled and fell against him—every day had its high point, he thought wryly—and then she righted herself, bunching up her fists and using them to thrust away from his chest.

"I was telling the truth when I said I loved you, Holly," he said, allowing her to keep the small distance she apparently needed, "so stop flaring your nostrils and clenching your fists and listen to me."

"You go straight to hell, Mr. Goddard!" she gasped out. "Or is it 'God' for short?"

David's jawline tightened painfully. "Dammit, Holly," he bit out, "can't you see that I was caught in this trap as much as you were? I came here to find out if you were helping Craig in any way and—"

"You mean you were spying on me, too? That you weren't just waiting for my brother to stumble into your net?" Right then he wanted to turn her over his knee and blister her delightful rear end. That was unthinkable, of course, but he did take some comfort in the fantasy.

"The president-elect was afraid you might be helping Craig sell secrets, Holly," he said evenly.

"Howard thought I was some kind of female James Bond?" She was seething now, showing her teeth. God, even though she was mad as hell and sweating, she was magnificent. "I don't believe it!"

"Believe it," David said.

"You lied to me the whole time!"

"Not the whole time. I meant it when I said I love you."

"Get out of my house!"

David stood stock-still. "Don't you want to know what's going to happen to Craig now that he's been taken into custody?"

That stopped her. She stood stiffly, attentively, her eyes searching his face. "Yes," she said in a whisper. "David, will they hurt him?"

"You've been watching too many espionage movies. They'll debrief him—" He paused, holding up both hands to stay the frantic questions he saw brewing in her green-blue eyes. "That only means that they'll find out what he knows and what he's told al-Qaeda, among other people he might have been dealing with. And then, because of the cocaine problem, they'll hospitalize him for a while. Whether or not he actually goes to prison will depend on a lot of factors that can't be determined right now."

"He was so afraid of being caught!"

David ached for Holly, wished that he dared take her into his arms and hold her. "Holly, being stopped was the best thing that could have happened to Craig. The cocaine alone would have killed him. And what was the situation doing to you? To Toby?"

She was gnawing at her lip again, her eyes bright with unshed tears. "I'm glad that Craig won't have to run anymore. I—I didn't realize how sick he was until he told me about the drug."

"I know," David said softly.

Holly stiffened, and her eyes flashed again. "I was going to turn him in myself, you know. I didn't need you to come here and pretend you loved me. I could have handled the situation."

"Could you, Holly? Do you have any idea how insidious cocaine addiction can be, what it can make a person do?"

He saw her tremble and knew she was bracing herself against him, against all he represented. In that instant, he accepted the fact that he'd lost her.

"Get out," she said. "And don't come back, David. Don't call and don't come to my classes."

"Your classes? Surely you're not going to teach this week—the press will be lying in wait for you, Holly. They'll eat you alive!"

"I can take care of myself," she said. And then she turned away and David didn't have the heart to turn her around to him again.

"I love you," he said gruffly. Then he drew a deep breath, struggled to control the burning in his eyes and left her. She switched the TV back on and climbed back onto the trampoline, bouncing with a vengeance.

As David passed through the kitchen, the housekeeper gave him a sympathetic look. He shrugged and without speaking opened Holly's back door to step out into a world that was never going to be quite the same again.

The moment David was gone, Holly sank to her knees on the trampoline, covered her face with both hands and let the sobs that had been scalding her throat have free rein. Claudette Colbert laughed merrily on the television screen, and Madge spoke softly from the doorway.

"Go after him, Holly. If you love that man, don't you let him get away. You'll be sorry all your life if you do."

Holly stopped crying and drew a deep breath. She would be sorry all her life that she'd *met* David Goddard, maybe, but she would never be sorry for sending him away. Damn his sneaky hide anyway. Let him go and use some other unsuspecting woman.

"I will not have that traitor mentioned under this roof again, Madge," she said, rising to her feet and dashing away her tears with the cuff of her jogging jacket. "If he calls or comes to the door, he is to be turned away. Do I make myself clear?"

There was a brief, tense silence. "Yes," Madge said finally, with resignation. "Clear enough."

Sorry that she'd had to speak so harshly to Madge, who had always been as good a friend as she was a housekeeper, Holly nevertheless left the room without apologizing. She went upstairs, stripped and showered.

At seven o'clock, she got into her car and drove downtown to teach her fruitcake class. The reporters were there, just as David had warned they would be, but so were the students. By sheer force of will, Holly taught the class as usual, the only deviation being that she didn't stay to gather up and clean the baking pans and mixing bowls.

Later, at home, Holly steeled herself and played back the messages her machine had been recording all day. With one startling exception, the calls were from news reporters. As if in a daze, Holly sat down to listen to the surprisingly ordinary voice of the next president of the United States.

"Hello, Holly. This is Howard. I'm sorry about Craig and all the fuss the press is probably stirring up. Maggie and I just wanted you to know that we hope you'll come to Washington for the shindig next month." Having said his piece, Howard hung up without another word and there were no more messages after that.

This is Howard…sorry about Craig…hope you'll come to Washington… The phrases echoed in Holly's overwrought mind and her broken heart. Maybe, just maybe, she would go to Washington. Maybe she would attend the balls and the parties and the swearing-in. Maybe she would tell Howard to his open and trustworthy face that she was just as loyal an American as the next person. "Do you solemnly swear," she imagined the Speaker of the House asking dear Howard, "that you will monitor the activities of your third cousin, the cookbook author, lest she undermine the security of this great country of ours?"

Howard, of course, would so swear.

Just then, Elaine arrived with Toby and, to Holly, she looked just a bit sheepish. Toby was carrying a dime-store fishbowl as though it were gold, frankincense or myrrh, and two goldfish hovered inside, staring stupidly.

"David gave me these," the little boy spouted before Holly could make any kind of comment at all. "He said I could take care of them for him, but I'm not s'posed to worry if they buy the farm 'cause they only cost seventy-nine cents a piece and they're spendable."

Expendable. Of course. The way Holly was expendable. The way Toby, though he hadn't made that painful discovery yet, was expendable. "Take the fish to your room, Toby," she said evenly.

When Toby was gone, she attacked an uncomfortable Elaine with, "You let David see Toby, didn't you? Why did you do that, Elaine, when you knew—"

"He only wanted to say goodbye!" Elaine broke in defensively. She looked pale and tired and a little harried, and Holly realized belatedly how hard this day had been for her friend.

"I'm sorry, Elaine. I shouldn't have jumped all over you that way."

Elaine managed a shaky smile. "We're all on edge, I suppose. I can't tell you how much I'm looking forward to putting on my old chenille bathrobe and curling up with Roy and a good book!"

Holly felt a touch of envy, somewhere in the deepest, darkest corner of her heart. Was she ever going to have anybody she could wear a chenille bathrobe in front of and "curl up" with?

It didn't seem very likely because she knew that she was never going to love a man the way she'd loved David Goddard. Never ever again.

"You can take the rest of the week off if you'd like," Holly offered in an unsteady voice.

"Not me," Elaine said, squaring her shoulders and trying to look intrepid. "I'm made of better stuff than that and so are you."

Holly smiled, even though tears were dangerously near the surface. "So you are. Thank you, Elaine, for everything."

Elaine hugged Holly briefly and patted her shoulder. "Anything for the boss," she said, and then she was leaving again, on her way home to Roy and the chenille bathrobe and a good book.

If Holly hadn't liked her friend so much, she would have hated her for being so lucky.

Chapter 9

Walt Zigman had seen that look before; it was a look that meant an agent had lost his spirit and maybe his grip. Damned shame it had to happen to a man like Goddard. He sat back in his desk chair and maneuvered his cigar stub from one side of his mouth to the other.

Goddard sat in the chair Walt knew the agents called the "hot seat," his long frame lank with an effort to hide tremendous pressure. "I told you she was clean," he said after a long, uneasy silence.

"Maybe you read palms or tea leaves, Goddard, but I don't. We had to know."

Goddard darted Walt a look meant to slice deep, and to Walt's surprise, it did. "Holly Llewellyn wasn't guilty of any crime. As far as I'm concerned, she's been harassed."

"Horsechips. She aided and abetted a suspected felon, Goddard. She's lucky we didn't bring her in, too."

Goddard was glaring now; his hands, gripping the arms of his chair, whitened at the knuckles. Though he hid the fact, Walt was pleased by the reaction; maybe this agent would be all right after all.

"Here." Goddard slapped a thin file folder down in the middle of a stack of memos and notes. Walt's whole life was one big memo these days, what with the transition from one administration to another and the inaugural festivities coming up in January. Security problems were everywhere and Walt Zigman didn't need another hassle.

"What's this?"

Goddard averted his eyes and shifted in his chair, but then he met Walt's gaze squarely. "My letter of resignation," he answered.

If there was regret in his voice, Walt didn't catch it. He wanted to swear. "You sure about this, Goddard? You're a good agent."

"I'm sure."

"What the hell are you going to do with your time, for Christ's sake? Walk dogs?"

Goddard made a visible attempt to keep his temper. "I'm qualified to practice law, in case you've forgotten."

"That little—that Llewellyn woman really got under your skin, didn't she?" Walt paused, sighed, lit the cigar stub and puffed industriously for a few moments. "Dammit, Goddard, we're swapping administrations here. We got an inaugural coming up in a little better than a month! I need every experienced agent I've got right now!"

Goddard was waving away the cigar smoke with one hand and Walt ground the stub out in an ashtray. "For what? Standing around in Saks while the new first lady tries on six hundred pairs of shoes?"

"You'll be assigned to the president himself, Goddard."

Goddard pointed one index finger toward the ceiling and spun it round and round in a contemptuous circle.

"Well, what the hell do you want?" Walt snapped, annoyed and a little insulted.

"I want out of the Service," David replied flatly. "I'll stay until after inauguration week is over, but I want the presidential assignments—no walking dogs. No strolls in the Rose Garden. It's strictly Oval Office and Air Force One, Walt, or I'm out of here."

"All right, all right, you're on presidential detail." Walt took up the folder Goddard had laid on his desk and extended it. "You keep this."

"You keep it," Goddard argued, standing up. "I meant it when I said I wanted out."

"What the devil do you plan to do after January?"

Goddard shrugged. "I told you, Walt. I intend to practice law."

Walt muttered a swearword and picked up the remains of his cigar again. "Take over for Erickson, then. He's got a root canal scheduled for this morning."

Goddard winced sympathetically. "Where?"

"In his mouth, dammit," Walt grumbled, tossing the folder containing his best agent's resignation letter into a deep drawer.

"I was asking where to find the president, Walt," came the strained and humorless response.

Walt didn't look up. "Oval Office," he bit out.

Holly was just getting through her days and nights, operating on automatic pilot, so to speak. She tried to see Craig, but he refused any contact with her or with her lawyer. Soon after that, he was transported to Washington, D.C., for the debriefing David had told her about.

It hurt, having to hear that on the evening news along with the rest of the world.

Christmas was fast approaching, though, and for Toby's sake, Holly tried her best to get into the spirit of things. She shopped, she baked, she decorated the house and put a wreath on the front door. But every time she so much as looked at the Christmas tree, she was filled with memories that brought tears to her eyes and a painful catch to her throat. David was gone, really gone. She knew because she had looked up his address in Elaine's records of the last cooking class and driven to his apartment.

Two college girls were living there now, and they couldn't tell Holly anything about David Goddard except that he must have had a dog because there were these "grungy" stains on the rug. Holly had turned away and gone blindly back to her car, sitting there in the parking lot for a full fifteen minutes with her forehead resting despondently against the steering wheel. She had already known that David had returned to his old life in Washington, D.C., so why was it such a crushing blow to find that strangers were living in his apartment? What would she have said to him if he had been there?

Holly hadn't known the answer to either question and now, kneeling on the floor of her own living room, struggling to wrap a last-minute gift for Toby, she still hadn't worked it all out.

The doorbell rang, and Holly sniffled and dashed a

stray tear from her cheek. Who could that be? After all, it was Christmas Eve, and nearly eleven o'clock at that.

She opened the door to find Skyler Hollis standing on the porch, looking uneasy and snow-dappled and rather earnest. For the space of a second, Holly had allowed herself the fantasy that David would be there in the glow of the porch light, and she hoped her disappointment didn't show.

"Sky," she said. "Come in."

"I hope you don't mind my coming by, Holly. I know it's late—"

Cautious because Skyler could be damnably persistent at times and because she didn't want to give him the wrong idea, Holly stepped back to admit him without saying anything.

He was carrying two beautifully wrapped packages in his arms. "I did my Christmas shopping last July," he explained. "I couldn't very well give Toby's to Mary Ann, so—"

Holly smiled because it was just like Skyler to do his Christmas shopping in July. He had probably addressed his cards then, too, though she hadn't received one. "Come in, Sky, and sit down. I think there might be some eggnog left."

He entered the living room ahead of her, put the two packages beneath the tree, then went to the hearth, ostensibly to examine Toby's as-yet-unfilled stocking, and confessed, "I've been worried about you, Holly, since that thing with your brother broke." He let the stocking fall back into place and turned to face her with the eyes of a concerned friend. "Are you all right?"

Holly shrugged and averted her gaze so that he

wouldn't see the tears that had gathered there. "I'm all right," she lied.

"Toby?"

Toby was resilient. In fact, he was rather enjoying the notoriety of having a "spy" for a father. "Toby is okay, too, Sky. How have you been?"

A smile broke across his face, warm and, to Holly, very reassuring. "I'm dating Mary Ann," he said.

Holly was pleased and she hugged Skyler impulsively. "That's wonderful."

Skyler was still grinning. "I'm opening another store, too—up in Colville. I've been wanting to spend more time there."

Colville was a good-sized town and very near the farm. Holly smiled, starting to ladle out a cup of egg-nog from the crystal bowl in the middle of the coffee table. Earlier, Roy and Elaine and Madge had all been by, and Holly had done her best to present them with some sort of celebration. "Your parents must be happy about that."

"Oh, none of that for me," Skyler said quickly, referring to the eggnog. "That stuff is fattening, you know."

Holly chuckled and took a sip from the cup herself. Lord knew, she spent so much time running on the mini-trampoline that she didn't have to worry about calories.

"You really ought to get away from Spokane for a while," Skyler said, watching her with a sort of gentle disapproval that implied she wasn't her usual self. "Hawaii, maybe, or—"

Holly laughed. "I can't go away, Skyler, much as I would like to. Toby is in school."

"All the same—"

She went to him, standing on tiptoe to plant a sisterly kiss on his cool, clean-shaven cheek. "Don't worry about me, Skyler. Please. I'm going to be just fine. You just concentrate on Mary Ann."

He returned her kiss, though her forehead was the target. "That guy is gone, isn't he?"

Holly's throat felt thick and sore again; she could only nod.

"He's a real fool," Skyler said. There was a long silence and then he started toward the door again, still wearing his coat. "I guess I'd better go," he said gruffly, his hand on the knob. "I've got a long drive to make."

"Be careful," Holly managed to say.

Skyler cleared his throat and nodded. When he met Holly's eyes, his gaze was full of something she had been getting too much of lately—sympathy. "I will. Merry Christmas, Holly."

Holly swallowed hard. "Merry Christmas, Skyler."

When he was gone, Holly walked back to the living room. The fire was burning low, the lights on the tree were glimmering and a Christmas carol was coming softly from the stereo. Holly swallowed again, squared her shoulders and methodically filled Toby's stocking until it bulged. For the first time in her entire life, she cried on Christmas Eve.

It seemed to Chris that her brother's smile was a little sad as he filled the girls' Christmas stockings and returned them to the hooks on the mantelpiece. He was looking at the two stockings that remained: his own and Chris's.

"I didn't know you still had these," he said gruffly.

Chris ached for him; though he hadn't said much

about the disaster in Spokane, she knew David well enough to guess that he'd fallen for someone out there— probably Holly Llewellyn herself—and lost her. Her own painful divorce was two years in the past, but enough of the hurt lingered for her to sympathize.

"Holidays are the worst, aren't they?" she prompted softly, perching on the arm of the sofa and watching her brother.

David was tracing the letters of his name, awkwardly written in glitter across the top of the old red corduroy stocking. "Remember the year Mom made these, Chris? She was so proud of them."

Chris closed her eyes momentarily, scrounging up a smile. "You were Joseph in the church play," she recalled aloud. "Mom made your robe from an old sheet with Batman all over it."

David laughed gruffly. "Yeah. You were an angel that year. Talk about miscasting." He fell silent, then turned to face his sister, his dark blue eyes full of pain. "Do you miss Dennis?"

The truth was that Chris rarely thought of her ex-husband. She was too busy with her girls, the house, the cover designs she painted for romance novels. "At Christmas I get a little sentimental. Most of the time, I revel in how much he and Mona deserve each other."

David laughed again, and the pain in his eyes faded a little. "I think the same thing about Marleen and her monkeys," he confessed.

"Something is hurting you," Chris prompted gently, folding her arms.

"Being a two-time loser, I guess," came the hoarse admission.

"Holly Llewellyn?"

David lowered his handsome head. "Not much gets by you, does it, Chris? You ought to be an FBI agent or something."

"Walt's daughter tells me you're resigning."

David cursed, but with less spirit than Chris would have liked. "Zigman has a big mouth."

Boldly, Chris went to her desk, picked up the telephone in both hands and thrust it toward her brother. "Call Holly and wish her Merry Christmas," she said.

"It's too late—"

Chris glanced at the clock on the mantelpiece. "It's only eleven out there. I'll bet she's still up."

David considered the telephone for a moment, as though it were some complicated equation, then turned resolutely away. "Shall I bring the girls' presents in from the garage?"

Chris sighed. From long experience she knew how stubborn her brother could be. She set the phone back in its place. "Let me check and see if they're asleep yet. Sometimes they pretend."

"How do you know if they're pretending?" David asked, so guilelessly that Chris had to laugh.

"Men! You tickle them, of course. If they giggle, they're playing possum."

David shook his head, grinning. Because his eyes had strayed to the telephone, Chris turned quickly and hurried up the stairs and into her daughters' room. She remained there, in the darkness, long after discovering that they were both asleep.

The telephone was ringing. Holly stared at it over her shoulder, parts of the Lego village she was trying to assemble still in her hands. She dropped a plastic palm tree and lunged for the receiver, telling herself that she mustn't let Toby be awakened by the noise.

"Hello?" she whispered, breathless with the foolish hope she couldn't seem to let go of.

Long-distance. The special ring had betrayed the call as long-distance. Holly's weary heart leaped within her.

"Hello?" she said again, because her caller seemed stumped for words.

"This is David," came the gruff, belated greeting.

Holly sagged onto the couch, dizzy with relief and with pain. "Oh," she said woodenly.

"Did I wake you?"

"N-no—I was putting out the Santa Claus things for Toby," Holly answered. Damn you, you should be here helping me, she added in her mind. For the moment, the fact that she had sent David away herself escaped her.

"How is Toby?"

God, the man was a conversational genius. Maybe that came from standing silent guard over presidents, ever-alert for any sort of danger. "He's doing okay," Holly replied. "He still has the fish."

"I hope their personalities have improved. They were definitely lackluster company when I had them."

Tears were streaming down Holly's face now, but they weren't audible, she hoped, in her voice. "What do you want from two goldfish? The old soft-shoe?"

David laughed. It was good to hear that sound, even if it was distant. "A medley of Elton John's greatest hits would have been nice."

"I'll buy them a little piano."

David's chuckle seemed to reach across the three thousand miles that separated them and caress Holly. "Have you forgiven me yet?"

"Quite honestly, no." It was sad to feel the anger again, the hurt. "Why concern yourself, David? You got your man and all that."

"It's my woman I'm concerned with."

Holly thrust out her chin, determined not to let him touch her with his voice. But she reddened to remember being his woman on that very couch and her body responded with a keen, embarrassing ache in her middle and a warm swelling in her breasts. "There are two college girls living in your old apartment," she said, and then hated herself for revealing that she'd gone there.

David must have sensed her discomfort, for he mercifully allowed the faux pas to pass. "Did they get the stains out of the rug?" he quipped.

Despite herself Holly laughed. "No. As a matter of fact, they didn't. They asked me if you had a dog."

There was a short, uncomfortable silence. "Holly," David finally ventured, "are you coming to Washington for the inauguration?"

Holly was winding and unwinding the phone cord around her finger. "I hadn't thought about it," she lied. The truth was that she had thought of little else; she'd been wondering if David would be at any one of the round of parties that were scheduled.

"Think about it."

"Why?"

"Dammit, you know why! Because I'll be in the president's hip pocket the whole time and I want to see you, that's why."

"Some Secret Service agent you are," challenged Holly hotly, flustered because he'd touched a nerve. "Do you always flirt with women while you're supposed to be protecting the chief executive?"

David sighed and it was a sound heavy with exasperation and strained patience. "I'll make time for you, don't worry."

"You're not going to make any kind of time, mister, so don't *you* worry!"

"Damn it all to hell, Holly, will you pull in your righteous indignation for one minute and listen to me?"

"No!" hissed Holly, remembering the lies, the pretense, the humiliation of finding out that she had been used. "You treated me like a…like a bimbo!"

He laughed. He actually had the gall, the temerity, to laugh!

"Merry Christmas!" Holly shouted and then she slammed the receiver back into its cradle.

After a few minutes spent wailing into a sofa pillow, Holly got hold of herself. She dried her tears and then stood up and went back to the Lego village, putting it together carefully. When it was done, she made sure that the red wagon was at just the right angle beneath the tree and that the football was displayed to proper advantage.

Then she burrowed on her hands and knees through the scratchy, fragrant branches, to unplug the tree lights and plunge a conscientious finger into the base of the stand to make sure there was enough water.

Later, upstairs, she put on a nightgown, brushed her teeth, washed her face and stumbled off to bed. Regrettably, no sugarplums danced in her head—only memories of David trying to fly his funny-looking model airplane in the park, David mixing fruitcake batter in the department-store class, David ushering Elaine and Toby through a pressing crowd of reporters and cameramen. David making love to her.

"Nerd!" she whispered, pounding one fist into the pillow. "Get out of my mind!"

David remained in Holly's mind until she slept; then he haunted her dreams. It seemed she had barely closed her eyes before Toby was bouncing gleefully on her bed, his tightly filled Christmas stocking in hand.

"Look, Mom!" he crowed, holding up the evidence. "Santa Claus came!"

Holly widened her eyes in feigned wonder; it was a game they played every Christmas morning. In truth, Toby had already added Santa to his list of fictional characters, along with the Hardy Boys, Superman and the Tooth Fairy. He was still undecided about the Easter Bunny.

Toby upended the stocking and the booty spilled out over the quilt—an orange, a bottle of bubbles, a deck of trick cards, a candy cane and at least a dozen other things. His delight uplifted Holly as nothing else could have.

"Can we go downstairs and open the presents?" the child demanded once the stocking goodies had all been inspected and mentally categorized in order of usefulness.

Holly pretended to be surprised. "I think we should eat breakfast first," she said.

Toby caught her hand in his and literally dragged her out of bed, giving her only a second to scramble for her robe and slippers before proceeding out into the hall and down the stairs.

The next half hour was happily absorbed in ripping away paper and ribbons. Toby received a model car and a Scrabble game from Elaine and Roy, along with gifts from Holly herself, from Madge, from some of his

friends at school. Skyler had given him a radio with—
he was a true friend, that Skyler—earphones.

"Aren't you going to open any of your stuff?" he
asked, surrounded by loot of every type. The eagerness
in his eyes made her choose the package he and Elaine
had wrapped in secret and put under the tree with a
converse sort of ceremony.

"This one has been driving me crazy," she confessed,
taking sidelong notes of the little boy's quick, delighted
grin. She opened the parcel to find a book she had
been longing to read tucked inside. And her pleasure
was real.

After that, Holly uncovered a frying pan from Skyler—that made her smile—and a bottle of her favorite
cologne from Elaine and Roy. There were other things,
too, sent by her mother and faraway friends, but nothing, she assured the little boy, was quite as wonderful
as the book he had chosen for her.

Toby was frowning, peering into the depths of the
tree. "What's those things?" he asked.

"What things?" Holly asked, honestly puzzled.

"In there. There's two presents in there, in the
branches!"

Holly smiled, thinking that Elaine must have hidden away an extra surprise or two for Toby. She liked
to do things like that. "Guess you'd better investigate,"
she said.

Toby drew out a sizable box—Holly couldn't imagine how she had missed seeing it—and then a smaller
one. Both were wrapped in gold foil.

"The big one's mine!" Toby crowed after reading the
tag. He was already tearing at the wrapping as he extended the other present to a confused Holly.

She looked down at the tag on her own gift and her heart stopped, then started again with an aching lurch. "Love, David," was written upon it in a typically firm hand.

Trembling just a little, Holly did not open her gift but, instead, watched Toby rip away a second layer of paper to reveal a plain box. Inside was a small robot, complete with hand-controls and a set of batteries.

Toby lifted round, shining eyes to Holly's face. "Who's this from?" he whispered, awed. It was obvious that he was considering shifting Santa Claus from the fiction list to the one peopled by Holly and his teachers and everyone else he could see and touch.

"From David, I think," Holly said, and thank heaven, Toby was too enthralled with the gift to notice the tremor in his aunt's voice.

"Wow," he said, dragging the word out for that emphasis peculiar to seven-year-old boys.

Holly's eyes were stinging a bit, and she averted her face for a moment before opening her own present with numb, awkward fingers. Inside was a small, elegant velvet box, and inside that was the most beautiful diamond engagement ring she had ever seen. Still trembling, Holly opened the note that had been rolled up and slipped through the ring itself. *"Marry me or I'll jump off the Washington Monument. Subtly, David."*

Holly couldn't help it. She laughed. She bit her lower lip to stop herself and that didn't help so she laughed again. Tears were streaking down her cheeks and Toby was looking at her in total confusion.

"What's-a-matter, Mom?" he asked, flushed with concern.

Holly closed the ring box firmly. "Nothing," she said. "Nothing is the matter."

"Was it a joke present?" Toby wanted to know, and his manner said that he wouldn't consider that untoward.

"Yes," Holly managed to say, taking the gift, box, wrapping paper and all, to the mantelpiece, where she tucked it behind a picture of her grandmother. Out of sight, out of mind, she told herself without much conviction.

All through that hectic day, all through the hurried breakfast, all through the drive to Elaine and Roy's apartment, all through Christmas dinner and the rousing trivia game that followed, Holly's mind and heart kept straying back to that ring and all it meant.

Of course, she couldn't marry David Goddard, as intriguing as the possibility was—not after what he had done. But she would take a certain pleasure in throwing that diamond in his face when she went to Washington next month to attend Howard's inauguration.

Chapter 10

Elaine was fairly dancing with excitement, her eyes bright and wide. She hugged Holly unreservedly, as other passengers pressed past them to board the airplane, and enjoined, "You have the best time anybody has ever had at an inauguration, Holly Llewellyn!"

Holly felt rueful and wary—perhaps it was a mistake to go to Washington after all—but she did return Elaine's hug. "Take care of Toby," she said.

"You know I will," Elaine scolded good-naturedly.

Holly wished she could back out at this late date but resigned herself to the fact that she couldn't. She squared her shoulders, drew a deep breath and entered the covered passageway leading to the airplane. She looked back once, wavering, but Elaine made a little shooing motion with her hands and winked encouragingly.

The flight was uneventful. Holly had a brief stopover in Denver, and then it was on to Washington, where a car and driver were waiting to take her to the White House—was this really happening to her? As a relative of Howard's—good heavens, she barely remembered him—Holly was to be accommodated in style at 1600 Pennsylvania Avenue.

Escorted by a grim-looking Secret Service agent who would obviously rather not have been bothered, Holly was quickly shuffled into a limo with tinted windows and driven to the most august address in the United States.

On the way, she tried to make conversation with the agent who sat in the back with her. A little chit-chat, she thought, might ease her nervousness about what was to come. "Jimmy Carter came to Spokane once," she ventured, "to speak at Riverfront Park. He rode past in a car like this one, with darkened windows, and I think he smiled at me because I saw a flash of teeth."

The chauffeur chuckled to himself, though his eyes were fixed on the crazy Washington traffic. But the Secret Service man only reacted with a look that questioned her sanity. She supposed that Jimmy Carter and his teeth were old news to this guy, but he could have been a little friendlier all the same. Holly resisted an urge to tap on his forehead with her knuckles and ask if there was anybody in there.

They entered the White House grounds through a back gate, snow crunching beneath the limo's tires as it came to a stop at a rear door. Holly drew in her breath and let it out as a long, Toby-like, "Wow."

The Secret Service agent cleared his throat, got out of the car and extended a hand to Holly. Reluctantly, she accepted it. This character had no personality at all, it seemed. He was certainly nothing like David.

Holly left the limo with as much dignity as she could summon. Perhaps David would behave in just this manner when he was on duty; for better or worse, she was about to find out.

In a small anteroom—Holly had no way of knowing what part of this fabled mansion they were in—another agent appeared. Like the first one, he wore a trim three-piece suit, a no-nonsense expression and a very small earphone that probably connected him to all sorts of small in-house intrigues.

Holly was more nervous than ever, and that made her chatter again. "George Washington actually slept here," she muttered, wide-eyed.

The agents exchanged a long-suffering look, probably thinking how unfortunate it was that the president-to-be had to have such a bumpkin for a cousin. "This way, Madam," one of them said, and Holly found herself being propelled through a series of rooms and up a rear staircase.

"Do you know David Goddard?" Holly tried again. Maybe these guys were at least semi-human.

The agents traded another look. Apparently the answer to that question was a state secret, for neither of them bothered to respond.

They were now on the floor where the first family resided. Holly decided charitably that that accounted for the reticence of the two men escorting her. She was deposited in a lovely room decorated all in blue. To her amazement, her baggage had already been brought up, and a small, plump woman in a maid's uniform was busy taking Holly's new evening gowns from the garment bag and hanging them carefully in the closet.

Here, perhaps, was a human being, though after the Secret Service agents, Holly didn't want to make any rash judgment.

"Hello," she ventured.

The maid, an elderly woman with a look of long service about her, smiled warmly. "Hello, Ms. Llewellyn. And welcome to Washington."

"Thank you," Holly said with a sigh of relief.

"I'm Mrs. Tallington, and I'll be helping you while you're with us. The first lady asked me to tell you that she will be in to greet you shortly."

So, Holly thought, Howard's Maggie is already referred to by that lofty title, even though the swearing-in isn't until tomorrow. "Have you worked here for a long time?" she asked as Mrs. Tallington examined Holly's blue chiffon, made a cluck-clucking sound and shook her gray head.

"Since JFK and Jackie," came the brisk answer. "They come and they go. Some are happier to leave than to arrive, I might add. This gown will need pressing."

Holly chuckled and relaxed enough to set her purse on a mahogany dresser and remove her winter coat. "I was afraid everyone here would be like those men who brought me upstairs."

A mischievous light twinkled in Mrs. Tallington's bright blue eyes. Her snow-white hair made a little knot on the top of her head, just visible through the gauzy fabric of her cap. "Don't speak ill of those who are probably standing right outside your door," she warned good-naturedly.

Drawing in a quick breath, Holly went to the door,

opened it a crack and peered out. The two agents looked back at her impassively, and she closed the door again with a resolute click.

Mrs. Tallington was chuckling. "A little unnerving, isn't it? But they're there to guard you; they mean you no harm. Just make yourself comfortable and pretend they're not around."

Holly had never been "guarded" before, and she was nonplussed. Once again she had misgivings about the wisdom of coming here, to this place where she didn't belong, where everything was so formal and intimidating.

"I'd like to see the room where Mr. Lincoln slept," she said to distract herself.

Mrs. Tallington nodded, her eyes twinkling again, toward a huge painting of the Great Emancipator himself. "You're in it," she replied matter-of-factly. "Some say they've seen Abe sitting on the edge of that very bed, taking off his shoes."

Holly shuddered despite her pleasant surprise at finding herself in a room once occupied by one of the greatest men in history. She certainly hoped that Mr. Lincoln would not deign to sit upon the side of the bed while she was in it—that would be most disconcerting.

There was a slight ballyhoo outside and then a knock at the door. Before Holly could issue any sort of invitation, Maggie swept into the room, all campaign-trail smiles, her glistening blond hair artfully coiffed, her dress a designer original.

"Holly, dear! How marvelous to see you!"

Holly stiffened, then worked up a smile. After all, this was Lincoln's bedroom and this was the first lady of the land. Such things had to be accorded due respect. "Hello, Maggie," she said.

Maggie bypassed Holly's cheek with a distant-cousin-by-marriage kiss. "Howard and I are so pleased that you could come!"

Mrs. Tallington, the wrinkled blue chiffon evening gown draped over one capable arm, ducked out of the room without a word. Holly watched her go, using the time to overcome her secret ire over what Howard and his suspicions had put her through.

The first lady drew back her guest's attention with a trilling, musical laugh. "Howard will apologize himself, of course," she said, "but I did want to tell you that we're both very sorry over what happened to poor Craig."

Holly was momentarily annoyed. They were very sorry. Did they think their third cousin from Spokane had come down in the last snowstorm? They had believed, actually believed, that Holly could turn on her own country. "Thank you," she forced herself to say.

Maggie dragged discerning eyes over Holly's rumpled woolen suit. "You'll want to change before meeting with the president, of course."

Which president? Holly wanted to ask, but she bit the perverse inclination back. The outgoing administration was probably out-gone anyway. "Of course," she answered.

Maggie smiled her blinding, trust-my-husband smile. "Wonderful. When you're ready, just tap at the door and the men stationed outside will see you to the Oval Office."

The Oval Office. Holly's knees weakened and she hoped she didn't sway visibly. Me? she thought. In the Oval Office?

Maggie noted with a glossy smile that her guest was properly overwhelmed by the magnitude of it all. With a cheery word of farewell, she swept out.

Holly wobbled her way into the bathroom that must have been added on sometime after Mr. Lincoln's demise, undressed and ran a hot bath. Half an hour later, she was presentable again, her hair neatly brushed, her makeup fresh. Wearing an expensive suit of beige and emerald, she drew a deep breath and tapped at the door, as instructed.

It opened to give Holly Llewellyn the shock of her life. David Goddard was smiling down into her face. "That outfit makes you look like a Midwestern schoolmarm," he muttered out of one side of his mouth.

Holly grappled inwardly for composure, then lifted her chin and retorted, "If it was good enough for *The Today Show,* buddy, it's good enough for Howard."

For a moment, before the intangible veil of officialdom fell over his eyes, making them expressionless, David allowed them to transmit a welcome that made Holly pinken slightly.

She was led to the Oval Office itself. There were Marines guarding the double doors, and beyond that point, there was a spacious outer office, populated by secretaries and advisors of various stations. One of them pressed a button on an intercom and said, "Mr. President, Ms. Llewellyn has arrived."

It was unsettling, the way everyone around there seemed to know Holly's name without her telling them. Did they know how much she owed on her charge cards and what kind of hairspray she used and whether or not her library books were overdue, too?

She flung one scathing, sidelong look at David, remembering just how personal a presidentially ordered investigation could get. "Rat," she whispered, and one side of David's firm mouth twitched almost imperceptibly.

"Send her in, send her in!" boomed Howard's jovial voice over the intercom.

Holly was escorted right to the doors—what did they think she was going to do? Bolt and run? Make a stirring speech in favor of Osama bin Laden?

"Let go of me!" she hissed.

Both agents immediately released their hold on her elbows. Though his face was completely expressionless, David's mouth twitched again and something danced in the blue depths of his eyes. "Give 'em hell, Llewellyn," he said, to the other agent's obvious distress.

And then Holly was inside that office of offices, alone except for Howard, and she couldn't hide her reaction to it all. After all, this was a place where dramatic decisions had been made. John F. Kennedy had discussed the Cuban missile crisis with Bobby. FDR had planned the New Deal. Abe Lincoln had listened to the ominous beat of Confederate drums from just across the Potomac....

"Wow," she said.

Howard, a genteel-looking, gray-haired man with a powerful build and a winning smile, stood up in gentlemanly deference. "My sentiments exactly," he said. "Actually, I'm just getting the feel of the place myself. This isn't my office yet."

Holly liked Howard for saying that. "Your predecessor—?"

"He's around somewhere," Howard said. "We both

want the transition to go as smoothly as possible and the president has been decent about this whole thing."

Howard gestured toward a long, comfortable-looking sofa, only one of several in the massive, overwhelmingly significant room, and Holly sat down gratefully with a smile.

But her smile faded as she considered the tremendous burdens that were about to be placed on this man's sturdy shoulders.

Howard had apparently guessed what she was thinking. "I'll do my best," he promised quietly and with conviction.

Holly's respect for the man deepened. "Waking up every morning, being responsible for much of the free world—I don't think I could do that."

The future president chuckled. "I can't make a decent wonton, so I guess we're even." He paused and cleared his throat in an I'm-about-to-say-something-momentous way. "Holly, Maggie and I are both very sorry about that investigation and the trouble it must have caused you."

Maggie's apology had been somewhat varnished and breezy, in Holly's opinion, but Howard's came across as the real thing. "You certainly had reason to doubt Craig," she admitted with dignity, "and I suppose you had no way of knowing that I would never take part in such a thing."

Howard watched her with kindly, rather tired eyes. "Thank you, Holly."

Holly bolted to her feet, conscious of the drains on this man's time and energy. She didn't want to be one of them; he had important things to do. "I'd better go and let you get back to your work. Do you think I could look around a bit?" She paused and chuckled nervously.

"It isn't every day that a cookbook author from Spokane finds herself in the White House, you know."

"Nor a lawyer from Oregon," quipped Howard, referring, of course, to himself.

Holly cocked her head toward the sturdy double doors and lowered her voice to a conspiratorial whisper. "Do those two goons have to be on my heels the whole time?" It felt good to refer to David Goddard as a "goon," unsuitable as the word might be for such a smooth operator.

Howard laughed his loud, ingenuous laugh. "I'm afraid so, Holly. They go with the territory."

"You mean, the whole time I'm in Washington—"

"The whole time you're in Washington," confirmed Howard with resignation.

Holly shook her head in irritated wonder and laid her hand on a knob touched by some of the greatest— but she wasn't going to ride that mental train again. Presidents, as had just been brought home to her, were as human as anybody else. Still, it was exhilarating to venture among such illustrious ghosts.

David was waiting, sans his partner, just beyond the doors. "I'd like a tour, please," she said, delighting in the brief flicker of irritation that moved in his eyes and tightened his splendid jawline a little.

They spent the rest of the morning visiting various parts of the White House, some accessible to tourists, some private. David might have been a stranger, so clipped were his explanations of this painting and that chair, and Holly told herself that it was just as well. After what he had done to her, who wanted intimate conversation?

She did. But she did a commendable job of hiding her disappointment at David's formal, distant manner.

It wasn't until he brought her back to Mr. Lincoln's bedroom that he said anything unagentlike, and even that was brief because the two men assigned to stand outside Holly's door and look intimidating were already zeroing in.

"I'm off duty at seven," he intoned. "Meet me outside the tourists' entrance."

"I will not—"

David was turning away. Damn, but he looked magnificent in his navy blue, don't-mess-with-me-I-guard-presidents suit. "Be there," he tossed back in parting.

Holly dodged inside her room and closed the door, impotently furious. The thing that made her maddest of all was knowing that even if it meant missing dinner with Maggie and Howard, she would be at the tourists' entrance at seven sharp.

David was pacing. He stopped occasionally to glare at his watch. Holly so enjoyed his discomfiture that had it not been for the two suits walking within lunging distance of each of her elbows, she would have hidden behind a statue and watched for a while.

"You're relieved," he said bluntly, his eyes darting from one impassive Secret Service face to the other.

"You got clearance for this, Goddard?" dared the taller one.

"Call upstairs and ask if you don't believe me," was David's response to the challenge.

If this was a bluff, the "goons" were calling it. One of them muttered something into the little device in his sleeve, his eyes never leaving David's face. Good heavens, Holly reflected, they don't even trust each other!

There was a buzzing sound, the response being discernible only if you happened to be wearing one of those communication contraptions, which, of course, Holly wasn't.

"You're clear, Goddard."

David's jawline tensed, then relaxed again. Was it possible that he found all this cloak-and-dagger stuff just as tiresome as Holly did? "Gee, thanks, Ranford," he bit out. And then as he pulled Holly into the protective curve of one arm, he added, "Don't wait up for us."

Holly found herself being ushered outside into the icy, snow-laced Washington wind and across a slippery parking lot. "Will they?" she asked, glancing back over one shoulder.

David opened the passenger door of a small green sports car and hustled her into the seat. "Will they what?"

Holly waited until he was behind the wheel before replying impatiently, "Will they wait up for us?"

David laughed. "No. They'll follow us. They'll sit across the street from my apartment building until we come out and then they'll tail us back to Pennsylvania Avenue. At which time they will collect you at the rear entrance and muscle you upstairs to your room. Neither of them will draw a calm breath until you're tucked in, safe and sound."

"I don't want to go to your apartment—"

David's perfect teeth flashed in the relative darkness. "Too bad," he replied.

"A lot of damned good it does to have bodyguards!"

Holly spouted, unnerved but tingly at the prospect of being alone with David Goddard. Distinctly tingly.

David only laughed. At the gate, he stopped to show his ID and the guard peered in, taking a long, level look at Holly.

"Do they always make such a big fuss about every little move a person makes?" Holly demanded, looking back as a limo followed them out, the gate slamming shut behind.

"Yes." David sighed. And he sounded tired and exasperated.

As they drove through the dark, snow-dusted streets of Washington and into an area Holly recognized as Georgetown, she glanced back at their one-car entourage and sighed. "Nobody will ever accuse those guys of being subtle. How do you stand it, David?"

"Stand it? I've done it myself a thousand times."

"Followed people? Who?"

"People who were taking a president's daughter out on a date, for one example."

He maneuvered the car into an underground parking area beneath one of the historic, renovated houses Holly had heard and read so much about. To hide her sudden case of jangly nerves, she sat up very straight in the seat and said, "This is quite an expensive car. It's good to know that civil servants are so well compensated for their work."

David grinned at her sarcasm, apparently unaffected by it. "Wait until you see my apartment," he baited her.

Holly was scowling as he parked the car and came around to collect her. As they hurried toward an elevator, she could hear the rhythmic click-click of the agents' shoes behind them. "They're not making any effort to be quiet, are they?"

"Why should they? They know that we know they're there."

"I thought you said they would sit outside, in the car," fretted Holly, looking back over one shoulder.

David thrust her into the elevator the moment the doors opened and took obvious delight in the fact that his colleagues were summarily shut out. "They'll stand outside my door for a while just to make sure we're not up to anything—" he paused, winking in a way that made Holly flush with quiet outrage "—un-American."

Holly gave him an arch look. "Why don't you just tell them that you've already checked me out, Agent Goddard?"

The man was impossible. Instead of getting mad, he laughed and said, "I've missed you, you tart-tongued little wench."

Holly bristled. "Tart-tongued little what?"

They had reached David's floor, the elevator doors whisking open to reveal an expensively carpeted hallway. He avoided answering by catching her hand in his and pulling her up to a door marked 17B.

It turned out to be a place that would raise the hackles of any taxpayer. The carpets were lush, the furniture was sturdy and obviously antique, and the lighted paintings on the walls had not come from the housewares department at Kmart. One of them, unless Holly was mistaken, looked like a Picasso.

A lulling, bubbling sound came from everywhere and Holly saw that there were no less than four sizable aquariums in the living room, every one of them populated by expensive tropical fish. The effect was quietly exotic.

Holly turned to David, desperately stalling, wondering why she had allowed him to bring her here at all. "You are overpaid, Mr. Goddard," she accused.

He laughed and touched her nose with a winter-chilled index finger. "Before you lodge an official complaint, may I say in my defense that my grandfather owned a large farm in Nebraska, and furthermore, that when it was sold at his death, I inherited half the money?"

Holly sagged a bit, tired and at a loss, but then rallied with a challenging, "Who got the other half?"

David's eyes danced and he grinned. "My sister, Chris. Are you disappointed?"

"Why would I be?"

He was easing her coat from her shoulders, and as ordinary as that gesture was, it seemed strangely sensual then. "I think you were hoping to add philandering to my other crimes. Be honest, Holly—for just a moment, you thought I was married, didn't you?"

The thought had crossed her mind. After all, if David would lie about his occupation and his feelings for her, he might have lied about his marital status, too. "I considered it. Then I realized that no woman in her right mind would ever put up with you."

Having laid her coat aside, David went to a beautifully carved bar and began rattling bottles and glasses about with a decorum suited to his surroundings. "Would you like something to drink?"

A drink might steady her nerves, Holly thought. Then again, it might lead her to make a fool of herself.

"White wine, please," she said primly, seated now on a plush sofa.

He brought the wine, holding a mixed drink of some sort in his other hand, and sat down, not on the couch beside Holly, but on a matching hassock nearby. Introspectively, David studied the amber depths of his glass.

"What did you think of your Christmas present?" he asked gruffly, still avoiding her eyes.

Reminded, Holly opened her purse and brought out the present in question, settling the small velvet box on the coffee table. "I think you shouldn't have given it to me," she replied coolly.

She ached at seeing his strong shoulders stoop just slightly. "My timing was less than perfect, I guess," he reflected, at length.

"Considerably less," Holly said softly, hurting because it was obvious that David did. "But Toby liked his robot."

Indigo eyes searched her face. "Holly, give me one more chance. Just one."

Holly tightened both hands around her wineglass, as though it could anchor her, enable her to ride out the emotional storm that was coming. "I didn't come to Washington so I could see you again, David," she said. And it was only after the words were out of her mouth that Holly realized she was lying.

Chapter 11

"Are you hungry?" David's question broke the uncomfortable silence.

Holly had eaten aboard the airplane but that, of course, had been some hours before. "A little."

David laughed, but it was a ragged sound, humorless and painful to hear. "God knows who you might have rubbed elbows with tonight if you hadn't come with me. The least I can do is take you to the best restaurant in town."

"No," Holly said quickly, glancing apprehensively at the door. "I don't want those men watching every lift of my fork." Or following me to and from the rest room, she added to herself.

David stood up to remove his suit coat. Nestled ominously against his broad chest was a holstered pistol. "Sorry," he said hoarsely, catching Holly's look of horrified surprise.

She looked away, reminded once again of all the things that stood between them, then heard the brisk click of a drawer and what she thought was the turning of a key.

"I make a mean omelette," David offered in a low voice.

Holly forced her eyes back to him, and to her abject relief, the gun was gone. She managed a shaky smile. "I hope it's better than your fruitcake," she ventured, and this time, David's responding chuckle was warm and real.

He executed a sweeping bow, reminiscent of a continental waiter. "This way, Madam," he said.

Against her better judgment, Holly rose from the sofa and followed him through a small, formal dining room and into the kitchen. There was a butcher-block table in the center of the room, and copper kettles hung from a black wrought-iron rack above that. The stove and sink were both within easy reach.

"Pretty nice," Holly approved, since she knew kitchens if she knew anything at all.

"Don't be too impressed," David warned with a half smile as he rolled up the sleeves of his white shirt and then went to the sink to wash his hands. "I wouldn't know an egg timer from hollandaise sauce. I only bought all this stuff to please my housekeeper."

"Is there anything I can do to help?" Holly asked, torn between attaching herself to this man like a barnacle and bolting out of the apartment on a dead run. The depths of her feelings for him were truly frightening; she had to remind herself that a relationship between them could never work.

"Yes," David responded, bringing an armload of ingredients from the fancy refrigerator, which had a sliding, opaque door. "Sit down at the table and relax."

Instead Holly claimed one of three high stools at the luncheon bar. There were louvered doors beyond them, opening into the dining room. She fixed her attention on the elegant refrigerator and tried to imagine it covered with memos and samples of a little boy's artwork. She couldn't, and that saddened her.

David's hands were busy chopping scallops crisp enough to appear in a *Bon Appetit* layout, but his eyes scanned Holly's face with a sort of weary tenderness. "You look as though you might just fall asleep in my culinary triumph," he observed.

Holly had no intention of falling asleep anywhere but in Mr. Lincoln's bedroom. "I'm all right," she said but an involuntary yawn belied her words.

David grinned and shook his head, moving on from the scallops to a mound of mushrooms. "Whatever you say," he replied.

Holly felt a blush rise in her face; it revived her a little, stinging the way it did. "I'm wide-awake," she insisted.

He stopped slicing mushrooms, bracing himself against the block table with his hands. "What do you think I'm going to do, Holly? Pounce on you if you so much as close your eyes?"

That made Holly laugh, however reluctantly. That was exactly what she'd thought, she realized. And it was a ridiculous notion. "I'm sorry," she said.

David went back to the project at hand, grinning mysteriously to himself. Holly would have given her Cordon Bleu diploma to know what he was thinking, but she was wise enough not to ask. Instead she just watched, yawning periodically, as David whisked eggs into a foamy froth, browned the scallops in butter, added the mushrooms and eggs at just the right moment.

They ate in the dining room, by candlelight, saying little. And good as the food was, Holly nearly disgraced herself by nodding off over her plate.

Exactly how it happened, and this was a very momentous "it," all things considered, was something that would always elude Holly. All her jet lag, all the rigors of the past couple of months, suddenly caught up with her. The room seemed to darken and the candlelight undulated and then David's arms were beneath her, strong and secure.

Holly yawned and made some senseless remark and David laid her gently down on a bed. "I can't…this isn't… Howard and Maggie…"

"Hush," he said, laying his fingers to her mouth and covering her with a satiny comforter.

"But—"

"Just sleep. As the president's cousin, you have a big day tomorrow. I'll make sure you're at the Capitol Building in plenty of time."

It was madness, but Holly believed him. And she was simply too tired to rally herself and get up. "It must have been…the wine…"

David chuckled and his lips touched her forehead, just briefly. "That and enough emotional trauma to devastate Jack Bauer. Sleep, sweetheart."

And Holly slept. She awakened a couple of hours later, confused and disoriented. When she remembered that she was in David Goddard's apartment, that the two agents assigned to her were probably still outside and coming to all sorts of scandalous conclusions, she sat bolt upright and gasped aloud.

It was a moment before she realized that David was not in the bed with her; when she made the discovery, Holly was both relieved and disappointed. "David?" she whispered, swinging her legs over the side of the bed. She was still completely dressed except for her shoes. "David?"

When there was no answer, she rose, not bothering to turn on a lamp, and groped her way out of the room. The living room beyond was dimly lit, but empty.

"David?" she ventured again. A small, cherrywood grandfather clock chimed three times. Good Lord, how was she going to explain this to the Secret Service, to Howard and Maggie? "David!" she yelled.

He materialized, a man made of shadows, at the end of the hallway. His hair was rumpled, his eyes were glass and his chest was bare. Holly didn't dare look any lower. "What?" he yawned.

"Take me back to the White House this minute! My God, what those men must be thinking—"

"'Those men' were called off hours ago. Go back to bed, Holly."

Go back to bed? Was the man insane? "May I point out that it is three o'clock in the morning? My reputation is at stake here!"

David yawned again and stretched his arms above his head and the play of the all too masculine muscles in his shoulders and naked torso unsettled Holly all the more. "Right. Three o'clock. Your reputation," he mumbled.

Holly glared at him for a moment. "The agents really left?"

"Yes."

"How did you manage that, may I ask?"

"I told them you and I were going to spend the night making love."

Holly flushed. "You didn't!"

"Oh, yes I did. And what they don't know won't hurt them. You're not the only one with a reputation to maintain."

"Very funny! Take me home this instant."

"I'm going back to bed. I would recommend, Ms. Llewellyn, that you do the same. If you don't, I may forget my good manners and—"

A jolt went through Holly's just-awakened system, and it wasn't an unpleasant one. "And what?"

"Don't ask." He turned to leave her, there in the middle of his living room.

"I'll take a cab!" she threatened in a high-pitched voice. "I mean it, David Goddard…"

Her announcement trailed off when he suddenly whirled on his heels and came toward her, an evil, teasing look in his eyes. "That's it," he said. "I warned you."

Holly trembled as he lifted her effortlessly into his arms. She should struggle. She should walk out. She should go down to the street and hail a cab. But she could do none of those things. She couldn't even speak.

David carried her back into the room where she had been sleeping only minutes before, stood her on her unsteady feet and began to undress her. "Maybe there is one way, lady, to convince you that I love you."

He removed the prim blouse and skirt she had changed into to meet him earlier, tossing each garment casually aside. Holly stood speechless before him in her camisole and her tap pants, overcome by the feelings she had been struggling against ever since Craig's arrest.

Her head fell back as David bared her breasts and caressed them, his thumbs chafing the nipples until they stood out in eager surrender. Simultaneously, she trembled and sighed.

Presently David removed the camisole entirely, as he had her other clothes, flinging it aside. And then her tap pants were sliding down over her quivering hips and thighs and they were gone, too.

"David," she choked in sweet desperation as he continued to caress her, more freely now, and with a boldness that made Holly ache to submit.

Finally he kissed her and if Holly Llewellyn had not been lost before, she was lost then.

David drew back from her mouth with obvious reluctance and muttered, "I must be the world's biggest fool—"

"Second biggest," Holly struggled to say as he placed her upon the bed and joined her there. Then he began doing the most delicious, wicked things to her.

He drew sweet nectar from her breasts, he touched and stroked her, mastering her in ways that exalted, ways that soothed. And he brought her to a soaring preliminary release that left her quivering like a string, unable to see and nearly unable to breathe.

David entered her gently, with a low groan and an urgency as old as the stars. In the ensuing minutes, Holly quite literally lost her mind, groping for it as explosions of shattering joy shook her, finding it in her own cries of release and in David's.

Holly's face was hot, but she kept her eyes straight ahead as her personal Secret Service contingent escorted her through the rear part of the White House and right to the door of Mr. Lincoln's bedroom.

Inside, she rested her back against the heavy, carved wooden panels and struggled to catch her breath and cool her flaming cheeks with hands still icy from the frigid weather outside.

Mr. Lincoln observed her pensively from within his costly frame.

"I couldn't help it, Abe! I'm crazy about the man!" Holly hissed defensively as she stomped into the bathroom, peeled off yesterday's clothes and ran herself a deep, hot bath.

By inauguration time, Holly was dressed again, her hair and makeup done to perfection. Nothing of the abandon of the night before showed in her face—she hoped.

Holly rode to the Capitol Building in a limo, as a part of a long motorcade.

"Sure is a cold day for standing outside," observed the chauffeur.

Holly was grateful for his attempt at conversation, for she needed something else to think about besides the way she had tossed and writhed in David Goddard's bed the night before. It didn't help that he'd drawn that damned veil down over his eyes the moment he had deposited her in the waiting hands of her bodyguards. That had been so impersonal, so cold, and Holly's pride was still stinging. "I'll be glad when it's over." She sighed. "Isn't that terrible? I mean, this is a historic occasion and everything."

"It is that, Ma'am," replied the driver kindly. "A historical day and all that, I mean. But that don't change the fact that it's cold as the devil's heart out there."

The Secret Service agents sitting on either side of Holly were a different set than she'd had the day before, but they were just as dour and silent. Thank God the driver wasn't intimidated by their presence.

"No," said Holly. "It don't."

That deliberate slip of grammar brought a look from one of the agents, anyway. Holly thought she saw a grin peer out from behind the rim of his retina, though it disappeared, of course, in less than a moment.

Reaching the crowded Capitol Building, Holly and her escorts left the car. A microphone had been set up at the top of the fabled steps, along with a canopy of sorts and a number of folding chairs. Maggie and Howard were nowhere in sight, though there were hundreds of guests milling about in the chill of that day, Secret Service agents moving among them. They were easy to spot, not only because of their conservative suits and their earpieces, but because their eyes moved constantly, searching every face, noting the rise of any arm.

When Howard and Maggie arrived, closely followed by the majority leader, they were surrounded by a bevy of agents, David among them. Like the others, he scanned the crowd incessantly, and Holly shivered, not because of the biting cold but because she knew in that instant that he would lay down his life for the president without hesitation. Just as promptly, he would take the life of anyone who was so foolish as to attempt an attack.

Holly barely heard the swearing-in itself; she was too busy watching David and trying to solve the mysteries he personified. She had every respect for his dedication to his job, of course, but it was very difficult to reconcile this cold-eyed man with the one who had made such thorough, gentle love to her the night before.

Tears of hopelessness began to burn behind Holly's eyes and ache in her sinuses. Like a fool, despite everything, she had entertained a fantasy or two concerning David Goddard and the future they might have together. Now, standing in the brutal wind, she had reality to deal with; David was always going to be the man who had come into her life as a liar, a pretender, an imposter. He was a man who wore a gun under his jacket, a man who would kill if he deemed it necessary.

Holly shivered again and clapped with numb hands as the new president lowered his right hand and turned to say a few words to the crowd. She didn't hear a word he said, so intent was she on David's immobile, watchful face. How could she have considered living with him, loving him for the rest of her life? Even if all the other problems could have been solved, there was still the ominous fact that he could be killed or crippled at any time. His work was dangerous.

"I'd like to leave now," Holly said to the agent standing at her right side. Without making any verbal response, he took her elbow in a firm hand and ushered her back to one of a dozen waiting limousines.

Safe in her room again some twenty minutes later, after declining an offhand, rushed invitation from Maggie to attend a state luncheon, Holly collapsed onto her bed with a pulsing headache.

Presently, Mrs. Tallington appeared with a tray and a look of sympathy. "Do you need a doctor, Madam?" she inquired.

Holly closed her eyes. She had taken two aspirin before lying down and she hoped they would be sufficient. "No, thank you," she said. "I'll be fine if I just rest awhile."

"Eating a little something might help," imparted the veteran, and then she was gone.

When Holly could sit up without feeling queasy, she inspected the contents of her tray. Beneath aged, mellow silver covers were generous servings of creamed crab, mixed vegetables and warm, crusty bread.

Knowing the wisdom of what Mrs. Tallington had said, she forced herself to eat, though most of the portions were larger than she could have handled even if she'd felt her best.

She slept—her dreams were damnably erotic replays of the night before—and when she awakened there were lengthy shadows in the room and the tray had been taken away. Her blue chiffon, pressed to meet Mrs. Tallington's impeccable standards, hung from a peg on the closet door.

Holly wished she had the nerve to thrust that gown and all her other clothes into her suitcases and make a dash for the airport. That would be so much easier than facing David again!

But she couldn't bring herself to do it. The biggest of all the inaugural balls was to be held that evening, and Holly was enough of an adventuress to really want to attend. After all, she would probably never have a chance to do anything like that again.

Holly took another long, leisurely, scented bath, washed and dried her hair, carefully painted her nails. She was wearing only a towel when the telephone at her bedside jangled, startling her so much that she jumped and had to clasp the towel in place again.

"Hello?"

"Holly, this is Howard. The staff tells me that you're a little under the weather."

Holly sighed, feeling troublesome and out of place. "I'm fine, Mr. President. Honestly. I think I was just a little tired."

"'Mr. President,' is it?" Howard chuckled. "Well now, Holly, I like the sound of that, but I'm still just Howard to you."

Still just Howard. Grinning, Holly shook her head in wonder but said nothing, waiting for her illustrious caller to go on.

"I've arranged for you to meet with Craig first thing tomorrow morning, Holly. He's ready to talk with you now."

Holly's knees went weak and she sank to the edge of the bed. "C-Craig? He's here?"

"He's at Walter Reed for the time being. Do you want to see him, Holly?"

Her throat tightened, memories of another Craig swirling in her mind: a laughing, responsible, healthy Craig. A devoted big brother. "Oh, yes," she said softly. "Yes, I want to see him."

"Good. We'll send you over there in a car, bright and early. In the meantime, young lady, you put on your dancing shoes and prepare to have yourself a good time at the shindig tonight."

Holly chuckled, though there were tears swimming in her eyes. "Being in the White House, going to an inaugural ball—I think I should wear glass slippers instead of dancing shoes."

"Can't dance in glass slippers," Howard retorted immediately. "You save a waltz for your old third cousin from Oregon, now."

"I will," Holly promised, and Howard rang off in his politely abrupt way.

Slowly, she set the receiver back in its cradle, drew a deep breath and went to the closet to find the special, strappy shoes she bought to wear with the blue chiffon. Turning one in her hand, Holly reminded herself that she was not Cinderella and that Howard was certainly not Prince Charming.

No, if Prince Charming attended the ball at all, he would be wearing an earpiece and a look fit to freeze-dry coffee beans.

The ballroom glittered with crystal chandeliers and silver punch bowls and guests one couldn't hope to encounter even on *The Today Show*. Holly spotted David almost immediately and spent the next fifteen minutes trying to ignore him.

The orchestra played and Holly danced with a pudgy, wheezing man a head shorter than she was. An emissary from some country Holly had never heard of, he spoke immaculate English.

Following that, she was waltzed around the enormous room by a man wearing a bright gold cummerbund and a dazzling array of medals. He was an ambassador from one of the Slavic countries.

When Howard and Maggie deigned to make their appearance, there was a hush and all eyes were upon them. Maggie looked every inch the first lady, and despite the unspoken strain between them, Holly was proud of her.

The president and first lady danced together then, the crowd moving back for them, the Secret Service agents looking on as alertly and unemotionally as ever, ready to pounce upon anyone foolish enough to make a wrong move.

Looking at David, Holly despaired. This was not the man who had loved her with such sweet ferocity the night before. This was a stranger, an automaton.

Some minutes later, Holly had her dance with the president of the United States, his last before retiring with Maggie from the festivities. "No glass slippers, I see," he teased as they waltzed, flashbulbs bursting all around.

Holly laughed. "No. I ordered a pair from Saks, but they didn't have my size."

Howard responded with a laugh of his own, but he looked tired. Holly thought of how the next four years would age him and felt sad.

"When you see your brother tomorrow morning, Holly, you tell him I'll do all I can to see he gets the help he needs."

"Thank you," Holly replied softly. "For both of us."

Howard nodded somberly. "I'm just sorry it had to come to this," he said. "You'll be with us a few more days, won't you?" he added a moment later, deliberately changing the subject.

Holly shook her head. "I've got to get home to my nephew and my work, I'm afraid. If I possibly can, I want to leave tomorrow, after I see Craig."

Howard responded politely, then the dance was over. A few minutes later he left the ballroom with Maggie and their Secret Service entourage, David included. Holly remained at the party for another half hour and then departed, leaving no glass slipper behind.

It was late and David was exhausted. Like several of the other agents assigned directly to the president, he had worn a tuxedo, and he was eager to hurl the thing into the depths of his closet and forget it existed.

Walt Zigman sat at his desk, as always, oblivious to the late hour. A widower, his children grown and gone, he had nothing better to do, David guessed. He hoped to God his own life would never come down to that.

He laid his identification card and the earpiece down on the desk.

"You told me you'd stay until inauguration week was over!" Walt blustered, his jowls quivering, his cigar bobbing between his teeth.

"I lied. I'm out, Zigman. Gone."

Zigman swore. "I knew it. I damned knew it."

David sighed and stuffed his hands into the pockets of his trousers. "I suppose Ranford gave you a full report on last night," he said, his eyes linked with Walt's.

"We didn't get it on tape, if that's what you're talking about, Goddard. Tell me something, though. What is it about this Llewellyn woman that makes her different from all the others?"

David had a headache; he rubbed his temples with a thumb and forefinger. "If I knew that, Walt, I might be able to put two sane thoughts together."

"She feel the same way you do?" Walt was apparently in a fatherly mood. His eyes were averted, though, and he was cleaning his fingernails with an unbent paperclip.

David had been struggling with that question all day. It had distracted him, making it hard as hell to keep his mind on the president and the endless crowds at the swearing-in and at the ball he'd just left. Holly had certainly responded in bed the night before, but come the rueful morning, her aquamarine eyes had been full of doubts. Misgivings. And a grudge that just might last a lifetime.

"It will be a long time before she trusts me completely, if she ever does."

There was a short, reflective silence.

"I'm sorry about this whole thing, Goddard, for what it's worth. I should have sent someone else."

"You didn't know I was going to fall in love with Holly," David said, his jaw growing taut of its own accord and then relaxing again. "I didn't either."

Walt reached out and collected the earpiece and the identification badge. "You keep in touch, Goddard. If things don't work out out there in Podunk, Washington, you come back here."

David had no answer for that. If things didn't work out in Spokane, he didn't know where he would go or what he would do. The only thing he could be certain of was that he was never going to come back to this job.

Leaving Walt's office, he squared his shoulders. Things would work out with Holly, dammit. He was going to *make* them work out.

Chapter 12

Holly was delivered to Walter Reed Hospital first thing the next morning, as promised. She was, of course, flanked by the usual Secret Service set of two, but at least they stayed outside of Craig's room, exchanging toneless rhetoric with the FBI man who guarded the door.

Craig sat alone in the room, wearing a striped bathrobe that was too big for him, his gaze fixed on the panoramic view offered by a huge window.

Holly lifted her chin and gave herself a silent order not to cry. Her brother looked so broken, so small and in so much trouble. "Craig?"

He turned, his eyes sunken and circled. His face, stubbled with a new beard, looked gaunt; he might have been a hundred instead of just thirty-six. "Hello, Holly," he said, and his voice was as hollow as his eyes.

"Are they treating you well?" she asked, and the words sounded stiff, stilted. Talking to this wasted remnant of a man was not the same as talking to her brother.

Craig shuddered and executed a rueful parody of a smile. "They're not shining lights in my face and telling me they have ways of making me talk, if that's what you mean."

Holly had no plans to ask about the cocaine habit that had brought him to this pass; the ravages of his withdrawal, which would probably go on for some time, were clearly visible in his face.

She forced herself to go to him, to lay one hand on his thin shoulder. Touching him seemed to work some magic—he became Craig again. Tears stung in her eyes and ached in her throat as she bent to kiss the top of his head.

"Oh, Craig, how did this happen?"

His shoulder stiffened beneath her hand. "The way it always happens, Holly," he said brokenly. "You try cocaine and you're on top of the world. You can do no wrong. You're Superman, you're James Bond. And then one day you find out that you've gotta have the stuff and there aren't any choices anymore."

Holly swallowed hard and reached up with one hand to surreptitiously wipe away her tears. Her falling apart was not going to do Craig any good; she had to be strong now. "Is there anything I can do?" she whispered. "Special doctors, anything like that?"

Craig shook his head. "Forget I was ever born," he said hoarsely, looking at the view again. "That's the best thing you can do for yourself and for Toby."

There was nothing to say to that. If and when Craig

overcame his cocaine problem, he might still be faced with a long prison term.

"You're still all tangled up with Goddard, aren't you?" Craig's question was so direct and so unexpected that Holly gaped at him for a moment, unable to answer. "He's bad news, Holly. For your own sake, walk away."

"That's going to hurt," she managed to say, at length.

Craig gave a humorless chuckle. "Lots of things hurt in this life, Holly. Too many things hurt. But Goddard used you and I don't want you to forget that. He'd use his own mother, if the Service asked him to. Believe me, I know."

Holly wound a finger in one of Craig's lank curls— once they had been so springy that she had teased him about them—and waited for him to go on.

"Find yourself a flesh-and-blood man, Holly," he complied after some time. "Goddard is a robot, like me. Like all the rest of them. He's nothing more than a hit man on the right side of the law."

Holly shivered. David wasn't a hit man! He wasn't!

"Lift your hand or a camera or a comb in the same room with the president or his lady sometime, Holly, if you don't believe me. You'll find yourself facedown on the floor with your hands cuffed before you catch your breath."

"There is a reason for that, Craig!"

He looked up at her. "Yes. But can you live with it, Holly? Can you live with guns and subterfuge and international intrigues that would curl your fingernails? Believe me, he knows things that he can't share with you, but they'll make him hell to live with all the same."

I love David, screamed some forlorn part of Holly's heart, I love him! "You needn't worry," she said aloud.

"Anything that David and I might have had was over the moment I found out that it was you he wanted, not me."

They were silent again for a while, lost in their own thoughts, their own griefs and regrets.

"I'd better go," Holly said finally. "I've got a plane to catch."

"Right."

She came around to look into his face. "Is there anything I can send you, Craig? Books? Magazines? Anything?"

"Books," he said, and for a moment there was a hint of the old Craig, an inveterate reader, in his eyes. He even chuckled. "Nothing about spies, though, okay?"

Near tears again, Holly bent to kiss his forehead. "No spies," she promised, and then she hurried out lest she break down in front of him.

It was a relief to board the airplane, to leave the White House and the Secret Service and everything else behind. Everything except David.

Holly buckled her seat belt and pretended to listen as a flight attendant explained the mysteries of oxygen masks and No Smoking signs. She wondered if she should have called David and said goodbye. Said *something*.

Vigorously, she shook her head in answer to her own questions. It was better this way, better to make a clean break and forget all about Agent Goddard and his novel investigating techniques.

The plane was barreling down the runway; Holly closed her eyes and braced herself for the lurching leap it would take when it left the ground. She hated that part of flying, along with the full reverse thrust of the engines upon landing; it always made her feel as though the craft would go tumbling end over end.

A hand closed over her fingers, which were clutching the armrest with painful force. She opened her eyes just as the plane lunged into the air and the landing gear ground into place.

David. David was sitting in the seat beside hers, big as life.

Holly blinked her eyes, certain that she was hallucinating, but he was still there when she looked again. Wearing tan corduroy slacks, a brown cashmere turtleneck and a cocoa-colored leather jacket.

"It's me, all right," he said calmly.

"What are you doing here?"

He peeled her fingers from the armrest and soothed them between his own, lifting her hand and inspecting her nail polish with a slight frown, as though he didn't quite approve of the shade. "Take a wild guess," he said.

Holly finally gathered the presence of mind to wrench her hand free. "Just go and sit in some other part of the plane. Or better yet, why don't you jump out over Kansas?"

David chuckled and settled into the seat with a comfortable sigh. "I've never liked Kansas. Besides, we won't be there for a while yet. We're probably over Maryland."

"Maryland would do just as well, I'm sure," Holly snapped, turning her head and looking out over the wing and a floor of cumulus clouds trimmed in pink and gold.

"Give me until Kansas to win you over." There was a wry, injured sort of humor in David's tone.

She swung her eyes around, giving him a look that

sliced deep. "Watch my lips," she said coldly. "We could fly to Hong Kong. We could fly to the moon. We could fly to *hell,* Mr. Goddard, and you couldn't win me over!"

The captain gave some garbled message over the speakers and the No Smoking and Fasten Seat Belt signs blinked out, making chiming sounds. The flight attendants reappeared with their smiles and their rattling service cart.

"You weren't even going to say goodbye?" David asked, and this time there was no hint of humor in his tone. He sounded hurt and more than a little bewildered.

For just a moment, Holly's impractical heart clogged her throat. She knew there were tears glistening in her eyes when she looked at him, but she couldn't help either the tears or the looking. "I didn't see any point," she managed to say.

His jaw tightened and he paled a little beneath his winter tan. Probably, Holly thought, it was a health-club tan, as artificial as the feelings he had claimed to have for her.

"I'm getting tired of playing the heavy. The investigation and Craig's arrest are both in the past—can't we go on from here?"

How Holly wished they could, but that would be asking too much. She might love this man—she *did* love this man with all her heart and all her soul—but what good was that without trust? And she was never, ever going to trust him.

"Maybe they're in the past for you," she said stiffly, shaking her head when a flight attendant stopped to offer liquid refreshments. After David had ordered and paid for a scotch and water, and the attendant had moved on, she finished, "I'm always going to remember, David. I'm going to remember your lies. I'm going to remember watching you handcuff my only brother in my kitchen."

"How about the way we made love, Holly? Are you going to remember that? Are you going to remember the things we said and did when our passion was so great that we couldn't bear it?"

Holly closed her eyes tight. "Don't!"

"Someone has to, Holly. What we had—what we have—is too rare and too precious to let go of without a fight. I've accepted that fact even if you haven't."

Holly snatched away his drink and took a gulp of it before handing it back, and David laughed.

"Face it, baby," he teased in an Edward G. Robinson voice, "you're stuck with a G-man!"

"I've already had to deal with all the 'G-men' I care to in this lifetime, thank you very much."

"We must be nearing Kansas. Do you still want me to jump?"

"More than anything." Holly sighed, unable to look at him now. If she did, she would tumble witlessly into those indigo eyes and the fall would be much deadlier than the one to Kansas. "What are you doing here, anyway? Don't you have to guard Howard or some visiting potentate?"

He hesitated and Holly sensed that he was hiding something—a possibility that infuriated her. "I've got some time off," he finally answered.

"I hope you're not going to Spokane," she replied in all honesty.

"I'm going wherever you go."

Holly sighed, sinking back into her seat. But when a flight attendant came by, she sat up straight again and announced in a clear voice, "Miss, this man is bothering me."

David laughed and the flight attendant looked him over in appreciative confusion, obviously wondering how a man like that could "bother" any woman in the unpleasant sense of the word.

"Is…is this true, sir?" asked the pretty attendant, not certain what to do.

"Oh, it's true all right," David confessed benevolently, rising from his seat and stepping into the aisle. He handed what remained of his drink to the stewardess and braced his hands against the back of the seat and the one just ahead. "And I'll go right on bothering you, Holly Llewellyn, because I love you. Because I need you."

Holly flushed with furious frustration and a need that rivaled the one he professed to feel. "You go to hell, Mr. Goddard," she replied, and then she fixed her eyes on the back of the seat in front of her and stared at the grubby tweed until it began to shift and undulate. When she dared to look, David was gone.

Holly felt a bereft sort of triumph. He meant to haunt her, he'd as much as said that straight out. He meant to follow her and pursue her until she gave in to him. And Holly was afraid she might do just that.

The airplane landed in Denver, where Holly was to catch her connecting flight to Spokane. Even before she looked back to confirm her suspicions, she knew that David was following her, she could feel him there, like a spectre.

She visited the rest room and the gift shop, trying to kill the hour layover, becoming more and more tense with every passing moment. Finally Holly whirled on David and hissed, "This is harassment! Leave me alone!"

He stepped closer, oblivious to the stream of people flowing around them on all sides, his eyes gentle. "Tell me you don't love me, Holly," he said quietly. "If you can truthfully say that, I'll go away."

Holly swallowed. That wasn't so hard, was it? Four little words, only four. *I don't love you.* She tried to say them and they would not pass her throat.

David waited patiently.

Holly tried again, failed again and turned away with a stifled sob, one hand to her face. David took her elbow in a firm grasp and escorted her into the nearest lounge. There, he settled her at a shadowy corner table, holding both her hands in his. At his request, a waitress in jeans and a Western shirt brought two cups of coffee.

Holly freed one hand to lift her cup to her lips; some of the steaming brew inside sloshed over to burn her hand and stain the tablecloth. David deftly removed the cup and set it aside to cool.

"I want one chance with you, Holly. Just one chance. Can you give me that?"

"Wh-what if I say no?"

"Then I'll get on the next plane to Washington."

"What about that speech you made on the airplane? What about the way you've been following me ever since we landed?"

David sighed raggedly and looked away for a moment. "I'm sorry. The last thing you need is pressure, I know that. But I was desperate."

"Why?" Holly whispered, and the word sounded pained.

"Because I love you—as, I believe, I have already mentioned on several occasions."

Holly was weary, her head full of dizzying, unrelented images—herself, dancing with the president; Craig, looking so lost and broken; David, carrying her to his bed, making love to her in a way that could still heat her blood. "I'm so confused," she muttered.

He squeezed her hand. "I know," he said softly. "Let me prove to you that I really do care, Holly. That's all I'm asking."

"How do you propose to do that, David?" Holly asked with a desperation that was more revealing than she could ever have guessed. "You'll always be the man who arrested Craig, the man who lied—"

"I'll always be the man who loves you," he reminded her.

And the man who carried Toby through a frightening crowd of reporters the day after Craig was arrested, Holly thought with disjointed hope. The man who set up the Christmas tree, the man who went out for chicken, the man who was hopelessly inept at flying model airplanes....

She gave herself a mental shake. "I don't think—"

"We'll date, that's all. We'll talk, get to know each other. And this time, it will all be on the level, Holly."

Her coffee had cooled; she took a steadying sip. Maybe David was right. Maybe there was a chance, if they could just approach the situation rationally and take their time. "No lovemaking," she ventured. "We have to start all over again, from square one. Agreed?"

David sighed. "Agreed," he replied with comic reluctance.

Their flight number was called and they left the

table, David pausing to pay the check. Holly was settled into her seat on the airplane, pretending to read a magazine, when he caught up with her.

"Very cute," he muttered wryly, falling into his seat on the aisle.

Holly peered at him over the rims of her reading glasses, which she was certain he had never seen before. "Have we been introduced?" she asked primly.

David laughed and rolled his eyes.

The condominium David selected as his new home was in a round building, three floors from the top, and every outer wall was a window. The view was phenomenal, including Riverfront Park, the Spokane River itself and the old brick railroad tower. Division Street was a double strand of diamonds glimmering in the first shadows of twilight.

He sat down on the lushly carpeted floor, drew his knees up and wondered whether he was doing the right thing, uprooting himself like this. Maybe he hadn't liked his job, per se, but he was going to miss the excitement of living in Washington. He was going to miss Chris and his nieces. And his friends.

He stood up again, taking in the spacious, as-yet-unfurnished living room. Holly was here; that was the important thing. Chris and the girls could visit as soon as school let out. And he would make new friends.

The telephone sat on the floor, looking forlorn in the empty vastness of the room. David moved toward it, then held himself back. He'd promised to go slowly with Holly, promised not to pressure her. And he had to abide by those promises.

He went into the kitchen and opened the refrigerator, which contained a quart of buttermilk and a red-and-white bucket with one chicken wing in the bottom. David gnawed at that as he wandered from one elegant room to another, pondering the lengths he'd gone to just to be near Holly and regretting none of them.

The telephone rang, echoing in the emptiness, and David ambled toward the nearest one, expecting to hear from the real-estate agency or maybe the law school, where he was registered for review classes.

"David?" The familiar shrill of that voice almost made him choke on the chicken he'd been munching. "God, if you knew what I've been through, trying to track you down! I practically had to bribe Chris—"

"Marleen," David said woodenly. "Marleen?"

"I'm on leave," she chimed in bright response, as though she had never walked out when he'd needed her. As though she had never torn his guts out and stomped on them.

"What does that have to do with me?" he managed to ask, hoping that he didn't sound as hollow as he felt.

"We were married!" she sang. "Doesn't that entitle me to call up and say hello, David?"

"I find it hard to believe that you called just to say hello. What do you want? Money?"

There was a silence. "David!" Marleen wailed in injured good humor. "What an awful thing to say! We loved each other once."

"How are your monkeys?"

"Well, if you're going to be that way—"

David closed his eyes and the old pain was a sickness within him. He wished that Holly were there. "Wait," he said. "I was just surprised, that's all."

"Good." Marleen sounded pleased and perhaps a

little relieved, which worried David. "Listen, sweetheart, I'm in L.A. right now, visiting the folks and all that." She paused, lowering her voice, presumably so the "folks" wouldn't overhear. "It's just a deadly bore, David, so I was wondering, well, since Spokane is a fairly short flight from here—"

"No," David broke in.

"No?"

David sat down on the floor, his head throbbing. He tossed the denuded chicken wing, because if he hadn't, he'd have tossed the telephone instead. "I mean, I'm just getting settled in here. And I'm flying back to Washington to sublet my place there and make arrangements for my furniture to be shipped. I really don't have time—"

"David, I was your wife!"

"You were the greatest single mistake of my life, Marleen," he said, thinking aloud.

He could almost see her pouting, see the tears welling in her enormous brown eyes.

"I guess I should have known I was going to get this kind of reception," she said. "Chris was positively cold when I called her."

David's head was pounding. "Look, Marleen, if you want money for some research project, apply for a grant. I really don't want to talk to you. And I sure as hell don't want to see you."

She sounded coy now, and just a little predatory. "Maybe you're scared, David. Scared that I might make you care again."

"If that's what you have in mind, don't waste your time. I'm in love with somebody else."

The moment that last sentence was out of his mouth, David knew it had been a terrible mistake. Marleen enjoyed a challenge, and saying that had been as good as flinging down a glove.

Having said too damned much already, David calmly and abruptly hung up the telephone. It rang again moments later; he lifted the receiver and dropped it into place.

The next morning, at twenty-five minutes after seven, he crawled, grumbling, out of the sleeping bag he had spread out in his future bedroom. The doorbell buzzed repeatedly as he groped into his jeans and stumbled, cursing under his breath, to open the door.

Marleen stood in the hallway, her big teeth bared in a smile that brought the jungles of Borneo to mind, her light brown, chin-length hair artfully rumpled.

"Mountain," she said, "meet Mohammed."

David groaned and rubbed his eyes. Maybe this was a bad dream. Maybe he was hallucinating.

"Aren't you going to ask me in?" Marleen wanted to know. "I could really use a cup of coffee and a hot shower."

"There are hotels all over town," David said, barring her way. "Check in to one."

"I don't have the money to do that. I spent it all to fly home from Borneo and then come up here."

David cursed, making no effort to keep his voice down, but Marleen only laughed and shouldered her way past him, a suitcase in each hand, her eyes sweeping the empty condominium.

"I'll pay for your hotel," he offered lamely. It was too late and he knew it; short of throwing Marleen out bodily, which he considered doing, his choices were limited.

"Oh, David, stop being so tiresome. I'm not here to cause you any trouble."

"Then why?"

"For old time's sake, that's all. And maybe for a slight—" she winced appealingly "—contribution."

"Anything for your monkeys, Marleen," David said with biting grandeur, his arms sweeping out from his sides.

"Stop calling them 'monkeys,'" came the controlled response. "They're chimpanzees and they are an important link to the past."

"Are they? As far as I'm concerned, they're small, noisy, furry beasts that pick bugs off each other's hides for a snack."

Marleen set down her suitcases, her eyes flashing even though she was still smiling determinedly. "I didn't expect you to be so bitter after all this time, David. I really didn't."

"Bitter? Me?" David retorted acidly. "Why would I be bitter, Marleen? Why the goddamned hell would I be *bitter?*"

She subsided a little, her chocolate-colored eyes wide and suspiciously moist. "I'm sorry that I hurt you."

"Oh, thank you. That makes everything all right. I can feel my ulcers and residual neuroses healing right now!"

Marleen sat down on one of her battered suitcases, a forlorn, elfin creature in a rumpled raincoat, her face in her hands. "Oh, David, don't do this to me," she whispered. "Please—"

David stormed away from her into his bedroom. He'd packed for the flight to Washington the day before, and he was going to leave early. Pale with rage, he showered, then dressed in slacks, a white sweater and a sports jacket.

When he reached the living room, his own suitcase in hand, the hopes he'd had that Marleen would just go away went up in smoke. Her baggage was still sitting there, and he could hear her humming in the kitchen, the sound blending in with the chortling of the coffeepot.

"Damn," he rasped, wondering what to do, how to get Marleen out of his house, out of his life. The answer was a four-figure drop in his bank balance; he wrote out a check with violent strokes of his pen, laid the payoff beneath the handle of one of her suitcases and walked out, slamming the door behind him.

Downstairs, he got into one of the cabs that were almost always on hand, muttering to himself. He would be gone for a couple of weeks, he supposed, making arrangements for his furniture to be moved, saying various goodbyes, giving away several hundred tropical fish.

Surely, by the time he'd driven his car across country—he needed the distance and monotony of the task to think—Marleen would have gone back to Borneo and her monkeys.

Chapter 13

The circular building towered over Riverfront Park. Holding Toby's model Cessna in both hands, Holly gazed up at it.

"Are we going to visit David?" Toby demanded eagerly, tugging at the sleeve of her pink Windbreaker. "Are we, Mom?"

The bright, springlike shine of that late January day caused a painful catch in Holly's heart, as did Toby's question. It had been a full week since she and David had parted at the airport, agreeing to start over again. He had called just once in that time, and that had only been to pass on his new telephone number and address; he hadn't suggested they get together. Holly's feelings about that were mixed.

Toby tugged at her sleeve again, more forcefully this time. "Mom?" he prompted. "Couldn't we? Please?"

She looked down at the little boy and smiled. "Okay. We'll ask if he wants to come down here and fly the plane with us."

"And ride the carousel!" Toby beamed. "Don't forget, you promised that we could ride the carousel!"

They walked across the rolling, snow-patched lawns of the park, Toby straining to rush ahead, Holly holding back a little, wondering if it was wise to approach David. After all, they had an agreement, and she still had contradictory feelings toward him, stemming from the way they'd met.

"Toby, maybe we shouldn't…" She hesitated when they reached the main door of the exclusive building. There was a doorman on duty, perhaps he wouldn't even let them pass.

"Come on, Mom," Toby insisted, dragging her up to the entrance.

As the doorman looked her over, Holly was painfully conscious of her battered blue jeans, her T-shirt and Windbreaker, her breeze-tumbled hair.

"May I help you?" asked the sentinel, his deep, rumbling voice ringing with genteel authority.

"My name is Holly Llewellyn and this is—"

The doorman's round face broke into a smile. "Go right up, Ms. Llewellyn. I can't say whether or not Mr. Goddard is at home, but I have orders to admit you at any time."

Holly was relieved; inwardly, she realized, she had been expecting to be turned away. Things were shaky between her and David, and there was always the possibility that he had decided their relationship wasn't worth the trouble.

She and Toby crossed the sumptuous, plant-filled lobby. There were two sets of elevators.

"What floor does David live on?" Toby queried when they were inside one of the elevators, his hand poised to punch the proper button.

"Seven," Holly answered immediately, then bit her lower lip. Her eagerness was showing, and she had to get it under control. Letting David Goddard see how easily he could sway her would be foolish.

They arrived on the seventh floor in a whisk and stepped out into a spacious entryway, decorated, like the lobby, with plants.

David's condominium apparently took up the entire floor, for there was only one door in sight. Holly's hand trembled a little as she reached out to ring the bell. She drew a deep breath and summoned up a brave smile just as the door swung open.

A lovely woman wearing a colorful robe answered the door. "Yes?"

Holly was speechless, her imagination running away from her. Toby, on the other hand, had the presence of mind to ask ingenuously, "Is this where David Goddard lives?"

Wide brown eyes swept over Holly's Saturday-in-the-park clothes. "Yes, it is. I'm afraid David isn't home right now, though."

Holly, having surrendered the airplane to Toby, wedged her hands into the pockets of her Windbreaker. A woman—good God, *a woman*. She tried not to panic or jump to conclusions, but her emotions were so raw where David was concerned that she had almost no control over them. "Are you his sister?" she dared to ask.

The woman laughed, running one hand through her soft brown hair. "Good heavens, no. I'm his wife."

"His wife?" Toby echoed, confused.

Holly was outwardly calm. She squared her shoulders, caught Toby's free hand in her own and turned back toward the elevator. Over one shoulder, she said, "I'm sorry we bothered you."

"No problem," Mrs. David Goddard responded lightly, with a shrug of her silk-clad shoulders. "Shall I tell David you were here?"

Holly debated with herself for a moment, gnawing at her lower lip. "No," she said finally. "Don't tell him anything."

The concern in Toby's upturned face wrenched at Holly's heart. He was too young to understand this sort of betrayal, and she wondered how she would explain it all to him.

"I didn't get your names!" sang out the remarkably calm wife of the man Holly loved as the doors were closing.

"Toby and Holly!" the little boy shouted just before the doors swept shut.

Holly let go of her nephew's hand and sagged against the elevator wall, her hands gripping the polished brass railing, her eyes squeezed closed against tears of rage and hurt.

"What's-a-matter, Mom?" Toby wanted to know.

Holly dragged in a steadying breath and lifted her chin. "Nothing, Tobe. Nothing at all. Let's go back to the park and fly your plane, okay?"

"Okay," Toby agreed somewhat sadly. "But I wanted David to be with us."

"So did I," Holly replied with despairing dignity.

"But sometimes things just don't turn out the way we hope they will."

Somehow, Holly got through the rest of that day, watching Toby's plane buzz in wide circles against a hurtfully blue sky, riding the fabled antique carousel, even choking down a hot dog. It was much later, when Toby had reluctantly taken his bath and tumbled into bed, that she sank into the chair at her desk in the kitchen, lowered her head to her arms and wept.

Being fooled once was bad enough; being fooled twice was devastating. Holly vowed that this was the last time, the very last time, that she would ever cry over David Goddard and his lies.

The trip across country had been a grueling one, and David was tired as he unlocked the door of his new condominium. He asked only one thing of the mysterious forces guiding the lives of mere mortals: that Marleen's failure to answer his telephone for the last week and a half meant that she was gone.

The movers had arrived ahead of him, and the furniture and crates they'd delivered looked ghostly in the dim light straying in through the open drapes. He paused a moment before flipping on the lights.

"Marleen?"

No answer. David shrugged out of his rumpled overcoat and flung aside the one suitcase he'd bothered to take with him. *There is a God,* he thought.

He checked the bedroom, which was full of boxes containing clothes and books, bed linens and towels. The bed had been set up, and he was grateful for that—now he wouldn't have to sleep on the floor or the couch.

"Marleen?" he ventured again. And that was when

he saw the note affixed to the headboard of his bed with a piece of tape.

He snatched it into one hand, a peculiar sort of dread niggling in the pit of his stomach. "Darling," Marleen had written in a hand that resembled the efforts of one of her beloved apes. "I've gone back to my work. Thanks for the check and your backhanded hospitality. By the way, Holly came by. Is she your new love? I think she was surprised to find me here, and she said not to tell you that she stopped in. Ciao, Marleen."

David crumpled the note into a ball and flung it away on the strength of a growled curse. What Holly must have thought, encountering Marleen, of all people, was all too obvious.

He picked up the trail of the phone cord and followed it until he found the telephone beneath a pile of rumpled bath towels. Marleen had always been a slob. Holly's number leaped to his mind, but his finger hesitated over the buttons. It was late and this debacle called for more delicate handling than a midnight telephone call. Flowers, at the least, and some very fast talking.

David stiffened as he drew his hand back from the telephone. Dammit, why was he ready to grovel and beg when he hadn't done anything wrong? Whatever impression Marleen might have given—and he suspected that she had played the moment for every possible ounce of drama—the fact remained that he wasn't involved with her and hadn't been in years. Holly was a rational person and she would understand. She had to understand.

Too exhausted to think about the situation further, David staggered into the bathroom and took a long, hot shower, before making his way back to the bed. Marleen hadn't bothered to make it up again before she left, but he didn't care. He flung back the comforter and collapsed, falling asleep within seconds.

The next day was Saturday, and he awakened late. Standing at the windowed wall of his kitchen, he looked out over Riverfront Park, a cup of coffee in his hand, pondering the best way to approach Holly.

The weather was cold and sunny and there were a number of inveterate outdoor people in the park. He could see the carousel turning, a colorful blur inside its glass walls, and the sight uplifted him.

Momentarily, his eyes were drawn back to a small figure dashing in mad circles on the grass. David squinted and bent forward, trying to see. He couldn't so he opened a sliding door and went out onto the balcony surrounding his condo on all sides, resting his arms against the wrought-iron railing.

With the small person was a slightly larger one. One with golden honey hair that shimmered in the sunshine of a false spring.

David grinned, went back inside, shutting the door behind him, and set his coffee cup aside with a resolute thump. He rummaged through boxes in the recreation room until he found his own model airplane, then put on a dark blue Windbreaker and went out.

He sprinted across the park until he was close enough to hear the buzz of Toby's plane, close enough to see them both. Toby was watching, his face upturned and bright with delight, while Holly skillfully executed swoops and dips and sharp turns with the radio-controlled toy.

Holly became aware of his presence by some sixth sense and turned to confirm the dizzying fact with her eyes. David was standing not twenty yards away, holding his airplane in his hands, watching her and Toby.

He looked fantastic in his jeans, navy blue pullover and windbreaker, but Holly wasn't going to let things like that sidetrack her. Not this time. Gritting her teeth, she worked the handset, guiding her airplane in his direction in a wide sweep. "Bombs away," she whispered with evil relish as she plunged the Lilliputian craft into a dive directed straight at his head. "Mom!" Toby bellowed, appalled.

David crouched, just barely escaping the airplane; it buzzed into another turn and came back toward him.

"Mom, don't!" Toby shrieked. "Don't! You'll hurt him."

"I want to hurt him," Holly replied grimly as David fell facedown in the snow-laced ground to avoid having a miniature Cessna embedded in his back. "Oh, boy, do I want to hurt him."

"Will you stop it!" David roared. Holly noted with satisfaction that the man had no sense of humor. "You're going to kill me!"

Holly brought the plane down again, letting it pass within inches of David's head. Toby, his face flushed with righteous indignation—he'd had lecture after lecture on how to operate that airplane safely—wrenched the controls out of her hands and guided the plane in for a smooth landing.

David sprang to his feet, his eyes snapping, a white line of annoyance edging his jaw. "If you're not happy to see me," he hissed, "just say so!"

Toby was looking frantically from one adult to the other, tears shimmering in his eyes, the handset shaking in his hands. "That was a crazy thing to do, Mom!" he shouted.

Looking down at him, Holly softened.

"You're damned right it was!" yelled David.

Holly shifted her gaze from Toby to David, piercing him with it. And then she turned on her heel and stomped away, toward the carousel, Toby scrambling along beside her like a puppy.

David halted her progress from behind, catching her elbow in his grasp and handing his airplane to Toby in one simultaneous motion. "If this wasn't a public place, lady, I would turn you over my knee," he said through his teeth.

Holly wrenched her arm free. "Stay away from me, you creep!"

"Mom!" Toby wailed, mortified.

She plunged one hand into the pocket of her jacket, pulling out a string of tickets. "Here!" she said to her nephew, with uncommon impatience. "Go and ride the carousel!"

Toby looked uncertain, his china-blue eyes again darting from Holly's face to David's.

"Go ahead, slugger," David urged in a gruff undertone, taking both toy planes from the little boy's arms. "Everything is going to be all right."

After one more glance at Holly, one so wary and concerned that it made her wince inwardly, Toby bounded off to enter the round building housing the carousel. The music of the calliope seemed ludicrous, in light of the situation.

His jaw still working with suppressed outrage, David set the planes aside and lifted his hands to his hips, watching Holly, his gaze burning into her face and finally forcing her to lift furious, tear-blurred eyes.

"What did Marleen tell you?" he asked when he had her full attention.

Holly shrugged, though she was on the verge of flinging herself at David Goddard kicking and scratching and hissing like a she-cat. Her whole body quivered with the need to attack, to hurt. "Only that she is your wife," she said, marveling at the calmness of her voice. She had expected the words to come out as a shriek.

"And you immediately decided that I had lied to you again," David muttered. Damn him, he didn't look the least bit apologetic; instead, he appeared angry enough to forget that this was a public place and make good on the threat he had issued earlier.

Some of Holly's indignation faded away, driving a slow, pink blush up over her cheeks. "When presented with the evidence, I naturally—"

"You naturally found me guilty!"

Holly retreated a step. "She said—"

"I can imagine what she said! The truth is that we've been divorced for years, just like I told you before!"

People were beginning to stare and the calliope music went merrily on. Holly was getting a headache. "She had on a bathrobe. She was in your apartment—"

"And I was on my way to Washington," David broke in again, more calmly this time, though his tone sliced deep.

Holly was about to start believing him again and she'd sworn she would never do that. She whirled away, stomped into the carousel building and bought herself a ticket. When the ride stopped, she climbed onto a ferocious-looking tiger, spotting Toby ahead on a white horse.

The carousel began to turn, going faster and faster. Holly was dizzy and ill all of a sudden, and she clasped the pole in front of her with both hands. When she opened her squeezed-shut eyes, David was perched, sidesaddle, on the black panther beside her, his chin propped in his hands.

Holly held on tighter, feeling the color drain from her face. "I don't think I...feel very well..." she managed to say.

David's face gentled, his eyes scanning her face. She could barely hear him over the shrill piping of the calliope. "Do you want me to tell them to stop this thing?"

Holly shook her head, then rested it against the pole she was still holding with a death grip. What was wrong with her? She had ridden this carousel a thousand and one times. Though it moved rapidly, it was not the sort of ride that could bring her breakfast burning up into her throat.

Finally, mercifully, the carousel stopped turning. Holly was trembling as David pried her hands loose from the pole and lifted her down. She might have stumbled, but he held her firmly, prepared to lift her into his arms and carry her, if necessary. She didn't dare let that happen.

Outside, she drew in fresh air in greedy gasps, praying that she wouldn't disgrace Toby by throwing up in public.

David ushered her to a brightly painted bench, sat her down and went off, returning within moments with a glass of water from a concession wagon several yards away.

"What's wrong?" he asked, bracing one foot against

the bench and watching her as she sipped the water, his arms folded across his chest.

"I don't…know," Holly confessed quite honestly. "I must have the flu or something."

"Or something," David muttered, and he sounded so wistful that Holly's eyes shot to his face.

Toby, evidently worried about Holly, had gotten off the carousel and gone to fetch the airplanes and their handsets. He stood a little way apart, watching with large, saucerlike eyes.

"Are you sick again, Mom?" he asked.

"Again?" David demanded, leaning forward slightly.

Toby came a few steps closer, still a bit wary of these two strange adults. "Mom's been getting sick a lot lately. I want her to go to the doctor."

"So do I," David said quietly. "Can you walk now, Holly, or shall I carry you?"

Holly stood up determinedly and nearly sank to the bench again, she was so dizzy. Her stomach was doing leaps inside her. How on earth was she going to drive home in this condition?

David smiled reassuringly at Toby, ruffling his hair, and then casually lifted Holly off her feet, holding her against his chest like a child. She was too queasy to resist.

"My car is…over there…" she offered.

"You're in no shape to drive," David said flatly, looking down at Toby. "Can you manage the planes, slugger?"

Toby swelled with confidence, reassured by David's calm manner. "Sure I can. Can you manage Mom?"

David threw back his head and laughed and Holly was soothed by the scent of his hair and skin, and by the strength of him. "I don't think anybody can manage your mom," he answered presently, "but I mean to try."

"Put me down," Holly said.

"No way," came the implacable answer. "You're going to my place and you'll take it easy until you feel better."

"I can walk!"

"I know, but I like carrying you."

"David, you are making a scene! Now, put me down this minute!"

David was striding off toward the condominiums, his hold on Holly as firm as ever. "You know something, woman?" he teased, his breath whispering through her hair. "You're getting completely out of line here. You need someone to take a firm hand—"

Holly stiffened again and made a strangled sound of furious protest. "I don't need anything of the sort!" she blustered. "I'm a grown woman, perfectly capable—"

David lowered his voice, even though Toby was already bounding ahead, out of earshot, eager to see the place where his hero lived. "We both know what you need, don't we?"

The queasiness had passed and Holly was not only able to walk on her own, she was desperate for it. "Damn you, David," she hissed in a scathing undertone, "you promised!"

He sighed and set her on her feet. "So I did," he said. Knowing that she wasn't going to bolt without Toby, he slowed his strides to stay in step with her. "Holly, could you be pregnant?"

Pregnant! Holly simmered, clenching her fists at her sides. This man was just full of heartening suggestions! But as she walked, she did some mental counting and subsequently felt the warmth seeping out of her face to pool in a hot puddle in the pit of her stomach.

"Oh, my God," she moaned, stopping cold.

David caught her arm and pulled her into motion again, propelling her into the building, through the lobby and into the elevator Toby was holding for them. Soon enough, they were inside David's lush, if cluttered, digs.

"I didn't think spies made this much money," Toby observed with the innocence of someone about to turn eight.

David and Holly both laughed. For Holly, it was involuntary. David, on the other hand, seemed relaxed, even happy.

He pressed Holly into a seat on the navy blue sofa she remembered from his apartment in Washington, D.C., and then abandoned her to take Toby on a guided tour of the new place.

Pardon me, Holly wanted to call out after him, *but I think I'm pregnant here. Aren't we even going to discuss it?*

She sank back against the sofa cushions, her heart in her throat, one tear slipping down her cheek. *Your chickens, Holly Llewellyn,* she thought with a bittersweet sort of joy, *have just come home to roost. You danced and now you're going to have to pay the piper. Your jig is up.*

Having run through all her favorite clichés, Holly wiped away the tear and sniffled, then sat up very straight.

"Stay off the balcony," she heard David telling Toby, in another room. "And don't fill up the hot tub."

"Right," Toby sang, eager to be obedient. Not for the first time, Holly resented his desire to please David; it wasn't an emotion she was proud of, but she seized it to keep from thinking about the baby that might, even now, be growing inside her. David's baby.

David came to her and sat down on the sofa beside her, drawing one booted foot up to rest on the opposite knee. "We can talk about this now," he said reasonably, "or we can wait until Toby isn't around. The choice is yours."

Holly swallowed hard. "Are all the choices mine?" she ventured softly.

David met her eyes directly. "Actually, no. If you are pregnant, the child is mine, too."

At least he didn't question that. Holly sighed and knotted her hands together in her lap.

He pried one free and held it tightly. "I'm sorry, Holly," he said in a voice so low that Holly had to strain to hear him. "I wanted you so badly that I didn't stop to ask if you were protected."

Again Holly sighed. She couldn't help being struck by his willingness to take responsibility so readily. "I wasn't taking the pill. I... I wasn't sleeping with anyone and—"

"It's all right, Holly."

"It isn't all right!" she argued sharply. Then, regretting her outburst, she struggled to take control of her emotions again, to lower her voice. "I'm single, David! And as much as I love Toby, raising him alone isn't easy! How will I manage two children?"

His thumb stroked the length of her fingers. "You would have the baby, then?"

She stared at him, her eyes wide. "Of course I would," she whispered.

"Thank God," he muttered, looking away again.

Holly saw a touching struggle for composure going on in his face and loved him desperately for it.

"I'm scared, David," Holly confessed after a long, painful silence.

He pulled her close and held her against the hard curve of his shoulder. "Me, too," he said hoarsely. "Me, too."

The marriage proposal that Holly both hoped for and dreaded was evidently not forthcoming. David got up off the couch as Toby came in, blurting out, "Geez, David, your place in fantastic!"

I would have had to say no anyway, Holly said to herself, searching for comfort within. *It's a good thing he didn't ask me again. It's a good thing.*

But if it was such a good thing, another part of Holly wondered, why was it that she had to turn her face away to hide a new crop of despairing tears?

I can't panic here, David thought as he pulled a plate of cold pizza from the refrigerator and slid it into the microwave oven. *I've got to remain calm.*

Toby sat at the table, looking up at him with trust and liking shining in his face. For the millionth time, David thought how much he would like to raise this kid, fly model airplanes with him and root for him at Little League ball games.

And the other child, the child that might be born—

He couldn't think about that child, he didn't dare. If it turned out that Holly wasn't pregnant after all, it was going to be the worst disappointment of his life. No, whatever he did, he had to keep his head and go slowly and patiently.

Patience, hell, David decided. He was going to walk

into that living room, get down on his knees and beg Holly Llewellyn to marry him.

When he got there, she was gone. After a moment of alarm, he heard her in the bathroom, throwing up.

And he had never loved her more.

Chapter 14

There was no way Holly could wait until Monday to find out whether or not she was going to have a baby, but she couldn't quite bring herself to put in an appearance at a hospital emergency room, either. Was there such a thing as an emergency pregnancy?

Holly's hands tightened on the steering wheel of the car. Beside her, the seat belt drawn across his small body, Toby slept peacefully. He'd fallen asleep at David's, and David had wanted them both to stay...

Holly pulled the car to a stop in front of an all-night drugstore and looked back at the huge cylindrical building towering against the night sky. The lights of David's condo burned like sweet beacons, pulling at her. God, how she'd wanted to stay. How she'd wanted to fall into David's arms, David's bed.

She let her forehead rest against the steering wheel.

Even now, it was all she could do not to go back, carrying Toby in her arms as David had carried him down to her car, and ask if he might not have room in his life for two—perhaps two and a half—more people.

But Holly couldn't do that, of course. Not until she knew what she truly felt and what she truly wanted. A baby might be the world's oldest reason for getting married; it was also the world's worst. And besides, David had not mentioned marriage again.

Grimly, Holly got out of her car and locked it, then hurried into the drugstore. There, she bought a home pregnancy test.

At home, she awakened Toby and half ushered, half carried him inside. "We should have stayed at David's," he yawned out as he groped his way up the stairs.

"Right," Holly said, smiling even though she was ready to cry. The paper bag containing her pregnancy test rattled a little in her hand.

"He has a hot tub," Toby argued sleepily. "Right in his bedroom."

"That clinches it," Holly teased. "A man with a hot tub in his bedroom is a person to be reckoned with."

A hot tub in his bedroom, she reflected as she went into the kitchen to check the answering machine and have one last cup of coffee. Or was it to put off taking that drugstore test and finding out whether or not she really was pregnant?

She poured a cup of cold coffee and put it in the microwave to heat. There was one message on the machine, from Elaine, if it could be called a message. Her friend sounded cryptic and excited and hesitant, all at once, but she hadn't really said anything.

With a sigh, Holly took her coffee from the microwave, was instantly nauseated by the smell of it and poured it down the sink. Then, resolutely, she snatched up the innocuous little bag that seemed to contain her, Toby's and David's fate, and she marched up the stairs.

"The test was positive," Elaine echoed with a sigh, her hands clenched tight around her coffee cup. "Well, Holly, clue me in—is that awful news or are we talking balloons and noisemakers here?"

Throughout the long, lonely Sunday just past, Holly had agonized over that very question. And she hadn't been able to come up with a clear answer. "I feel panic-stricken," she confessed. "I also feel like shouting for joy."

"Have you told David?"

Holly had reached for the telephone a thousand times on Sunday, for her car keys a thousand more. But in the end, she had not been able to face David. She was too afraid of leaning on him, too afraid of needing him for the wrong reasons. And too afraid, when she could bring herself to face it, that he would either reject her outright or offer to marry her for the sake of the baby.

"No," she said finally.

"I won't give you the he-has-a-right-to-know speech, Holly," Elaine replied, her voice gentle. "I don't think you need that right now."

"I've given it to myself a hundred times." She paused and assessed her friend. "You have something to tell me, don't you?" she prompted, remembering the brief, disjointed message Elaine had left on the machine over the weekend.

Elaine's pretty face seemed a little drawn. "This is a lousy time to bring it up, but yes, I do have something to tell you. I've been offered a fantastic job, Holly—an editorial position with a regional magazine."

Holly knew what was coming then, and though she would hate losing Elaine, she couldn't help being happy for her. It was the kind of job her friend had always wanted, the kind of job she had been trained for. "That's wonderful, Elaine," she said softly.

Elaine's wide green eyes lifted to Holly's face. "You're not angry?"

"You were the best assistant anybody could have hoped to have, Elaine. But you've outgrown this job. It's time for a change."

"I'll stay until the new book is indexed," Elaine offered, and though she was smiling, there were tears shimmering in her eyes.

"No need. I can do that myself. You just go out there and set local publishing on its ear!"

Elaine laughed and sniffled, both at the same time. "To think I dreaded this so much. Poor Roy—I cried and fretted all weekend, I was so sure you would be upset. That offer couldn't have come at a worse time."

Holly sighed. "I'm not sure I agree, Elaine. The truth is, I think it might be time for my life to take on a new direction, too."

Elaine's eyes widened. "What are you saying, Holly?"

"I seem to be making the decision even as we talk, but thinking about it, I realize that I've wanted to make several changes for a very long time. I hate traveling so much, for one thing, having to leave Toby behind, and, well, cookbooks aren't much of a challenge anymore. I'd like to find out if I can write something different, Elaine. Something completely different."

"Such as?" Elaine prodded with a genuine interest that touched Holly and gave her courage.

"Maybe a novel," she blurted out bravely.

"Wow!" Elaine beamed. "And I thought you were going to resign yourself to motherhood!"

"Motherhood is wonderful, Toby has already proven that beyond any shadow of a doubt. But I know I need something more. Is that terrible?"

"Of course it isn't terrible. But—" Elaine paused, turning her coffee mug in an idle circle "—I'm still old-fashioned enough to think that kids need a father as well as a mother. Holly, are you going to marry David?"

An awkward silence fell. "You know that he gave me a ring at Christmas, I suppose," Holly ventured after a time.

Elaine all but smirked. "I guessed as much. After all, I was the one who hid his packages in the tree so you wouldn't fly mad and send them back in the next mail." She paused, then frowned, her eyes on Holly's left hand. "But I don't see a diamond."

"I gave it back," Holly confessed brokenly. "I was so angry with him, so hurt over that whole deception. And then Craig's arrest—"

"You've dealt with all that now?"

Holly sighed. "I thought I had. I love David so much, Elaine. I think I have from the first. And the more I saw him, the less those things seemed to matter."

"So what's the problem now?"

"There are several problems, actually. I don't know whether David even wants to marry me now. And I'm wondering how much of my—my caring for him is really caring and how much is panic at the idea of having a baby all by myself."

Elaine looked exasperated. "The solution is simple,

Holly. You need time to think, time to get your head together, as the kids say. I mean, with all that's happened to you in the past few months, how can you expect to have a handle on everything?"

Holly tangled her fingers in her hair as if to pull it out by the roots. "Think! How can I think, Elaine? That man sends me into fits of confusion every time I see him."

"Then don't see him for a while," Elaine said flatly. "Call a time-out. Give yourself a chance to catch your breath."

"That might be easier said than done," Holly fretted, lifting her own coffee cup to her mouth. She felt her stomach leap at the smell and set the cup back down without taking a sip.

Her grimace made Elaine grin. "Everything is easier said than done," she agreed, patting Holly's hand. "But what the hell?"

"Yeah," Holly replied with a wry arch of one eyebrow. "What the hell?"

The two women spent the rest of that day determining what had to be done to wrap up Holly's lucrative career as a cookbook author. There was one more set of classes to teach at the department store and the manuscript on Middle Eastern cooking had to be edited and then indexed. The newspaper column could be stopped with a month's notice.

Elaine had already gone home, taking a copy of the new manuscript with her, when the telephone rang. Holly drew a deep breath and answered it with a hello meant to sound cheerful. Except it came out a little hollow.

"Did you see your doctor?" David demanded without preamble, his voice gentle but gruff with weariness.

Holly closed her eyes a moment, stung by David's tone. He was hoping that she would say she wasn't pregnant, that he would be let off the hook. "Not yet," she said. "I have an appointment tomorrow morning."

"You're certainly casual about this, I'll say that for you!" David snapped. "I've been sweating blood ever since Saturday and you say you 'have an appointment tomorrow'!"

A tear slid down Holly's cheek. So much for never crying over David Goddard again. "I'm not being 'casual,' David, believe me," she managed to say. "I bought one of those home tests."

"And?"

"And—" Holly drew a deep breath to steady herself "—and it was positive."

There was a shattering silence at the other end of the line. "Are those things conclusive?" David finally asked, and there was no anger in his tone, but there was no happiness, either.

"I don't know," Holly admitted wearily. "I've never used one before."

"Very funny," came the ragged response.

"I wasn't joking, David."

He sighed; in her mind, Holly could see him leaning back in his chair, his thumb and forefinger to his temples. "I'd like to go with you tomorrow," he said finally, and still there was nothing in his voice to tell Holly what he was thinking.

She thought she knew that all too well. He was probably castigating himself for getting involved with a woman who didn't have enough sense to use birth control. "That won't be necessary, David," she said coldly, hanging up in his ear.

The telephone immediately rang again.

"Don't hang up on me, Holly," David warned. "I hate it."

Holly didn't hang up, but she did begin to cry, helplessly and with all the attendant noise. "Please, David... don't insist on going to the doctor's office with me... I couldn't bear it..."

"Holly." The word was a reprimand, but it was unbelievably gentle.

"I mean it, David!" Holly wailed. "I can't think clearly when you're around... I..."

He spoiled the intangible comfort he had just offered by swearing in a brutal undertone and then snapping, "Neither of us was thinking clearly from the beginning! Why start now, Holly?"

"David!"

"You should have stayed here the other night, Holly," he went on, quietly cruel. "What the hell? We could have made love until dawn. After all, the damage has been done!"

Damage. The word sliced through Holly like a knife. How could he call their baby, their precious child "damage"? "I hate you, David Goddard," she hissed into the receiver, keeping her voice down only because Toby might be near enough to hear. "Do you hear me? I hate you and I never want to see you again!"

The silence was charged. Holly braced herself for David's answer, but in the end, he gave none. There was a soft click and the line went dead.

In the morning, Holly kept her appointment with her doctor and was told for a certainty that she was pregnant. The baby would be born, she was blithely informed, in late September or early October.

Holly stumbled out of her doctor's office, vitamin prescriptions in hand, stricken by a combination of joy and despair. David was waiting beside the elevator doors.

"Well?" he asked simply, his voice hoarse. Holly was too distracted to even attempt to read the expression in his navy blue eyes. She nodded, her throat too thick to permit speech.

"When?" he prompted, not unkindly.

"Fall," she croaked.

The elevator arrived and David ushered Holly inside. But she didn't look at him, and as far as she could tell, he didn't look at her, either. How could this be? They had made this baby together, in passion so intense that Holly ached to remember it, and now they had nothing to say to each other. Nothing at all.

Out on the busy streets, people were rushing by, it seemed to Holly, in a colorful, threatening blur. Where had she left her car? Had she even brought the car?

No. She'd taken the bus. She remembered now. She had definitely taken the bus.

She tried in vain to recall which stop to wait at for another. Considering that she had lived in Spokane all her life and taken buses into virtually every part of it since the age of eleven, it was annoying to forget the routes and schedules now.

David's hand was strong on her elbow. "Come on," he said gruffly.

Holly looked at him with dazed, tear-blurred eyes. "Where are we going?"

"My place."

That snapped her out of it. She wrenched her arm

free and went rigid. "Why, David? To do more 'damage'?"

Pain moved deep in his eyes, but was overcome so quickly that she thought she'd imagined it. "To talk," he said firmly, and his hand again closed around her arm.

"I don't want to talk to you, David. I don't want to talk to anybody. I just want to lie on my bed and cry."

The statement seemed to wound him; he looked away, scanning cloud-dappled blue skies for a moment. "All right," he said after a long time. "All right. But, please, let me get you a cab."

It seemed the least he could do, after fathering a baby he didn't want. "Thank you," Holly replied woodenly.

But when she reached her house, high on the South Hill, she did not lie down on her bed and cry. Elaine was there, working on the manuscript, and Madge was cleaning furiously. Both of them were trying so hard to be subtle that Holly forgot her misery for the time being and burst out laughing.

"Yes!" she yelled, spreading her hands wide of a body that would soon swell to pearlike proportions. "I'm pregnant!"

Faced with the certainty, her friends did not seem to know whether to celebrate or commiserate. Thinking it enough that she wasn't flying apart in pieces, Holly gave them no clue. She simply sat down at her desk and turned on her computer and began working on the last of the cooking columns she was required, by contract with the local newspaper, to write.

For the next two weeks, Holly lived in a frenetic kind of limbo, working day and night, praying that David wouldn't call or come by and leaping every time the telephone or doorbell rang.

David didn't call, though. And he didn't come by. Holly was resigned to the fact that, despite his earlier claims to love and want her, she was going to have this baby alone. And raise it alone.

The fates seemed to respect her secret grief, however, and even to aid her in holding up the front she maintained for Elaine and Madge and Toby. Everything went well; Holly's agent accepted her decision to switch from sure-thing cookbooks to novels that might or might not sell, the newspaper was gracious, though they said their readers would miss her columns, and the department-store people didn't give her any flak, either, beyond reminding her that her contract called for one more set of lessons to be taught.

Yes, everything was fine. Until the night Toby ran away.

David was developing a hatred for coffee. He scowled at his empty cup and set it in the sink, looking out over the lights of the city and despairing. Why was he beating the books, night after night, like some college kid? For what?

He sighed raggedly and ran one hand through his hair. For his sanity, that was for what, he admitted to himself. If he didn't bury himself in classes by day and law books by night, he would go crazy. Perversely, he wondered what Holly was doing at that moment. What she was thinking and feeling.

Love for her clenched within David in a spasm so painful that it nearly bent him double. He had to leave her alone; he had to, no matter what the cost. A long talk with Holly's assistant, Elaine Bateman, had convinced him of that. And yet it was the hardest thing he had ever had to do—his every instinct ran counter to this endless, agonizing waiting.

The doorbell rang and David's heart lunged to the pit of his stomach and then swelled into his throat. Let it be her, he thought desperately as he strode to the door and reached for the knob.

Forcibly, David stopped just short of opening it, drew a deep breath and tried to compose himself. It was crucial to say the right thing, to do the right thing— The bell rang again, insistently, and David grinned as he turned the knob and pulled the door open.

Toby was standing before him, head down, jacket askew, his toy Cessna in one hand and the robot David had sent at Christmas in the other.

David scanned the hallway, puzzled, but saw no sign of Holly. Then, hiding the alarm he felt, he crouched to look into the little boy's averted face. It was tear-stained and pink from the cold outside.

Toby looked at him then and David ached at the despair he saw in that small face; it seemed to crumple before his very eyes.

"Don't you want to marry Mom and me?" the child wailed, flinging his arms around David's neck, the plane and the robot thumping to the floor.

David held him and rose to his feet, too overcome to respond immediately. After a time, though, he cleared his throat and asked, "Does your mom know where you are, slugger?"

The small head shook against his shoulder.

David had already guessed the answer to that question, of course, but it made an opening. "I think we'd better call her and tell her you're safe. Right now."

"Okay," sniffled Toby.

His shirt sodden with Toby's tears, David ruffled the little boy's hair and set him gently down on the sofa. This would be the first call he'd made to Holly in weeks, but his fingers didn't hesitate over the buttons as they usually did.

She answered, frantic, on the first ring. "Toby?"

"He's here with me," David said gently. "And he's all right."

"Thank God!" Holly wept. "Oh, thank God! I thought—"

David had to close his eyes for a moment. For some damned, inexplicable reason, he felt like crying himself. He didn't speak because he didn't dare.

"When did he get there?" Holly demanded, sniffling. "What did he say?"

The little boy's words echoed in David's heart. *Don't you want to marry Mom and me?*

"He hasn't said anything much," David lied gruffly, for Holly's sake as well as his own. "How the devil do you suppose he got all the way down here by himself?"

Holly sighed; David could see her in his mind, her wonderful aquamarine eyes puffy, her hair tangled from repeated, nervous ruffling. "I shudder to think," she said.

"Shall I bring him home or do you want to come and get him?" Either way, David despaired in silence, how am I going to be able to bear seeing you? Can that possibly be worse than *not* seeing you?

Holly's answer surprised him. "C-could you keep him, just for tonight?"

David glanced back at Toby, who was watching him from the sofa, his lower lip jutting out in some kind of little-kid defiance. "Keep him?" he echoed, and Toby's eyes widened.

"Evidently it was important to him to see you, David. Maybe you can find out what made him do this."

"I'll try," David promised hoarsely, and then he said goodbye to Holly and turned back toward the child, folding his arms across his chest.

"Okay, slugger. What's the deal? How did you get down here alone?"

Toby was scrambling out of his jacket, ready to stay for the duration, but there was a challenge in his eyes. "Everybody thinks I'm too little to do anything," he complained. "Just like that dumb baby."

Bingo, thought David, but he didn't smile. He didn't want Toby to think that running away in the middle of the night was clever.

"What dumb baby is this?" he asked.

"The one Mom's going to have. She won't want me anymore, that's for sure."

"Oh? And on what do you base that conclusion, counselor?"

Toby squared his shoulders. At least he'd had supper before setting out on the crosstown journey—half of it was still on his striped T-shirt. "I'm not really hers, you know," he said.

"Mmmm."

"She's really my aunt."

"Right. You just call her 'Mom' to make her feel good, huh?"

Toby considered and seemed to find the idea magnanimous enough to claim. "Yeah."

"She loves you, Toby. And no matter how many babies she has, that is never going to change."

The uncertainty in Toby's face was painful to see. "You really think so?"

"I really think so. Now, how did you get here?"

"You won't believe it."

"Indulge me," David replied.

"I walked."

"All the way from the South Hill?" David was horrified, though he did a creditable job of hiding it.

"All the way from the South Hill," Toby confirmed proudly. But his grin faded away. "If Mom loves me so much, how come she said you could keep me?"

"She just meant for tonight, slugger. She's a smart lady—she figured that if you wanted to see me badly enough to run away, well, then she should let you see me."

"Oh. Are you going to marry us? Mom and me and the baby?"

David reeled inwardly but again managed to recover. "I'd like that a lot, Toby, but sometimes things don't go the way we want them to, no matter how hard we try. And right now, you'd better be thankful that I'm *not* married to your mom."

"Why?" demanded Toby, a study in disbelief.

"Because I'd give you the worst spanking you've ever had in your whole life, that's why. Running away is an ultra-dumb thing to do."

Toby pondered this carefully, his face working as he weighed getting spanked against having David for a father. "I guess al-Qaeda could have got me," he said after due consideration.

"What do you know about al-Qaeda?"

"I know they were after my dad."

David went to the sofa and sat down beside Toby, making a big deal of stretching his legs and crossing his booted feet on the glass top of the coffee table. "They're not going to bother you, Tobe," he said after a long time.

Toby looked relieved. "Good. I thought they might think my dad told me a secret or something."

David put one arm around the little boy and held him close. He could understand the depths of Holly's feelings for this child, for he already loved Toby as if he were his own.

"Would you really have spanked me if I'd been your kid?" Toby asked when the silence grew too long for comfort.

"You'd better believe it," David replied honestly. "There are certain things a guy just doesn't do, and running away is one of them."

Blue eyes the size of Frisbees looked up into David's face. "I think I'd still like to be your kid anyway," he said.

David laughed because if he hadn't, he'd have cried.

"You'll probably like the baby better'n me, just like Mom."

"Neither of us will like the baby better than you, Toby."

Toby snuggled close, beneath David's arm. "Babies can't fly Cessnas or nothin'," he said derisively. And then he fell asleep.

David removed Toby's shoes, slipped a pillow beneath his head and covered him with a down-filled quilt from one of the extra bedrooms. He tried to go back to his books—the Bar Exam was only weeks away—but try as he might, he couldn't concentrate.

He kept losing himself in dreams that would probably never come true.

Chapter 15

Elaine had been right in saying that what was needed was time, Holly reflected as she stepped onto the department-store escalator. She was munching on caramel-covered popcorn and peanuts—her third box that day—and she frowned as she emptied the last of it into the palm of one hand. The minute the morning sickness had passed away, the strange cravings had begun. And caramel corn wasn't the only thing she felt compelled to gorge on, unfortunately. Sometimes she wanted smoked oysters rolled in peanut butter....

Holly made a face and then thumped the box against her hand so that the prize would fall out. It was in a white packet, whatever it was, and she tore the paper away as she strolled toward Cookware, where she would teach her last class.

It was an omen! The prize turned out to be an enormous ring with a plastic solitare. Grinning, Holly tucked it into her pocket.

Tonight's project was shawarma, and the members of her class were at their tables, sleeves rolled up. She scanned their faces as she did every night, hoping to see David among them and, paradoxically, hoping not to.

David had not called her or put in an appearance at her house since the morning he had brought Toby home. Even then, he'd only said that the little boy was worried about being shunted aside when the baby came. And the word *baby* had been like a barrier between them, impossible to surmount.

Holly was saddened as she dropped her caramel-corn box surreptitiously into a wastebasket and shrugged out of her coat. Determinedly, she smiled at her students. "Looks like everyone is ready to start."

There were nods, grins and expressions of nervousness all around. And then they began.

It was just as the class was ending that David appeared, his hands wedged into the pockets of a Windbreaker emblazoned with the Gonzaga University logo, his eyes carefully avoiding Holly's gaze.

She felt a shivering sort of exhilaration, followed by plunging doubts. Just because David was there, well, that didn't mean that he was ready to make any sort of declaration or renew their relationship. He might even have come to say goodbye, having decided to return to Washington….

This was a considerate class. Each and every student cleaned up his or her own mess, leaving nothing for Holly to do but sneak the occasional glance at David, who was leaning against a refrigerator door, his arms folded, his navy blue eyes touching upon everything except Holly herself.

She smiled as the last goodbyes were said and her students departed, certificates in hand. And then she was alone. With David.

"Time to take the bull by the horns, kid," she told herself, drawing on all her courage as she plunged a hand into her coat pocket. Win, lose or draw, there could be no more guesswork and no more emotional sparring. If David Goddard wasn't going to declare himself, then Holly would state her own case and see what happened.

"Hello," she said, walking over to him and stopping within touching distance.

David gave her a wry look. Obviously he wasn't going to make this easy.

"Thank you for taking such good care of Toby that night," she said hoarsely. She was clenching her fingers so tightly that the small object she held dug into her palm.

"You're welcome," he said.

Holly sighed and rolled her eyes. Now or never, she thought, drawing a deep breath that dizzied her. And then she extended her hand, the plastic ring lying in her palm.

"Will you marry me, David?" she choked out.

He looked as though she had flung a shawarma on him. His face contorted for a moment and he no longer leaned so indolently against the door of that display-floor refrigerator. No, David stood erect now, Secret-Service alert. His throat worked, but he said nothing.

Holly wanted to die. "You haven't mentioned getting married lately, so I thought I'd bring it up," she said lamely.

Suddenly, so suddenly that Holly jumped, David pulled her against his hard chest, that chest she had so missed the scent and feel and strength of, and he laughed. His hands touched her shoulders briefly and then entwined themselves in her hair, mussing it.

"God, Holly, how I love you," he muttered.

"Does that mean you're going to accept my proposal?" she asked softly, searching his face with wide, cautious eyes.

"How could I refuse?" he asked gruffly, his breath warm against her face, his eyes meeting hers with a direct sort of tenderness that made her shiver with the love of him, the need of him. "Holly, are you sure? Have you thought about this?"

"Yes. To the detriment, I might add, of everything I was supposed to be thinking about instead."

"What made you decide?"

"I didn't need to decide because I already knew. I just needed to *know* I knew."

David rolled his eyes—they were shining with laughter—and then he kissed her. Salespeople and customers were probably looking on, but Holly didn't care. She kissed him back.

She was breathless, moments later, as she caught his hand in hers and tried to wedge the caramel-corn diamond onto his finger. It didn't fit, of course, but David accommodatingly wore it on his pinkie.

"I wonder if accepting an expensive gift like this," David teased, "obligates me to submit to lewd and improper demands."

Holly laughed. "You bet it does," she answered. "Your place or mine, handsome?"

"What about Toby?" he asked, so seriously that

Holly's already fathomless love deepened with a painful jolt.

"Toby is spending the night with a friend."

A grin broke over David's wonderful, magnificent face. "You planned this!"

Holly laughed. "Do you really have a hot tub in your bedroom?" she asked. "Rumor has it that you do."

His hand fitted itself to the small of her back and Holly found herself being propelled through Cookware and onto the down escalator. "Rumor is entirely correct," he answered. "All the same, I think you should confirm it with your own eyes."

The hot tub made a lulling, bubbling sound in the semi-darkness, filling the room with a tropical sort of heat. Holly luxuriated in contentment as David's hands slowly divested her of her clothes, pausing now and then to stroke and caress whatever prize he had just uncovered.

"I love you," he said, bending his head to one breast and circling the instantly responsive nipple with the tip of his tongue.

Holly groaned and then, somehow, found the strength to push him away. "Oh, no, you don't, fella. You're not going to stand there in all your clothes and make me crazy."

A compliant sort, David was soon standing there without his clothes. And making her crazy.

She went to stand beside the hot tub, looking down into its churning depths. Then David was behind her, drawing her back against him, running his hands from her waist to her breasts. He seemed to be weighing them in his palms, and Holly moaned and let her head fall back against his shoulder as his thumbs coaxed her nipples to a new level of response.

When Holly thought she could bear no more of that, when she was sure she would have to turn to him and demand that he take her, he retraced his path, lingering at her hips for a delicious moment and then knitting his fingers together over her abdomen.

His teeth caught at her earlobe and she quivered against the sinewy length of him, the hair on his chest tickling her naked back. "I want this to last forever," he breathed and again she trembled. "Cold?" he queried as an afterthought.

"Hardly," Holly managed to say.

All the same, David lowered her gently into the hot tub. The warm, moving water seemed to intensify the raging need in her senses to an almost unbearable degree, but Holly hadn't the strength to lift herself out.

Kneeling behind her, David took her hands in his and positioned them so that they were cupped behind her head. And then he began, idly, to toy with her breasts again, now bathing them with warm water, now caressing them, now plying the nipples between skilled fingers. Holly moaned and her own fingers uncurled, but she did not try to lower her arms.

"David," she finally managed to say, "oh, David—make love to me—now—"

He drew her up out of the water and placed her on the tiled edge. Even in the half darkness, she could see the glittering hunger in his eyes, a hunger he appeased at her breasts until Holly was writhing with need, her body still slick and warm from the brief episode in the hot tub.

"I—"

"David," Holly tangled her hands in his thick, dark, rumpled hair. "Now."

"I might hurt you—the baby—"

The concern in his voice caused Holly to free her hands and capture his muscle-corded thighs instead, urging him toward her. "I need you, David. I love you. And we've already waited long enough."

With a moan, he lowered himself to her and sought her solace with his manhood. His welcome was such that, with a rasped exclamation, he surged inside her, deeply but gently. Holly drew her knees up and felt his powerful hips moving slowly against her inner thighs.

She watched him until she could no longer bear the shadowy beauty of him and then closed her eyes. Patches of golden light exploded behind her lids as new feelings blossomed within her like flowers.

David, in turn, was nearly incoherent. "I thought this—would never—happen again—oh, God, Holly— how I need you—"

Holly muttered some wicked sweetness and her reward was a breathtaking increase in the pace of their lovemaking. Their bodies rose and fell in fierce unison, fever after fever raging within Holly and then breaking, each one making her wilder. Her fingernails raked David's back, as his possession and her own became one and the same and they both cried out as the tender anguish bonded them, fusing them into one being with its heat.

David collapsed beside her, his body trembling, his breath a primitive, tearing sound. "Good Lord, woman," he managed after some time, "I'm not sure I can bear up under a lifetime of that."

Holly stretched languidly, an evil wanton in the

warm, lush darkness. "You'll 'bear up' just fine," she said, winding a finger in the moist down curling upon his chest.

He laughed, turned her onto her side and gave her bottom a playful swat. "Vamp," he said. "Just for that, I think I'll carry you to my bed and prove your theory."

"You couldn't carry me if you had to," challenged Holly in a sensuous, stretching purr. "Your knees are too weak."

"Is that so?" he asked in a rumbling whisper. And then, as Holly had hoped, he rolled to his feet, pulled her after him and lifted her into his arms. Feigning a dark passion, he dropped her from shoulder height onto the bed.

"Ummm," Holly crooned, stretching her arms upward. David came to her and never let her go throughout that long, glorious night.

Epilogue

Holly Goddard glared at her computer screen, muttering. This book had started out as a mystery, and her agent had liked what she had seen of it, but now it seemed to be taking an unexpected direction.

"It's Saturday," Holly grumbled to herself. "In some religions, Saturday is a day of rest."

"Did you say something?" David asked from the doorway of the study they shared. He was wearing blue jeans, a maroon sweatshirt, a denim jacket—and a baby girl in the carrier on his back.

Born in late September, Miss Autumn Goddard was already spending most Saturdays in the park with David and Toby. Her cheeks were pink and her round, indigo eyes sleepy as they peered out of the tiny snowsuit she wore.

Holly was filled with such tenderness that she ached. She forgot the problems she was having with her novel and went to plant a kiss on Autumn's plump cheek before lifting her out of the carrier to cuddle her for a moment.

"Where's Toby?" she asked.

David grinned, sliding back the hood of Autumn's snowsuit, revealing a head of curly, Holly-gold hair. He kissed the baby's forehead briefly before answering, "Downstairs, doing his homework with Marcus."

Marcus was Toby's newest and "bestest" friend; since he and Holly had moved into David's condo, the very day of the wedding, the two little boys had been a package deal. If you wanted one, you had to accept the other.

"Don't you have any homework to do, counselor?" Holly teased as she carried Autumn into the bedroom that adjoined her own and David's. "You have a big case coming up this week, if I remember correctly."

David dodged the question by disappearing into the kitchen, but he was back soon enough, Autumn's naptime bottle in hand.

Holly had already undressed their daughter, changed her diaper and bundled her into a cuddly pink sleeper. Autumn extended her tiny hands at the sight of the offered bottle and was asleep after a few gurgling swallows.

"About your case," Holly prodded, in the living room. Dammit, if she had to work on Saturday, then David was going to be right there in the study with her, plugging away at *Snider vs McCulley*.

Showing not the slightest sign of industry, David sat down on the raised hearth of the fireplace and stared indolently down at his right sneaker, his chin resting on one knee. "I've got that case down pat and you know it."

"Is that so?"

"Yes," David replied flatly, his eyes sparkling as they met hers. "You have to work so you want me to suffer right along beside you—misery loves company and all that."

"I'll be misery and you be company," Holly grumbled, assessing the situation. Toby was downstairs, visiting Marcus. Autumn was asleep. She blushed at the course her thoughts were taking.

David grinned. "And you'll love me?" he leered.

"Anytime I get the chance," Holly admitted.

He assumed his best attorney manner, frowning pensively, standing up to pace back and forth along the hearth as though it were a jury box. "What about your book, Mrs. Goddard?" he demanded soberly. "How do you intend to meet your deadline if you don't write?"

Holly shrugged, her legs curled beneath her on the navy blue sofa. "I made up the deadline myself. There's no reason to be picky, here."

"Picky?" David boomed, looking suitably shocked, even horrified. He shook his head as he continued to pace, his hands locked behind his back. "Have you no dedication, Mrs. Goddard? No ambition? No—"

Holly giggled at the picture he made. "Don't tease me, David," she wailed. "My plot is so hopelessly snarled that I'll never get it undone and my characters won't do anything I tell them to!"

David stopped, bending slightly to peer into Holly's face. "Exactly what kind of scene are you trying to write, anyway?" he demanded in that same ponderous, lawyerlike tone.

Holly gave him a once-over from beneath coyly lowered eyelashes. "A love scene, of course," she purred.

"Aha!" he cried, pointing one index finger into the

air. "In that case, Madam, we are able to ascertain the exact nature of your problem!"

Holly pretended to peer around him. "We?" she echoed.

"Speaking as the prosecution, of course," he admitted.

"Of course. And what, pray tell, is the 'exact nature of my problem,' counselor?"

"Research, of course. A pitiable, contemptible lack of research."

"I see," Holly said, assuming a look of deep chagrin.

"No, Madam," David went on sternly, "I don't think you do see. This is a matter of the gravest importance."

Holly giggled again. "You don't really say things like that in the courtroom, do you?"

"No," David confessed. "I saw it in an old Henry Fonda movie. Now, exactly how do you plead? Guilty or not guilty?"

Holly deliberately batted her eyelashes. "Of what am I accused, sir?"

He sank to his knees before her with a comical thump, his eyes gleaming. "Neglecting your research," he replied.

Thinking of the weeks after Autumn's birth when there had been no lovemaking at all, and the hesitant quality in David's touch even now, Holly's playful mood was dampened. "Or perhaps of neglecting my husband?" she prompted softly.

He bent forward and kissed her. "Never that," he whispered.

"I know it was hard for you—"

David laid an index finger to her lips. "Having a baby was no piece of cake, either, I'll wager. Still, Autumn is almost two months old. Time is passing us by. Maybe we should start another baby right away."

Holly laughed and wrapped her arms around his neck. "I love you, you maniac."

"And I love you. But, as a writer, that doesn't excuse you from doing proper research." He stood up, drawing Holly with him, pulling her against the appealing, granitelike length of him. His face was serious, though, despite his earlier teasing. "Tell me the truth. Does it... does it hurt when I make love to you?"

She stood up on tiptoe to kiss his chin. "No. It feels glorious."

"Really?"

"Would I lie about something as important as research?" She slid her arms around his waist and felt him tremble as their bodies touched, her soft curves a temptation to his hard lines and angles.

"I certainly hope not," he gasped, gazing deep into her eyes, finding things she might have hidden once but was willing to share now. His hands came tentatively to burrow into her silky hair. "Oh, Holly," he breathed. "Holly. Every day, I wake up and I think I can't possibly love you any more than I already do. And every day, you prove me wrong."

Holly's eyes misted with happy tears. "Do you love me enough to help me with my research?" she whispered.

David laughed and swatted her firm, round bottom with both hands. "Oh, at least that much. I'm in the mood to be magnanimous here."

Holly gave him a long look. "Then what's holding you back? Carry me off to your bed and slake your savage passion at my heaving breasts."

David grinned and feigned a beleaguered look. "God, I hope that isn't a direct quote from your manuscript, woman," he teased. "If it is, you'd better go back to writing about crumpets and tacos."

Holly wriggled against him in reply, and he groaned, lifting her into his arms. "If we're going to research savage passion, I guess we'd better get started."

Their passion was not savage, but tender, mounting with every kiss, every caress, every surrender of a garment. Though they had made love several times since Autumn's birth, David was still afraid of hurting her.

As Holly lay beneath him, her blouse and bra gone, her breasts proudly bared to him, David bent his head and kissed each impudent peak. "Allow me, Madam," he taunted in a rumbling voice, "to slake my savage something or other."

The kisses felt so good that Holly stretched, crooning and thrusting herself upward for more. "Please, do," she said and she whimpered with pleasure as he began to lose his restraint and enjoy her freely, now nibbling, now suckling with the fierce hunger Holly craved.

Finally, leaving breasts moistened and tuned to passion by his lips and his tongue, David traced a path of kisses over her collarbone and up her neck to the sensitive hollows beneath her ears.

"Are you taking notes?" he demanded, working his way back down to a breast, attending to it briefly, and then moving on to the heaving ridges of her rib cage.

"C-copious notes," Holly choked out as he circled her navel with a leisure that was positively torturous. She moaned with sweet despondency as his kisses continued. "Th-that isn't at all p-pertinent to my wo-work, sir."

He chuckled, the sound far away and yet so near as to be a part of Holly. "Want to bet?" he asked, his hand stroking her inner thigh, pressing her legs to part.

Research was the furthest thing from Holly's mind then—moments later, she didn't even have a mind, for she had been driven out of it. Only later, after a series of shattering releases, after David had finally given in to her pleading and entered her, his body at once taming and exalting hers, was she free to grope her way back toward sanity.

He lay beside her afterward, his head pillowed on her breasts, his legs still entangled with hers. Smiling to herself, Holly wound a lock of his hair around her finger and speculated, "I think I've got it. I know what I was doing wrong now."

"Believe me," David rasped, still too weak, apparently, to rise from her breast, "you didn't do anything wrong."

Holly laughed. "I was talking about my book, silly."

David growled with pretended outrage and rolled onto his back, hauling Holly up to sit astride him. It was so good, this easiness between them, this lack of restraint or caution. Tears of sheer joy blurred Holly's vision.

David frowned and caught them on his thumbs when they fell. "What is it, love?"

Holly was anxious to reassure him, and she gave a sniffling laugh. "I'm afraid I've used you shamelessly," she confessed.

"How so?"

"I'm not writing a romance; I'm writing a mystery. The love scene I was talking about consists of one kiss, nothing more."

David glared at her, pretending outraged honor. "Wench," he said in gravelly tones, "you'll have to pay for that."

"I will?" Holly questioned, the picture of innocence. "How?"

He shifted slightly and then entered her with an authority that made her gasp with pleasure. His hands rose with brazen idleness to cup her breasts. And that was answer enough.

Holly began to move upon him, slowly, sweetly, a creature of fire and instinct. "You are completely—oh, God—without conscience—"

David matched her pace and then began to set one of his own. "Completely," he agreed, pressing his head back into the pillows and closing his eyes. Several glorious, heated minutes passed, and then they were both crying out for each other, even though they were already joined, seeking each other with desperate hands and hoarse, tender words.

The finding was sweet indeed.

Turkeys. David's fancy refrigerator, with its sliding opaque door, was covered with construction-paper turkeys. Holding a fussy Autumn against her hip with one arm, Holly opened the appliance's door with the other and reached inside for milk.

The draperies had not been drawn, and as Holly sat at the table, rocking her hungry daughter in her arms while the bottle heated, she looked out over the sparkling lights of the city, thinking.

Impatient for her midnight feeding, Autumn flung back her gossamer-tufted head and wailed.

"Shhh," Holly whispered against a tiny neck scented of talcum powder and baby lotion. "You'll wake up Daddy and Toby."

Autumn was unimpressed with that possibility. Her

wail intensified to a series of piercing shrieks. Chuckling softly, Holly took the bottle from its warmer and did the gyrations required to hold a furious baby and test the heat of the milk at the same time.

"This looks like a job for Super-lawyer," yawned David, clad in a velour bathrobe, as he took both baby and bottle from Holly and plopped down in a chair. A moment later, Autumn was imbibing greedily.

"Fine thing," Holly scoffed with mock indignation. "I do all the work and you get the credit."

David only grinned, watching his daughter with such adoration in his eyes that Holly wasn't sure she could bear it. Or the feelings inspired in her.

"There was a letter from Craig today," she said quietly, leaning back against the counter, her arms folded. She felt like a housewifely bundle of chenille and love.

David's eyes darted to her face, wary. "Oh? How is he?"

"He's getting better," Holly answered gently. "They haven't decided yet exactly what to try him for. It might be a long time before they do."

There was a silence; obviously David didn't know what to say. And Holly didn't want Craig or anyone else to stand between them.

She went to David and made a place for herself on his knee, unsettling the ravenous Autumn only slightly. Wrapping one arm around David's neck, Holly intoned, "Kiss me, you fool!"

He laughed and responded accordingly.

* * * * *

Also by Brenda Jackson

For additional books
by *New York Times*
bestselling author
Brenda Jackson,
visit her website,
brendajackson.net.

TALL, DARK…
WESTMORELAND!

Brenda Jackson

To the love of my life, Gerald Jackson, Sr.,
and to everyone who has ever sent me a letter
or email to let me know how much you've enjoyed
the Westmorelands. This book is for you!

Withhold not good from them to whom it is due,
when it is in the power of thine hand to do it.
—*Proverbs* 3:27

Chapter 1

There has to be another way for a woman to have fun, Olivia Jeffries thought as she glanced around at everyone attending the Firemen's Masquerade Ball, an annual charity event held in downtown Atlanta. Already she was gearing up for a boring evening.

It wouldn't have been so bad if she hadn't arrived from Paris just yesterday, after being summoned home by her father. That meant she had to drop everything, including plans to drive through the countryside of the Seine Valley to complete the painting she had started months ago.

Returning to Atlanta had required her to take a leave of absence from her job as an art curator at the Louvre. But when Orin Jeffries called, she hadn't hesitated to drop everything. After all, he was only the greatest dad in the entire world.

He had wanted her home after making the decision to run for public office, saying it was important that she was there not only for his first fund-raiser but also for the duration of his campaign. There would be a number of functions he would need to attend, and he preferred not to go with any particular woman on a regular basis. He didn't want any of his female friends to get the wrong idea.

Olivia could only shake her head and smile. Her divorced father had taken himself off the marriage block years ago. In fact, she doubted he'd ever allowed himself to be there in the first place. He dated on occasion, but he'd never gotten serious about any woman, which was a pity. At fifty-six, Orin Jeffries was without a doubt a very good-looking man. His ex-wife, who was Olivia's mom in genes only, had left a bad taste in Orin's mouth. A taste that the past twenty-four years hadn't erased.

Her two older brothers, Duan, who was thirty-six, and Terrence, who was thirty-four, had taken after her father in their good looks. And as in the case of their father, the thought of marriage was the last thing on their minds. In a way, she followed in her dad's footsteps as well. Finding a husband was the last thing on hers.

So there you had it. They were the swinging single Jeffries, although for the moment, nothing was swinging for her, Olivia thought. There were a few people at this ball who seemed to be having fun, but most, like her, were looking at their watches and wondering when proper etiquette dictated it would be okay to leave.

Whoever had come up with the idea of everyone wearing masks had really been off their rocker. It made her feel like she was part of the Lone Ranger's posse. And because all the money raised tonight was for the new wing at the children's hospital, in addition to the mask, everyone was required to wear a name badge on which was printed the name of a nursery rhyme character, a color of a crayon or a well-known cartoon or comic-book character. How creative.

At least the food was good. The first words out of her father's mouth when he'd seen her at the airport the day before had been, "You look too thin." She figured the least she could do was mosey on over to the buffet table and get herself something to eat. Hopefully, in a little while she could split.

Reginald Westmoreland watched the woman as she crossed the room, making her way over to the buffet table. He had been watching her for over twenty minutes now, racking his brain as to who she was. Mask or no mask, he recognized most of the women at the ball tonight. He knew almost every one of them because for years he had been immersed in the science of "lip-tology." In other words, the first thing he noticed about a woman was her lips.

He could recognize a woman by her lips alone, without even looking at any other facial feature. Most people wouldn't agree, but no two pairs of lips were the same. His brothers and cousins had denounced his claim and had quickly put him to the test. He had just as quickly proven them wrong. Whether you considered it a blessing or a curse, the bottom line was that he had the gift.

And there were other things besides her lips that caught his attention, like her height. She had to be almost six feet tall. And then he was struck by the way she fit into her elegantly designed black and silver beaded dress, the way the material clung to her shapely curves.

He had noticed several men approach her, but she had yet to dance with any of them. In fact, it seemed that she was brushing them off. Reginald smelled a challenge.

"So, how is the campaign going, Reggie?"

Reginald, known to all his family as Reggie, turned to look at his older brother, divorce attorney extraordinaire, Jared Westmoreland. Just last week Jared had made the national news owing to a high-profile settlement he'd won in favor of a well-known Hollywood actor.

"It officially kicks off Monday. But now that Jeffries has decided to throw his hat into the ring, things should be rather interesting," he said, referring to the older man who would be his opponent. "With Brent, I have a good campaign manager, but I still feel it might be a tight race. Jeffries is well-known and well-liked."

"Well, if you need any help, let me know, although I'm not sure how much time I can spare now that Dana's expecting and all."

Reggie rolled his eyes. Just last month Jared had found out he was going to be a father. "Dana is going to be carrying the baby, Jared, not you."

"I know, but I'm the one who's been getting sick in the morning, and now I'm getting cravings. I never liked pickles until now."

Reggie couldn't help but smile over his wineglass. "Sounds like a personal problem to me." At the moment, his attention strayed from whatever Jared was saying. Instead, his gaze focused on the other side of the room. He noticed the woman whom he'd been watching sit down at a table. He had yet to see a man by her side, which meant she had come to the party alone.

"Umm, I wonder who she is?" he asked.

Jared followed Reggie's gaze and chuckled. "What's wrong? Don't you recognize the lips?"

Reggie shifted his gaze from the woman to his brother and frowned. "No, she's someone new. I definitely haven't met her before. Her lips don't give her away."

"Then I guess the only thing left for you to do is go over there and introduce yourself."

Reggie grinned. "I know they don't call you the sharpest attorney in Atlanta for nothing."

"Don't you know sitting alone at a party isn't good for you?"

Olivia swung her head around at the sound of the deep, throaty masculine voice to find a tall, handsome man standing beside her. Like everyone else, he was wearing a mask, but even with it covering half of his face, she knew he had to be extremely good-looking. In the dim lighting, her artist's eye was able to capture all his striking features that were exposed.

First of all, there was his skin, flawlessly smooth and a shade of color that reminded her of rich, dark maple syrup. Then there was the angular plane of a jaw that supported a pair of sexy lips. The same ones that bestowed a slow smile on her. Apparently, he realized she was checking him out.

"In that case, I guess you need to join me," she replied, trying to remember the last time she'd been so outrageously forward with a guy and quickly deciding never. But the way the evening was going, she would have to stir up her own excitement. And now was as good a time as any to start. Maybe it was the fact that the party was so unrelentingly boring that made her long for a taste of the wild and reckless. The other men who had approached her hadn't even piqued her curiosity. She had no desire to get to know them better. But this man was different.

"I don't mind if I do," he said, easily sliding into the chair beside her while his eyes remained locked with hers. Her nose immediately picked up the scent of his cologne. Expensive. She quickly checked out his left hand. Ringless. Her gaze automatically went back to his face. Beautiful. Now he was smiling in earnest and showing beautiful white teeth.

"You're amused," she said, taking a sip of her punch but wishing she had something a little stronger.

Whoever he was, he was certainly someone worth getting to know, even if she was returning to Paris in a few months. That made it all the more plausible. It had taken her two years to get on full-time at the Louvre, and the hard work was just beginning. Once she returned, she would be working long hours, with little time to get her painting done. That was why she had brought her paints to Atlanta with her. She was determined to capture something worthwhile on canvas while she was here. The man sitting beside her would be the perfect subject.

"Flattered more than amused," he said, his voice reaching out and actually touching her, although she barely registered his words in her mind, because she was too busy watching the way his mouth moved. Sensuously slow.

She couldn't help wondering who he was. She had been gone from Atlanta a long time. After high school she had attended Pratt Institute in New York before doing her graduate work at the Art Institute of Boston. From there she had made the move to Paris, after landing a job as a tour professional, a glorified name for a tour guide.

He had to be around her brother Terrence's age, or maybe a year or so younger. She wondered if he would give her his real name, or if he would stick to the rules and play this silly little game the coordinators of the ball had come up with. His name badge said Jack Sprat. No wonder he was in such fine shape, she thought. Even in the tuxedo he was wearing, she saw broad, muscular shoulders and a nice solid chest. All muscles. Definitely no fat.

"So, Jack," she said, smiling at him the same way he was smiling at her. "What is such a nice guy like you doing at a boring party like this?"

He chuckled, and the sound sent goose bumps over her body. "Waiting to meet you so we can start having some fun." He glanced at her name badge. "Wonder Woman."

The smile that touched the corners of her mouth widened. She liked him already. "Well, trust me when I say, it's a *wonder* that I'm here at all. I really want to be someplace else, but I promised the person who paid for this ticket that I'd come in his place. And since it's all for charity, and for such a good cause, I decided to at least make an appearance."

"I'm glad you did."

And Reggie meant it. He'd thought she had a beautiful pair of lips from afar, but now he had a chance to really study them up close. They were a pair he would never forget. They were full, shapely, and had luscious-looking dips at the corners. She had them covered in light lip gloss, which was perfect; any color would detract from their modish structure.

"We've exchanged names, and I'm glad to make your acquaintance, Jack," she said, presenting her hand to him.

He grinned. "Likewise, Wonder."

The moment their hands touched, he felt it and knew that she did, too. Her fingers quivered on his, and for some reason, he could not release her hand. That realization unnerved him. No woman had ever had this kind of effect on him before, not in all his thirty-two years.

"Are you from Atlanta?"

Her voice, soft and filled with Southern charm, reclaimed his attention.

"Yes, born and raised right here," he said, reluctantly releasing her hand. "What about you?"

"Same here," she said, looking at him as if she could see through his mask. "Why haven't we met before?"

He smiled. "How do you know that we haven't?"

Her chuckle came easily. "Trust me. I would remember if we had. You're the type of man a woman couldn't easily forget."

"Hey, that's my line. You stole it," he said jokingly.

"I'll give it back to you if you take me away from here."

He didn't say anything for a minute but just sat there studying her face. And then he asked, "Are you sure you want to go off with me?"

She managed another smile. "Are you sure you want to take me?" she challenged.

Reggie couldn't help but laugh loudly, so loudly, in fact, that when he glanced across the room, his brother Jared caught his gaze and gave him a raised brow. He had five brothers in all. He and Jared were the only ones still living in Atlanta. He also had a bunch of cousins in the city. It seemed Westmorelands were everywhere, but he and Jared were the only ones who were here tonight. The rest had other engagements or were off traveling someplace.

A part of Reggie was grateful for that. He was the youngest of the Atlanta-based Westmorelands, and his brothers and cousins still liked to consider him the baby of the family, although he stood six-seven and was the tallest of the clan.

"Yes, I would take you in a heartbeat, sweetheart. I would take you anywhere you wanted to go."

And he meant it.

She nodded politely, but he knew she was thinking, trying to figure out a way she could go off with him and not take any careless risks with her safety. A woman couldn't be too trusting these days, and he understood that.

"I have an idea," he said finally, when she hadn't responded and several moments had passed.

"What?"

He reached into his jacket pocket and pulled out his cell phone. "Text someone you know and trust, and tell them to save my number. Tell them you will call them in the morning. When you call, they can erase the number."

Olivia thought about what he'd suggested and then wondered whom she could call. Any girlfriends she'd had while living here years ago were no longer around. Of course, she couldn't text her father, so she thought about her brothers. Duan was presently out of the city, since his job as a private investigator took him all over the country, and Terrence was living in the Florida Keys. She and her brothers were close, but it was Terrence who usually let her get away with things. Duan enjoyed playing the role of older brother. He would ask questions. Terrence would ask questions, too, but he was more easygoing.

Perhaps it was Duan's inquisitive mind that made him such a stickler for the rules. It had to be all those years he'd worked first as a patrolman and then as a detective for Atlanta's police department. Terrence, a former pro football player for the Miami Dolphins, knew how to have fun. He was actually the real swinging single Jeffries. He owned a nice club in the Florida Keys that really embodied the term *nightlife*.

Her safest bet would be to go with Terrence.

"Okay," she said, taking the phone. She sent Terrence a quick text message, asking that he delete the phone number from which the message was sent after hearing from her in the morning. She handed the phone back to him.

"Feel better about this?" he asked her.

She met his gaze. "Yes."

"Good. Is there any particular place you want to go?"

The safest location would be her place, Olivia thought, but she knew she couldn't do that. Her father was home, going over a campaign speech he would be giving at a luncheon on Monday. "No, but I haven't been out to Stone Mountain in a while."

He smiled. "Then Stone Mountain it is."

"And we'll need to go in separate cars," she said quickly. She had begun to feel nervous because she had never done anything like this in her life. What was she thinking? She got a quick answer when she met his gaze again. She was thinking how it would probably feel to be in this man's arms, to rub her hand across that strong, angular jaw, to taste those kissable lips and to breathe in more of his masculine scent.

"That's fine," he said in a husky voice. "You lead and I'll follow."

"And we keep on our masks and use these names," she said, pointing to her name badge.

He studied her intently for a moment before nodding his head. "All right."

She let out a silent breath. Her father was well-known in the city, and with the election just a couple of months away, she didn't want to do anything to jeopardize his chances of winning. Anything like having her name smeared in the paper in some scandal. Scandals were hard to live down, and she didn't want do anything that would be a nice addition to the *Atlanta Journal-Constitution*'s gossip column.

"Okay, let's go," she said, rising to her feet. She hoped she wasn't making a mistake, but when he accidentally brushed up against her when they headed for the exit, she had a feeling anything that happened between them tonight could only be right.

Reggie, as a rule, didn't do one-night stands. However, he would definitely make tonight and this woman an exception. The car he was following close behind was a rental, so that didn't give him any clues as to her identity. All he did know was that she was someone who wanted to enjoy tonight, and he was going to make sure she wasn't disappointed.

She'd indicated that she wanted to go someplace in Stone Mountain, and she was heading in that direction.

He wondered if they would go directly to a place where they could be alone, or if they would work up to that over a few drinks in a club. If she wanted a night on the town first, there were a number of nightclubs to choose from, but that would mean removing their masks, and he had a feeling she intended for these to stay in place. Why? Was she as well-known around the city as he was? At least after Monday he would be. Brent Fairgate, his campaign manager and the main person who had talked him into running for the Senate, had arranged for campaign posters with his picture to be plastered on just about every free space in Atlanta.

Returning his attention to the car in front of him, he braked when they came to a traffic light. Just then his cell phone rang. He worked it out of his pocket. "Hello?"

"Where are you?"

He gave a short laugh. "Don't worry about me, Jared. However, I do apologize for not letting you know I was leaving."

"That woman you were with earlier isn't here, either. Is that a coincidence?"

Reggie shook his head, grinning. "I don't know. You tell me."

There was a pause on the other end. "You sure about what you're doing, Reggie?"

"Positive. And no lectures please."

"Whatever," came his brother's gruff reply. And then the call was disconnected.

The traffic began moving again, and Reggie couldn't help but think about how his life would change once the campaigning began. There would be speeches to deliver, interviews to do, television appearances to make, babies to kiss and so on and so forth. He would be the first Westmoreland to enter politics, and for him, the decision hadn't been an easy one to make. But Atlanta was growing by leaps and bounds, and he wanted to give back to the city that had given him so much.

Unlike his brothers, who had left town to attend college, he had remained here and had gone to Morehouse. And he had never regretted doing so. He smiled, thinking that the good old days were when he got out of college and, a few years later, when he opened his own accounting firm. At the time, his best buddy had been his cousin Delaney. They were only a few months apart in age and had always been close. In fact, he was the one who had helped Delaney outsmart her five overprotective brothers right after she finished med school and needed to get some private time. He had let her use his cabin in the mountains for a little rest and relaxation, without telling Dare, Thorn, Stone, Chase or Storm where she was. Lucky for him, his cousins hadn't broken his bones, as they had threatened to do, when they discovered his involvement. The good thing was that Delaney had met her desert sheikh and fallen in love at his cabin.

Reggie's attention was pulled back to the car in front of him when Wonder Woman put on her blinker to turn into the parking lot of the luxurious Saxon Hotel. He smiled. He liked her taste, but given that they were wearing masks, he wondered how this would work. And then he got an idea and immediately pulled his cell phone out of his jacket pocket to punch in a few numbers.

"Hello?"

Reggie could hear babies crying in the background.

"This is Reggie. What are you doing to my nieces and nephew?"

He heard his brother Quade's laugh. "It's bath time, and nobody wants to play in the water tonight. What's up? And I understand congratulations are in order. Mom told me you've decided to run for the Senate. Good luck."

"Thanks." And then, without missing a beat, he said, "I need a favor, Quade."

"What kind of favor?"

"I need a private room at the Saxon Hotel here in Atlanta tonight, and I know Dominic Saxon is your brother-in-law."

"So?"

"So make it happen for me tonight, as soon as possible. And I need things kept discreet and billed to me."

There was a pause on the other end. "You sure about this, Reggie?"

He shook his head. It was the same question Jared had asked him moments ago. "Yes, Quade, I'm sure. And I don't expect any lectures from you, considering when and how my nieces and nephew were conceived."

"Go to hell, Reggie."

He smiled. "Not in front of the babies, Quade. And as far as going to hell, I'll go, but only after I get a night of heaven. So make it happen for me, Quade. I'll owe you. I'll even volunteer to fly in one day and babysit."

"Damn, she must be some woman."

Reggie thought about those lips he wanted so desperately to taste. "She is."

"I'll see what I can do." And then the call was disconnected.

Smiling and feeling pretty certain that Quade would

come through for him, he watched as Wonder Woman parked her car, and then eased his car into the parking spot next to hers. As soon as she turned off the engine, he got out of his car and glanced around, making sure there weren't a lot of people about. She had parked in an area that was pretty empty, and he was grateful for that.

When he got to her side of the car, she rolled down the window and looked a little flushed. "Sorry. I guess I didn't think this far ahead."

He bent down and leaned forward against her door and propped his arms on the car's window frame and smiled at her. She smelled good, and she looked good. His gaze shifted from her eyes to her lips and then back to her eyes again. He couldn't wait to taste her lips.

"Don't worry. Tonight will end the way we want," he said, with certainty in his voice and all the while thinking that if Quade didn't come through for him tonight, he was liable to kill him. At her confused expression, he said, "I've made a call, and it will only be a few moments. I'll get a call back when things get set up."

Olivia eyed the man staring at her and tried to ignore the stirring in the pit of her stomach. She couldn't help wondering just who was he and what kind of connections he had. They had to be big ones if he was able to get them a room at the Saxon from the parking lot. Would they have to do the normal check-in?

One part of her brain was screaming at her, telling her that what she was contemplating doing was downright foolish and irresponsible. No good girl, certainly not one who'd been raised to be a proper young lady, would think about having a one-night stand with a stranger.

But then the other part of her brain, the one that

was daring, as well as wild and reckless, urged her on. Go ahead, Libby. Have some fun. Live a little. You haven't been seriously involved with a man for almost two years. You've been too busy. You deserve some fun. What will it hurt as long as you've taken every precaution to make sure you're safe?

And at the moment she was safe. Terrence had this man's phone number, and the hotel was definitely a respectable one. And it was one she had selected, not him. But she had to admit, she felt a little silly with the two of them still wearing their masks. At least she had taken off her name badge.

"So, Wonder Woman, what's your favorite color?"

She couldn't help but smile. He evidently felt the tension and was making an attempt to ease it. "Lavender. What's yours?"

"Flesh tone."

She grinned. "Flesh tone isn't a color."

"Depends on who's wearing it," he said softly, and then his eyes flickered to her lips. She felt the intensity of his gaze just as if it was a soft caress. Suddenly, she felt the need to moisten her lips with her tongue.

"I wish you hadn't done that," he whispered huskily, leaning his body forward to the point where more of his face was in the window, just inches from her face.

A breathless sigh escaped from her lips. "What?" she asked in a strained voice.

"Tasted your own lips. That's what I want to do. What I'm dying to do."

"What's stopping you?"

Reggie thought that was a dare if ever he'd heard one. Deciding to take her up on it, he leaned his body in closer. She was tilting her head toward his face when suddenly his cell phone rang.

Damn. He reluctantly pulled back and pulled the cell phone from his jacket.

Olivia took that time to take a deep breath, and then she listened to his phone conversation.

"Yes?" he said into the phone.

She watched a huge smile brighten his face, and at the same time, she felt intense heat gather at the junction of her thighs.

"Thanks, man. I owe you one," he said. She then watched as he clicked off the phone and put it in his pocket. He glanced over at her. "Okay, Wonder Woman. Everything is set. We're on the sixteenth floor. Room sixteen thirty-two. Ready?"

She exhaled slowly. A part of her wanted to tell him that, no, she wasn't ready. She wanted to know how he'd arranged everything from a parking lot. Another part of her needed to know how he was capable of making her feel things that no other man had ever made her feel before. How was he able to get her to take risks when she was the least impulsive person that had ever lived? At least she had been risk averse until she'd seen him at the party tonight.

She met his gaze, knowing this would be it. Once she got out of the car and walked into that hotel with him, their night together would begin. Was that what she really wanted? He was staring at her, and his gaze seemed to be asking her that same question.

She drew in a deep breath and nodded her head and said, "Yes, I'm ready."

He then opened the car door for her. "You go on ahead, and I'll follow within five minutes. The bank of elevators you should use is the one to the right of the check-in desk," he said.

"Okay."

He watched as she placed the strap of her purse on her shoulder before walking away. He smiled as she gracefully crossed the parking lot and headed toward the entrance to the hotel. He couldn't help but admire the way she looked in her dress, a silky number that swished around her legs whenever she made a movement. And she had the legs for it. Long, shapely legs that he could imagine wrapped around him, holding him inside her body during the heat of passion.

He was so into his thoughts that when she suddenly stopped walking, his heart nearly stopped beating. Had she changed her mind? Moments later he gave a deep sigh of relief when he realized she had stopped to remove her mask. He wondered if she would take the risk and turn around to let him see her face, voluntarily revealing her identity. He got his answer when she began walking again without looking back. He had a feeling that that was how the entire night would go. Identities and names would not be shared. Only passion.

He would respect her wishes, and when he joined her in the hotel room, his mask, too, would be back in place.

There was no doubt in his mind that this would be a night he would always remember.

Chapter 2

Olivia was grateful that no one seemed to pay her any attention when she walked into the huge lobby of the Saxon. It had always been her dream to spend a night in what had to be one of the most elegant hotels ever built. It was more stylish and extravagant than she had expected. There were only a few Saxons scattered about the country, in the major cities, and all had a reputation of providing top-quality service.

When she stepped onto the elevator that would carry her to the sixteenth floor, she couldn't help but again wonder about the man behind the mask and the connections he seemed to have. Reservations were hard to get because the hotel was booked far in advance, even as much as a year.

As she stepped out of the elevator and walked down the spacious hall, she studied the decor. Everything had a touch of elegance and class. With an artist's eye, she absorbed every fine detail of not only the rich and luxurious-looking carpet on the floor but also of the beautiful framed portraits that lined the walls. She would bet a month of her salary at the Louvre that those were original Audubon prints. If they devoted this much time and attention to the hallways, she could only imagine what one of the rooms would look like.

She wondered what Jack Sprat thought of her taste, since she was the one who'd guided him here. Of course, she would pay tonight's bill, since coming here was her idea. Connections or no connections, this place was her choice and not his, so it would only be fair. The last thing she wanted to do was come off as a thoughtless, high-maintenance woman.

Moments later she stood in front of room 1632. She didn't have a key and could only assume the door was unlocked. There was only one way to find out. She turned the handle and smiled when it gave way without a problem. She slowly opened the door and stepped into the room. Quickly closing the door, she glanced around, her eyes widening. This had to be a penthouse suite. She hadn't expected this, wasn't even sure she would be able to pay for it. She had figured on a regular room, which, though costly, would have been within her budget.

She was paid well, and loved Paris, but eventually she intended to return to the United States. She planned to open an art gallery in a few years, and that took money. Every penny she earned went into her special savings. Her father and brothers had promised to invest in the venture, but she felt that it was her responsibility to come up with the majority of the capital for her gallery. This little tryst was going to cost her. She would have to dip into her savings to pay for this suite. She wondered if just one night with a stranger could possibly be worth the sacrifice.

She crossed the room, drawn to the stately furnishings. She had stayed in nice hotels before, but there was something about a Saxon that took your breath away. Besides the elegant luxury that surrounded you, there was also the personalized service, culinary excellence and other amenities, which she had often heard about, but had yet to experience.

She walked through the sitting area to the bedroom. Her gaze moved from the plush love seat in the room to the bed. The bed was humongous and stately; the covering was soft to the touch. It felt as if you could actually lose yourself under it. The bedcoverings and curtains were done in an elegant red and a single red rose had been placed in the middle of the bed. Very romantic.

The connecting bath was just as stunning, with a huge Jacuzzi tub that sat in the middle of the floor, surrounded by a wall-to-wall vanity the likes of which she'd never seen in a hotel. Everything was his and hers, and the bathroom was roomy, spacious.

Nervously, she walked out of the bathroom and back into the bedroom and sat down on the edge of the bed.

When she was growing up, people had often said she was spoiled and pampered, and in a way, she had been. Being the only girl in the house had had its advantages. She had been only three years old when her mother left her father, ran off with a married man and destroyed not one, but two families. She would always admire her father for doing what had to be done to hold their family together. He'd worked long and hard hours as a corporate attorney and still had been there for her piano recitals and art shows and her brothers' Little League games. And one year he had even gotten elected president of the PTA. It hadn't been easy, and everyone had had to pitch in and help. And she could now admit that her brothers had made it easier for her.

Leaving home for college had been good for her. Against her father's and brothers' wishes, she had worked her way through college, refusing the money they would send her. She'd needed to encounter the real world and sink or swim on her own while doing so.

She'd learned how to swim.

She glanced at her watch. Chances were that Jack Sprat was on his way up, so now was not the time to get nervous. She had come on to him at the party, and he had come on to her. They were here because a night together was what they both wanted. So why was she thinking about hightailing it all of a sudden? Why were butterflies flying around her stomach? And what was with the darn goose bumps covering her arms?

She stood and began pacing. He would be here at any moment, so she stopped and took the time to put her mask back on. In a way she felt silly, but at the same time mysterious.

Olivia glanced at her watch again. She felt her body heating up just thinking about what would happen when he did arrive. To say she was fascinated by a complete stranger would be an understatement. If anyone had told her that within less than forty-eight hours of returning to Atlanta, she, Olivia Jeffries, would be involved in an affair to nowhere, she would not have believed them. Usually she was very conservative, but not tonight.

She caught her breath when she thought she heard

footsteps coming down the hall. An anticipatory shiver ran down her spine, and she knew that in just a minute he would be there.

Reggie walked down the hallway, deep in thought. Some people engaged in casual affairs to pass the time or to feel needed. He was not one of them, and for some reason, he knew that the woman waiting on him in the hotel room wasn't, either. He would admit that there had been a few one-night stands in his history, back in the day at Morehouse, when he hadn't had a care in the world other than studying, making the grade and getting an easy lay. But now as a professional who owned a very prestigious accounting firm and as a political candidate, he picked his bed partners carefully. He hadn't been involved in any long-term affairs since right after college—and that disastrous time with Kayla Martin a few years ago, which he preferred to forget. He'd pretty much stuck to short-term affairs.

His family constantly reminded him he was the last Westmoreland bachelor living in Atlanta, but that was fine with him. Settling down and getting married were the furthest things from his mind. He was glad it wouldn't be an issue in his campaign, because his opponent, Orin Jeffries, was a long-term divorcé, and from what he'd heard, the man had no plans of ever remarrying.

Finally, he stood in front of room 1632. Only pausing for a brief second, he reached out to open the door and then stopped when he remembered his mask. Glancing up and down the hall to make sure it was empty, he pulled the mask out of his pocket and put it on. Then, after drawing a deep breath, he opened the door.

* * *

The moment he opened the door, his eyes, that is, the portion of them that Olivia could see through his mask, met hers. They felt possessive, as if he was stamping ownership on her, when there was no way he could do that. He didn't know her true identity. He knew nothing about her other than that it seemed her need for him was just as elemental and strong as his need for her. It was a tangible thing, and she could feel it, all the way to her toes.

Yet there was something in the way he entered the room, not taking his eyes off her as he pushed the door closed behind him. And then giving the room only a cursory glance. Without a single word spoken between them, he swiftly crossed the room and drew her into his arms.

And kissed her.

There was nothing to be gained by any further talking, and they both knew it. And the moment his mouth touched hers, lightly at first, before devouring it with a hunger she felt deep in her belly, she moaned a silent acceptance of him and their night together.

This was sexual chemistry at its most potent. He was all passion, and she responded in kind. She kissed him, not with the same skill and experience he was leveling on her, but with a hunger that needed to be appeased, satisfied and explored.

The kiss intensified, and they both knew it wouldn't be enough to quench the desire waiting to be unleashed within them. Sensations were spreading through her, seeping deep into her bones and her senses. Urges that she had tried desperately to control were now threatening to consume her.

He reluctantly pulled his mouth away, and she watched as a sensuous smile touched his lips. "Tonight is worth everything," he whispered softly against her moist lips. "Not in my wildest imagination would I have thought of this happening."

Neither would I, Olivia thought. The masks were silly, but they had a profound purpose. So were the pretend names. With them, they were free to do what they pleased, without inhibitions or thought of consequences. If their paths were to cross again, after tonight, there would be no recognition, no recrimination and no need for denials. What happened in this hotel room tonight would stay in this hotel room tonight.

Reggie's gaze studied Olivia as he fought to catch his breath while doing the same for his senses. Kissing her, tasting her lips, had been like an obsession since the moment he'd laid eyes on her. The shape, texture and outline of her lips had a provocative effect on him. Some men were into the shape and size of a woman's breasts; others into her backside. He was definitely a lips man. The fullness of a pair, covered in lipstick or not, could induce a state of arousal in him. Just thinking of all the things he could do with them was enough to push him over the edge.

And then, losing control, he leaned down and kissed her again, and while his tongue dominated and played havoc with hers, he felt her loosen up, begin to relax in his arms. She wrapped her arms around his neck while her feminine curves so effortlessly pressed against him in a seamless melding of bodies. They fit together perfectly, naturally. There was nothing like having soft female limbs and a beautiful set of lips within reach, he thought.

The hand around her waist dipped, and he felt the curve of her backside through the gown she was wearing. A firm yet soft behind. He needed to get her out of her gown.

Pulling his mouth away, he swept her into his arms. At her startled gasp and with a swift glance, he met the eyes staring at him through the mask, and then his lips eased into a smile. So did hers. And with nothing left to be said, he walked to the bedroom.

Instead of placing her on the bed, he held her firmly in his arms and sat down on the love seat, adjusting her in his lap. She pulled in a deep breath and caught hold of the front of his jacket.

He smiled down at her. "Trust me. I'm not going to let you fall." She loosened her hold on him yet continued looking into his eyes, studying his features so intently that he couldn't help asking, "Like the part you can see?"

She smiled. "Yes. You have such an angular jaw. It speaks of strength and honesty. It also speaks of determination."

He raised a brow, wondering how Wonder Woman could tell those things about him from just studying his jaw. He stopped wondering when she reached out and her finger traced that same jaw that seemed to fascinate her.

"It's rigid, but not overbearing. Firm, but not domineering." She then smiled. "Yet I do see a few arrogant lines," she said, tapping the center of his jaw.

He had sat down with her in his arms, instead of placing her on the bed, so as not to rush things with her, to give her time to collect herself after their kisses. He refused to rush their lovemaking. For some reason, he wanted more, felt they deserved more. He was never one for small talk, but he figured he would take a stab at it. But now her touch was making it almost impossible not to touch. Not to undress her and give her the pleasure they both wanted. And then it came to him that the reason he was here with her had nothing to do with lust. He'd gone months without a woman warming his bed before. What was driving him more than anything was her appeal, her sexiness and his desire to mate with her in an intimate way. Only her.

He stood while cradling her tightly in his arms and moved toward the bed and gently placed her in the middle of it, handed her the rose and then he took a step back so she could be in the center of his vision. He wanted the full view of her.

Her shoulder-length hair was tousled around her face, at least the part of her face he could see. Her dress had risen when he'd placed her on the bed. She had to know it was in disarray and showing a great deal of flesh, but she didn't make a move to pull anything down, and he had no intention of suggesting she do so. So he looked, got his fill, saw the firmness of her thighs and the shapeliness of her knees. And he couldn't help but notice how the front of the dress was cut low, showing the top portion of her full and firm breasts. He was a lips man first and a breasts man second. As far as he was concerned, he had hit the jackpot.

Olivia wondered how long he would stand there and stare. But in a way, it reassured her that he liked what he saw. No man had taken the time to analyze her this way. She might as well make it worth his while. She placed the rose to one side and reached down and unclasped her shoes before slipping them off her feet. She tossed one and then the other to him. He caught them perfectly, and instead of dropping them to the floor, he tossed them onto the love seat they had just vacated.

She was surprised. He had recognized a pair of stilettos by Zanotti. They had been another whim of hers. Shoes were her passion, and she appreciated a man who knew quality and fine workmanship in a woman's shoes when he saw it. He moved up another notch in her book.

Now it was time to take off the rest. Because she never wore panties with panty hose, that would be easy. Instead of removing her panty hose last, she decided to take them off first. He wouldn't be expecting it, and the thought of catching him off guard stirred something inside of her. With his eyes still on her, she lifted her bottom off the bed slightly to ease down her panty hose, deliberately giving him a flash to let him know that once they were gone, there would not be any covering left. After she'd removed them, she rolled the hose up in a ball and tossed them to him. As with her shoes, he made a perfect catch, and then, while she watched him, he brought the balled-up nylon to his nose and took a whiff of her scent before placing it in the pocket of his jacket.

Her gaze had followed his hands, and now it moved back to his face. She saw the flaring of his nostrils and the tightening of his fists by his sides, and she saw something else. Something she had noted earlier, when he had walked across the room to her, but that now had grown larger. His erection. There was no doubt in her mind, unclothed and properly revealed, it would put Michelangelo's *David* to shame. Her artistic eye could even make out the shape of it through his pants. It was huge, totally developed, long and thick. And at the moment, totally aroused. That was evident by the way the erection was straining against the fly of his pants.

He shifted his stance. Evidently, he'd seen where her gaze had traveled, and she watched as his fingers went to the zipper of his tuxedo pants and slowly eased it down. She could only stare when, after bending to remove his shoes and socks, he stepped out of his pants, leaving his lower body clad only in a pair of sexy black briefs. She knew they were a designer pair; their shape, fit and support said it all. The man had thighs that were firm, hard and muscular. She didn't have to see his buns to know they were probably as tight as the rest of him. There was no need to ask if he worked out on occasion. The physical fitness of his body said it all.

And he looked sexy standing there, with a tux jacket and white shirt on top and a pair of sexy briefs covering his lower half. She figured he had decided to remove the clothes from the same part of his anatomy as she had. They were both undressing from the bottom up.

She held her breath, literally stopped breathing, when his hands then went to the waistband of his briefs. And while her gaze was glued to him, he slowly pulled the briefs down his legs.

Damn.

The man, thankfully, had no qualms about exposing himself, and for that she was grateful, because what her eyes were feasting on was definitely worth seeing. He was truly a work of art. And while her focus was contained, he went about removing the rest of his clothes. She wasn't aware of it until he stood before her, totally naked in all his glorious form.

Her gaze traveled the full length of his body once, twice, a total of three times before coming back to settle on his face. He was a naked, masked man, and she would love to have him pose for her as such. On canvas she would capture each and every detail of him. He was pure, one hundred percent male.

"It's your turn to take off the rest of your clothes, Wonder."

His words, deep and husky, floated around the already sexually charged room.

She forced her gaze from his thick shaft and moved it to his face as, on her knees, she reached behind herself and undid the hooks of her dress before pulling it over her head. It was simple, and she was naked, since she hadn't worn a bra.

Now he saw it all. And like she had earlier, his gaze moved to her lower part, zeroing in on the junction of her thighs. Suddenly she felt awkward. She wondered what he was thinking. She kept her body in great shape, and her Brazilian wax was obvious.

She met his gaze when he returned it to her face. She smiled. "I'm done."

"No, baby," he said in a tight and strained voice. "You haven't even got started."

Reggie pulled in a deep breath, meaning every word he'd just spoken. Never in his life had he been so hard and hot for a woman. Never had he wanted to eat one alive. As far as he was concerned, there would not be enough time tonight to do everything he wanted to do. So there was none to be wasted. But first...

"Is there anything you have an aversion to doing?" he felt the need to ask.

He watched how she lifted her gaze a moment, and then she said in a soft voice, "Yes. I'm not into bondage."

He chuckled. "Then it's a good thing I left my handcuffs at home." And because he saw the slight widening of her eyes, he smiled and said, "Hey, I'm just teasing. I would be crazy to tie your hands since I prefer you putting them all over me."

As far as Olivia was concerned, that was the perfect invitation. She scooted close to the edge of the bed and reached out and splayed her hands across his chest. She smiled when she heard his sharp intake of breath. And she was fascinated by the way his muscles flexed beneath her hands and by the warmth of his skin beneath her fingers.

"You're into torture?" he asked huskily, his tone sounding somewhat strained.

"Why? Do you feel like you're being tortured?" she asked innocently, shifting one of her hands lower to his stomach.

"Yes." His answer was short and precise. His breathing seemingly impaired.

"You haven't seen anything yet, Jack Sprat."

And then her hand dropped to that part of him she'd become fascinated with from the moment she'd seen it. It was large, heavy and, for tonight, it was hers. Her hand closed up, contracted and then closed up again, liking the feel of holding it, stroking it.

Breathing at full capacity, Reggie could no longer handle what his mystery woman was doing to him and pulled back and reached down for his pants to retrieve a condom packet from his wallet. Ripping the packet with his teeth, he proceeded to put the condom on.

He glanced up to see her lying back on the bed, smiling at him, fully aware of the state she'd pushed him to. He moved so quickly, it caught her off guard, and then he was there with her in the bed, pinning her beneath him on the coverlet and immediately taking her mouth captive, devouring it like he intended to devour her. And when he pulled back, he moved down to her breasts, taking the nipples in his mouth, doing all kinds of things to them with his tongue until she cried out. She pleaded with him to stop, because she couldn't take any more.

But he definitely wasn't through with her yet. Intent on proving that she wasn't the only one with hands that could torture, he used his knee to spread her legs. He then settled between them, determined to fit his erection in the place where it was supposed to be.

There was so much more he wanted to do—devour her breasts, lick her skin all over—but at that moment, the one thing he had to do before his brain exploded with need was get inside of her.

He pulled his mouth away from her breasts, and breathing hard, he stared down at her, determined to see what he could of her eyes through the mask. "This is crazy," he said, almost choking for both breath and control of the words.

"Might be," she said, just as short of breath. "But it's the best craziness I've ever experienced. Let's not stop now."

He stared at her. "You sure?"

She stared back. "Positive."

And with their gazes locked, he entered her.

He felt her small spasms before he even got into the hilt, and when her inner muscles clenched him, he pressed deeper inside of her. She was tight, but he could feel her opening wider for him, like a bloom. "That's it. Relax, let go and let me in," he said.

And as if her body was his to command, it continued to open, adjust, until it was a perfect fit and curved around him like a glove. And at that moment, while buried deep inside of her, he just had to taste her lips again. He leaned forward, took her mouth and began swallowing every deep, wrenching moan that she made.

And then he began moving back and forth inside of her, thrusting, then retreating, then repeating the process all over again, each thrust aimed with perfect accuracy at her erogenous zone. He lifted her hips, and she dug her fingertips deep into his shoulders and cried out with each stroke he took.

It was at that moment that he actually felt her body explode. Then the sensations that had rippled through her slammed through him as well. He threw his head back; and he felt the muscles in his neck pop; and he breathed in deep, pulling in her scent, which filled the air.

Shudders rammed through him, and he squeezed his eyes shut as his body exploded. His orgasm came with the force of a tidal wave, and he continued to thrust inside her as his groans mingled with her cries of pleasure. And with their bodies fully engaged, their minds unerringly connected, together they left Earth and soared into the clouds as unadulterated pleasure consumed them.

"I need to leave," she said softly.

Reggie turned his head on the pillow and looked over at Wonder. He doubted he could move. He could barely breathe. It was close to morning. They'd made love all night long. As soon as they had ended one session, they'd been quick and eager to start another.

He knew she had to leave. So did he. But he didn't want their one and only night together to end. "You do know there is no reason why we can't—"

She quickly turned toward him and placed a finger

on his lips. "Yes, there is. I can't tell you my true identity. It could hurt someone."

He frowned. She wasn't wearing a ring, so quite
naturally, he had assumed she wasn't married. What
if she...

As if reading his mind, she said, "I don't have a husband. I don't even have a boyfriend."

"Then who?" he asked quickly, trying to understand
why they couldn't bring their masquerade to an end. He
probably had more to lose than she, because his campaign for the Senate officially began Monday.

"I can't say. This has to be goodbye—"

Before the words were completely out of her mouth,
he reached out and pulled her into his arms, knowing
this would be the last time he would kiss the lips he had
grown so attached to.

Moments later he released her mouth, refusing to
say goodbye. She wiggled out of his arms and began
re-dressing. He watched her do so, getting turned on
all over again.

"I'm getting money out of the ATM to pay for the
room," she informed him.

He frowned at her words. "No, you're not."

"I must. It was my idea for us to come here," she said.

"Doesn't matter. Everything has been taken care of,
so they won't take any money from you at the front
desk. Last night is on me, and I don't regret one minute of spending it with you."

Olivia slipped back into her shoes and gazed across
the room at him. He was lying in bed, on top of the
covers. Naked. So immensely male. "And I don't regret anything, either," she said, meaning every word.
She was tempted to do as he wanted—cross the room,

remove his mask and remove hers as well—but she couldn't. She couldn't even trust herself to kiss him goodbye. It had to be a clean break for both of them. "And you sure you don't want me to pay for the room?" she asked.

"Yes, I'm sure."

"At least let me give you something toward it and—"

"No," he said, declining her offer.

She didn't know how much time passed while they just stared at each other. But she knew she had to leave. "I have to go now," she said, as if convincing herself of that.

He shifted on the bed to take the rose, and offered it to her. She closed the short distance between them to retrieve it. "At least let me walk you to the door," he said.

She shook her head. "No. I'll see myself out."

And then she quickly walked out of the bedroom.

Reggie pulled himself up in the bed when he heard the sound of the hotel door closing. He sat on the edge of the bed, suddenly feeling a sense of loss that touched his very soul and not understanding how such a thing was possible.

He stood up to put on his clothes, and it was then that he snatched off the mask. It had served its purpose. He reached for his shirt and tie and noticed something glittering on the carpet. He reached down and picked it up. It was one of the diamond earrings that she had been wearing.

He folded the earring in the palm of his hand. He knew at that very moment that if he had to turn Atlanta upside down, he would find his Wonder Woman.

He would find her, and he would keep her.

Chapter 3

"So, Libby, how was the party?"

Olivia, who had been so entrenched in the memories of the night before, hadn't noticed her father standing at the bottom of the stairs. She glanced down at him and smiled. "It was simply wonderful." He didn't need to know that she was speaking not of the party per se but of the intimate party she'd gone to at the Saxon Hotel, with her mystery man.

It had been just before six in the morning when she slipped into her father's home, and knowing he was an early riser, she had dashed up the stairs and showered. She had also put in a call to Terrence, leaving a message on his cell phone that it was okay to delete the text message she had sent to him the night before. And then she had climbed into bed. By the time her head had hit the pillow in her own bed, she had heard her father moving around.

best sleep in years. She had
...tomach, and the last person
...when she took the stairs to
...chen was her father. Typically,
...g church services on Sunday, he hit
...lub with his buddies for a game of golf.
...was he still here?

...rin met his daughter on the bottom stair and gave
her a hug. "I'm glad you enjoyed yourself. I felt kind
of bad that I couldn't attend the ball with you, but I did
have to work on that speech."

She looked up at him and, not for the first time,
thought that he was definitely a good-looking man, and
she was glad he took care of himself by eating right and
staying active. "No problem, Dad."

Not wanting him to ask for details about the party,
she quickly asked a question of her own. "So why are
you home and not out on the golf course?"

He smiled as he tucked her arm in his and escorted
her to the kitchen. "Cathy threatened me with dire consequences today if I left before she got the chance to
come over and go over my speech."

Olivia smiled but didn't say anything for a moment.
Cathy Bristol had been her father's private secretary
for almost fifteen years, and Olivia couldn't help but
wonder when her father would wake up and realize
the woman was in love with him. Olivia had figured
it out when she was in her teens, and when she'd gotten older had asked her brothers about it. Like her dad,
they'd been clueless. But at least Duan and Terrence had
opened their eyes even if her father hadn't. Cathy was
a forty-eight-year-old widow who had lost her husband

over eighteen years ago, when he died in a car a
leaving her with two sons to raise.

"So when is Cathy coming? I'd love to see her.

Her father smiled. "Around noon. I'm treating he.
lunch here first before I put her to work."

"To review your speech?"

"Yes," he said when they reached the kitchen and he
sat down at the table. "She's good at editing things and
giving her opinion. As this is my first speech, I want
to impress those who hear it. It will be one of those fo-
rums in which all the candidates speak."

Olivia nodded as she grabbed an apple out of the
fruit bowl on the table and sat down across from him.

Orin frowned. "Surely that's not all you're having
for breakfast."

"Afraid so," she said before biting into her apple.

"You're so thin," he pointed out. "You should eat more."

Olivia could only smile. There was no way she could
tell her father that she had eaten quite a lot last night.
After making love several times, they had ordered room
service, eaten until their stomachs were full and then
gone back to bed to make love some more.

Deciding to get her father off the subject of her
weight, she said, "So, tell me something about this guy
who has the audacity to run against my father."

Orin leaned back in his chair. "He's one of those Westmorelands. Prominent family here in Atlanta. He's young,
in his early thirties, and owns an accounting firm."

Olivia nodded. She recalled the name, and if she
wasn't mistaken, Duan and Terrence had gone to school
with some of them. They were a huge family. "So what's
his platform? How do the two of you differ?"

"On a number of issues, we're in agreement. The

main thing we differ on is whether or not Georgia can support another state-financed university. He thinks we can, and I don't. We have a number of fine colleges and universities in this area. Why on earth would we need another one? Besides, he's inexperienced."

Olivia couldn't help but smile at that, because her father didn't have any political experience, either. In fact, she and her brothers had been shocked when he'd announced he was running for a political office. The only thing they could come up with as to the reason was that his good friend and golfing buddy Senator Albert Reed was retiring and wanted someone to replace him whom he knew and could possibly influence. Not that her father was easily influenced, but he was known to give in under a good argument, without fully standing his ground.

"And young Westmoreland will run on his name recognition since he has a couple of celebrities in the family. One of his cousins is a motorcycle racer, and another is an author."

And your son just happens to be a very well-known former NFL player, she wanted to say. Who you have called upon to appear at a couple of rallies. So you are just as bad.

Olivia said nothing but listened as she took another bite of her apple. At least she tried to listen. More than once her mind took a sharp turn, and she found her thoughts drifting to breath-stopping memories of the tall, dark and handsome man she had met and spent a wonderful night with. She could vividly recall his kisses and the way he had been methodically slow and extremely thorough each time he'd taken her mouth in his, eating away at her lips, unrestrained, unhurried and not distracted.

And there were the times his mouth had touched her

everywhere, blazing a trail from her nape to her spine, then all over her chest, tasting her nipples and making her intensely aware of all her hidden passion—passion he'd been able to wrench from her.

The only bad thing about last night was the fact that she had lost one of the diamond earrings she had purchased a year ago in Paris. The earrings had been a gift to herself when she landed her dream job. She would love to get it back, but knew that wouldn't be happening. But she would be the first to admit that the night spent in her one-time lover's arms had been worth the loss.

The ringing of the doorbell claimed her attention and brought her back to the present.

"That must be Cathy," Orin said. He quickly rose from the table and headed to the front door.

Olivia studied her father and couldn't do anything but shake her head. He seemed awfully excited about Cathy's arrival. Olivia couldn't help wondering if perhaps her father had finally awakened and smelled the coffee and just wasn't aware he'd been sniffing the aroma. She had been around her brothers long enough to know that when it came to matters of the heart, men had a tendency to be slow.

She turned in her seat when she heard a feminine voice, Cathy's voice. Olivia smiled when she saw the one woman she felt would be good for her father and again wondered why her father hadn't asked Cathy to be his escort for some of these functions. Cathy was very pretty, and Olivia thought, as she glanced at the two of them walking into the kitchen, that they complemented each other well.

Brent Fairgate waved his hand back and forth in front of Reggie's face. "Hey, man, are you with us, or are you somewhere in la-la land?"

Reggie blinked, and then his gaze focused on the man standing in front of him, before shifting to the woman standing beside him, Pam Wells. Brent had hired Pam as a strategist on a consulting basis.

"Sorry," he said, since there was no use denying they hadn't had his attention. "My mind drifted elsewhere for a moment." There was no way he was going to tell Brent that he was reliving the memories of the prior night. Brent was the most focused man that Reggie knew. Reggie was well aware that Brent wanted him to be just as focused.

"Okay. Then let's go back over the layout for tomorrow," Brent said, handing him a folder filled with papers. "The luncheon is at the Civic Center, and both you and Jeffries will be speaking. The order will be determined by a flip of a coin. You got the speech down pat. Just make sure you turn on your charm. Jeffries will be doing likewise. Without coming right out and saying it, you will have to make everyone see you as the voice of change. You will have to portray Jeffries as more of the same, someone who represents the status quo."

"Okay. Give me some personal info on Jeffries, other than he's the Holy Terror's father," Reggie said.

Early in his professional football career, Terrence Jeffries had been nicknamed the "Holy Terror" by sportscasters. Reggie understood that Terrence was now a very successful businessman living in the Florida Keys.

"He also has another son, who's a couple years older than the Holy Terror," Pam replied. "He used to be on the Atlanta police force, but now he owns a private investigation company. He's low-key and definitely not in the public eye like Terrence."

Reggie nodded. "That's it? Two sons?"

Pam shook her head. "There's also a daughter, the youngest. She's twenty-seven. An artist who lives in Paris. I understand she's returned home for the campaign."

Reggie lifted a brow. "Why?"

Pam smiled. "To act as her father's escort for all the fund-raisers he'll be expected to attend. From what I understand, he hasn't dated a lot since his wife up and left him."

Reggie frowned. "And when was that?"

"Over twenty-something years ago. He raised his kids as a single father," said Pam.

Reggie nodded, immediately admiring the man for taking on such a task. He was blessed to have both of his parents still living and still married to each other. He couldn't imagine otherwise. He had heard his siblings and cousins talk about the hard work that went into parenting, so he admired any person who did it solo.

"As you know, Orin Jeffries is a corporate attorney at Nettleton Industries. He's worked for them for over thirty years. And he's almost twenty-five years older than you. He'll likely flaunt the age difference and his greater experience," Brent added.

Reggie smiled. "I'm sure that he will."

"Do you need me to look over your speech for tomorrow?" Brent asked.

Reggie met his friend's gaze. "I haven't written it yet." Concern touched Brent's features, and not for the first time, Reggie thought his best friend worried too much.

"But I thought you were going to do it last night, right after you came home from the Firemen's Masquerade Ball," Brent said.

Reggie sighed. There was no way he was going to

mention that he hadn't made it home from the ball until this morning, because he had made a pit stop at the Saxon Hotel. Actually, it had been more than a pit stop. The word *quickie* in no way described what he and Wonder Woman had done practically all through the night. They had refused to be rushed.

Before Brent could chew him out, Reggie said, "I'll do it as soon as the two of you leave. If you want to drop by later and look it over, then feel free to do so."

A stern look appeared on Brent's face. "And don't think that I won't."

Reggie rolled his eyes. "Just don't return before six this evening."

Brent raised a brow. "Why?"

"Because I need to take a nap."

Brent chuckled. "You never take naps."

Determined not to explain anything, Reggie said, "I know, but today I definitely need one."

As soon as Pam and Brent left, Reggie called and checked in with his parents. Usually on Sunday he would drop by for dinner, and he didn't want his mother to worry when he didn't make an appearance.

After convincing Sarah Westmoreland that he was not coming down with a flu bug and that he just needed to rest, he was ready to end the call, but she kept him on the phone longer than he'd planned to give him a soup recipe…like he would actually take the time to make it. Not that she figured he would. She was just hoping he had a lady friend available to do his bidding.

He couldn't help but smile as he climbed the stairs to his bedroom. His mother's one wish in life was to live to see her six sons all married and herself and his father surrounded by grandchildren. A bout with breast cancer a few years ago had made her even more determined to see each one of her sons happily married.

Her dream had come true—almost. Jared's recent announcement that he and his wife, Dana, would become parents in the fall meant that all of James and Sarah Westmoreland's sons—with the exception of him— were married and either had kids or were expecting them. Quade had blown everyone away with his triplets. But then multiple births ran in the Westmoreland family.

When he reached his bedroom, he began stripping off his clothes, remembering when he had stripped for an audience of one the night before. He had been aware that Wonder Woman's eyes had been directed on him while he'd taken off each piece...the same way his eyes had been on her.

As he slid between the covers, he promised himself that once he woke up, he would have slept off the memories and would be focused on the present again. That morning he'd thought about trying to find his mystery woman, and he still intended to do that, but he owed it to Brent and his campaign staff to stay focused and put all his time and energy into winning this election.

But still...

He thought about the lone earring he had in his dresser drawer. On the way into the office, he would stop by Jared's favorite jewelry store, Garbella Jewelers, to see if they could possibly tell him anything about the earring, like who had made it and, possibly, from which store it had been purchased. Checking on something like that shouldn't take too long and wouldn't make him lose focus.

As he felt himself drifting off to sleep, his mind was

flooded with more memories. He wondered how long this fascination, this mind-reeling, gut-wrenching obsession with his mystery woman, would last.

He wasn't sure, but he intended to enjoy it while it did.

Olivia sat in the chair across the room, and her observant eye zeroed in on her father and Cathy. She tried not to chuckle when she noticed how they would look at each other when the other one wasn't watching. Boy, they had it bad, but in a way, she was glad. Sooner or later, her father would realize that Cathy was the best thing to ever happen to him. Even now, after working as his secretary for over fifteen years, their relationship was still professional. She knew in time that would change, and she would do her part to help it along.

"Dad?"

Orin looked up from his seat behind his desk and glanced over at her. Cathy was standing next to his chair. They'd had their heads together while Cathy critiqued his speech. "Yes, sweetheart?"

"Why did you send for me to be your escort for all these fund-raising events when you had Cathy right here?"

As if on cue, Cathy blushed, and her father's jaw dropped as if he was surprised she would ask something like that. Before he could pick up his jaw to respond, Cathy spoke, stammering through her explanation.

"Th-there's no way Orin can do something like that. I'm his secretary."

Olivia smiled. "Oh." What she was tempted to say was that secretary or no secretary, Cathy was also the woman her father couldn't keep his eyes off. She couldn't wait until she talked to Duan and Terrence.

And then, as if by luck or fate, since it also seemed

to be on cue, her cell phone rang, and when she stood and pulled it out of her back jeans pocket, she saw the call was from Terrence.

Knowing it was best to take the call privately, she said, "Excuse me a moment while I take this." She quickly walked out of the room and closed the office door behind her.

"Yes, Terrence?"

"What the hell is going on with you, Libby? Why did you text me from an unknown number and then call this morning and ask that the text be deleted?"

Olivia nervously licked her lips. One thing about Terrence was that he would ask questions, but if she gave him a reason that sounded remotely plausible, he would let it go, whereas Duan would continue to ask questions.

"Last night I went to this charity party in Dad's place and met a guy. He asked me to follow him to a nightclub in Stone Mountain, and I did, but I felt I should take precautions."

"That was a good idea. Smart girl. So how was the club?"

"Umm, nice, but it didn't compare to Club Hurricane," she said, knowing he would like to hear that she thought the nightclub he owned in the Keys was at the top of the list.

"You're even smarter than I thought. So how's Dad? He hasn't dropped out of this Senate race yet?"

Olivia smiled. Terrence and Duan were taking bets that sooner or later, when Orin Jeffries got a taste of what real politics were like, he would call it quits. At first she had agreed with them, but now she wasn't so sure. "I don't know, Terrence. I think he's going all the way with this one."

"Umm, that's interesting. I still think Reed pushed Dad into running for his own benefit. I'm going to give Duan a call. We might need to talk to Dad about this."

"You might be too late. The first forum is tomorrow, and he's giving a speech. He's been working on it for two days. The only good thing coming out of all this is that he and Cathy are working together," she said.

"Libby, they always work closely together. She's his secretary."

"Yes, but they are working closely together in a different way, on issues other than Nettleton Industries business. In fact, she's over here now."

She could hear her brother chuckle. "Still determined to play Cupid, are you?"

"I might as well while I'm here, since I have nothing else to do." She thought of Jack Sprat. She had been tempted earlier to pull out her art pad and do some sketches to pass the time. She had thought about drawing her mystery man with the mask and then playing around to see if she could draw sketches of how she imagined he might look without the mask. She had eventually talked herself out of it.

"Well, I'll be coming home in a couple of weeks, so stay out of trouble until then, sport."

She laughed. "I can't make you any promises, but I'll try."

Chapter 4

Brent had given his speech a thumbs-up, so Reggie felt confident it would go over well. He walked around the luncheon reception, greeting all those who had arrived to attend the forum. This would be the first of several gatherings designed to give voters a chance to learn each candidate's agenda. He had met Orin Jeffries when he'd first arrived and thought the older man was a likable guy.

A number of his family members were present and a number of his friends as well. These were people who believed in him, supported him and were counting on him to make changes to some of the present policies.

A career in politics had been the last thing on his mind and had never been his heart's desire, until recently. He'd become outraged at the present senators' refusal to recognize the state's need for an additional college. More and more young people were making the decision to acquire higher learning, and the lower tuition costs of state universities compared to private universities were a key factor in the process. It was hard enough for students to get the funds they needed to go to college, but when they were refused entrance into schools because of campus overcrowding, that was unacceptable. Anyone who wanted a college education should be able to get one. Georgia needed another state-run college, and he was willing to fight for it.

The University of Georgia was the oldest public university in the state and had been established by an act of the Georgia General Assembly over two centuries ago. Just as there had been a need for greater educational opportunities then, there was a need now. In fact, land had been donated for that very purpose ten years ago. Now some lawmakers were trying to use a loophole in the land grant to appropriate the land to build a recreation area—a park that would be largely composed of a golf course.

Reggie was aware that getting elected would only be the first hurdle. Once he got in the Senate, he would then have the job of convincing his fellow lawmakers of the need for an additional state university as well.

He glanced at his watch. In less than ten minutes, lunch would be served, and then halfway through lunch, each person seeking office would get an opportunity to speak. There were about eight candidates in attendance.

Deciding he needed to switch his focus for a moment, he thought about his visit to Garbella Jewelers that morning. Mr. Garbella's assessment of the earring was that it was a fine piece of craftsmanship. The diamonds were real and of good quality. He doubted the piece had been purchased in this country. He thought the way the diamonds were set was indicative of European jewelry making. Mr. Garbella had gone on to say that the pair had cost a lot of money. After visiting with the jeweler, Reggie was more determined than ever to find his Wonder Woman and return the missing earring to her.

Quade and his cousin Cole, who'd both recently retired—Quade from a top security job with the government and Cole from the Texas Rangers—had joined forces to start a network of security companies, some of which would include private investigation. He wondered if they would be interested in taking him on as their first client.

He looked at his watch again before glancing across the room and meeting Brent's eye. He had less than ten minutes to mingle, and then everyone would be seated for lunch. He hated admitting it, but he felt in his element. Maybe a political career was his calling, after all.

Olivia waited until just moments before the luncheon was to begin to make an entrance and join her father. According to his campaign manager, Marc Norris, her entrance was part of a coordinated strategy. He wanted her to ease into the room and work one side of it while her father worked the other. Subtle yet thorough.

When he had mentioned his strategy that morning while joining Olivia and her father for breakfast, she had gotten annoyed that the man assumed she didn't have any common sense. Evidently, Norris doubted she could hold her own during any discussion. But not to cause any problems, she had decided to keep her opinions to herself.

She saw noticeable interest in her from the moment she stepped into the room. Most people knew that Orin Jeffries had a daughter, but a number of them had forgotten or shoved the fact to the back of their mind in the wake of his two well-known sons. Practically everybody in the country knew of the Holy Terror, whether they were football enthusiasts or not. Since retiring from football, Terrence had been known for his work in a number of high-profile charities. He also commentated on a popular radio talk show, *Sports Talk,* in South Florida, which might go into syndication the next year. Duan had made the national headlines a few years before, when his undercover work as a detective had resulted in the exposure of a couple of unsavory individuals who'd been intent on bringing organized crime to Georgia.

But it didn't bother her in the least that her brothers' good deeds had somehow made people forget about her. Besides, she hadn't lived in this country in four years, returning only on occasion to visit, mainly around the holidays.

She began mingling, introducing herself as Orin Jeffries's daughter, and actually got a kick out of seeing first surprise and then acknowledgment on many faces. One such incident was taking place now.

"Why, Olivia, how good it is to see you again. It's been a while since you've been back home. But I do remember you now. You must be extremely proud of your father and brothers."

"Yes, I am, Mrs. Hancock, and how is Beau? I understand he's doing extremely well. You must be proud of him."

She watched the older woman's eyes light up as she

went into a spiel about her son. She was a proud mother. Olivia knew Beau from school. Unless he had changed over the years, Beau Hancock was an irrefutable jerk. He'd thought he was the gift to every girl at Collinshill High School.

She glanced down at her watch. She had ten minutes left before everyone would take their seats for lunch. She had called the Saxon Hotel on the off chance that someone from housekeeping had come across her diamond earring and turned it in. That hadn't been the case. A part of her was disappointed that it had not been.

There was still one section of the room she needed to cover. Mrs. Hancock, in singing Beau's praises, had taken up quite a bit of her time. Now she was again making her way through the crowds, speaking to everyone, as Norris had suggested.

"You're doing a marvelous job working the room," Senator Reed whispered. The older man had suddenly appeared by her side.

She forced a smile. For some reason, she'd never cared for him. "Thanks."

She had already met several of the candidates since entering the room, but she had yet to meet the man who would be her father's real competition, Reggie Westmoreland.

As she continued mingling and heading to the area where Reggie Westmoreland was supposedly rubbing elbows with the crowd, her curiosity about the man who opposed her father couldn't help but be piqued. She started to ask Senator Reed about him but changed her mind. The senator's opinion wouldn't be the most valuable.

"You look nice, Olivia."

She glanced up at the senator, who seemed determined to remain by her side. He was a few years older than her father, and for some reason, he had always made her feel uncomfortable.

"Thanks, Senator." She refrained from saying that he also looked nice, which he did. Like her father, he was a good-looking man for his age, but Senator Reed always had an air of snobbery about him, like he was born with too low expectations of others.

"It was my suggestion that your father send for you." When she stopped walking and glanced at him, with a raised brow, he added, "He was in a dilemma, and I thought bringing you home to be his escort was the perfect answer."

She bit back a retort, that bringing her home had not been the perfect answer. Being in that dilemma might have prompted her dad to ask Cathy to attend some of those functions with him. No telling how things would have taken off from there if the senator hadn't butted in.

She was about to open her mouth, to tell Senator Reed that her father was old enough to think for himself, when, all of a sudden, for no reason at all, she pulled in a quick breath. She glanced up ahead, and no more than four feet in front of her, there stood a man with his back to her.

The first thing she noticed about him was his height. He was taller then the men he was talking to. And there was something about his particular height, and the way his head tilted at an angle as he listened to what one of the men was saying, that held her spellbound.

He was dressed in a suit, and she could only admire how it fit him. The broadness of his shoulders and the tapering of his waist sent a feeling of familiarity through her. She stopped walking momentarily and composed herself, not understanding what was happening to her.

"Is anything wrong, Olivia?"

She glanced up at Senator Reed and saw concern in his eyes. She knew she couldn't tell him what she was thinking. There was no way she could voice her suspicions to anyone.

She needed to go somewhere to pull herself together, to consider the strong possibility that the man standing not far away was her Jack Sprat. Or could it be that she was so wrapped up in the memories of that night that she was quick to assume that any man of a tall stature who possessed broad shoulders had to be her mystery man?

"Olivia?"

Instead of saying anything, she shifted her gaze from the senator to look again at the man, whose back was still to her. It was at that precise moment that he slowly turned around, and his gaze settled on her. In a quick second, she pulled in a sharp breath as she scanned his face, and her gaze settled on a firm jaw that had an angular plane. Her artist's eye also picked up other things, and they were things others would probably not notice—the stark symmetry of his face, which was clear with or without a mask, the shape of his head and the alignment of his ears from his cheeks. These were things she recognized.

Things she remembered.

And she knew, without a doubt, that she was staring into the face of the man whom she had spent the night with on Saturday. The man whose body had given her hours upon hours of immeasurable pleasure. And impossible as it seemed—because they'd kept their masks in place the entire time—she had a feeling from the way he was staring back at her just as intently as she was staring at him that he had recognized her, too.

"Olivia?"

She broke eye contact with the stranger to gaze up at the senator. The man was becoming annoying, but at the moment, he was the one person who could tell her exactly what she needed to know. "Senator Reed, that guy up there, the one who turned around to look at me. Who is he?"

The senator followed her gaze and frowned deeply. "The two of you had to meet eventually. That man, young lady, is the enemy."

She swallowed deeply before saying, "The enemy?"

"Yes, the enemy. He's the man that's opposing your father in his bid for the Senate."

Olivia's head began spinning before the senator could speak his next words.

"That, my dear," the senator went on to say, "is Reggie Westmoreland."

It was her.

Reggie knew it with every breath he took. Her lips were giving her away. And he wasn't sure what part of him was recognizable to her, but he knew just as sure as they were standing there, staring at each other, that they were as intimately familiar to each other as any two people could be.

It was strange. He'd been standing here with Brent, his brother Jared, his cousins Dare and Thorn, and Thorn's wife, Tara. They'd all been listening to Thorn, a nationally known motorcycle builder and racer, who was telling them about an order he'd received to build a bike for actor Matt Damon. Then, all of a sudden, he'd felt a strange sensation, followed by a stirring in the lower part of his gut.

He had turned around, and he'd looked straight into her face. His Wonder Woman.

He couldn't lay claim to recognizing any of her other facial features, but her lips were a dead giveaway. Blatantly sensual, he had kissed them, tongued them, licked them and tasted them to his heart's content. He knew the shape of them in his sleep, knew their texture, knew what part of them was so sensitive that when he'd touched her there, she had moaned.

She looked totally stunning in the stylish skirt and blouse she was wearing. The outfit complemented her figure. Even if he hadn't met her before, he would be trying his best to do so now. Out of his peripheral vision, he noted a number of men looking at her, and he understood why. She was gorgeous.

He lost control, and his feet began moving toward her.

"Reggie, where are you going?" Brent asked.

He didn't respond, because he truly didn't know what he could say. He continued walking until he came to a stop directly in front of the senator and the woman. The senator, he noted, was frowning. The woman's gaze hadn't left his. She seemed as entranced as he was.

He found his voice to say, "Good afternoon, Senator Reed. It's good seeing you again."

It was a lie, and he realized the senator knew it, but he didn't care. Approaching him would force the man to make introductions, and if it took a lie, then so be it.

"Westmoreland, I see you've decided to go through with it," replied the senator.

Reggie gave the man a smile that didn't quite reach his eyes. "Of course." He then shifted his gaze back to the woman. The senator would be outright rude not to make an introduction, and one thing Reggie did know about the senator was that he believed in following proper decorum.

"And let me introduce you to Olivia Jeffries. Olivia, this is Reggie Westmoreland," the senator said.

At the mention of her name, Reggie's mind went into a tailspin. "Jeffries?" he replied.

"Yes," the senator said as a huge, smug smile touched his lips. "Jeffries. She's Orin Jeffries's daughter, who is visiting from Paris and will remain here during the duration of the campaign."

Reggie nodded as his eyes once again settled on Olivia. He then reached out his hand. "Olivia, it's nice meeting you. I'm sure your father is excited about having you home."

"Thank you," replied Olivia.

They both felt it the moment their hands touched, and they both knew it. It was those same feelings that had driven them to leave the party on Saturday night and to go somewhere to be alone, with the sole purpose of getting intimately connected. Reggie opened his mouth to say something, and then a voice from the microphone stopped him.

"Everyone is asked to take a seat so lunch can be served. Your table number is located on your ticket."

"It was nice meeting you, Mr. Westmoreland," Olivia said, not sure what else to say at the moment.

She honestly had thought she would not see him again, not this soon, not ever. And now that he knew their predicament—that she was the daughter of the man who was his opponent in this political race—she hoped that he would accept the inevitable. Nothing had changed. Even with their identities exposed, there could never be anything between them beyond what had happened Saturday night.

"It was nice meeting you as well, Ms. Jeffries," said Reggie. And then he did something that was common among Frenchmen but rare with Americans. Bending slightly, he lifted her hand to his lips and kissed it before turning and walking away.

Chapter 5

Olivia found that every time she lifted her fork to her mouth, her gaze would automatically drift to the next table, the one where Reggie Westmoreland was sitting. And each time, unerringly, their gazes would meet.

After their introduction, she had excused herself to the senator, smiling and saying she needed to go to the ladies' room. Once there she had taken a deep breath. It was a wonder she hadn't passed out. With his mask in place, Reggie Westmoreland had been handsome. Without his mask, he took her breath away. While standing in front of him, she'd had to tamp down her emotions and the sensations flowing through her.

His eyes were very dark, almost chocolate, and their shape, which she had been denied seeing on Saturday night, was almond, beneath thick brows. It had taken everything in her power to force her muscles to relax.

And when he had taken her hand and kissed the back of it before walking off, she'd thought she would swoon right then and there.

"Libby, are you okay? You've barely touched your meal," her father said, interrupting her thoughts.

She glanced over to him and smiled. "Yes, Daddy, I'm fine."

"Westmoreland is the cause of it," said Senator Reed, jumping in. "She met him right before we took our seats. He probably gave her an upset stomach."

Her father frowned. "Was he rude to you, sweetheart?" he asked, with deep concern tinged with anger.

She was opening her mouth to assure her father that Reggie hadn't been rude when Senator Reed said, "He was quite taken with her, Orin."

She ignored the senator's comment, thinking that he didn't know the half of it. Instead, she answered her father. "No, he wasn't rude, Dad. In fact, although we spoke only briefly, I thought he was rather nice." She smiled. "Quite the charmer."

"The enemy is never nice or charming, Olivia. Remember that," the senator said, speaking to her like she was a child. "I strongly suggest that during this campaign, you stay away from him."

She was opening her mouth to tell the senator that she truly didn't give a royal damn about what he would strongly suggest when her father spoke.

"You don't have to worry about Libby, Al. She's a smart girl. She would never get mixed up with the likes of Westmoreland."

The likes of Westmoreland? Was there something about Reggie that her father and the senator knew but that she didn't? she wondered. Granted, that might be true, since she had arrived in the country on Friday. But still, she heard intense dislike in her father's voice and pondered the reason for it. Did it have to do only with the campaign, or was there more? Marc Norris was the only other person at their table, and he wasn't saying anything. But then Norris didn't look like the type to gossip. She didn't know him well. In fact, she had just met him on Friday evening.

"Well, if I didn't know better, I'd think Olivia and Westmoreland had met before," replied Senator Reed.

The senator's words almost made her drop her fork. She had to tighten her grip on it. She thought about Reggie. Had their reaction to each other been that obvious?

There was a lag in the conversation at the table, and she knew from the brief moment of silence that the men were waiting for her to respond one way or the other. So she did. "Then it's a good thing that you know better, Senator, isn't it?"

She said the words so sweetly, there was no way that he or anyone else could tell if she was being sincere or smart-alecky. Before any further conversation could take place, one of the sponsors of the event got up and went to the podium to announce that the speeches were about to begin.

"Okay, Reggie. What's going on with you and that woman at the other table? The one you can't seem to keep your eyes off," Brent said in a whisper as he leaned close to Reggie.

Reggie lifted a brow. "What makes you think something is going on?"

Brent chuckled. "I have eyes. I can see. You do know she's Jeffries's daughter."

Reggie leaned back in his chair. He couldn't eat another mouthful, although he hadn't eaten much. He was still trying to recover from the fact that he and his mystery woman had officially met. "Yes, the senator introduced us. And grudgingly, I might add. He didn't seem too happy to do so," Reggie said.

"Figures. He probably wants her for himself." At Reggie's surprised look, Brent went on to explain. "Reed is into young women big-time. I once dated someone who worked at his office. He tried coming on to her several times, and she ended up quitting when the old man wouldn't give up no matter how many times she tried turning him off. The man takes sexual harassment to a whole new level."

Reggie's jaw tightened. The thought that the senator could be interested in Olivia, even remotely, made his blood boil. "But he's friends with her father."

"And that's supposed to mean something?" Brent countered, trying to keep his voice low. "I guess it would mean something to honorable men, but Reed is not honorable. We don't have a term-limit law here, so it makes you wonder why he isn't seeking another term. Rumor has it that he was given a choice to either step down or have his business—namely, his affairs with women half his age—spread across the front pages of the newspapers. I guess since he's still married and his wife is wealthier than he is, although she's bedridden, he didn't want that."

Reggie shook his head. "Well, he shouldn't concern himself with Olivia Jeffries."

"And why is that?"

Reggie didn't say anything for fear of saying too much. In the end, he didn't have to respond, because it was his turn to speak.

* * *

"You gave a nice speech, Dad. You did a wonderful job," Olivia said once she and her father got home.

"Yes, but so did Westmoreland," Orin said, heading for the kitchen. "He tried to make me look like someone who doesn't support higher education."

"But only because you are against any legislation to build another state university," she reminded him.

"We have enough colleges, Libby."

She decided to back away from the conversation because she didn't agree with her father on this issue. The last thing she wanted was to get into an argument with him about Reggie Westmoreland and his speech. If nothing else, she had reached the conclusion at dinner that neither her father nor the senator wanted her to get involved in any way with the competition.

She glanced at her watch. "I think I'm going to change and then go to the park and paint for a while."

"Yes, you should do that while you still have good sunlight left. And feel free to take my car, since I won't need it anymore today. That rental car of yours is too small," Orin said, already pulling off his tie as he headed up the stairs.

She could tell he was somewhat upset about how the luncheon had gone. Evidently, he had assumed, or had been led to believe, that winning the Senate seat would be a piece of cake. It probably would have been if Reggie Westmoreland hadn't decided to throw his hat into the ring at the eleventh hour.

And she had to admit that although her father's speech had been good, Reggie's speech had been better. Instead of making generalities, he had hammered down specifics, and he had delivered the speech eloquently.

And it had seemed that as his gaze moved around the room while he was speaking, his eyes would seek her out. Each time they'd done so and she'd gazed into them, she'd felt she could actually see barely concealed desire in their dark depths. She had sat there with the hardened nipples of her breasts pressed tightly against her blouse the entire time.

And all she'd had to do was to study his lips to recall how those same lips had left marks all over her body, how they, along with his tongue, had moved over these same breasts, licking, sucking and nibbling on them.

After the luncheon was over, instead of dallying about, she had rushed her father out, needing to leave to avoid any attempts Reggie might have made to approach her again. She would not have been able to handle it if he had done so, and it would only have raised Senator Reed's suspicions. For some reason, the older man was making her every move his business.

Olivia had changed clothes and was gathering her art bag to sling over her shoulders when her cell phone rang. Not recognizing the local number, she answered the call.

"Hello?"

"Meet me someplace."

She got weak in the knees at the sound of the deep, husky voice. She really didn't have to ask, but she did so anyway. "Who is this?"

"This is Reggie Westmoreland, Wonder Woman."

Olivia pulled into the parking lot of Chase's Place, wondering for the umpteenth time how she had let Reggie Westmoreland talk her into meeting him there. The restaurant, he'd said, was closed on Mondays, but since he knew the owner, there would not be a problem with them meeting there for privacy.

When she'd indicated she did not want to be seen meeting with him, he'd told her to park in the rear of the building. She hated the idea of everything being so secretive, but she knew it was for the best.

Of all the never-in-a-million-years coincidences, why did she have to have an affair—one night or otherwise—with the one man her father could not stand at the moment?

Doing as Reggie had advised, she drove around to the rear and parked beside a very nice silver-gray Mercedes, the same one she'd seen Reggie driving Saturday night. After getting out and checking her watch for the time, she walked up to the back door of the restaurant and knocked. It opened immediately. A man who was almost as tall as Reggie and just as handsome opened the door and smiled at her before stepping aside to let her in.

"Olivia?" he asked, continuing to smile, as he closed the door behind her.

She was so busy studying his face, noting the similarities between him and Reggie, that she almost jumped when he uttered her name. Like Reggie, he was extremely handsome, but she didn't miss the gold band on his finger. "Yes?" she said finally.

"I'm Chase Westmoreland," he said, extending his hand. "Reggie is already here and is in one of the smaller offices, waiting for you. I'll take you to him."

"Thanks." And then, because curiosity got the best of her, she asked, "Are you one of Reggie's brothers?"

The man's chuckle floated through the air as he led

her down a hallway. "No, Reggie has five brothers, but I'm not one of them. I'm his cousin."

"Oh. The two of you favor one another," she pointed out.

"Yes, all we Westmorelands look alike."

After walking down a long hallway, they stopped in front of a closed door. "Reggie is in here," Chase said, grinning. "It was nice meeting you."

Olivia smiled. "And it was nice meeting you as well, Chase." And then he was gone. She turned toward the closed door and took a deep breath before turning the handle.

Reggie stood the moment he heard voices on the other side of the door. This was the only place he could think of where he and Olivia could meet without fear of a reporter of some sort invading their privacy. The political campaign had begun officially today, and already all the sides were trying to dig up something on the others.

He'd told Brent that he wanted a campaign that focused strictly on the issues. He wasn't into dirty political games. He felt the voters should get to know the candidates, learn their stance on the issues and then decide which offered more of what they were looking for. If they wanted something different, then he was their man, and if they were used to the do-nothing agenda that Reed had implemented over the past four years, then they needed to go with Jeffries, since it was a sure bet that he was Reed's clone.

As soon as the door opened, his heart began hammering wildly in his chest, and the moment Olivia walked into the room and their gazes met, it took everything he possessed not to cross the floor and pull her into his arms and taste those lips he'd enjoyed so much a couple of nights ago.

Instead of coming farther into the room, she closed the door behind her and then leaned back on it, watching him. Waiting. His hands balled into fists at his sides. He smiled and said, "Wonder Woman." It wasn't a question; it was a statement. He knew who she was.

The butterflies in Olivia's stomach intensified as they flew off in every direction. As she looked across the room at the extremely handsome man, she couldn't help but pose the one question that had been on her mind since they'd met earlier, at the luncheon. "How did you recognize me?" she asked in a soft-spoken voice.

He smiled, and she actually felt her heart stop. She felt her body begin to get hot all over. "Your lips gave you away. I recognized them. I would know your lips anywhere," he said. His voice was deep and throaty.

Olivia frowned, finding that strange. But it must have made some sense, at least to him, because he *had* been able to recognize her.

"What about you? You recognized me also. How?" he asked.

"I'm an artist, at least I am in my spare time. I study faces. I analyze every symmetrical detail. Although you were wearing a mask, and I couldn't see the upper part of your face, I zeroed in on the parts I could see." She decided not to tell him that there was more to it than his face. It had been his height that had first drawn her attention, and the way he'd tilted his head and his broad shoulders. If she could find the words to describe him, they would be, in addition to *handsome—tall, dark... Westmoreland.*

"I guess both of us can see things others might miss," he said.

"Yes, I guess we can," she agreed.

The room got silent, and she could feel it. That same sexual chemistry that had overtaken them that night, that had destroyed their senses to the point where they hadn't wanted to do anything else but go somewhere and be alone together, was still potent.

"Please come join me. I promise not to bite."

His words broke into her thoughts, and she couldn't help but smile. It was on the tip of her tongue to say, yes, he did bite and that she'd had numerous passion marks on her body to prove it. However, she had a feeling from the glint in his eyes that he'd realized the slipup the moment she had. His eyes darkened, and she felt heat settling everywhere his gaze touched.

She breathed in a deep breath before moving away from the door. She glanced around. The room was apparently a little game room. It had a love seat, a card table, a refrigerator and a television.

"This is where my cousins and brothers get together to play cards on occasion," said Reggie, breaking into her thoughts. "They used to rotate at each other's homes, but after they married and started having kids, they couldn't express themselves like they wanted whenever they were losing. So we decided to find someplace to go where we could be as loud and as colorful as we wanted to be."

She nodded and remembered how things were when her brothers used to have their friends over for poker. Some of their choice words would burn her ears. She then crossed the room to sit on the love seat.

He remained standing and was staring at her, making her feel uncomfortable. She cleared her throat. "You wanted to meet with me," she said, reminding him of why they were there.

He smiled. "Yes, and do you know why?"

"Yes," she said, holding his gaze. "It wouldn't take much to figure out that now that you know my father is one of the men you'll be running against in a few months, you want to establish an understanding between us. You want us to pretend that Saturday night never happened and that we've never met."

He continued to stare at her intently. "Is that what you think?"

She blinked. "Yes, of course. Under these circumstances, there's no way we can be seen together or even let anyone in on the fact that we know each other."

"I don't see why not. I'm running against your father, not you, so it shouldn't matter," he said.

Olivia felt her heart pounding hard in her chest. "But it does matter. Orin Jeffries is my father, and he and his campaign staff consider you the enemy," she said truthfully, although she hadn't meant to do so.

Reggie shook his head. "It's unfortunate they feel that way. I'm not his enemy. I'm his opponent in a Senate race. It's nothing personal, and I was hoping no one would make it such."

Olivia didn't know what to say. She knew Senator Reed, who seemed to be calling the shots as to how her father ran his campaign, could be ruthless at times. She had overheard the whispered conversations that took place at her table during lunch. She knew that the man had no intentions of letting this be a clean campaign, and that bothered her because it was so unlike her father to get involved in something so manipulative and underhanded.

"I'm sorry, but it will be personal. I don't agree, but politics is politics," she heard herself saying, knowing it wasn't an acceptable excuse. "If I became involved with you in any way, it would be equal to treason in my father's eyes. Things are too complicated."

"Only if we let them be. I still say us meeting and going out on occasion don't involve your father, just me and you."

She shook her head as she stood. It was time to go. She really should not have come. "I need to go."

"But you just got here," he said softly in that sexy voice that did things to her nervous system.

"I know, but coming here was a mistake," she said.

"Then why did you?" he asked softly.

She met his gaze and knew she would tell him the truth. "I felt that I should. Saturday night was a first of its kind for me. I've never left a party with someone I truly didn't know, and I've never had a one-night stand. But I did with you because I felt the chemistry. One of the reasons I came today was that I needed to see if the chemistry between us was real or a figment of my imagination."

"And what's your verdict?" he asked, holding her gaze.

She didn't hesitate in responding. "It's real."

"Does that frighten you?"

"It does not so much frighten me as confuse me. Like I said, I've never responded to a man this way before."

"And what was the other reason you came tonight?"

"We never took our masks off, and I needed to know how you were able to recognize me today. I got the answers to both of my questions, so I should leave now."

"But what about me? Aren't you interested in knowing why I wanted to see you again? Why I asked for us to meet?" He was staring intently at her, and his gaze seemed to touch her all over.

"Why did you want to see me?" she asked.

He slowly moved across the room to stand in front of her, and her pulse began beating rapidly, and heat began to settle between her thighs from his closeness. "Your lips were one reason."

"My lips?" she asked, raising a brow. He seemed to be searching her face, but she could tell his main focus was her lips.

"I claimed them as mine that night," he said in a husky whisper. "I just needed to know if they still are."

And before she could catch her next breath, he pulled her into his arms and captured her mouth with his.

They were still his.

This was what he needed to know. This was the very reason he had kept breathing since Saturday, Reggie thought as he hungrily mated with Olivia's mouth. The memories that had consumed him over the past forty-eight hours had nothing on the real thing. And she was responding to his kiss, feasting on his mouth as greedily as he was feasting on hers. Their masks were gone but not their passion.

He hadn't expected the fires to ignite so quickly, but already they were practically burning out of control. Her body was pressed fully against his, and he could feel every heated inch of her, just like he was certain she could feel every inch of him. Hard. Aroused. He knew he needed to pull back from her mouth to take a much-needed breath, but he couldn't. He had thought of kissing her, dreamed of kissing her, ever since the morning they'd parted. His tongue was tangling with hers, and it seemed he couldn't get enough.

Instantly, he knew the moment she began withdrawing, and he pulled back, but not before tracing the outline of her lips with the tip of his tongue while tamping down on the stimulating effect the kiss had had on him.

"I really do need to leave." Her words lacked conviction, and he couldn't help but notice that she had wrapped her arms around his neck and hadn't yet released him. He also took note that her mouth was mere inches from his, and she hadn't pulled back.

Making a quick decision for both of them, he said, "Please stay and let's talk. Will you stay a while longer if I promise not to kiss you again? There's so much I want to know about you. I won't ask you anything about your father and his campaign, just about you."

"What good would it do, Reggie?" she asked, saying his name for the first time. The sound of it off her lips produced flutters in the pit of his stomach.

"I think it will appease our curiosity and maybe help us make some sense as to why we became attracted to each other so quickly and so deeply," he responded. "Why the chemistry between us is so strong."

Olivia pulled her arms from around his neck, thinking that what he was suggesting wasn't a good idea, but neither was kissing. But then she really didn't want to leave, and she had to admit that she'd wondered why they had hit it off so quickly and easily. But it didn't take a rocket scientist to figure out some of the reasons. He was an extremely handsome man, something she had recognized even with the mask. And his approach that night had not been egotistical or arrogant. She had somehow known he was someone she could have fun with and whose company she could enjoy.

And those things had been verified in the most intimate way.

"And we'll just talk?" she asked, making sure they understood each other.

"Yes, and about no one but us. That way you can't feel disloyal to your father."

She inhaled deeply. "But I still do," she admitted openly.

He didn't say anything for a moment. "Let me ask you something." At her nod, he asked, "If we would have met at any other time and if I was not your father's political opponent, would he have a problem with you dating me?"

She knew the answer to that, since her father had never been the kind of dad who cross-examined his children's dates. He had always accepted her judgment in that area. Now, her brothers had been another matter, especially Duan. "No, I think he wouldn't have a problem with it," she said truthfully.

"That's good to know, and that's why we should move forward on the premise that the campaign should not affect our relationship." His voice and smile conveyed that he truly believed what he was saying.

"But how can it not?" she asked, wishing things were that simple.

"Because we won't let it," he responded. "First of all, we need to acknowledge that we are in a relationship, Olivia."

She shook her head. "I can't do that, because we really don't have a relationship. We just slept together that night."

"No, it was more than that. It might have been a one-night stand, but I never intended *not* to find you after you left the Saxon on Sunday morning. In fact, I took this to a jewelry store this morning to see if I could trace where it was originally purchased," he said, pulling her diamond earring from his pocket. "It might have taken me a while, but eventually, I would have found you, even if I had to tear this town up doing so," he said, handing the earring to her.

She took it and studied it, remembering just when she had purchased the pair. It had been when she'd gotten her first position at the Louvre Museum. These diamonds had cost more than the amount of her first paycheck. But it had been a way for her to celebrate.

"Thank you for returning it." She slipped the earring into her pants pocket and then looked back at him. "So, what do you want to talk about?"

"I want to know everything about you. Over dinner. In here. Just the two of us."

She licked her lips and noticed immediately how his gaze had been drawn to the gesture. "And you promise no kissing, right?"

He chuckled. "Not unless you initiate it. If you do, then I won't turn you down."

She couldn't help but smile at that. "You mentioned dinner, but the restaurant isn't open today."

"No, it isn't, but Chase will make an exception for us. Will you join me here for dinner so we can talk and get to know each other?"

She was very much aware that if her father knew she was here, spending time with Reggie, he would think she was being disloyal, but she knew she truly wasn't. If at any time Reggie shifted the conversation to her father, as if pumping her for information about him, she would leave. But for now, she owed it to herself to do something that made her happy for a change, as long as she was not hurting anyone. If Duan or Terrence had been caught up in a similar situation, there was no way her father would have asked them to stop seeing that person. She should not be made the exception.

Olivia knew Reggie was waiting for her answer. "And our time here together will be kept confidential?"

He smiled. "Yes. Like I said, this is about you and me, and not the campaign. As far as I'm concerned, one has nothing to do with the other."

"Then, yes, I'll join you here for dinner," she said after taking a long, deep breath.

Chapter 6

"I know your favorite color is lavender, but tell me something else about Olivia Jeffries, and before you ask, I want to know everything," Reggie said as he sat in the chair at the table while Olivia sat across from him, on the love seat, with her feet curled beneath her. They were both sipping wine and trying to rekindle that comfort zone between them.

Chase had been kind enough to take their food order and had indicated that he would be serving dinner to them shortly. He had given them a bottle of wine, two wineglasses, a tablecloth and eating utensils. Together, the two of them had set the table.

Reggie wondered if being here with him reminded her of how intimate things had been between them on Saturday night. They had shared dinner then, but only after spending hours making love, to the point where they were famished.

"I'm the baby in the family," she said, smiling. "I have two older brothers."

"And I know the Holy Terror is one of them," Reggie said, grinning. "He went to school with a couple of my cousins and two of my brothers. In fact, my brother Quade was on his football team in high school. I understand the Holy Terror has mellowed over the years."

Olivia chuckled. "It depends on what you mean by 'mellowed.' Both of my brothers tend to be overprotective at times, but Duan is worse than Terrence, since he's the oldest. Duan is thirty-six, and Terrence is thirty-four."

"And you are?" he asked, knowing a lot of women didn't like sharing their age.

"I'm twenty-seven. What about you?"

"Thirty-two."

Reggie took a sip of his wine and then asked, "Is Duan the one you sent the text message to on Saturday night?"

"Are you kidding?" she said, chuckling. "Duan would have been on the first flight back home, and he would not have erased your number. He would have had you thoroughly checked out. He has a lot of friends in law enforcement. He used to be a police detective. Now he owns a private investigation company. I sent the text message to Terrence. I can handle him a lot easier than I can Duan."

Reggie nodded. "So why is a beautiful girl like you living so far away from home, in Paris?"

She smiled. "Working. I've always wanted to work at the Louvre Museum in Paris, and I was hired right out of grad school as a tour guide. I had to start at the bottom, but I didn't mind if that's what it would take to work my way up the ladder to be an art curator. It took me almost four years, but I finally made it. I've been a curator for almost a year."

"Congratulations," he said and meant it.

"Thanks."

"So do you plan to make Paris your permanent home?" he asked, watching her sip her wine. He liked the way her lips curved around her glass. He had noticed this detail about her on Saturday night, and it had been a total turn-on...just like it was now.

"I love living over there. I miss being home sometimes, but I've managed to return for the holidays. My brothers and I make it a point to be home for Christmas. But my dream is to return home in a few years, when I've saved up enough money to establish an art gallery." She smiled wistfully.

He nodded. "So over the years, you've come home only during the holidays?"

"Yes."

He wondered if that had anything to do with the fact that her mother had walked out on them a couple of days before Christmas, according to Brent. Reggie could only imagine how disruptive that particular Christmas had to have been for them. "And how long do you plan to stay this time?"

She didn't say anything at first, just stared into her wineglass for a while. Finally, she said, "Until the election is over."

She glanced up and met his gaze, and he breathed in deeply and said, "We won't let that matter now, remember?" he reminded her gently.

"Yes," she said softly. "I remember." She shifted positions in her seat. "So, now, tell me about Reggie Westmoreland."

He took another sip of his wine and then leaned forward in his chair, resting his arms on his thighs. "I'm the youngest son of my parents. Multiple births run in my family. My father is a fraternal twin. My uncle John and my aunt Evelyn have five sons and one daughter."

"Chase is one of their sons?" she interrupted.

He smiled. "Yes, and Chase is a twin. His twin, Storm, is a fireman. So in their birth order, my cousins are Dare, who is the sheriff of College Park, Thorn, who races and builds motorcycles, Stone, who is a writer and writes adventure novels as Rock Mason, the twins Chase and Storm, and Delaney, the only girl. Delaney and I are the same age and are very close."

"I've heard about Thorn, and, of course, I've read a few Rock Mason novels. And I remember reading years ago about your cousin Delaney and how she married a sheikh. That's awesome."

"Yeah, we all think it is, although I have to say, her brothers weren't too happy about it at first, especially with her leaving the country to live in the Middle East. But her husband, Jamal, is a real nice guy, and everyone looks forward to her trips home. All my cousins are married with children."

"What about your siblings? I understand there are quite a few. Are there twins on your side, too?" she asked.

"Yes. My oldest brother is Jared, and he is a divorce attorney here in the city. Spencer lives in California and is the financial adviser in the family. Durango lives in Montana and is a park ranger. He's thinking about retiring to play a bigger role in his horse-breeding busi-

ness. And then there are the twins—Ian and Quade. Ian
owns a resort on Lake Tahoe, and Quade used to work
for the government, but now he owns a number of security firms around the country. Quade and his wife
are the parents of triplets, and they live in Carolina, although they have another home in Jamaica."

"Wow! You weren't kidding when you said multiple
births run in your family. Are your brothers married?"

"Yes, and happily so. I'm the only single Westmore-
land living in Atlanta. My father has a brother, Uncle
Corey, who lives in Montana. He also has triplets,
Casey, Clint and Cole, and they are all married."

At that moment, there was a knock on the door, and
seconds later Chase entered with their food. "Everything smells delicious," Olivia said, getting to her feet
to help place the plates on the table.

Chase smiled. "I hope the two of you enjoy it," he
said, then left them alone again.

Once they were seated at the table, Reggie glanced
over at her and smiled. "I'm glad you decided to stay."

Olivia returned his smile.

During dinner Olivia was so tuned in to Reggie that
she could only stare at him and listen to everything he
was saying. He told her about the other family of Westmorelands, the ones living in Colorado, whom his father
had discovered when he decided to research the family history a year ago. A family reunion was being held
later this month in Texas, where both the Atlanta-based
Westmorelands and the Denver-based Westmorelands
would be getting together and officially meeting for the
first time. It sounded exciting, especially to someone
whose family was limited to two brothers and a father.

Both of her sets of grandparents were deceased, and both of her parents had been only children.

"Would you like some more dessert?" he asked.

Reggie's question reclaimed her thoughts, and she smiled over at him. He had kept his word, and although the attraction they shared was there, flowing blatantly between them, they had been able to harness it while sharing information about each other. A part of Olivia wasn't sure why they had decided to spend time together when nothing would ever come of it, but they had. Once again, the desire to be together, if only to breathe the same air and share conversation, had driven them to defy what others around them felt they should do.

"No, thanks. I do have to leave. I told my father I was going to the park to paint."

"I'm glad you agreed to meet with me and I'm sorry if I placed you in an awkward position."

"You didn't," she said. "I mentioned to Dad that I was going to the park before you called. I just didn't tell him of my change of plans, because he was resting."

"Would you have done otherwise?" he asked her.

She knew she would be honest and said, "No, he would have forbidden it. And that's the reason why, as much as I enjoyed sharing dinner and conversation with you, Reggie, we can't do it again. I hope you understand."

He met her eyes. "No, I don't understand, because like I said earlier, Olivia, the campaign doesn't concern our relationship."

"The press won't see it that way, and they would have a field day with the story of you and I being involved. I refuse to sneak around to see you." She stood. "I need to go."

Reggie stood as well. He knew he couldn't detain her any longer, but he was more determined than ever to see her again and spend time with her. And he didn't want them to sneak around, either. There had to be a way, and he was determined to find it. "I enjoyed our time together, Olivia."

She held out her hand to him. "So did I. Thank you."

Reggie took the hand she offered, felt the heat the moment he touched it and knew she felt the heat as well. His fingers tightened on hers, and they both were aware of the sensations flowing between them. This wasn't the first time such a thing had happened. It always did when they came in contact with each other.

It was she who tugged her hand away first. "And thanks again for returning my earring."

"You're welcome."

And then Olivia turned and moved toward the door. Before she opened it, she glanced back over her shoulder, saw his unwavering stare, deciphered the intense desire in his eyes. She still felt the heat of his touch on her hand.

She wanted to go back to him, wrap her arms around his neck, but she knew she could not. She would not regret the time she'd spent with him on Saturday night or today. But she was realistic enough to know that as long as Reggie Westmoreland was her father's opponent in the Senate race, her father would never accept her dating a Westmoreland. So from this day forward, she would have fond memories of their times together, but they would have to sustain her throughout the campaign and later, when she returned to Paris.

"Olivia?"

She had already opened the door to leave when

she heard him call her name. Swallowing deeply, she stopped and turned around. "Yes?"

"No matter what, you will forever be my Wonder Woman."

She felt the tightness in her throat and fought the tears that had begun clouding her eyes. *And you, Reggie Westmoreland, will forever be the man that I wished I'd had the opportunity to get to know better,* she thought.

Their gazes held for the longest time, and then she turned and walked out the door and closed it behind her.

Olivia was surprised to find her father had already gone to bed by the time she returned home. At some point, he had come downstairs and fixed a pot of vegetable soup, which he'd left warming on the stove for her. A part of her felt awful about her deceit. She'd been served a delicious full-course meal at Chase's Place, while her father had been home, eating alone.

She quickly realized that he'd not eaten alone when she noticed two of everything in the sink and the lipstick on the rim of one of the coffee cups. She smiled. The lipstick was the shade Cathy usually wore, which meant there was a good possibility that her father's secretary had joined him for dinner.

She went upstairs and was about to undress for her shower when her cell phone rang. "Hello."

"Hey, Libby, I heard you were home."

"Duan! Where are you? How have you been?"

She heard her brother's deep laugh. "Still asking a thousand questions, are you? I've been fine. How are things there?"

"Umm, so-so. Dad gave his first speech today, and

I thought it was great, but he feels his opponent did better."

"Well, did his opponent do better, Libby?"

His question threw her. Why would Duan ask her something like that? "Let's just say that they both did well, but Westmoreland made a direct hit on all the issues, whereas Dad just skated across the surface, like Senator Reed used to do."

"Politics as usual," Duan said. "I told Dad that I don't know squat about politics, but I'd think the people would want some fresh and innovative ideas. With Senator Reed tagging along, there's no way Dad can represent change."

Olivia nodded. She was glad she wasn't the only person in the family who thought that.

Duan went on. "And it's a shame that he's running against Reggie Westmoreland. I heard he's a nice guy. His cousin Dare is the sheriff of College Park. I've worked with Dare before, and I like him. Most of the Westmorelands that I know are good people."

"Dad thinks he's the enemy," Olivia said.

"I'm sorry that Dad feels that way. I was hoping this would be a clean campaign. I bet it's Senator Reed who's trying to make it dirty."

She could hear the dislike in her brother's voice. "So you will make it home for the barbecue next Saturday?" she asked him. In two weeks there would be a massive outdoor cookout in Atlanta-Fulton County Stadium for people to come out and meet all the candidates. Their father had asked her and her brothers to be there for the event so that the Jeffries family could show a united front.

"Yes, I'm in Detroit, but I hope to have everything wrapped up by then."

"Good." She looked forward to seeing both of her brothers. "Be safe, Duan."

"I will."

After leaving Chase's Place, Reggie decided to stop by and visit with his parents. He'd always admired his parents and the strength of their marriage. Everyone in the family knew the story of how James and Sarah Westmoreland had met and how it had been love at first sight. He couldn't help but chuckle when he thought about it now.

His mother and his aunt Evelyn had been the best of friends since childhood and had both been born and raised in Birmingham, Alabama. After graduating from high school, Evelyn had come to Atlanta to visit her aunt for the summer. During her first week in the city, she'd gone on a church picnic and met John Westmoreland. It had been love at first sight, and deciding not to waste any time, John and Evelyn had eloped the following week.

Evelyn had called Sarah to tell her the news, and being the levelheaded person that his mother was, Sarah could not believe or accept that someone could meet and fall in love at first glance. So Sarah had gone to Atlanta to talk some sense into Evelyn, only to meet John's twin brother, James, and fall in love with him at first sight as well. Two weeks later Sarah and James had married.

That had been nearly forty years ago, and his parents' marriage was still going strong. There had been his mom's cancer scare a few years back, when she'd been diagnosed with breast cancer. But thankfully, she was now doing fine, although she made sure never to miss her annual checkups. His mother was a strong and determined woman who had the love and admiration of her family.

Although Reggie knew it was his mother's desire to see her last son happily wedded, he was in no hurry. He had a good career as an accountant, with a very prestigious client list, and in a couple of months, he would know if his future would include politics.

His thoughts then shifted to Olivia Jeffries. He had enjoyed the time they had spent together tonight. In bed or out, she was someone he liked being with, and it bothered him that she had refused to see him again because of her father. The last thing they needed was to let anyone or anything get in the way of what could be a promising relationship. He understood that she would be leaving the country to return to Paris once the election was over, but Saturday night and today had proven that they were good together. He had actually enjoyed sitting in the coziness of that room at Chase's Place with her while they did little more than engage in conversation with each other.

He had enjoyed studying her while she talked, watching her lips move with each and every word she enunciated. And she had been wearing the same perfume she'd had on Saturday night. It had been hard sitting there across from her, knowing that he had tasted every inch of her skin, had been inside her body and had brought her pleasure.

By the time he pulled into his parents' driveway, he knew there was no way he could willingly walk away from Olivia Jeffries. He didn't like the thought of the two of them sneaking around to see each other so her father wouldn't find out, but at the moment he didn't care. The bottom line was that he wanted to see her again and would do anything and everything in his power—even blackmail—to make it happen.

If Olivia thought she had seen or heard the last of him, she was sorely mistaken.

Chapter 7

"I see you had a guest for dinner last night, Dad."

Olivia watched her father actually blush across the breakfast table and thought it was kind of cute that he seemed a little embarrassed.

"Ahh, yes, Cathy stopped by, and I invited her to stay for dinner."

"Oh, and why did she come by? Are the two of you working on another speech?"

"No, no," her father was quick to say. "She thought I wasn't in a good mood after yesterday's luncheon and wanted to cheer me up. She stopped by the bakery and brought me my favorite Danish. I thought that was kind of her."

"I think so, too, but then Cathy is a kind person. I like her."

Her father lifted a brow. "Do you really?"

Olivia looked over at him. She could tell her response was important to him. "Yes, and I always have. Over the years I thought she was not only a good secretary to you but a nice person, too. When I was younger and was dealing with a lot of girl stuff, I would often call Cathy."

Her father looked surprised. "You did?"

"Yes. Come on, Dad. You have to have known it was hard for me being the only girl in the house, and I couldn't talk to you, Duan and Terrence about *everything*."

"No, I guess not. I'm glad she was there for you then," her father said.

"Yes, and I'm glad she's here for you now, Dad."

Olivia watched as Orin's blush deepened. "Everything between me and Cathy is strictly business."

She was forced to hide her smile behind the rim of the coffee cup she'd brought to her lips. "Of course, Dad. I wasn't insinuating anything."

Half an hour later, after her father had left for work, Olivia decided to get dressed and go to the park and paint like she had planned to do the day before. She was about to head downstairs when her cell phone rang. For some reason, she knew who the caller was without looking. Her heart skipped several beats before she clicked the phone on. "Hello."

"Please meet with me again, Olivia."

She closed her eyes and breathed in deeply as the sensuous sound of his voice floated through her. "Reggie, I thought we decided that we wouldn't see each other again."

"I thought so, too, but I couldn't sleep last night. Thoughts of you kept invading my mind. I want to see you, Olivia. I want to be with you. Meet me today at noon. The Saxon Hotel. The same room number."

Her mind was suddenly flooded with memories of everything that had taken place in that room. And he wasn't the only one who'd been unable to sleep last night. Her body had been restless. Hot. She had dreamed of him several times, and at one point she had sat on the edge of the bed for what seemed like hours, recovering from the pleasurable memories that had swept through her, interrupting her night and filling her with a need she had never felt...until meeting Reggie.

"Will you come, Olivia? Please."

His voice was deep, quiet, yet persuasive. The sound of it poured over her skin like warm cream, and she couldn't fight it, because deep inside she wanted to be with him as much as he wanted to be with her.

She needed to see him again, to know, to understand and to explore the pull between them. Was it just sexual, or was it something else? Despite her decision not to become involved with him, she knew that she had to be with him at least one more time. These memories she was collecting would have to be enough to sustain her for the rest of her life.

"Yes," she said finally. "I'll meet you at noon."

Reggie paced the hotel room, glancing at his watch every so often. It was a few minutes before noon. He had had a news conference at nine but hadn't counted on a slew of reporters bombarding him after the news conference was over. Nor had he counted on the rumor that had quickly spread that his accounting firm, which employed over a hundred people, was facing possible bankruptcy and definite layoffs.

It was a lie that could easily be proven false, but not before mass pandemonium erupted at his business, and he'd spent part of the morning calming his employees' fears. He didn't have to think twice about where the lie had been generated, which made him angrier than hell. He'd never suspected that Orin Jeffries would allow his campaign staff to stoop so low.

For a moment he'd thought he would have to cancel this meeting with Olivia, but a part of him had refused to do it. She had consented to meet with him, and he would have moved heaven and hell to be here. Now he couldn't help wondering if she would show up. What if she had changed her mind? What if—

At that moment the door opened and Olivia walked in and his entire body went completely still. It seemed as if his heart picked that exact moment to stop beating. He was very much aware of how good she looked dressed in a pair of black tailored slacks and a light blue linen blouse.

She closed the door behind her and leaned against it, saying nothing but holding his gaze as intently as he was holding hers. He could now admit that although he had been drawn to her lips, the total package was what had captured his interest. She had the kind of presence that demanded attention, and just like at the Firemen's Masquerade Ball and yesterday, she was getting his again today. In droves.

In addition to checking her out, he was trying to get a read on her but couldn't. The sexual chemistry had hit the airwaves the moment she had walked through the door. With them, it couldn't be helped. But what about her attitude? he wondered. She had said yesterday that she didn't want them to become involved. Yet when he had defied her wishes and had called and asked her to meet with him here, she had accepted.

What was she expecting from him? What was he expecting from her?

He definitely knew what he wanted, but wanting and expecting were two different things. For the moment he was just glad to have her here, in this hotel room, alone with him. Had she come to spend time with him or to chew him out for having the audacity to call and ask her to meet with him? He was certain he was about to find out.

"Hello, Olivia."

"Reggie." And then, with her gaze still locked firmly with his, she moved away from the door and walked toward him.

His heart somehow began beating again, and it was only when she came to a stop directly in front of him that he allowed his gaze to shift and took note of the cut of her blouse. The low, square cut showed the nice swell of her breasts. They were breasts he had tasted before and was dying to taste again. Not surprisingly, something primal stirred inside him. His heart rate increased, and he breathed in deeply as a way to slow it down.

He cleared his throat. "I ordered lunch," he heard himself say and watched as she glanced behind him to see the table that had been set for two. "I'll call them to deliver the food when we're ready to eat," he said and drew a somewhat shaky breath.

She reached out and smoothed her hand along the back of his neck. "Are you hungry now, Reggie?" she asked, her voice an octave lower than he remembered.

He swallowed thickly. The feel of her fingers on his skin was pure torture. "It's up to you, since you're my guest."

A smile touched her lips at the corners. "In that case, we can wait. I'd rather do this now." And then she leaned up on tiptoe and connected her mouth to his.

At that moment whatever control he had been holding on to broke, and he instantly swept her into his arms without disconnecting their mouths. He wanted to head directly for the bedroom, but at that moment the only thing he could do was stand there with her in his arms and savor her this way, not sure when or if he would be granted the opportunity to do so again. He intended to make this their day, just like Saturday had been their night.

On the way to the hotel, Brent had tried to pin him down as to where he was going. He had told his friend that he was to be disturbed only if there was an emergency. He could tell Brent had wanted more information, but none had been forthcoming. What he did on his personal time was his business, and this lunch was on his personal time. And he was feasting on what he enjoyed most. Olivia's mouth.

He wasn't sure what had changed her mind since yesterday, when she had been adamant about not getting involved with him, but he was just glad she had. There was only so much a man could take.

He finally pulled back from her mouth. It was then that she nuzzled against his ear. The tip of her tongue trailed a path beneath it, and then she whispered, "I want to make love with you again—"

Before she could finish her words, he headed in the direction of the bedroom, sidestepping the table set for two. She laughed when he gently tossed her on the bed, then captured her laughter with his mouth when he quickly joined her there. And then it was back on. The heat was blazing. They didn't have a moment to waste, and they both knew it. As they lay fully clothed in bed, with their mouths joined in the most intimate way, their tongues dueled, tangled and mated. She refused to stay still. She was moving all over the place, and he eventually placed a thigh over hers. She had become wild, so bold and wanton. And he loved it.

She pulled her mouth back and met his gaze, their hearts pounding loudly in the room. "Make love to me, Reggie. Now," she said.

She didn't have to say the words twice. He moved off the bed and quickly undressed, trying not to rip the buttons off his shirt in his haste. And then, when he was completely naked, except for the condom he had taken the time to put on, he went for her, pulled her toward him to remove her blouse and bra before tackling her shoes, slacks and panties.

When he had pulled the latter two down her hips to reveal the lushness of her feminine mound, he knew he had to taste her right then. He tossed the items of clothing aside and held down her hips at the same time that his mouth lowered to her, kissing her intimately, with a hunger and greed that made her tremble and moan incoherently. But he didn't let up. His tongue was desperate to reacquaint itself with the taste it had relished on Saturday, and he intended to get his fill. And her body responded, generating the sweetness he wanted, and he mercilessly savored her.

He felt her hands lock around his head as if to hold his mouth in place, but that wasn't needed. He wasn't going anyplace until he got enough, and that wouldn't be anytime soon. He proved his point by plunging his tongue deeper inside of her, absorbing the wetness of her sensuality, which was being produced in abundance just for him.

Reggie finally pulled back and licked his lips, while his eyes traveled down her entire body, taking in every inch and every curve, the texture of her skin and the fullness of her breasts, which seemed to be begging for his mouth.

Leaning upward, he brushed his lips against a taut nipple, liking the sound of the quick breath that got caught in her throat. He proceeded to sample her nipples, finding both tantalizingly hot.

"Come inside me, please."

Olivia's tortured moan had Reggie moving his body over hers. When his heated shaft was at the opening of her feminine mound, he met her gaze, and then, with a hungry growl, he pushed deep inside of her.

Olivia closed her eyes as pleasure washed through her. What was there about being joined to Reggie that made her feel such joy, such mind-blowing pleasure and such spellbinding ecstasy? She felt him lift her legs, and she wrapped them around his waist while he thrust inside of her with whipcord speed and precision. Everything about him was affecting her in an elemental way, and she could barely stifle her moans as she was consumed by a tide of red-hot passion. It was only with him that she could feel not only taken but possessed. Only with him could she be not only driven but also contained. And he was making love to her without any restraint and with a voracious need, which was fueling her own. And every time the hard muscles of his stomach pressed against hers, pinning her beneath him, she trembled from the inside out.

And then an orgasm rammed through her. Never before had she felt anything so profound. She cried out his name. And he used his tongue, lips and mouth to absorb her cries of pleasure, her moans of passion. Instead of letting up, he pressed on and thrust deeper.

The flames ignited, flared and then burned in the very center of her, and when an explosion ripped through her a second time, he was there, and she felt his shaft expand before exploding in his release. And as passion tumbled her over into the depths of turbulent, sensual waters, she cried his name once more before she felt herself drowning in a sea of ecstasy.

Propped up on his elbow, Reggie stared down at Olivia. In the middle of the day, she had actually drifted off to sleep. He smiled, understanding why. He had shown her no mercy in taking them both through waves and waves of pure pleasure. Somewhere in the back of his mind, he heard the sound of his cell, but at that moment he chose to ignore it. His main focus, his total concentration, was on the most beautiful creature he had ever laid eyes on.

He glanced over at the clock on the nightstand. They had been in the room for two hours already—two hours of nonstop lovemaking in which he would get hard again before even coming out of her. They would start another bout of lovemaking right on the tail end of the previous one. Nothing like this had ever happened to him before. He felt totally obsessed with this woman.

He could vividly recall the first moment he had seen her at the Firemen's Masquerade Ball. He had known then, just like he knew now, that she was the one that he would make his. At the time he just hadn't known the depth to which he would do so. Now he did.

And he also understood why his brothers and cousins seemed so happy these days, so blissfully content. They had been able to find that one person who they knew was their soul mate. The question of the hour was, how was he going to convince Olivia that she was his? Especially considering the fact that they were sneaking around just to be together.

He wanted to introduce her to his family. He especially wanted her to get to know his mother and his brothers' and cousins' wives. He wanted to take her to the Westmoreland family reunion, which would be held in Texas at the end of the month. He wanted to take her to one of Thorn's motorcycle races later this year. There were so many things he wanted to share with her. But the most important thing of all was his life.

There was no need to tell her that he loved her, because she wouldn't understand that one thing about being a Westmoreland was recognizing your mate when you saw her or him. Although, he thought, with a smile, he would have to admit some of his cousins and brothers had refused to accept their fate at first. But in the end it hadn't done any good. Love had zapped their senses just the same. And it had done the same thing to him. It had hit him like a ton of bricks on Saturday night, and like his parents, he had fallen in love at first sight.

She had her defenses down now, but he wouldn't be surprised if they were back up before she left the hotel today. It didn't matter. He was not going to let her deny them what was rightfully theirs to have. She didn't know it yet, but in time she would. No matter what the situation was between him and her father regarding the campaign, it had no bearing on the two of them.

He noticed her eyes fluttering before they fully

opened, and then she was staring up at him. She had to be hungry now. He would feed her, and then he would make love to her again.

Or so he thought. Suddenly she lifted her body and pushed him back onto the covers to straddle him, placing her knees on the sides of his hips to seemingly hold him immobile. She tilted her head back and looked down at him. And smiled. He felt the effects of that smile like a punch to his gut, and his shaft suddenly got hard, totally erect.

"I thought you would be hungry," he said, reaching out and placing the palm of his hand at the back of her neck.

"I am," she whispered, holding his eyes with her own. "For you."

He drew her head down to brush his lips against hers. "And I for you."

When he released her mouth, she glanced at him with a confused look in her eyes. "What are you doing to me, Reggie Westmoreland? How do you have the ability to make me feel wild and reckless? Make me want to yield to temptation?"

A hot rush of desire sent shivers through his body. "I should be asking you the same thing, Olivia Jeffries."

And then she lowered herself on him, and he knew it was a good thing he'd already donned a new condom, because there was no way he could have said stop when she embedded him inside of herself to the hilt. The look on her face told him that she was proud of her accomplishment. She had wanted, so she had taken.

And then she began moving, slowly at first and then with a desperation that sent fire surging through his loins and made it feel as if the head of his shaft was about to explode. But she kept moving, dangling her twin globes in front of his face with every downward motion.

He reached out and grabbed hold of one, brought it to his mouth, and she threw her head back as she continued to ride him in a way he had never been ridden before. The woman had power in her thighs, in her hips and in her inner muscles, and she was using them to make shivers race all through him.

In retaliation, he covered her breasts with his kisses, using his lips and tongue to push her over the same edge that he was close to falling from. And when an explosion hit, he bucked until they were almost off the bed, but then her thighs nearly held him immobile. His body was locked so tightly with hers, he wondered if they would be able to separate when the time came. And at that moment he really didn't care if they couldn't. He would love to stay inside of her forever, in the place where he would one day plant his seed for their child.

That thought triggered another explosion inside of him, and he groped hard for sanity when Olivia came apart on top of him. Her inner muscles clamped him tightly, and she drew every single thing she could out of him. His lungs felt like they were about to collapse in his throat when he tried to keep from hollering out. Burying his face in her chest, he found a safe haven right between her breasts. He knew from this day forward that whatever it took, one day he would make her totally, completely and irrevocably his.

"We never ate lunch, did we?" Olivia asked as she slid back into her slacks.

"No, and I owe you an apology for that," Reggie said, pulling up his pants. He stopped what he was doing and stared at her, watched how she was struggling with the buttons on her blouse.

"Come here, Olivia."

She glanced over at him and smiled before crossing the room to him. "I don't know why I wore this thing when it has so many buttons. It's not like I didn't know that you would be taking it off me."

He didn't say anything as he took over buttoning her blouse. She was right. It did have a lot of buttons. That wouldn't have been so bad if his attention hadn't been drawn to her flesh-toned bra. "Your bra is my favorite color," he said, smiling down at her.

"I figured as much when I put it on," she said, grinning. "You were right. Flesh tone is a color."

"If you're hungry, we can still—"

"No. I noticed your cell phone went off a few times. You need to get back to work."

He chuckled. "Have you noticed the time, Olivia? The day is practically over. We've been here for five hours. It's past five o'clock." And he really wasn't bothered by it. "There. All done," he said, dropping his hands to his sides before he was tempted to do something, like pull her into his arms and kiss her.

"Thanks. Now I definitely need to know something," she said, looking up at him.

"What?"

"Do you have stock in this place?"

Another smile touched his lips. "Wish I did, but no."

"Then what kind of connections do you have?" she asked, with an expression on her face that said she was determined to know.

"My connection is my brother Quade. Dominic Saxon is his brother-in-law. Both recently became fathers. Quade has triplets—a son and two daughters and Dominic's wife, Taylor, gave birth to a son a few months ago."

"Oh. Proud fathers, I gather."

Reggie smiled. "Yes, they are."

He slipped into his shirt while he watched her stand before the dresser's mirror to redo her makeup. Although he knew he would probably get some resistance, he decided to go ahead and have his say. "I got the room again for this Saturday night, Olivia."

Olivia met his gaze in the mirror before slowly turning around to stare at him. He had just issued an open invitation, and it was one he wanted her to accept. She continued to stare into his dark eyes, and then she shifted her gaze to study his face. There was something, something she couldn't decipher, in his eyes and on his face.

"Coming here today was risky, Reggie," she finally said softly.

"I know," was his response. "But I had to see you."

"And I had to be with you," she said honestly.

Too late she wondered why she would admit such a thing to him, but deep down she knew the reason. She wanted him to know that she had wanted to be here and that she thought their time together was special.

Reggie crossed the room to her, and without giving him the chance to make the first move, she reached up and drew his mouth down to hers. And he kissed her with a gentleness that he had to fight to maintain.

When she released his mouth, he gazed down at her. "Sure you had enough?"

She licked her lips. "For now." She then smiled. "I'll get the rest on Saturday."

He lifted a hopeful brow. "You will come?"

She smiled. "Yes, I will come."

Although he knew they needed to finish getting dressed and be on their way, he reached out, caught her around the waist and pulled her gently into his arms, immediately reveling in the way her body seemed to cling to his, perfectly and in sync. And then he lowered his mouth to hers for a kiss that would keep him going strong until Saturday night, when they would come together once again.

Chapter 8

"Cathy will be calling you later today, Libby."

Olivia lifted her gaze from her cereal bowl to glance over at her father, with a questioning look on her face. "For what reason?"

"To schedule all those fund-raisers that you and I will need to attend over the next couple of weeks, beginning this Saturday."

Panic shot through Olivia. "Not this Saturday night, I hope."

Her father quirked a thick brow. "No, it's Saturday midday at the home of Darwin Walker and his wife."

She nodded. Darwin and Terrence used to play together for the Miami Dolphins. Last year Darwin, who, like Terrence, had retired from the NFL, moved to Atlanta after accepting a coaching position with the Falcons.

"And why are you concerned about Saturday night? Do you have plans or something?" Orin asked.

Olivia swallowed. She hated lying to her father, but there was no way she could tell him the truth. Running for political office had made him somewhat unreasonable, especially when it came to Reggie. She was convinced that the only reason he didn't like Reggie was that he was the main person standing in the way of him becoming a senator. However, she intended to do as Reggie had suggested and believe that the election had no bearing on what was developing between them.

She met her father's gaze. "Yes, I have plans. I ran into a friend at the party Saturday night, and we're getting together again this weekend." At least what she'd said wasn't a total lie.

Her father's features softened. "That's good. I've been feeling badly about asking you to put your life in Paris on hold to come here and be my escort for all these campaign events. I'm glad you've managed to squeeze in some fun time."

If only you knew just how much fun I've had thanks to Reggie, she thought.

Both she and her father resumed eating, and the kitchen became quiet. There was something she needed to ask him, something she truly needed to know. The issue had been bothering her since she'd heard about it yesterday.

She glanced across the table at her father. He had resumed reading the paper and was flipping through the pages. She hated interrupting, but she had to. "Dad, can I ask you something?"

"Sure, sweetheart," Orin said, looking up to meet her gaze and placing the newspaper aside. "What is it?"

"Reggie Westmoreland," she said and watched her father's jaw flex.

"What about him, Libby?"

"Did you authorize any of your staff members to put out that false statement about his company facing bankruptcy and layoffs?"

Her father frowned. "Of course not. Why would I or my staff do something like that?"

"To discredit him."

His features tightened. "And you believe I would do something like that or give my staff permission to do so?"

"I don't want to believe that, but I'm not naive. I know how dirty politics can be, Dad."

Orin leaned back in his chair. "Are you taking up for Reggie Westmoreland?" he asked, studying her features.

She sighed deeply. "No, Dad, I'm not taking up for anyone. Such tactics can backfire, so my concern is actually for you."

What she didn't say was that she was sure Reggie was aware of the rumor, which had circulated yesterday, but he hadn't mentioned it to her. Although he had to have been upset about it, Reggie had given her his full concentration and had kept his word not to mix his competition with her father and his relationship with her.

Now it was her turn to study her father's features, and she could see that what she'd said had him thinking. Was he so disjointed from his campaign staff that he truly didn't know what was going on? Did he not know what they were capable of?

"I'm having a meeting with my campaign staff this morning, and if I discover that someone on my staff is connected to yesterday's story in any way, they will be dismissed."

She came close to asking if that included Senator Reed. She had a feeling he was behind the rumor. "Thanks, Dad. I think it will be in your best interest in the long run."

"Where were you yesterday, Reggie? I tried reaching you all afternoon," Brent said, looking across the breakfast table at his friend. They were sitting in Chase's Place, where they had met for breakfast.

Reggie shrugged. "I was busy. Did anything come up that you couldn't handle?"

"Of course not." Brent set his coffee cup down, and his blue eyes studied Reggie intently. "But it would have been nice if I'd been able to contact you. Someone from *Newsweek* called to do an article on you. We're not talking about a local magazine, Reg. We're talking about *Newsweek*. You know how long I've been trying to get you national coverage."

Yes, Reggie did know, and he felt badly about it. But at the time all he could think about was that he wanted to spend uninterrupted time with Olivia. "I'm sorry about that, Brent."

"You're seeing her, aren't you?"

Reggie lifted a brow and met Brent's stare. "It depends on who you're referring to."

"Orin Jeffries's daughter."

Reggie leaned back in his chair. He and Brent had been friends for a long time, since grade school, actually. After attending college at Yale, Brent had worked for a number of years in Boston before moving back to Atlanta a few years ago to care for his elderly parents. A couple of months ago, Reggie had been the best man at Brent's wedding.

As far as Reggie was concerned, other than his brothers and cousins, there wasn't a man he trusted more. He met his best friend's eyes. "Yes, I'm seeing her."

Brent let out a deep sigh. "Do you think that's smart?"

Reggie chuckled. "Considering the fact that I plan to marry her sometime after the election, yes, I would have to say it's smart."

Brent's jaw dropped. "Marry!" And then he quickly glanced around, hoping no one had heard his outburst. After turning back around, he nervously brushed back a strand of blond hair that had fallen onto his face. "Reggie, you just met the woman on Monday at that luncheon."

"No," Reggie said, smiling, as he absently swirled the coffee around in his cup. "Actually, we met before then."

Brent lifted a brow. "When?"

"Saturday night, at the Firemen's Masquerade Ball."

"Saturday night?"

"Yes," replied Reggie.

"That wasn't even a week ago. Are you telling me you decided once you saw her at a party that you were going to marry her?"

"Something like that. And at the time I didn't know who she was. I found out her true identity on Monday, at that luncheon, the same time she found out mine." Reggie could only smile. Brent was staring at him like he had totally lost his mind. "Trust me, my friend, I haven't lost my mind. Just my heart."

Brent took a sip of his orange juice. His expression implied that he wished the juice was laced with vodka. "Do the two of you understand the implications of what you're doing? Hello," he said, putting emphasis on that single word. "Her father is your opponent in a Senate race."

"We're aware of that. However, we've decided that has nothing to do with what's going on between us," Reggie said.

"And you love her?" Brent asked incredulously.

"With all my heart and then some," Reggie answered truthfully.

He had thought about it a lot last night. To be honest, he hadn't been able to think about anything else. As crazy as it might seem to some people, yes, he had fallen in love with her. He had never been totally against marriage, especially since his family over the past seven years—starting with Delaney—seemed to be falling like flies into matrimony. He just knew he wouldn't ever settle down until the right woman came along. Because of his career and his decision to get into politics, he hadn't expected that to happen anytime soon. He thought he would at least be in his late thirties when he tied the knot, although he knew his mother wished otherwise.

"And she feels the same way?"

Brent's question invaded Reggie's thoughts. "Not sure. I've never asked her. In fact, I haven't even shared my feelings with her yet. It will be best to wait until after the campaign."

Brent took another gulp of his orange juice. "I swear, Reggie, you're going to give me heart failure."

Reggie smiled. "Don't mean to. I'm sure you remember when you met Melody. What did you tell me? You claimed you had fallen in love with her instantly."

"I did. But her father wasn't my political opponent," Brent countered.

"Shouldn't matter, and we intend not to let it affect our relationship, either. So wish us luck."

Brent couldn't help but smile. "Hey, man, what you need are prayers, and I'll be the first to send one up for you."

Olivia stepped off the elevator and glanced around. Over the years, not much in her father's office had changed. The placement of the furniture was still the same. She remembered coming here as a child after school and sitting on the sofa and watching television—but only after she had completed her homework. Duan and Terrence had been into after-school sports, so instead of letting her go home to an empty house, her father had hired a private car to pick her up from school and bring her here.

"Libby, it's good to see you. You didn't need to come in to meet with me."

Olivia couldn't help but return Cathy's warm smile. "I didn't mind. I wanted to get out of the house, anyway."

That much was true. She had tried to paint, but the only subject that had readily come to mind was Reggie, and she couldn't risk her father finding sketches of him all over the place. She slid into the chair next to Cathy's desk.

"If you wanted to see your dad you're too late. He stepped out. I think he went over to his campaign headquarters," Cathy was saying, with a concerned expression on her face. "He was on the phone earlier with his campaign staff, and he wasn't a happy camper. He suspects someone released that false information on Westmoreland yesterday. Now it says in this morning's paper that your father's campaign is turning to dirty politics."

Olivia sighed. She'd been afraid that would happen. "Well, I'm glad Dad is addressing it. Otherwise, it could backfire even more if whoever is responsible keeps it up."

"I agree."

Olivia liked Cathy. She was attractive, responsible, and Olivia knew the woman had her father's interests at heart. At least her father was beginning to notice Cathy as a woman, although he was moving way too slowly to suit Olivia. "Well, as you can see, I brought my planner," she said to Cathy. "Dad wants me to pencil in all those important dates of those campaign events. I still don't understand why he just didn't ask you to go with him."

Cathy blushed. "Your father would never do that. I'm his secretary."

Olivia rolled her eyes. "You're not just his secretary, Cathy. You're his right hand in more ways than one, and I'm sure he knows it. Frankly, I'm concerned about him and the election. Sometimes I think he wants to become a senator, and other times I'm not sure. What's your take on it?"

Cathy hesitated in responding, and Olivia knew it was because she thought that to say anything negative about Orin or the campaign might be construed as disloyalty. "I think that if it had been left up to your father, he would not have run," Cathy said hesitantly.

"Then why did he?"

"Because Senator Reed talked him into it."

Olivia shook her head, still not understanding. "My father is a grown man who can make decisions on his own. Why would he let Senator Reed talk him into doing anything? That doesn't make sense. It's not like they have a history or have been friends for a terribly long time. It's my understanding that they met playing golf just a few years ago."

Cathy shook her head. "No, their relationship goes back further than that."

Olivia blinked, surprised. She had a feeling Cathy knew a lot more than she was telling. Definitely a lot more than Olivia or her brothers knew. "So, what's the relationship?"

Cathy, Olivia noted, was nervously biting her lips. "I'm not sure it's my place to say, Libby," she said.

Olivia knew that if she didn't get the information from Cathy, then she would never get it. Deciding to go for broke, she said in a low and soft voice, "I know you love Dad, Cathy." At the woman's surprised look, Olivia lowered her voice even more. "And I'm hoping Dad realizes, and very soon, what a jewel he has in you, not only as an employee, but, more importantly, as a woman who, I know, has his back. But I'm honestly worried that something is going on that my brothers and I wouldn't agree with, and if that's the case, then we need to know what it is."

Cathy stared at her for a long moment. "Your father feels indebted to the senator."

Olivia raised a brow. "And why would he feel that way?"

Cathy didn't say anything for a long while. "Because of your mother," the older woman said.

Olivia's head began spinning. "How does my mother have anything to do with this? My brothers and I haven't heard from her in over twenty-something years. Are you saying that my father has? That he and my mother are in contact with each other?"

"No, that's not what I'm saying."

With a desperate look in her eyes, Olivia took hold of the woman's hand. "Tell me, Cathy. You need to tell me what's going on and what my mother has to do with it."

"Years ago, your mother ran off with another man, a married man," Cathy said.

Olivia nodded. She knew all that. Although she had been only three then, years later she had overheard one of her grandparents talking about her mother in whispers. "And?"

"The man's wife had a child."

"Yes, I know that as well," Olivia said. "I also know the woman was so torn up about what happened that eventually she and her child moved away."

"Yes, but what you probably don't know is that eventually, a couple of years later, that woman committed suicide. She could never get over losing her husband."

Olivia gasped. Cathy was right. She hadn't known that. "How awful."

Cathy nodded sadly in agreement. "Yes, it was. And what's even worse, when she decided to stall her car on the train tracks and just sit there waiting for the train to come, she had her child in the car with her. They were both killed."

Tears she couldn't hold back sprang into Olivia's eyes. It was bad enough that her mother's actions had broken up a family, but they had also caused a woman to end her own life and that of her child.

"I didn't want to tell you," Cathy said softly, handing Olivia a tissue.

Olivia dabbed at her eyes. "I'm glad you did. But what does all that have to do with Senator Reed?"

Now it was Cathy who reached out to hold Olivia's hand. "The woman who committed suicide was his sister, Libby, and your father feels responsible for what eventually happened to her and her little girl because of what your mother did."

The first thing Olivia did when she got home was to pull out her sketch pad and watercolors, determined to go to the park. Painting always soothed her mind, and she needed it today more than ever.

She had come home soon after her conversation with Cathy; otherwise, she would have gone looking for her father just to cry in his arms. It just wasn't fair that he felt responsible for the choices his wife had made over twenty years before, choices that had ultimately led to a sad tragedy. And if Senator Reed was intentionally playing with her father's conscience, he would have to stop.

Once at the park, she found several scenes she could concentrate on and tried her hand at doing a few sketches, but her concentration wavered. A part of her wanted to call her brothers and tell them what she'd found out, but she resisted doing so. They would be in town next weekend, and she would tell them then. They would know how to handle the situation. She loved her father and if he really wanted to enter politics and become a senator, then he had her support. But if he was being railroaded into doing something out of misplaced guilt, then she definitely had a problem with that.

For the first time in years, she thought about the woman who had given birth to her. The woman had walked out of her, her father's and her brothers' lives without looking back. When Duan had gotten old enough, he had tried contacting her, to satisfy his need to know why Susan Jeffries's maternal instincts had never driven her to stay in contact with the three kids she had left behind. Instead of finding a woman who regretted what she had done, he had found a selfish individual who had been married four times and had never given birth to another child. Instead, she had been living life in the fast lane and was the mistress of a race-car driver, apparently working on hubby number five. That had been six years ago. There was no telling what number she was on now.

The more Olivia thought about her mother, the more depressed she became, and she found that even painting couldn't soothe her troubled mind. It was strange that the happiest of her days were those she'd spent with Reggie. Not just sharing a bed with him, but sharing a bit of herself like she'd never shared with a man before. They would talk in between their lovemaking. Pillow talk. She felt so good around him.

A child's laughter caught her attention, and she glanced across the pond to see a mother interacting with a child that appeared to be about three, the same age she'd been when her mother left. The woman seemed to be having fun, and the exuberance on the face of the little girl left no doubt that she, too, was having the time of her life. That's what real mothers did. They put smiles on their children's faces, not sad frowns that lasted a lifetime.

Aware that she had begun thinking of her poor excuse for a mother again, she shifted her thoughts back to Reggie. She would love to see him now, be held by him and kissed by him. It was hard to believe that they had met less than a week ago, but since then they had shared so much.

Half an hour later she was still sitting on the park bench, thinking about Reggie. They had spent most of yesterday together. Would he want to see her today? Would he meet her somewhere if she were to call, just to hold her in his arms and do nothing more?

Olivia swallowed. There was only one way to find out. She took her cell phone out of her bag and dialed his number.

"Hello. This is Reggie Westmoreland."

The sound of his sexy voice oozed all over her. "Hi. This is Olivia. I didn't want to call you, but I didn't have anyone else to call."

"Olivia, what's wrong?"

She swiped at a tear. "Nothing really. I just need to be held."

"Where are you?"

"At a park. I came here to paint and—"

"What's the name of the park?"

"Cypress Park."

"I know where it's located. I'm on my way."

"No, it's out in the open. Is there a place near here where we can meet?" she asked.

There was a pause, and then he said, "Yes, in fact, there is. My cousin Delaney and her husband, Jamal, own a town house a few blocks away. It's on Commonwealth Boulevard. Delaney's Square."

"A town house just for her?" Olivia asked.

"Jamal was the first tenant and decided to buy out the others so he, Delaney and the kids could have their privacy whenever they came to town. I have a key to check on things when they're not here. Go there now, sweetheart. I'll be waiting."

Olivia recognized Reggie's car parked in front of a massive group of elegant buildings, all townhomes, around ten of them, on a beautiful landscaped property.

She strolled up the walkway to the center building; her pulse rate increased with every step she took. When she reached the front door, she glanced around. She lifted her hand to knock on the door, but before her knuckles could make contact, the door opened and Reggie was there. He captured her hand in his and gently pulled her inside and closed the door behind her.

Olivia looked up at him, and he gently pulled her into his arms. He wrapped his arms around her waist and pressed her face to his chest.

She inhaled deeply. He smelled of man, a nice, robust scent that sent shivers down her spine. This was what she needed. To be held in his arms. Riding over here, she kept thinking about how it would feel to be in his arms again. Her life was in turmoil, and right now he was a solid force in her mixed-up world.

Suddenly, she felt herself being lifted in his arms, and she linked her arms around his neck. "Where are you taking me?" she asked when he began walking.

"Over here, to the sofa, so I can hold you the way I want to, and so you can tell me what's bothering you."

Olivia pressed her lips together, not sure she could do that without implicating her father, and that wouldn't be good. He didn't need to know that her father had felt compelled to enter the Senate race because Senator Reed, a man he felt indebted to, had encouraged him to do so, and that her father's heart might not be in it.

Reggie adjusted her in his arms when he sat down on the sofa and angled her body so that she could look up at him. "What happened, Olivia? What happened to make you call me?"

She hesitated and then decided to tell him some of what was bothering her, but not all of it. "I was at the park and saw this mother and child. The little girl was about the age I was when my mother walked out on my dad, my brothers and me. Seeing them made me realize how easy it was for my mother to walk away without looking back."

"And she's never tried contacting you?" Reggie asked, softly stroking the side of her face with the pad of his thumb.

Oliver shook her head. "No, she never has."

Reggie tightened his hold on Olivia, and she clung to his warmth. She wasn't sure how much time passed before she lifted her head to look at him. He looked at her, studied her face. "Are you okay?" he asked softly.

She nodded. "I am now. But I have to go. Dad will worry because it's getting late."

He stood with her in his arms and let her slide down his body until her feet touched the floor. For a long moment, she stood there and stared at him, realizing that he hadn't kissed her yet. He must have read her mind, because he lowered his mouth to her. She craned her neck to meet him halfway and let out a deep sigh when their lips met.

His tongue was in her mouth in a flash, moving around in a circular motion before winding around hers, taking it in total possession. She wrapped her arms around his neck and groaned out loud when he deepened the kiss. Sensations throbbed within her, and she felt a shiver pass through her body.

Moments later, she pulled back from the kiss, gasping for breath. Nobody could kiss like Reggie Westmoreland. She was totally convinced of that. They had to stand there a moment to catch their breaths. In a way, it did her heart good to know he had been just as affected by the kiss.

"Do you want me to show you around before you go?" Reggie asked her in a ragged voice, taking her hand in his.

Olivia glanced around. The place was absolutely beautiful, with its sprawling living room that was lavishly decorated in peach and cream, its bigger-than-life dining room and kitchen and its spiral staircase. Fit for a king. And from what she'd read, Sheikh Jamal Ari Yasir would one day inherit that title.

"Yes, I'd love to see the rest of it."

Reggie showed her around, and she was in total awe of the lavishly decorated bedrooms and baths, and when they toured one of the beautifully decorated guest rooms, with a huge four-poster bed, he didn't try to get her in it. Instead, he looked at her. "Saturday night will be ours. Today you just needed me to hold you," he whispered.

His words went a long way to calm her, soothed her troubled mind and actually made her feel special, mainly because she had called and he had come. "Thank you for coming, Reggie."

He looked down at her and pulled her closer to him. "I will always come when you call, Olivia."

She met his gaze, thinking that was a strange thing

to say. They didn't have a future together. At the end of two months, she would be returning to Paris.

"Come on. Let me walk you to your car," Reggie said huskily as he placed his arms around her shoulders.

Olivia regretted that her time with Reggie was about to end and appreciated that he had been there for her when she had needed him. That meant a lot.

Chapter 9

The following week Olivia kept busy by attending several functions with her father. She had decided not to discuss her conversation with Cathy with him. Instead, she would meet with her brothers and get their take on the matter when they came to town later that week.

She had to catch her breath whenever she thought of the times she and Reggie had spent together, especially on Saturday night. On Wednesday he had called and asked her to have a midday snack with him at Chase's Place. It was then that she had met Chase's wife, Jessica, who was expecting the couple's first child. Jessica, who liked to bake, had treated her to a batch of brownies, which had been delicious. Olivia wondered what Reggie had told Chase and Jessica about their relationship, and if they knew that she was the daughter of his opponent in the Senate race.

Olivia couldn't help but note over the past few days that her father seemed excited about this weekend. He would have his three children home to attend the huge barbecue that was being planned for all the candidates on Saturday evening.

Tonight she would attend yet another political function with her father. All the candidates would be there. She and Reggie would have to pretend they barely knew each other. They had talked about it on Wednesday, and she knew he wasn't overjoyed at the thought of that, but he had promised to abide by her wishes. She wasn't crazy about them sneaking around to see each other, either, but under the circumstances, it was something they had to do.

She smiled as she continued to get dressed, thinking that sneaking around did have its benefits. It made them appreciate the time they were together, and they always found ways to put it to good use. It would be hard tonight to see him and not go over to him and claim him as hers. And a part of her felt that he was hers. Whenever they were together, he would use his mouth to stamp his brand all over her, and she would do likewise with him.

She tried not to think about the day when the campaign would finally be over and she would have to return to Paris. She was even thinking about calling the Louvre to see if she could extend her leave for a couple more weeks. She wanted to be able to be with him in the open after the election. She didn't want to think about how he and her father would feel about each other then, depending on which one of them was victorious.

She glanced at her watch. She needed to hurry, because the last thing she wanted was to make her father late to a campaign event. Besides, although she had just seen Reggie yesterday, she was eager to see him again.

Reggie clung to his patience when he glanced at the entrance to the ballroom. He had thought about Olivia most of the day and couldn't wait to see her. Last night he had begun missing her and wished he could have called her to ask her to meet him somewhere. This sneaking around was unpleasant, and his patience was wearing thin. He wasn't sure he would be able to hold out for another month. Because her brothers would be arriving in town this weekend, she'd said it wouldn't be wise for her to try to get away for a tryst at the Saxon on Saturday night, after the barbecue. The fact that Duan and Terrence Jeffries would be in town until next Wednesday meant his and Olivia's time together would basically be nonexistent.

"And how are you doing this evening, Westmoreland?"

Reggie turned to look at Senator Reed. The one man he really didn't care to see. "I'm fine, Senator. And yourself?" he asked, more out of politeness than a sense a caring.

"I'm doing great. I think, for you and Jeffries, it will be a close election."

Reggie wanted to say that this view was not reflected in the most recent poll, which indicated that he had a substantial lead, but he refrained from doing so. "You think so?" he said.

"Yes, but what it all will eventually boil down to is experience."

Reggie smiled.

"And the candidate I endorse," the senator added.

What the senator didn't add, Reggie quickly noted, was that he was not endorsing him. That was no surprise. The man had already endorsed Orin Jeffries and was working with Jeffries's campaign. "Sorry you think that, Senator, since I'm equally sure that I don't need or want your endorsement."

"And I'm equally sorry you feel that way, because I intend to prove you wrong. I will take great pleasure when you lose." The older man then walked away.

"What was that about?" Brent asked when he walked up moments later.

"The good senator tried convincing me of the importance of his endorsement."

Brent snorted. "Did you tell him just where he could put his endorsement?"

Reggie chuckled. "Not in so many words, but I think he got the picture."

Brent glanced to where the senator was now standing and talking to a wealthy industrialist. "There's something about that man that really irks me."

"I feel the same way," Reggie said. He was about to tilt his glass to his lips when he glanced at the ballroom entrance at the exact moment that Olivia and her father walked in. He immediately caught her gaze, and the rush of desire that sped through his body made him want to say the hell with discretion, cross the room and pull her into his arms. But he knew he couldn't do that.

Brent, who was standing beside Reggie, followed his gaze. "Do I need to caution you about being careful? You never know who might be watching you two. I don't trust Reed. Although he's backing Jeffries, I wouldn't put anything past him."

Reggie's gaze remained on Olivia's face for a minute longer, until she looked away.

Senator Albert Reed frowned as he watched the interaction between Olivia and Reggie. He had a strong feeling that something was going on between them, but he didn't have any proof. And that didn't sit well with him. He had suggested to Orin that he send for his daughter under the pretense that she could be an asset. But the truth was that he really wanted Olivia for himself.

He had discovered that women her age enjoyed the company of older men, especially if those men were willing to spend money on them. With his wife bedridden, he had needs that only a younger woman could fulfill.

When he had seen all those pictures of Olivia that Orin had on the wall in his study, he had made the decision that he wanted her as his next mistress. Getting her into his bed would be the perfect ending to his quest for revenge against the Jeffries family for what Orin's slut of a wife had done. Orin felt guilty, and as far as Senator Reed was concerned, his guilt was warranted. He should have been able to control his unfaithful wife.

He took a sip of his drink as he continued to watch Olivia and Reggie looking at each other. Umm, interesting. It was time to take action. Immediately.

"I'm sure England is just beautiful this time of the year."

Olivia nodded as Marie Patterson rattled on and on to the group of four women about her dream to one day spend a month in England. Then Olivia took a sip of her drink and glanced around the room, her gaze searching for one man in particular. When she found him, their gazes met and held.

She knew that look. If they had been alone, she would have crossed the room to him and wrapped her arms around his neck while he wrapped his around her waist. He would have brought her close to him and pressed his hard, muscular body against hers to the point where she would cradle his big, hard erection at the junction of her thighs.

"So, what about Paris, Ms. Jeffries? I understand you've been living there for a while. Is the weather there nice?"

Olivia swung her attention back to Mrs. Patterson when the woman said her name. She took a quick sip of her wine to cool off her hot insides before answering. "Yes, the weather in Paris is nice."

When the conversation shifted from her to the latest in women's fashion, Olivia's gaze went back to Reggie. He was talking to a group of men. Because the men had that distinguished Westmoreland look, she could only assume that they were relatives of his—brothers or cousins.

She was about to turn her attention back to the group of women around her when Senator Reed, who was standing across the room, caught her eye. He was staring at her. For some reason, the way he was looking at her made her feel uncomfortable, and she quickly broke eye contact with him.

Reggie had endured the party as long as he could and was glad when Brent indicated he could leave. He headed for the door, but not before finding Olivia. He smiled at her and nodded. He knew she would interpret the message.

He had been in his car for about five minutes when she called. "Where are you, sweetheart?" he immediately asked her.

"The ladies' room. I'm alone, but someone might walk in at any minute. You wanted me to call you?"

"Yes," he said hoarsely. "I want you."

The depths of his words almost made Olivia groan. She turned to make sure she was still alone in the ladies' room. "And I want you, too," she whispered into her cell phone.

There was a pause. And then he said, "Meet me. Tonight. Our place."

Olivia inhaled deeply. Meeting him later wouldn't be a problem, because her father was a sound sleeper. She knew it would be their last time together for a while. Her brothers would be arriving sometime tomorrow. She could pull something over on her dad, but fooling her brothers was a totally different matter. "Okay, I'll be there. Later."

She then clicked off her cell phone.

"Did you enjoy yourself tonight, Libby?"

Olivia glanced over at her father as they walked up the stairs together. "Yes, I had a good time, and the food was excellent."

Orin couldn't help but chuckle. "Yes, it was good, and I was glad to see you eat for a change, instead of nibbling."

When they reached the landing, he placed a kiss on her forehead. "Good night, sweetheart. I'm feeling tired, so I'm going on to bed. What about you?"

"Umm, I may stay up a while and paint. Good night, Dad. Sleep tight."

He chuckled. "I will."

As soon as Olivia walked into her room and closed the door behind her, she began stripping out of her clothes, eager to get to the Saxon Hotel and meet Reggie. Going to her closet, she selected a dress. She felt like going braless tonight. Within minutes she was slipping her feet into a pair of sandals and grabbing her purse. Opening the door, she eased out of her room, and within seconds she was down the stairs and out of the house.

She couldn't wait until she was with Reggie.

Reggie stood when the door to the hotel room opened and Olivia walked in. Without saying anything, she tossed her purse on the sofa and then crossed the room to him. The moment she was within reach, he pulled her into his arms and swept her off her feet.

On other nights he had stamped his ownership all over her body, but tonight he wanted to claim her mouth, lips and tongue and locked all three to his. At the party she had been so close, yet so far, and he had wanted her with a force that had him quaking.

He pulled his mouth back. He was moving toward the bedroom when she began wiggling in his arms. "No. Here. Let's make love in here."

The moment he placed her on her feet, she went for his clothes, pushing the shirt off his shoulders and greedily kissing his chest. He was tempted to tell her to slow down, to assure her that they had all night, but he knew that they didn't. She would need to leave before daybreak.

Her hands went to the buckle of his pants, and he watched as she slid down the zipper before easing her hand inside to cup him. He threw his head back and released a guttural moan as sensations spiraled through him, almost bringing him to his knees. And when she began stroking him, he sucked in a deep breath.

"I want this, Reggie," she said as she firmly held his shaft.

"And I want to give it to you," he managed to say, slowly backing her up to the wall.

When they couldn't go any farther, he reached out and pulled down the straps of her dress and smiled when he saw she wasn't wearing a bra. Her breasts were bared before his eyes. He licked his lips. "Are you wearing anything at all under this dress?" he asked when his mouth went straight to her breasts.

"No."

"Good."

He lifted up the hem of her dress and planted his hand firmly on her feminine mound. "And I want this."

Taking a step back, he tugged her dress the rest of the way down, and the garment drifted to the floor. His gaze raked up and down her naked body. "Nice."

He then removed his clothes, and, taking a condom out of his wallet, he put it on. Then he reached out and lifted her by the waist. "Wrap your legs around me, Olivia. I'm about to lock us together tightly, to give you what you want and to get what I need."

As soon as her legs were settled around his waist and his shaft was pointing straight for the intended target, he tilted her hips at an angle to bury himself deep inside of her and then drove into her. She arched her back off the wall, and his body went still. Locked in.

A perfect fit. Silence surrounded them, and they both refused to move.

Flames roared to life within him, and he felt himself burning out of control, but he refused to move. Instead, he held her gaze, wanting her to see what was there in his eyes. It was something he couldn't hold in any longer, but first he wanted to see if she could read it in his gaze.

Olivia stared back at Reggie. She saw desire, heat and longing. She felt him planted deep inside of her. But it was his gaze that held her immobile. In a trance. And she knew at that moment why she kept coming back, kept wanting to be with him when she knew that she shouldn't.

She loved him.

The result of that admission was felt instantly: her body shivered. In response, Reggie, she noted, never wavered in his relentless stare, and then he spoke in a deep, husky voice. "I love you."

She immediately stifled a deep sigh before reaching up and placing her arms around his neck and saying, "And I love you."

Reggie's lips curved into a smile before he leaned down and sank his mouth onto hers as his body began moving, slowly, then fast, in and out of her with powerful thrusts, stirring passion, fanning the fire and then whirling them through an abyss of breathless ecstasy. Over and over again, he made love to the woman he loved and captured her moans of pleasure in his mouth. And when she shattered in his arms and he followed her over the edge, he knew he wasn't through with her yet.

They had just begun.

He tightened his hold on her, and on weak legs, he

moved toward the bedroom. For them, time was limited tonight. Their passion was raging out of control. But moments ago they had let go and claimed love, and when they tumbled onto the bed together, he knew that tonight was just the beginning for them.

"Wake up, sweetheart. It's time to go."

Olivia lifted her eyes and gazed up at Reggie. He was standing beside the bed, fully dressed. "What time is it?" she asked sleepily, forcing herself to sit up.

"Almost four in the morning, and I got to get you home," he said.

She nodded. Although they had driven separate cars, it was the norm for him to follow behind her and see her safely inside her house. Excusing herself, she quickly went to the bathroom, and when she returned moments later, he was sitting on the edge of the bed.

He reached out his hand to her. "Come here, baby."

And she did. She went to him, and he pulled her down onto his lap and kissed her so deeply and thoroughly, she could only curl up in his warmth and enjoy. When he finally lifted his mouth from hers, he gazed down at her lips.

"You have beautiful lips," he whispered softly.

"Thank you."

His gaze then moved to her eyes. "And I meant what I said earlier tonight, Olivia. I love you."

She nodded. "And I meant what I said earlier, too. I love you." She didn't say anything else for a minute, and then she added, "Crazy, isn't it?"

"Not really. My dad met my mom, and they were married within two weeks. Same thing with my aunt

and uncle. Westmorelands believe in love at first sight."
He paused for a second. "This changes everything."

She lifted a brow. "What do you mean?"

"No sneaking around."

She wondered why he thought that. "No, Reggie. It
changes nothing." She eased out of his arms and began
getting dressed.

"Olivia?"

She turned to him. "My father is still running against
you, and the election is not until the end of next month
and—"

"You would want us to sneak around until then?" he
asked incredulously. When she didn't answer, he said,
"I want you to meet my family. I want you to attend
my family reunion with me in Texas in a few weeks. I
want you by my side and—"

"I have to think about my father. He would not want
us to be together," she said.

"And I told you in the beginning, this doesn't involve
your father. You are a consenting adult. You shouldn't
need your father's permission to see me."

"It's not about his permission. It's about me being
there for him, Reggie. I owe my father a lot, and I refuse to flaunt our affair in front of him," she persisted.

"And I refuse to sneak around to see you any longer.
That's asking a lot of me, Olivia. I love you, and I want
us to be together."

"But we are together, Reggie."

He was silent for a moment, and then he said, "Yes,
behind closed doors. But I want more than that. I want
to take you out to dinner. I want to be seen with you. I
want to do all those things that a couple does together
when they are in love."

Olivia sighed. "Then you will have to wait until after the election."

They stared at each other for the longest time. Then Reggie said quietly, "When you're ready to let nothing get in the way of our relationship, our love, let me know, Olivia."

Then he turned and walked out of the hotel room. As soon as the door closed behind him, Olivia threw herself on the bed and gave in to her tears.

Olivia slowly walked out of the Saxon Hotel, with a heavy heart. She'd told a man that she loved him, and then she'd lost him in the same day. She had stayed in the hotel room and cried her eyes out, and now she felt worse than ever.

Crossing the parking lot, she stopped walking when she glanced ahead and saw Reggie leaning against her car. She stared at him, studied his features, not wanting to get her hopes up. Inhaling deeply, she moved one foot in front of the other and came to a stop in front of him.

They stood, staring at each other for a long moment, and then he reached out and pulled her into his arms and kissed her.

Moments later he pulled back slightly and placed his forehead against hers. "I love you, and I want you with me, out in the open, not sneaking around, Olivia. But if that's the only way I can have you right now, then that's what I'll take."

Olivia felt a huge weight being lifted off her shoulders, but she knew it was at Reggie's expense. He deserved to have a woman by his side, one that he could take to dinner, take home to meet Mom and invite to his home.

Leaning closer, she snuggled into his arms, close to his warmth and his heart. She knew that this was the man that would have her heart forever.

Chapter 10

"You've been rather quiet, Libby. Aren't you glad to see us?"

Olivia glanced over at Duan and forced a smile. "Yes. I missed you guys."

"And we missed you," Terrence said, coming to join them at the breakfast table. "So why haven't you been your usual chipper self the past couple of days?"

She sighed, thinking there was no way she could tell her brothers what was really bothering her. But she could tell them what Cathy had shared with her. "I'm fine. I'm just in a funky mood right now. It will pass soon," she said.

Her brothers had flown in yesterday for the barbecue to be held that afternoon. It was an event she wasn't looking forward to, because she knew that Reggie would be there. It would be hard to see him and not want to be with him.

"There is something I need to talk to you two about while Dad is at campaign headquarters. It's something that Cathy told me, and it might explain why Dad decided to run for the Senate."

Duan raised a brow. "What?"

She then told her brothers everything that Cathy had shared with her. She saw Duan's jaw flex several times.

"I knew there was a reason I didn't like Senator Reed," Duan said.

"Same here," Terrence said. His eyes had taken on a dark look, and she now understood why the sportscasters had dubbed him the Holy Terror when he played professional football.

"I think we should talk to Dad to make sure he's entered politics for the right reason," Duan said. "If he did then he has our blessings. If he didn't, then I think he should reconsider everything before going any further."

Olivia nodded. "I agree."

"And what do the three of you agree on?"

Olivia, Duan and Terrence glanced up. Their father had walked into the kitchen, and he had Senator Reed with him. Olivia looked at her brothers. "It's nothing that we can't talk about later, Dad," she said quickly. She then glanced at Senator Reed, who was looking at her oddly. "Good morning, Senator."

The man had a smug look on his face when he responded. "Good morning, Olivia." He then slid his gaze to her brothers. "Duan. Terrence."

They merely nodded their greeting.

Her father studied her and her brothers and then reached into his pocket and pulled out an envelope. "Can you explain this, Olivia?" he asked, tossing several photographs on the table.

Olivia picked them up and studied them. They were photographs taken of her in Reggie's arms two nights ago in the parking lot of the Saxon Hotel. Several were of them kissing. "Who took these?" she asked, glancing at her father.

It was Senator Reed who spoke. "We have reason to believe Westmoreland himself is responsible. It seems you put more stock in the affair than he did. I was able to get these before the newspapers printed them."

Olivia glanced back at the photographs, and when Duan held out his hand for them, she handed them over to him. The room got quiet while Duan looked at the pictures before passing them on to Terrence.

"Were you having an affair with Westmoreland, Libby? Knowing he is my opponent in the Senate race?" Orin asked his daughter, as if he was insulted by such a possibility.

Refusing to lie, Olivia lifted her chin. "Yes. Reggie and I met at the Firemen's Ball two weeks ago. It was a masquerade party, so we didn't know each other's identity."

"But what happened once you found out?" her father asked quietly.

She sighed deeply. "Once we found out, it didn't matter. Our involvement had no bearing on your campaign," she said.

Senator Reed chuckled. "And I'm sure he convinced you of that. It's obvious he wanted to make a spectacle of you and your father. It's a good thing I stepped in when I did."

Olivia glared at the man. "You would like my father and brothers to believe the worst of Reggie, wouldn't you?" she said in a biting tone. "Well, it truly doesn't matter, because it's what I don't believe that does."

"And what don't you believe, Libby?" Duan asked, standing next to her.

She glanced up at her oldest brother. "What I don't believe, Duan, is that Reggie had anything to do with this." She turned back to her father. "And knowing that only makes me wonder who does."

At that moment the doorbell rang. "I'll get it," Terrence said, walking away, but not before gently squeezing his sister's elbow, giving her a sign that she had his support.

"So if you don't believe Westmoreland sent out these photos, Libby, then who did?" Orin asked his daughter.

"That's what I'd like to know," said a male voice behind them.

Olivia swung around. Terrence had escorted Reggie into the kitchen.

Orin frowned. "Westmoreland, what are you doing here?"

Reggie looked at Orin. "Someone thought it was important that a courier deliver these to me before eight in the morning," he said, throwing copies of the same pictures Olivia had just seen on the kitchen table. "I figured someone was trying to play me and Olivia against each other, and I wasn't having it."

Reggie then turned to Olivia. "I had nothing to do with those photos, Olivia."

"I know you didn't," she said softly.

"Well, the rest of us aren't so gullible," Senator Reed snapped.

Duan stepped forward. "Excuse me, Senator, but

why are you here? What goes on in this family really doesn't concern you."

The man seemed taken aback by Duan's words. "If it wasn't for me, those pictures would have been on the front page of today's paper. I saved your father the embarrassment of this entire town knowing that his daughter is having an affair."

Terrence's smile didn't quite reach his eyes as he came to stand beside Duan. "You do mean his *grown* daughter, don't you?"

"She is having an affair with *him*," Senator Reed said, almost at the top of his voice, pointing at Reggie.

"And what business is it of yours?" Olivia snapped.

"It is my business because I had your father bring you home for *me*," Senator Reed snapped back. The entire room got quiet, and the senator realized what he'd said. Five pairs of eyes were staring at him. "What I meant was that I—"

"We know exactly what you meant, Al," Orin said in a disgusted voice, seeing things clearly now. "And just to set the record straight, I didn't ask my daughter to come home for you. The only reason I summoned Olivia home was to be here with me for the campaign."

Seeing he had lost his footing with Orin, Senator Reed said, "Aw, come on, Orin. You know how I spout off at the mouth sometimes. Besides, why are you getting mad at me? She is the one who is sneaking around with your opponent behind your back. She reminds you of your ex-wife, don't you think?"

Before anyone could blink, Orin struck the senator and practically knocked him to his knees. "Get up and get out, and don't ever come back. You're no longer welcome in my home, Al," Orin said, barely holding back his rage.

The senator staggered to his feet. "Fine, and you can forget my endorsement," he said heatedly, limping toward the door.

"I don't need it," Orin shot back. "I plan to pull out of the race."

When the door slammed shut, Olivia quickly moved over to her father. "Dad, are you going to pull out because of what I did?" she asked softly.

Orin pushed a strand of hair out of her face. "No, sweetheart. Your old man realizes that he's not cut out to be a politician. Al had convinced me that running for office was what I needed to do, but it was not truly what I wanted to do. I never really had my heart in it."

He glanced down at the pictures on his kitchen table and then over at Reggie. "I hope for your sake that you care for my daughter, Westmoreland."

Reggie smiled as he came to stand beside Olivia. "I do. I'm in love with her, sir," he said.

Orin's features eased into a satisfied smile. "And the way she defended you a few moments ago, I can only assume that she's in love with you, too."

"I *am* in love with him," Olivia affirmed.

"Good." Orin then looked at his two sons. "It seems our family will be increasing soon. What do you think?"

Duan chuckled. "He loves her. She loves him. It's all good to me."

Terrence smiled. "As long as they don't decide to marry before today's barbecue. I was looking forward to checking out the single ladies there today."

Orin rolled his eyes and shook his head. He then offered Reggie his hand. "Welcome to the family, son," he said.

* * *

The barbecue was truly special. Orin made the announcement that he was pulling out of the Senate race, and he gave his endorsement to Reggie. In the next breath, Orin announced that there would be a Jeffries-Westmoreland wedding in the very near future.

With Olivia by his side, Reggie introduced her to all the many Westmorelands in attendance.

"Just how many cousins do you have?" she asked him a short time later.

He smiled. "Quite a number. Just wait until you meet the Denver Westmorelands at the family reunion in a few weeks."

"Have you met them all?" she asked curiously.

"No, but I'm looking forward to doing so."

Olivia nodded. So was she. She and Reggie had discussed her move back to the States, and a wedding was planned for next month after the election. She was truly happy.

Reggie held her hand as they walked around the grounds, greeting everyone. She smiled, thinking she was beginning to like the idea of becoming a politician's wife.

"You know what I think?" Reggie whispered to her when they claimed a few moments to be alone.

She glanced up at him. "No, what do you think?"

He smiled. "I think we should go to the Saxon Hotel tonight and celebrate. What do you think?"

She chuckled. "I think, Reggie Westmoreland, that you are a true romantic."

He pulled her into his arms. "If I am, it's because I've got a good teacher." And then he sealed his words with a kiss.

Epilogue

The following month, in a church full of family and friends, newly elected senator Reginald Westmoreland and Olivia Marie Jeffries exchanged vows to become man and wife. Reggie thought Olivia was the most beautiful bride he had ever seen. His mother was crying. The last Atlanta-based Westmoreland was now married.

At the reception, when they made their rounds to speak with everyone, Reggie got to spend time again with his new cousins, the Westmorelands of Denver. Everyone had met and gotten acquainted at the family reunion. Talk about a good time. And it was great knowing there were more Westmorelands out there. Everyone on both sides was looking forward to spending time together, getting to know each other and having family reunions each year.

"I can't believe how the men in the Westmoreland

family favor each other," Olivia said, glancing across the room at five of Reggie's cousins from Denver— Jason, Zane, Dillon and the twins, Adrian and Aidan. They were just five of the tons of cousins from Colorado, and she had liked all of them immediately, including the women her age.

Olivia had enjoyed the family reunion and getting to know Reggie's family. And they had accepted her with open arms. She felt blessed to be a part of the Westmoreland clan.

Later that night Reggie presented his wife with her wedding gift. They had flown to the Caribbean right after the wedding reception to spend a week at the Saxon Hotel that had recently been built in St. Thomas.

"This, sweetheart, is for you," Reggie said, handing her a sealed envelope. They had just enjoyed dinner in the privacy of their room.

"Thank you," Olivia said, opening up the envelope. It contained a key. And then she glanced at the card. She suddenly caught her breath and then stared over at Reggie as tears sprang into her eyes. "I don't believe it."

"Believe it, darling. You once told me what you wanted, and as your husband, I want to make it happen for you. Years ago I bought the building and when my first partner and I dissolved our business partnership, I kept the building. I think it would be perfect for your art gallery. It's in a good location."

She got out of her seat and went around the table to thank Reggie properly. He pulled her into his lap and kissed her with the passion she had gotten used to receiving from him.

"Thank you," she said through her tears. "I love you."

"And I love you, my Wonder Woman."

Reggie gathered her into his arms, and when she leaned up and caught his mouth with hers, he shivered as a profound need rushed through him. This was their wedding night. They were in a Saxon Hotel. And they were in each other's arms.

Life was wonderful.

* * * * *

We hope you enjoyed reading

STATE SECRETS

by #1 *New York Times* bestselling author

LINDA LAEL MILLER

and

TALL, DARK...WESTMORELAND!

by *New York Times* bestselling author

BRENDA JACKSON

Both were originally Harlequin® Special Edition
and Desire stories!

Powerful heroes...scandalous secrets...burning desires.

From passionate, suspenseful and dramatic
love stories to inspirational or historical,
Harlequin offers different lines to
satisfy every romance reader.

New books available every month.

NYTHRS0518

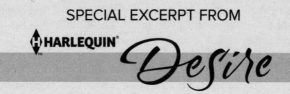
Spencer Jameson wasn't accustomed to being ignored.

He'd been back in Washington, DC, for three weeks. The plan
was to buzz into town for just enough time to help out his oldest
brother, Derrick, and then leave again.

That was what Spence did. He moved on. Too many days
back in the office meant he might run into his father. But dear
old Dad was not the problem this trip. No, Spence had a different
target in mind today.

Abigail Rowe, the woman currently pretending he didn't
exist.

He followed the sound of voices, careful not to give away his
presence.

A woman stood there—*the* woman. She wore a sleek navy
suit with a skirt that stopped just above the knee. She embodied
the perfect mix of professionalism and sexiness. The flash of bare
long legs brought back memories. He could see her only from
behind right now but that angle looked really good to him.

Just as he remembered.

Her brown hair reached past her shoulders and ended in a
gentle curl. Where it used to be darker, it now had light brown

highlights. Strands shifted over her shoulder as she bent down to show the man standing next to her—almost on top of her—something in a file.

Not that the other man was paying attention to whatever she said. His gaze traveled over her. Spence couldn't exactly blame him, but nothing about that look was professional or appropriate. The lack of respect was not okay. As far as Spence was concerned, the other man was begging for a punch in the face.

As if he sensed his behavior was under a microscope, the man glanced up and turned. His eyebrows rose and he hesitated for a second before hitting Spence with a big flashy smile. "Good afternoon."

At the intrusion, Abby spun around. Her expression switched from surprised to flat-mouthed anger in the span of two seconds. "Spencer."

It was not exactly a loving welcome, but for a second he couldn't breathe. The air stammered in his lungs. Seeing her now hit him like a body blow. He had to fight off the urge to rub a hand over his stomach. Now, months later, the attraction still lingered…which ticked him off.

Her ultimate betrayal hadn't killed his interest in her, no matter how much he wanted it to.

If she was happy to see him, she sure hid it well. Frustration pounded off her and filled the room. She clearly wanted to be in control of the conversation and them seeing each other again. Unfortunately for her, so did he. And that started now.

Don't miss
REUNION WITH BENEFITS by HelenKay Dimon,
*part of her **JAMESON HEIRS** series!*

Available June 2018 wherever
Harlequin® Desire books and ebooks are sold.

www.Harlequin.com

HARLEQUIN Desire

Powerful heroes…scandalous secrets…burning desires.

REUNION WITH BENEFITS

HELENKAY DIMON

Save **$1.00**

on the purchase of ANY
Harlequin® Desire book.

Available wherever books are sold,
including most bookstores, supermarkets,
drugstores and discount stores.

Save $1.00

on the purchase of any Harlequin® Desire book.

Coupon valid until August 31, 2018.
Redeemable at participating outlets in the U.S. and Canada only.
Not redeemable at Barnes & Noble stores. Limit one coupon per customer.

52615737

5 65373 00076 2 (8100)0 12362

Canadian Retailers: Harlequin Enterprises Limited will pay the face value of this coupon plus 10.25¢ if submitted by customer for this product only. Any other use constitutes fraud. Coupon is nonassignable. Void if taxed, prohibited or restricted by law. Consumer must pay any government taxes. Void if copied. Inmar Promotional Services ("IPS") customers submit coupons and proof of sales to Harlequin Enterprises Limited, P.O. Box 31000, Scarborough, ON M1R 0E7, Canada. Non-IPS retailer—for reimbursement submit coupons and proof of sales directly to Harlequin Enterprises Limited, Retail Marketing Department, 225 Duncan Mill Rd., Don Mills, ON M3B 3K9, Canada.

U.S. Retailers: Harlequin Enterprises Limited will pay the face value of this coupon plus 8¢ if submitted by customer for this product only. Any other use constitutes fraud. Coupon is nonassignable. Void if taxed, prohibited or restricted by law. Consumer must pay any government taxes. For reimbursement submit coupons and proof of sales directly to Harlequin Enterprises, Ltd 462, NCH Marketing Services, P.O. Box 880001, El Paso, TX 88588-0001, U.S.A. Cash value 1/100 cents.

® and ™ are trademarks owned and used by the trademark owner and/or its licensee.

© 2018 Harlequin Enterprises Limited

NYTCOUP0518